PRAISE FOR THE NOVELS
OF J. KATHLEEN CHENEY

THE SEAT OF MAGIC

"[A] killer sequel . . . intriguing and fun, the mystery unfolds like a socially conscious tour through a cabinet of curiosities."

—*Kirkus Reviews*

"[M]esmerizing."

—*Publishers Weekly*

"Those who enjoy alternate history—Edwardian- or Victorian-era historical fiction with a touch of magic and mythology—will be delighted with this story." —*Booklist*

"This second entry in the Golden City series is even better than its predecessor: Readers will be completely enthralled with the characters and the organic development of their relationship . . . a sheer delight." —*Romantic Times*

continued . . .

THE GOLDEN CITY

"Cheney's alternate Portugal, a society of delicate manners, gaslights, and under-the-sea artworks, provides a lush backdrop for an intricate mystery of murder, spies, selkies, and very dark magic. A most enjoyable debut."   —Carol Berg, author of the Novels of the Collegia Magica

"[A] masterpiece of historical fantasy. . . . The fascinating mannerisms of the age and the extreme formality of two people growing fonder of each other add a charmingly fresh appeal that will cross over to romance fans as well as to period fantasy readers."
—*Library Journal*

"[P]ulls readers in right off the bat. . . . Oriana's 'extra' abilities are thoroughly intriguing and readers will love the crackling banter and working relationship between Oriana and Duilio."
—*Romantic Times*

"An ambitious debut from Cheney: part fantasy, part romance, part police procedural, and part love letter to Lisbon in the early 1900s. . . . [The author] does a lovely job connecting magical, historical, and romantic elements."   —*Kirkus Reviews*

Books by J. Kathleen Cheney

The Golden City

The Seat of Magic

THE
SHORES
OF
SPAIN

A Novel of the Golden City

J. KATHLEEN CHENEY

A ROC BOOK

ROC
Published by the Penguin Group
Penguin Group (USA) LLC, 375 Hudson Street,
New York, New York 10014

🐧

USA | Canada | UK | Ireland | Australia | New Zealand | India | South Africa | China
penguin.com
A Penguin Random House Company

First published by Roc, an imprint of New American Library,
a division of Penguin Group (USA) LLC

First Printing, July 2015

LIBRARY OF CONGRESS CATALOGING-IN-PUBLICATION DATA:

Cheney, J. Kathleen.
The shores of Spain: a novel of the Golden city/J. Kathleen Cheney.
p. cm.
ISBN 978-0-451-47291-5
I. Title.
PS3603.H4574S56 2015
813'.6—dc23   2015003240

Printed in the United States of America
10 9 8 7 6 5 4 3 2 1

Set in LTD Kennerley
Designed by Spring Hoteling

For my family, for all their support.

ACKNOWLEDGMENTS

First, I'd like to thank Kat Sherbo, my acquiring editor, who believed in this series from the beginning. I'd also like to thank the other editors who've worked on this—Danielle Stockley and Jessica Wade—and all the copy editors who've worked so hard on these books. The art department has done an amazing job with my covers, including the photographer, Juliana Kolesova, the designer, Katie Anderson, and the model who came back for three covers in this series. I truly appreciate all the hours and heart you've all put into this.

Secondly, I'd like to thank everyone who's read multiple versions of these books, especially my husband, Matt Cheney, my agent, Lucienne Diver, and the multiple members of Codex who went through parts of these three books, most notably Beth Cato. Thanks, all!

And a hat tip goes out to the superb staff of the Old School Bagel Café on Covell, my second office, where much of this series was written. Thanks for the friendly smiles, the coffee, and those tasty honey-oat bagels.

Finally, I'd like to thank all the book reviewers and bloggers who've supported my work with kind words and encouraged me as I made my way along this rocky road. It's impossible to get by in this world without friends.

THE
SHORES
OF
SPAIN

CHAPTER I

Marina Arenias curled up in one of the upholstered chairs in the front sitting room of the Ferreira home, the room in the house with the best light even now, past sunset. She had no idea how long it would be before Joaquim returned to escort her back to her flat on Virtudes Street. After dinner, he'd retreated with her father to the Ferreira library, where they would probably debate history and philosophy long into the night. She hoped he didn't forget about her.

The letter she held came from her sister, Oriana, the new Portuguese ambassador to the Ilhas das Sereias. Oriana and her husband had been there for almost three months now, and Marina missed her sister sorely. She wished she could go to Oriana for advice at times . . . although she would probably just ignore whatever Oriana recommended.

Smiling ruefully at that thought, Marina popped open the wax seal and settled her rump more firmly in the comfortable chair.

Dearest Marina, the letter began.

She imagined it in Oriana's voice, which made her feel young and meek. Oriana had always been the bold one, always jumping to Marina's defense. Marina had never had that sort of nerve.

Duilio and I will be leaving Quitos soon to visit Grandmother on Amado. I know you wish you could be here with us.

In some ways, Marina did wish she could be there. She'd spent her first twelve years in that house on the beach beyond the town of Porto Novo, and they'd been happy ones. Her mother, contrary to custom, had chosen to live with her mate's family rather than the other way around. Her own family, the Paredes line, hadn't approved of her choice of mate. Not only was Marina's father educated, but he was also a practicing Christian, both qualities her mother's traditional family deplored. It had been an unconventional relationship, yet her parents had seemed quite happy together.

Her mother died when Marina was eight, while away investigating something for the Ministry of Intelligence. The world had seemed bleak after that, but Marina had bounced back with the resilience of a child. She'd had her father and grandmother to console her, and Oriana looked out for her in their mother's stead. Life went on. Marina hadn't understood until years later what a toll the loss of their mother had taken on Oriana.

I will relay your affections to Grandmother, the letter continued, *and will write once we're there to tell you everything that's changed. I'll probably see some of your childhood friends while there, and will relay any messages they have for you.*

Oriana didn't mention her own childhood friends because she hadn't had many. Not that she wasn't friendly—she simply hadn't had time for friends. After their mother's death, Oriana had taken it on herself to make certain that Marina kept up with her schooling, even though Oriana had only been twelve. Because Marina was small and meek, other girls teased her, calling her *webless* and other names. Oriana had always come to her defense.

The true turning point in their lives had come when their mother's eldest sister, Jovita Paredes, requested that the girls visit the main island of Quitos to get to know their mother's family. Despite his misgivings, their father gave in, but once they were there, everything had gone wrong. Their father had been accused of sedition, jailed, and exiled without even a chance to speak with his daughters. Effectively orphaned, Marina and Oriana became wards of the state. They had to live with two of their aunts and their spoiled cousins, forbidden to return to their grandmother's home on Amado.

Marina hated her life there. Her aunts found fault with everything she did. Worse, they forbade her to practice her religion; Christianity wasn't *allowed* on Quitos. Oriana tried to protect her from her aunts' venom and her cousins' ridicule, but Oriana couldn't always be there, particularly not after she took a job at a factory. She'd wanted to save money so that when Marina came of age they could move out of their aunts' household, perhaps even back to Amado.

That was why Marina lived in Portugal now. By the time she was eighteen she'd grown so frustrated with her mother's family that she decided to run away to find her exiled father. Marina had scraped together every last royal she had to cross to Amado on a ferry. She waited until Oriana was away, thinking her aunts wouldn't hold Oriana at fault. Once on Amado she hadn't contacted her grandmother for fear of getting her in trouble. Instead, Marina begged captains of the various human ships to take her to Portugal to find her father, offering to work for her passage. She hadn't understood then what manner of trouble she could have found herself in. But God had been merciful, and an English captain felt moved by her obvious distress to let her work in his ship's kitchen until the ship reached Portugal.

Marina sighed softly. *The only daring thing I've ever done in my life.*

It *had* all worked out for her. She liked Portugal. She fit in far better here than she ever had at home. Here she wasn't expected to be a leader or politician or spy. She wasn't sure what she did want to do with her life, but it wasn't one of *those* professions—the careers considered acceptable for females from her family line. Here in Portugal she had choices.

Back on the islands she wouldn't have been likely to attract a mate either. She didn't have the money to support a male, nor did her lineage make a match advantageous for a male's family. In Portugal, though, she'd found a male who very much suited her tastes—Joaquim Tavares. So no matter how much she'd missed her sister and grandmother, she was very happy to be in Portugal with her father.

She turned her eyes back to the letter. Oriana went on to tell an amusing story about visiting a street market in the capital city of Praia Norte with Duilio. Apparently the guards hadn't noted the approach of an old woman who, curious about the human man in the marketplace, managed to snatch off his *pareu*, leaving Duilio wearing nothing more than a revolver strapped to his thigh.

Marina clapped her hand over her mouth to keep from giggling aloud.

She shouldn't laugh. It would have been mortifying to Duilio, especially since etiquette forbade him to demand his garment back. Instead he'd had to wait for Oriana to retrieve the *pareu* from the old woman. The embassy guards should have prevented the incident, but they'd made the mistake of assuming a woman was harmless because she was elderly.

A soft cough sounded at the sitting room's doorway, alerting Marina to Lady Ferreira's return. The lady had gone down to the kitchens to discuss something with the cook—likely a flimsy excuse to allow Marina privacy to read her letter.

"Lady, did Oriana write to you about the . . . um . . . *incident* in the market?"

Lady Ferreira laughed merrily as she approached. "Certainly. An amusing tale, but not one that needs to be spread about here in the Golden City."

The lady settled gracefully in the matching chair on the other side of the window, the deep brown fabric of her gown glistening in the lamplight. To ward off the chill coming off the window glass, she adjusted her ivory shawl around her shoulders. Marina reminded herself firmly not to covet the thing. It looked to be of silk and cashmere—or perhaps wool—with intricate embroidery all along the edges. It had likely cost more than all of Marina's current garments combined. Marina's father, with his successful business in the city, was well-to-do. Her father's wife, Lady Alma Pereira de Santos, had managed to turn her own limited funds into a comfortable fortune. The Ferreiras were, by comparison, shockingly wealthy.

"Is your father still talking with Joaquim?" Lady Ferreira asked once she was comfortable.

"Yes, although I've no clue what they're talking about," Marina said, a hint of vexation creeping into her voice.

Lady Ferreira chuckled. "Perhaps they're discussing you."

Marina shook her head. "I'm sure it's politics."

Lady Ferreira gazed at her for a moment, her warm brown eyes sympathetic. "Young men have their passions," she said.

Marina felt childish and petulant now. "I know. The referendum is very important to him, and I do understand why."

Joaquim had a revolutionary streak. He believed in the equality of all peoples regardless of kind, religion, or birth. He regularly conferred with Prince Raimundo—they'd become unlikely friends over the past six months. Despite the prince's station, Marina was sure that Joaquim treated him no differently than he would a fellow police officer, a beggar chance-met on the street, or a pagan sereia whose child had been murdered. That was one of the things she loved about him.

The upcoming referendum would determine whether the princedoms of Northern Portugal and Southern Portugal would once again be one country. Not only would reunification mean one monarchy, one government, and one military; it would also trigger the drafting of a new constitution, a chance for the new country to redefine itself, perhaps into a more republican mode. That was the outcome Joaquim prayed for. Unfortunately, Marina wouldn't be voting in that referendum. No woman in the Portugals would.

As important as it was, Marina wanted Joaquim to spend less time worrying over the future of the government and more time thinking about *their* future. "I wish it was over so we could all move on with our lives."

Lady Ferreira didn't disagree with that. "Dear, Joaquim only acts when *he* is ready, you know. He was always the most stubborn of my boys."

Marina blinked. Had she spoken her worries aloud? Too often they showed on her face, she knew. "But what about when *I* . . ."

She stopped herself. It was one of the truths of living in the human world, another thing that was different from her homeland. There, she would have been the one to court Joaquim. If she'd had her way, their courtship would have progressed much more quickly. Oriana had courted Duilio less than a week before taking him as her mate, while Joaquim had been courting Marina for six months now and had done nothing more forward than hold her hand. Engagements in Portugal sometimes lasted two or three years, she'd heard.

Lady Ferreira's fingers touched her cheek. "Dear, give him time. Consider him a pearl of great value, one worth selling all you have to possess."

What is wrong with wanting to possess the pearl now? Marina sighed. "I know, lady."

Lady Ferreira waved one hand airily then. "He would be pleased that I even know that parable."

Actually, Marina was a little surprised herself. Lady Ferreira's adherence to the Church was nominal at best. Like Marina, the lady wasn't human; she was a selkie. Unlike most of her kind, though, the lady had been raised among humans and must have been exposed to that parable in her childhood. She sometimes professed it a mystery how Joaquim had grown up so religious. Of all the boys from the Ferreira household, Joaquim was the only devout one.

Marina understood how different influences in life could affect one's beliefs. Although her own grandmother and father were Christians, her older sister—Oriana—had chosen the religion of their mother. Since Oriana's husband, Joaquim's cousin Duilio, wasn't terribly devout, he hadn't minded taking a pagan to wife. Joaquim, on the other hand, wouldn't have been able to accept that. Fortunately, Marina held to her father's religion, despite pressure from her mother's family to deny her chosen faith. She'd only learned later that the Christianity practiced on the islands was different than that of Portugal, shifted to better suit the culture of the sereia, with greater emphasis placed on the Virgin as the instrument of God and intercessor.

Marina folded up the letter. The rest of it could wait. "I will tell him we were discussing it,"

The lady turned in her chair to face Marina more directly then. "I confess I did come in here with an ulterior motive. I wanted to see whether you could influence Joaquim."

Oh dear. "To what?" she asked cautiously.

"With Duilio and Oriana gone, when I marry, this house will stand empty. I would prefer that Joaquim move into the house, but I cannot get him to agree."

"Will you and Joaquim's father not move in here?" Marina had assumed that when Lady Ferreira married, she and Joaquim's father would move into this house. The Tavares house was much smaller than the Ferreira one.

"He wants to stay closer to his business," Lady Ferreira said, "and since I've never been particularly attached to this place, I don't feel any need to stay. This was Alexandre's house. Never mine."

Alexandre Ferreira had been dead two years or so. Some members of society had been scandalized when Lady Ferreira suddenly dropped her mourning six months before. Still, it was considered appropriate for a woman to leave off her mourning if she intended to remarry. It hadn't taken long before it became clear that Lady Ferreira planned to wed her first husband's cousin—Joaquim's father—who'd been a widower for decades.

Marina surveyed the elegant sitting room, its sofa and chairs in ivory and beige, the fine carpet under that, the silver-framed photographs on the mantel. "But you've worked so hard to make it beautiful."

Lady Ferreira laughed shortly. "Things, dear. I purchased *things*. They are not my children."

Marina licked her lips, trying to see this as Joaquim would. He might have lived in this house for eight years, but he was only a *cousin* of the Ferreira family. "I suspect Joaquim would feel like an interloper, like he has no business living here. The house should belong to Mr. Ferreira, shouldn't it? Not a cousin."

Lady Ferreira's head tilted and she gazed inscrutably at Marina.

Marina swallowed, feeling as though she'd failed some test. She didn't know what the lady had expected her to say, but her answer hadn't been the correct one.

"Duilio will be away for a couple of years at a minimum. Joaquim could act as . . . a caretaker," the lady suggested.

That was *not* what she'd originally meant, Marina was certain. Lady Ferreira had been saying that Joaquim should move into the house *permanently*. "I can talk to him, I suppose," she said after a moment. "It would save him the cost of his rent if he did."

She had only been to Joaquim's flat once, in the company of Oriana and Duilio; Joaquim's landlady would be scandalized if an unmarried woman went up there alone. It was a cozy place, nearly as shabby as her own, but full of Joaquim's books and possessing a masculine feel she'd found quite charming. It was *his* place, and it would be difficult for Joaquim to give it up.

He doesn't like change.

Masculine voices sounded in the hallway and, before Lady Ferreira could add more, Joaquim stood in the doorway, Marina's father behind him.

Tall and lean, and with dark hair going gray at the temples, her father had a distinguished air. He looked very much the Portuguese gentleman in his elegant evening attire. Most people would never guess he wasn't human. "Marina, darling," he began, coming to kiss her cheek in farewell when she rose. "I'm sorry we didn't get much of a chance to chat. Shall we talk in the morning?"

Since she worked for him in his office, it was a rhetorical question. "Yes, Father. Please tell your wife I hope she feels better in the morning."

Lady Pereira de Santos had left the Ferreira house not long after dinner, claiming a need for rest. That had been a common occurrence lately; the lady was pregnant. It would be a strange thing to have a half brother or sister, particularly one so much younger than herself, but Marina enjoyed the prospect of watching her so-serious father chase after a toddler.

"I will do so," her father promised, and then took his leave of Lady Ferreira before departing.

Joaquim came to Marina's side then, holding out one arm for her to take. She'd thought him terribly handsome from the moment she met him. He was tall and strong, with straight dark hair and brown eyes that hinted at his mother's Spanish blood, a square jaw that betokened firmness of purpose, and a wide brow that spoke of wisdom. Well, she hadn't *known* all those things about him from her first glance, but it hadn't taken long to learn his true character.

"Are you ready to go?" he asked. "Your father and I talked longer than I realized."

A lock of Joaquim's hair had fallen across his forehead, and Marina's fingers itched to push it back into place. "No need to worry," she assured him. "Lady Ferreira and I were chatting."

Reminded of his foster mother's presence in the room, Joaquim kissed the lady's cheeks before bidding her good night, and Marina followed suit. Then they made their way out of the house, pausing at the entryway so Marina could wrap her plain black shawl about her shoulders to keep at bay the chill of the early spring evening.

"So, what were you discussing?" Joaquim asked once they were walking along the Street of Flowers. The traffic on the street slowed once the sun went down, so the walkways weren't crowded, although the tram continued its circuit up toward the palace on its high hill.

Marina glanced at Joaquim's face as they passed under one of the streetlights, trying to decide where to start with the issue of the house. "Pearls."

She could use her *call* on him, her feeble version of sereia magic. Lady Ferreira knew that, and she wondered if that was what the lady expected—for Marina to convince Joaquim by influencing him magically. *He would hate that I used my gift to sway him.*

And he might never trust her again.

No, she decided. Joaquim would move into that house when *he* was ready. It would not be because Marina Arenias coerced him into it.

"Do you like pearls?" he asked as they paused at a corner to let a carriage rattle past.

So Marina walked on, one gloved hand on Joaquim's dark sleeve, telling him all about her favorite pair of gold and pearl combs back on the islands, a pair her mother had once owned. She completely forgot to ask Joaquim about his conversation with her father.

CHAPTER 2

❦

THURSDAY, 16 APRIL 1903; ILHAS DAS SEREIAS

The ferry belched out steam as it made its passage between the islands of Quitos and Amado. Judging by words stamped on the side of the hull, Duilio guessed it had come from England, brought here to the islands of the sereia through a series of arcane trades. Most of the newer machinery he'd seen on the islands was of English origin, where once it would have been predominantly Portuguese. Normally he would be the first one poking around and asking questions of the ship's captain, but it wasn't his place to do so. Not here.

Here it was the man's place to be quiet. *To be seen but not to do.*

Oriana had warned him of that, as had her father, but Duilio hadn't grasped how pervasive that attitude was until he'd been on the main island of Quitos for a couple of weeks. It was the most traditional of the islands of the sereia, and as a male he had almost no rights—a shocking change for a Portuguese gentleman of wealth and social standing.

They'd spent the last three months there, in the sereia capital of Praia Norte, persuading the local government to accept Oriana as the Portuguese ambassador. The islands hadn't hosted an ambassador from either Northern or Southern Portugal for almost two decades, and most trade between the two peoples had died out. The embassy's primary charge here was to resurrect that trade, a problematic mission given the lingering lack of trust between the two peoples.

Oriana currently stood with her back against the wall of the ferry's cabin, the remainder of the ambassadorial entourage taking up the aft of the upper deck. She wore a pensive expression as she watched the island of Quitos grow more and more distant, her full lips pressed together and her arms folded over her chest. Her burgundy-highlighted hair had been pinned into a coronet of braids, but the two combs emerging from that crown were actually slender knives, a concession to the danger in which she'd stood since their arrival here. The tension in her shoulders had eased once they reached open waters, but hadn't fled completely.

The four guards accompanying them kept anxious watch on the other travelers crowding the ferry's upper deck, but the curious passengers seemed willing to keep their distance. Judging by their fine garb and glossy hair, Duilio guessed that most of the sereia he saw there traveled between the two largest islands for reasons of business. A few, like Oriana, wore a vest as well as the *pareu*, and one elderly woman had on a fine jacket with elaborate blue and yellow embroidery down the plackets. Even so, the majority of the passengers, all female save for a handful of children, only wore the *pareu*—little more than a length of fabric wrapped about their waists.

Fortunately, the embassy guards were well trained not to stare at the display of bared skin. Their Portuguese uniforms seemed extravagant by comparison to the local mode of dress. The brass-buttoned blue jackets with braid across the chest and lighter blue trousers with a red stripe down each side looked starchy and unapproachable—as did their rifles and sabers. But since they represented the governments of the two Portugals here, the standards of the army must be upheld, even when the locals dressed far less formally.

Duilio glanced down at his bare feet ruefully. His situation was different. He'd agreed to adopt native garb to show that the Portuguese took the customs of the sereia seriously. No one ever mistook him for a sereia male, of course. He lacked gill slits on his neck and webbing between his fingers, both traits that gave the sereia advantages in the water. And his feet were unmistakably human. The sereia had coloring on the lower halves of their bodies that mimicked the scales of a fish—a tuna, actually—so anyone looking downward would immediately know he wasn't native to these islands.

He'd adapted quickly to wearing the *pareu*, though, a stark change for someone accustomed to the habitual multilayered dress of a Portuguese gentleman. Despite the afternoon sunshine, a chill came off the water today, so he also wore a black linen vest, the open front embroidered in gold along the edges. It covered most of the Paredes tattoo that ran from over his heart to his left shoulder, but enough of that could be seen to guarantee that any sereia would know he was claimed. Bangles clattered about his ankles, he wore bands of rose gold around his upper arms, and his hair hadn't been properly cut in half a year now. It hung on his neck in curls. If his old valet, Marcellin, were here, the man would have had an apoplectic fit. It pleased Oriana, though, so Duilio put up with the peculiar attire and overlong hair.

Even so, there were times he honestly missed wearing trousers. He didn't miss his valet frittering on about every wrinkle and speck of dust, but he missed *trousers*.

Oriana came around to the side of the ferry to join him. She touched his arm, her gold bangles clattering, and gestured toward the shores of Amado. "My grandmother's house is on that beach."

Duilio followed her finger. Amado was a volcanic island, reminding him greatly of Madeira, the only one of his people's islands he'd visited. A ridge of mountains formed the island's spine, covered in forest save for the jagged peaks. He could, however, see a narrow strip of sand where Oriana pointed, dotted with a handful of white-plastered houses. They didn't look much different from houses on some of the beaches along the Portuguese coast.

Amado, the so-called Portuguese island, also offered him a respite from the social strains of living on Quitos. Of all the six islands of the sereia, Amado was the most *liberal*. On Amado males were allowed to be educated, speak out of turn on occasion, and even own property. He hoped their time here wouldn't be as stressful as the last three months had been, either for him or their four remaining male guards.

Duilio shot a glance at Lieutenant Costa, who leaned against the ferry's white-painted rail. He worried them the most. The young man removed his shako to run a hand through his short blond hair, but quickly replaced it, cheeks flushing, when he noted one of the ferry's sailors looking his way with an appreciative smile. Costa was healthy and handsome and not terribly clever—the worst sort of guard for them to have brought to these islands. Here males were in short supply, and sereia females could use their *call* to seduce a human male they found interesting. Because of his selkie blood, Duilio had some immunity to that magic, but the young lieutenant didn't. According to his captain, Costa hadn't slept well for the last few weeks, besieged by dreams. Oriana feared that a sereia had gotten to him, although the young man denied it. Duilio only hoped they could get Costa back to human shores before he gave in to some unknown sereia's seduction.

In truth, on Quitos they'd endured a constant barrage of *calling*, and not just attempts at seduction. It wasn't unusual for a sereia to *call* in the course of the day, much as any human woman might sing to herself back in Portugal. Happiness, sorrow, and vexation all tore at the men's senses, although usually with a touch light enough for them to recognize that the impulses weren't their own. Most sereia strove for politeness near the grounds of the various embassies, strung together along one street. Even so, there were always those who didn't care, or those who wanted to cause chaos.

But Amado was less populated, and that would minimize the *calling* to which the men were exposed. Duilio hoped the passengers of this ferry were representative of the population of the island. So far their fellow travelers had refrained from *calling* altogether, despite the novelty of having humans to practice on.

By that point the ferry had passed the small secluded beach and now headed for the island's main harbor, where rough stone breakwaters limited the waves. They slid the last distance into the first pier and rocked against the wooden pilings. An intrepid young sailor in a white *pareu* and vest—the same one who'd been admiring Costa—jumped over the water to the planks and wrapped the mooring line around a bollard. Then she jogged back toward the aft of the ferry to catch a second line, her bangles jangling.

Oriana moved to the railing to peer along the wooden planks toward the beach. Duilio joined her, laying one hand on the back of her vest. "Do you see her?"

Oriana lifted her chin toward the shore. "Yes, she's there with that open carriage." She added the hand sign for *relief*, and turned to her guards. "We'll debark last."

By now the men knew not to look to Duilio to corroborate Oriana's orders; he might be her deputy, but *she* was the ambassador. So they patiently watched until the last of the ferry's passengers straggled off the gangplank and onto the pier. Then it was their turn, two guards going ahead and two behind. The guards' presence was more than just posturing, for today they would enter the perilous phase of their tenure as ambassadors, taking on their secondary mission.

Today they began the hunt to learn who'd murdered Oriana's mother.

CHAPTER 3

Grandmother Monteiro waited for them at the head of the pier. It had been almost five years since Oriana had seen her, but she hadn't changed much. She was a tall woman, her lean figure still straight and erect, and her dark eyes sharp. Like Oriana's own, her nails were filed down to sharp points, curving over the ends of her fingers—as much a marker of wealth as the rose-gold bangles at her wrists and ankles. Her white hair was massed atop her head in neat braids. The blue jacket she wore over her yellow *pareu* matched the embroidery about the *pareu's* hem. Oriana stopped an arm's length away. The two guards in the lead moved off to one side of the pier, but Duilio stopped behind her and waited for them to acknowledge his presence.

Oriana inclined her head. "Honored Grandmother."

Her grandmother's lips curved in a smile. "My child. And who is this you bring to the house of Monteiro?"

Oriana swept her hand to one side, and Duilio obediently stepped up next to her. "Honored Grandmother, this is my mate, Duilio, of the house of Ferreira."

And perfectly on cue, Duilio sank to his knees and bowed to the ground at her grandmother's feet. After only a second, her grandmother reached down and touched the top of his head. "Welcome, child."

Oriana let loose a breath she hadn't realized she'd been holding.

What a relief. She hadn't expected her grandmother would reject him, not for a moment. Even so, her grandmother's ready acceptance of him was reassuring. Oriana knew she'd made foolish mistakes in her past, but Duilio wasn't one of them.

And her grandmother's warm welcome made a stark contrast to the complete lack of welcome she'd had from the Paredes family on Quitos. None of her three aunts and neither of her cousins had acknowledged Oriana's arrival on the island in any way. Legally she was dead, and therefore they no longer had ties to her. Oriana was grateful that the Monteiro side of her family, as small as it was, was more understanding.

Duilio pushed back up to his knees and smoothly came to his feet, a smile on his face. This was the first time Oriana had asked him to perform the full obeisance, and he'd done it without flinching. Her grandmother reached up and put a finger on his chin, tilting his head down so that she could peer up into his face. He complied, his lips pressed together and warm brown eyes dancing with laughter.

She eyed him narrowly and then released him, a further sign of approval. "Come, children," she said then, including the guards in that address. "I have a carriage waiting."

The carriage's driver wore the blue-and-white-patterned *pareu* of the Monteiro servants, along with a blue vest that hid her dorsal stripe. Sailors and dockworkers strolled past the carriage and along the harbor's main street. White plastered buildings with dark wooden trim clustered across that street, mostly cafés and shops. Farther down, the street ran past the harbormaster's offices and along the main docks for trading ships. The hub of all foreign trade on the islands, the harbor of Porto Novo always bustled with activity.

A venerated elder on this island, her grandmother had never feared being exposed. Oriana, on the other hand, found it unnerving. She'd become accustomed to closed coaches in the last three months, ones with shades drawn so that the guards could better protect them. She cast a glance at Duilio, who signed discreetly with one hand that his seer's gift for sensing danger wasn't triggered by this mode of transportation. So she climbed into the carriage and settled next to her grandmother. In the seat behind them, Duilio squeezed in with two guards, leaving the other pair to ride on the carriage's tail. Once the driver was sure they were all settled, she shook the reins and the horses set off.

As they passed the docks, Oriana peered at the ships, trying to estimate the balance of trade. A handful of English ships were moored at the piers, along with two Spanish ships, one also flying the yellow and red streamers of Catalonia. And at the far end, two small-ish Portuguese freighters flew their country's blue and white flag— one from Northern Portugal and one from Southern Portugal. It was a welcome sight after all their efforts to reestablish trade. They would have to make a point of visiting with the Portuguese captains while they were here.

The docks swarmed with human men unloading their cargos, voices lifted to carry over the raucous calls of the seagulls. Just as boisterous, sereia shore crews in their short tucked-up *pareus* loaded that cargo onto wagons to cart it to the nearby warehouses. The docks of Amado were among the few places where human men and sereia females treated one another as equals. By the rules of old treaties, the sereia dockworkers swore not to entice any man off those ships, and not to *call* them in any way. In turn, the human captains knew to keep certain crew members aboard those ships. Any male who did stir up trouble on the docks—or any male who was particularly handsome—might never return. Despite the wide differences be-tween human and sereia cultures, the harbor's rules had held steady for generations. It was *business.*

As the carriage moved away from the docks, they passed older houses, sprawling affairs with plastered walls and tiled rooftops very unlike the granite buildings in the Golden City that rose three or more stories, crammed together like sardines in a tin. Here the houses were built up the mountainsides, too steep to run them close together.

Oriana glanced back at Duilio. He was watching those mountains with eager eyes. One of the advantages he'd gained from being half selkie was good lungs. He enjoyed climbing. She didn't, but was willing to join him so long as they could go slowly enough for her. She suspected at least one extended hike was in their future, perhaps along one of the aqueducts that brought freshwater down from the mountain springs to the shores.

When they finally reached the edge of Porto Novo, Oriana made the gesture that told Duilio he could talk. "Honored Grandmother," he said immediately, "Oriana pointed out the beach where you live. Is it far?"

The driver cast a glance over her shoulder, but didn't comment on the male talking out of turn behind her. Here on Amado it wasn't *that* unusual.

Oriana's grandmother turned in her seat to glance back at the three men crowded onto the bench behind her. "There's no need for such formality, child," she said to him. "You've met the requirements of custom. You may simply call me Grandmother now."

"I am honored," Duilio said, inclining his head.

Her grandmother smiled and gestured toward Oriana. *Pretty,* her hands said—a reference to Duilio's behavior rather than his appearance. Then she pointed at the next spine of the mountains that slid down to the sea ahead of them. "It's just beyond that ridge. Not as far as it seems."

"You don't travel back and forth every day, do you?" Oriana asked. Her grandmother was nearing eighty, and rattling along these dirt and gravel roads had to be hard on her constitution.

"Not every day, child." She patted Oriana's knee and turned back to gaze at the men. "I imagine that the last few months have been difficult for all of you."

The two guards glanced at each other as if startled to be addressed. Duilio just smiled secretively. "It has been challenging, Grandmother, although in different ways for each of us."

"Duilio's greatest challenge has been refraining from speaking," Oriana informed her, making the sign for the chattering of seagulls with one hand. Duilio just grinned.

"I believe that males have as much right to be heard as their mates," her grandmother said to him. "It's a common belief here on Amado. Please don't be afraid to ask questions."

That was one of the great differences between Quitos and Amado. On Quitos, traditional ways held sway. Because of their comparative rarity, sereia males were seen as creatures to be protected. They were to be cared for, and weren't to involve themselves in *demanding* activities like government or business. Once they had a mate, they cared for the children and stayed in the home. It was a near parallel to the role of women in Portugal, although not exact. In Portugal there wasn't a dearth of women as there was of males here, so poor women there had no choice but to work.

Duilio leaned forward, eager to take advantage of the chance to ask questions. "Your son was educated, I understand. What percentage of males pursue that here?"

Her grandmother sighed. "Less than twenty percent, even now. The poorer the family, the less likely the sons will be educated. You attained a university degree, did you not?"

Oriana suspected her father had included a great deal about Duilio in his letters to her grandmother.

"Yes," Duilio admitted. "I studied law and serve as Oriana's legal advisor here."

"And you've traveled abroad, my son told me," her grandmother continued. "Most males here would be jealous."

"I'm fortunate," Duilio admitted. "My family is wealthy. Many human males would envy those opportunities just as much as sereia males."

"True," she countered. "My son was also born into a wealthy family, one with enough political consequence that I could afford to have an eccentric child."

Oriana reined in her urge to laugh. Hearing her father described as an *eccentric child* would bring her secret amusement for years to come. The carriage passed over the ridge, finally giving them a view down into the bay. The surrounding slopes were steep and heavily wooded, but on the beach there were a handful of houses widely spaced apart—homes of some of the wealthiest families on Amado.

Even from this distance Oriana could see her grandmother's house, the familiar outline of it with its two courtyards and terraces. She and Marina had slept out under the stars on those terraces many nights. It was the closest thing she had to a home.

The advance guard had arrived with the luggage on an earlier ferry, so their bags waited in a fine bedroom with a view of the sea. Oriana had warned Duilio that the furnishings would be minimal given their proximity to the water. A delicately carved bench in dark wood stood to one side of the doorway, and two matching chairs waited near the windows with a small table between them, but there was no bed. Only the elderly or the infirm used beds here. Instead, above a shallow indentation in the floor, the bedding hung neatly from hooks on the wall, meant to be laid out and picked up every day so that it could air properly. The room's heavy wooden shutters each had a screened inner shutter that would let in a fresh breeze and sunlight, but not seagulls. Duilio threw those open and surveyed their luggage, deciding what to unpack first.

This was one of the rare times when he did miss his valet, who'd moved up in the world and was now valet to a prince. It would be nice to have someone unpack for him. But this was his duty here, to make sure Oriana had everything she needed.

She emerged from the bathing room and came to wrap her arms

around him, setting her chin on his shoulder. Her sharp nails pricked his bare waist. "Leave it," she urged. "We can sort it out after dinner."

"I don't want to make a poor impression," he admitted, indicating his *pareu*, wrinkled during the ride from the harbor.

"Grandmother's not overly critical," Oriana whispered against his ear. She'd unbraided her hair and now wore it loosely tied back, a hint of informality. "You'll be fine."

So they went to dinner without changing. In the dining room, a fine linen tablecloth covered with whitework embroidery lay atop a wooden table surrounded by chairs whose backs bore intricate carvings of vines and leaves. Very different from the wicker furniture more common on Quitos. Duilio would definitely call the décor in this room, at least, *Portuguese*.

Grandmother Monteiro assessed Duilio, her dark eyes bypassing his rumpled *pareu* altogether, and then sat at the head of the table, directing them to sit to either side of her. She waited until the servants had brought in the first course, potato and kale soup, before asking, "So, now that we're alone, is it true that you're half selkie, young man?"

Duilio supposed that to a woman of her age, *young man* was an acceptable description for a man who'd recently turned thirty. "Yes, Grandmother."

Her dark eyes narrowed. "You don't seem uncivilized, but my son told me your mother was raised among humans."

"That's true." The sereia commonly perceived selkies as savages, since they chose to live on the ocean. "Most people back home have no idea that my mother isn't human."

Grandmother Monteiro gestured, signing acceptance by touching her chin. It didn't necessarily mean she believed him, but that she chose not to argue the point. Duilio inclined his head to grant her that. It had taken him a while to learn some of the finer points of sereia gestures. Their people used hand signals to communicate underwater, but those same signs were also used on land, an augmentation to their words that went beyond facial expressions. It added a second level to dialogue that often belied the words spoken aloud. Oriana had begun teaching him those long before they'd accepted the assignment as ambassadors to the Ilhas das Sereias, mostly so he could understand what her father was signing.

"My son speaks well of Lady Ferreira," Grandmother Monteiro added. "He says your family has proven supportive, especially now that their marriage has been made public."

Oriana's father had been secretly married for almost eight years to a Portuguese noblewoman. But he'd recently accepted Portuguese citizenship, and the newspapers, fascinated by the dozens of New Portuguese—mostly sereia who'd lived secretly in the Golden City for years—had exposed his marriage. It was scandalous enough that a woman of the aristocracy would wed a commoner, her man of business, but when it became public that the man in question was also nonhuman, many of Lady Pereira de Santos' friends had abandoned her. Fortunately, Duilio's mother cared nothing about the opinions of society. "My mother finds them both charming company, as well as the lady's daughter."

"And speaking of daughters," Grandmother Monteiro said, "I hope that I may have a great-granddaughter eventually?"

Oriana's eyes met Duilio's across the table and he winked at her, *permission* rather than any salacious commentary. Sereia tradition held that once a woman became pregnant, she would signal that to others by folding the tucked-in edge of her *pareu* differently. Oriana hadn't done so yet, wanting to break the news to her family first. "Actually, Grandmother," she admitted, "we are expecting our first child."

Her grandmother pressed her webbed hands together, almost as if in prayer. "I am pleased, child, and I hope for nothing but health for you." She turned to Duilio. "Are you good with children?"

Because she expects me to raise those children. "I had a much younger foster brother," he said, "and I did well with him. I hope to care for our children well."

And so the meal went on, a chance for Oriana's grandmother to catch up not only on Oriana's recent history but on that of her father and her sister, Marina, who also lived in the Golden City now. The conversation ranged from there to the nascent movement for women's suffrage in Portugal and how it compared to the male suffrage movement on the islands, and then the views of the various countries in which Duilio had lived. It was normal dinner conversation, carefully avoiding the issue they'd come to this house to discuss. Oriana and her grandmother would likely handle that in a more private venue.

After the meal, Duilio excused himself to return to their room, but stopped first to determine how the guards were settling into their temporary posting. Lieutenant Benites had taken over one of the sitting rooms, transforming it into the guard contingent's office and armory. She glanced up from her work and rose when she saw him standing there. The young lieutenant was quicker than Lieutenant Costa, who rose from his chair belatedly with a flush on his cheeks.

"Mr. Ferreira, is there anything you need?" Benites asked. A stocky young woman from a small town outside Lisboa, she had a perpetual half smile on her face. She did, however, approach her assignment with great seriousness.

In Duilio's opinion, she also carried out her duties better than her male counterpart. *And she's considerably smarter than Costa.* "No, Lieutenant. I only wanted to be sure you had everything in hand."

The lieutenant nodded once. "Yes, sir. The layout the ambassador drew for us is quite accurate, so we'll be able to proceed with the duty roster as planned. Having seen the house now, though, I would like our hostess' permission to put a guard on the roof instead of the terrace."

They'd only brought a dozen guards to Amado, so they would be stretched thin for the next month. That had been one of their concerns in coming here. While there had been little official notice of the arrival of the new Portuguese mission, someone certainly had noted Oriana's return to her homeland. It hadn't taken long before threats began to appear, usually sent via the mail, but a few delivered directly by members of the sereia government. They usually suggested that Oriana should return to Portugal for her own safety. Someone in the government found her presence threatening.

The embassy on Quitos was a solid building behind a wrought-iron fence, tidy and defensible, but this house was on an open beach. Surely they could spot anyone approaching either by land or water from the rooftop. The lieutenant's idea was a good one, Duilio decided, provided the rooftops were accessible.

"I'll inquire into that in the morning," he promised. He could ask Grandmother Monteiro directly, but he would go through Oriana first.

Captain Vas Neves, the officer in charge of the embassy's guards, entered their office then, nodding to him before striding past and setting her Kropatschek rifle among the others neatly lined up against one wall. Vas Neves was a hard-faced older woman, tall and lean, with gray hair scraped back into a tight bun at the nape of her neck. Duilio knew little of her background save that she'd grown up in the former colony of Portuguese East Africa, the daughter of a big-game hunter there. She rarely spoke of her past, but, given what he'd observed of the guards at their target practice, she'd inherited her father's deadly aim with firearms.

It hadn't been a popular decision to place a woman in charge, not within the upper ranks of the army, but grudging consent had finally been won. Women were far less vulnerable to the *call* of a sereia than men. That had prompted Prince Raimundo to argue for the creation of a contingent of female guards, a shocking suggestion back home. He'd further shocked his constituents by arguing that the women should wear uniforms identical to the men's—with trousers, not skirts—granting them greater freedom of movement. The prince had finally won out over the army's objections, but the obstacle of finding and training the women in the short months before they set sail remained. Thus the ambassadorial staff had arrived on Quitos with a guard contingent that still had a dozen male members. Those remaining male soldiers spent their time guarding Duilio rather than Oriana, but he would be relieved when they packed them back to Portugal. *They* were too much at risk here, and Duilio was perfectly willing to trust the female members of the guard with his safety.

He turned to the captain. "So, Captain, are your soldiers settled in?"

"We've had a couple of issues with the baggage and one dispute with a servant, but Lady Monteiro's head of staff has sorted them out for us. Nothing serious," Vas Neves said, one hand lying comfortably on her pistol. The guard's main challenge had been to distinguish between what was an actual threat and what was normal behavior for a very different culture. They'd avoided triggering any incidents so far, but the past three months in Quitos *had* been nerve-racking. "Quarters are assigned," the captain went on, "and Benites has the duty rosters well in hand. We've also sent word of the ambassador's presence here to the Portuguese ships in harbor, and will let you know if the captains wish to arrange a visit."

Obviously they had everything under control, so he wasn't needed here. "Thank you, Captain. Let me know if there's anything we can do to make this easier for your personnel. This is supposed to be a retreat for us all."

The captain nodded and Duilio left the officers plotting their next few days. Duilio walked along the white hallways, nodding to sloe-eyed Corporal Almeida as he passed her duty station in the hall outside his and Oriana's bedroom. Once inside, he crossed the room to unlatch the inner shutters, allowing the cool evening breeze in through the screens.

For a moment, he stood inhaling the sea air.

Oriana might joke about his frustration over not being allowed to speak, but in truth *this* was far more difficult. He was accustomed to *doing*, not to standing by while Oriana did all the work. The last three months had been an eye-opening experience. Oriana had done this often enough while she was in the Golden City, forced to wait while he'd gone off to investigate. He could do it too.

He sighed and turned his eyes to the bedding hanging from hooks on the wall. *I have chores to do.*

CHAPTER 4

The library of the Monteiro beach house was on the second floor. The décor was simple; centuries of living with the sea had taught the sereia to choose furniture and bedding that was easy to move to higher ground or abandon. A much larger collection of books waited at her grandmother's mountain house, a location safer from the whims of the sea gods.

Gold draperies hung on those walls not covered by book-laden shelves. The fabric shimmered in the lamplight, making the room look rich and reminding Oriana of the opulent libraries she'd seen back in Portugal. A braided rug in mixed blues warmed her bare feet. There was a large rosewood table for opening out the folio-sized texts and a high-backed bench under a pendant lamp meant for more casual reading.

Her grandmother gestured toward the leather-bound books on one of the shelves at eye level. "If you'll pull out those, please, child."

Oriana pulled down the volumes on that shelf and stacked them neatly on the table. When the shelf was empty, she could see a small hole cut in the paneling behind it. Her grandmother handed her a dowel and, following her instructions, Oriana inserted the dowel in the hole and used it to push the paneling aside. It slid back to reveal a shelf in the stone wall behind the paneling. On that shelf was a strongbox made of cast iron with heavy rivets along the seams.

Oriana shot a glance at her grandmother. "When did you put that in here?"

"The shelf was here long before you were born, child," Grand-mother said, laughter in her tone. "The strongbox came from Amer-ica about ten years ago. There's a good trade in them here. Many fear that the bank in Porto Novo would have no choice but to hand over our belongings should the government on Quitos demand it. I trust them with my money, but not this."

Oriana peered at the strongbox. "Is it waterproof?"

"No, although it is supposed to be fireproof, should they ever try to burn this house down."

What a horrible thought.

Her grandmother selected a key from her ring and used it to unlock the box. The door swung open to reveal a pile of papers and, atop that, a single book bound in leather, the spine sewn with red thread. Her grandmother plucked out the book and handed it over. Gooseflesh prickled along Oriana's arms when it touched her hands.

"I haven't read the thing," her grandmother said. "Your father advised me not to. That way I can deny any knowledge of its con-tents."

That was probably wise. As her grandmother locked the safe again, Oriana ran her fingers over the journal's aged cover gingerly, not wanting to snag the delicate leather with her pointed nails. It smelled musty, like any other book one might find in a library. Given all the trouble this thing had caused, it should smell of blood and pain.

Her grandmother began replacing the books Oriana had removed. "I have the original letter that your father sent with it in there also. When I go back up to the mountains, I take the contents of that box with me, so the journal's never been out of my possession all this time."

Oriana swallowed, her throat tight. "I see."

Her grandmother turned back to her, one book in her hand. "In case there's a need to testify about whether it's your mother's or a fake," she clarified. "Now it's in your hands, child. I'll leave you to decide what's best to do with it."

Her father had read part of this journal and reached the conclusion that his mate hadn't died of food poisoning as he'd been told, but had been murdered. Lygia Paredes had worked for the Ministry of Intelligence, vetting new applicants, yet when Oriana's father went to that body to beg them to investigate her death, he'd been arrested, falsely charged with sedition, and exiled from the islands—ample reason for her to believe the book held a secret worth killing for. "Has the Ministry of Intelligence searched your house for this?"

"No," her grandmother said. "The ministry may suspect I have it, but if they *had* found it, it would be gone."

A good point. Oriana stepped closer to the lamp on the wall and opened the journal, picking a spot randomly. She peered at the handwriting and smiled fondly; her mother's hand had never been particularly neat. But what she read there seemed odd. She cast a quick glance back at her grandmother, who was setting the last volumes back onto their shelf, completely masking the sliding panel. "Father noticed there was something wrong with this?"

"Yes," her grandmother said. "He never told me what, though."

Her father hadn't found this journal until four years after her mother's unexpected death. All that time it had lain under the floorboards in the Paredes house on Quitos, waiting for him. Clearly, Lygia Paredes hadn't trusted any of her sisters with the journal. She'd hidden it well, in a place where only her mate knew to look. Even so, Oriana doubted that her mother had foreseen the consequences of his discovery—his exile and her daughters being left without a parent.

Two of their Paredes aunts, Valeria and Vitoria, had taken Oriana and Marina in, saving them a state upbringing, at least. But they'd never been happy there. Their aunts were unfriendly, their two cousins spoiled, and Oriana had been pushed relentlessly to join the Ministry of Intelligence. Her aunts told her that it was her destiny to serve, not to take a mate and bear children. When Marina ran away years later, their aunts spun out a tale that convinced Oriana her younger sister was dead, murdered by sailors on a human ship. They'd even produced a body, although it had been in the sea long enough that it was unidentifiable. The dead girl, however, had been of the same petite build as Marina, so Oriana believed their fabrication. Heartbroken and craving revenge, she'd relented and joined the ministry, only to be given one insignificant assignment after another. None of her three aunts—neither Valerian or Vitoria, nor the eldest Paredes sister, Jovita—had done anything to advance Oriana's career, despite holding high positions in the ministry themselves.

Oriana peered down at her mother's scrawl and blinked back tears. The pages of this book *must* contain a terrible secret for it to be worth all that pain. She closed the journal, not sure she was ready to address that pain tonight.

"I loved your mother too," her grandmother said softly. "She was very good to my son, and I would have been happy for them to live here forever."

Oriana smiled, recalling better days in this house.

"Now, there's another thing I need to discuss with you, child," her grandmother added, settling on the high-backed bench. "And I'd prefer not to put it off."

"Of course, Grandmother." Oriana dutifully tucked the journal under one arm and went to join her.

Duilio had everything unpacked by the time Oriana returned with a slender book clutched in her hand. The bedding was laid out as Oriana liked, their clothing neatly organized on shelves in the dressing area, and the shutters closed to keep the chilly night air outside where it belonged. For the month that they planned to stay, it would be comfortable enough.

"Oh, thank you," Oriana said absently as she took in the fruit of his labors.

He gestured toward the book, suspecting it had caused her melancholy tone. "Is that it?"

She licked her upper lip. "Yes."

"Have you started reading it?"

She sank down on the carved bench near the door. "I read just a bit and . . . there's something wrong."

What does that mean? Duilio sat next to her. "Your father said there's no name in that journal to reveal who killed your mother. Nothing specific."

"That's not what I meant." She opened the journal to a page near the center and pointed to the words. Untidy printing in black ink filled the page, some letters capitalized, others not. "Look at this sentence," she said. "Doesn't it strike you as odd?"

Duilio stared down at words telling of Lygia Paredes' fondness for food with mushrooms, fish and prawns, and cheese. Had Oriana's mother pursued a secondary career as a food critic? "I thought this was about her suspicions regarding the spy within the ministry."

Back in the Golden City, Oriana had been hounded by a woman from the Ministry of Intelligence who used the name Iria Serpa. The woman had ordered Oriana to leave the city, but the ship that should have taken her back to the islands instead left her chained out on a rocky island to die. Only later had they learned that Iria Serpa was not who she claimed. She was a Canary, from that branch of distant cousins of the sereia who served the Spanish crown—a foreign spy hidden within the ministry itself. They'd assumed the journal would show that Oriana's mother had discovered that fact . . . not an interest in fine cuisine.

"That's what I meant." Oriana shook her head. "She rambles in places, talking about the most inane things. She didn't even care for mushrooms. Too bland."

He'd been known to ramble about inane things himself, but when he did, it was usually as a diversion. Duilio stared down at the words on the page, waiting for his brain to sort out what was out of place.

"I'm sure that's what convinced my father something was wrong," Oriana said, "but I can't figure out why she did it."

It was a good sign, to his mind. Oriana's mother *had* been hiding information.

Duilio went to his traveling desk near the windows and sat down, the journal in his hand. Oriana came to gaze over his shoulder while he pulled a fountain pen out of one of the drawers. "Do you mind if I make some small marks in this?"

She shook her head, even though it bothered her to write in books. She set one curved nail against her lip, a gesture of anxiety.

Duilio placed a small dot underneath each capitalized letter in the awkward sentence about food. Most were the initial letters in the words, but in the middle of the word *peixe*, the letter I was capitalized. He took a blank sheet of stationery paper and transcribed the capitalized letters onto it. "Did your mother ever work with codes?"

Oriana leaned over him, setting her chin atop his head. The lily-of-the-valley scent of her perfume surrounded him. "I don't know," she said. "I was only twelve when she died."

"Did she like puzzles?" he asked instead.

Oriana took a breath to speak, thought better of it, and after a moment said, "Mother used to make up puzzles for Marina to solve when she was a girl. I was never good at them, but Marina was. I wasn't patient enough."

He wasn't going to dispute that claim, but Oriana did have patience when needed. "I'm having trouble imagining Marina besting you," he said instead.

Oriana laughed ruefully. "Don't let her guise of helplessness fool you. She lets people think she's compliant because that's often the easier path to getting her way, but she's very clever, and tenacious as a crab when she wants something."

He had to bow to her familiarity with her sister. "Well, I think this is a cipher, an encrypted message where one substitutes one letter for another. Figuring it out is primarily logic. If Cristiano were here he could break it in five minutes. It will take me considerably longer." His young foster brother, Cristiano Tavares, had recently received his degree in mathematics from the university in Coimbra. He loved this type of challenge. "Given some time, you and I can work it out."

"So it's not just . . . rambling?"

"Absolutely not," he reassured her. "I think she meant for someone to pull out all the capitalized letters and decipher the message." He flipped through several pages each direction and saw that the odd pattern of capitalization continued throughout. "There's quite a bit here. I'd need to figure out on which page she started this and work through to the end."

Oriana went and sat down on the bench again, her shoulders slumping. "Thank the gods."

He turned in his chair to face her. "Were you doubting your father's claims?"

"Father didn't believe there was anything specific in the journal," she said, "but if Mother went to all this trouble, there *must* be. If we have her guidance, it will be easier to find out who feared being exposed and had her killed."

Even better, the embedded cipher meant that the journal was more than a toothless threat. It could be used to blackmail the culprit or culprits in return for Oriana's continued safety. Duilio hoped it didn't come to that, but was relieved to know that possibility existed.

They'd discussed what to do with the journal once they had it in their hands. If it named a specific member of the ministry as Iria Serpa's protector, they could advise the ministry that they had a collaborator in their midst. Unfortunately, they still weren't sure whom to trust. Even Oriana's aunts were suspect, since Lygia Paredes had hidden the journal from them.

Duilio closed the journal, slid the book inside his traveling desk, and locked it. Then he joined her on the bench. "Why don't we start off in the morning?" he suggested. "We'll go through it from the beginning and figure it out together."

Oriana sighed and pressed her hands over her face.

Duilio slid one hand under her vest onto her bare back, her skin warm under his fingers. She didn't want to dive into this puzzle right away. She'd wanted a few days without the worries that had plagued her for the last few months, days without decisions to be made. "We *can* put if off for a while."

She dropped her hands to her lap, but didn't reply.

He leaned forward, gazing at her downturned face. If this wasn't about the journal, her grandmother must have said something in the library that she hadn't wanted to hear. "What else is bothering you?"

Oriana turned partway toward him. "She wants to adopt me."

Why would that upset her? "What does that mean?"

"She wants me to have this house, all her property. She wants me to *live* here."

Despite being her granddaughter, Oriana couldn't inherit anything. She was legally dead. In the eyes of the sereia government, the Oriana Paredes who'd come to Quitos to serve as Portugal's ambassador was a completely different Oriana Paredes than the one who'd been left chained on an island to die for unstated crimes the previous fall.

"What of our term as ambassadors?" he asked.

Oriana shook her head. "I explained that we have the rest of our term to serve," she said. "It's after that time that she wants me to live here. Given her age, though, she wants to start the paperwork on the adoption right away."

"I understand."

"Do you?" she asked, a line between her brows. "She wants us to *live* here, Duilio. I don't know what to say to her."

He suddenly grasped what was bothering her. *He* would have to live under the expectations of sereia society. So far he'd followed their rules assiduously. He'd been silent and dutiful, and that rankled. When a new ambassador replaced Oriana, he would have more freedom to do as he wished, although he'd still need to be cautious so as not to damage Oriana's reputation. Living on Amado would, at least, be an improvement over living on the main island.

But it also meant being far from his family. "What is the chance of going back and forth between here and the Golden City?"

"I don't know," she admitted. "Would you hate me for that? Being trapped here?"

He ran his fingers through the burgundy-tinged curls that tumbled down her back. "I'm not trapped. I'm with you."

"Don't pretend it's that easy, Duilio," she said softly.

"It *is* that simple for me," he said. "I will go where you go; I will live where you live."

She sighed and then sniffed. "And what if *I* don't want to be trapped here?"

Ah, she's not sure how she *feels about this.* Oriana always needed more time to decide about anything. They had talked about traveling after her term ended, and possibly returning to the Golden City to live. Now all those plans were endangered. "Let's take a few days and talk it over. Surely she can wait that long."

"I think so." Oriana leaned her head against his shoulder.

He slid one hand under the open front of her vest. "Forget about the journal and your grandmother for now."

She let him push the vest off her shoulders. In a *pareu* and nothing more, her dorsal stripe showed above the edge of the black fabric. He traced one finger along the rippled line of brilliant blue that separated the glittering black of her stripe from the human-colored portion of her back. Below the waist of her *pareu*, that human coloration gave way to a perfect imitation of silver scales, a source of endless fascination for him. She shivered at his touch. "You're not supposed to be demanding."

The core truth of these islands: the woman should always have the upper hand. "No one's here to see me," he reminded her.

Oriana smiled. "Please me, then."

CHAPTER 5

Oriana awoke feeling uncharacteristically muzzy. The room dipped and dove as she breathed the chilly sea air streaming in through the shutters. She'd thought she was past the worst of the morning sickness. She remained still, hoping her stomach would settle into its proper place. The heady scent of lilies filled the room, odd this early in the year.

Duilio's head lay on her breast, and she raised one hand to touch his hair. When she first told him how he would be expected to behave on the islands, she hadn't believed his quick acceptance. Yet so far he'd done everything expected of a mate, including growing out his hair, which made it long enough that she could run the tips of her fingers through it, the webbing between her fingers snagging occasionally on his curls. He hadn't even balked at being tattooed. She ran a finger along one line of his tattoo, only then noting an orange stain on her fingertips and webbing.

She lifted her hand away. *What is that?*

His hair bore a dusting of the yellow-orange substance as well. She pushed at his shoulder and he mumbled in his sleep.

"Duilio, wake up." He didn't have the excuse of pregnancy for his sleepiness. He never came awake quickly, not unless his limited seer's gift perceived a threat. He did move his head to his own pillow, though, allowing her to ease up onto her elbows.

The blankets were heavily dusted with yellow-orange pollen.

Oriana tried to sit up without disturbing the blankets further. She ended up with her back flat against the wall, gazing down on her still-sleeping mate. "Captain Vas Neves! Captain, I need you!"

Startled into wakefulness, Duilio shook himself, but she laid a hand on his shoulder. "Don't move," she whispered. "It's in your hair."

Duilio blinked dazedly but obeyed, trusting her assessment of the situation. She could see the pollen now in her own curls, which meant a thorough washing was in order. *Annoying.* The bedroom door opened, but Lieutenant Benites peered inside rather than the captain. "The captain is off duty, Madam Ambassador."

Oriana gazed up at the young woman. "Someone's been in this room, Lieutenant, while we slept. There's no other explanation for this pollen everywhere."

The lieutenant's hazel eyes swept across the rumpled blankets of their bedding, flicked toward the open shutter, and took in the bathing and dressing area. Then she closed the door again. Oriana could hear the lieutenant's voice as she ordered another guard to fetch the captain. The door opened a second time and Benites stepped back inside. "Corporal Almeida's gone for the captain, madam. What do you need me to do?"

"Oriana," Duilio interrupted.

She held up one hand to forestall him. "We need to roll this blanket up without dislodging any of the pollen. If this is what I think is—*gornarva* pollen—it induces sleep."

"Oriana," Duilio tried again. "Did you get up during the night at all?"

She spared him a glance. He was up on his elbows as she'd been a few moments ago, the yellow-dusted blanket still covering his chest. There was an orange blotch on the tip of his nose, matching his stained fingers. His eyes were fixed on a spot across the room near the door to the bathroom. "No," she answered. "Did you?"

"No," he said, his voice tight. "Look at my desk."

Oh gods. We've been robbed. The desk's lid was up, but Duilio had been careful to lock it the night before. She'd seen him do it. Her first impulse was to jump up and search for the journal, but they needed to clear this mess before a wind came in through the open shutters and disturbed the pollen, putting them all back to sleep. "Duilio, stay here."

He didn't argue, but his jaw clenched in frustration.

Oriana waved the lieutenant over and waited while the young woman carefully lifted the edge of the blankets so that Oriana could shimmy out from underneath them. Then she clambered to her feet and dashed into the dressing room. Unfortunately, the abrupt motion turned her stomach, and she had to stop at the basin to retch up its meager contents.

She quickly rinsed out her mouth and washed her hands. Then she grabbed one of her blue-embroidered *pareus* off the dressing room shelves and wrapped it around her waist. She snatched one of Duilio's as well and returned to the bedroom.

"What exactly is *gornava*?" He eyed the orange-yellow dust warily.

She knelt next to him and began carefully rolling up the blanket. "A carnivorous plant whose pollen, in sufficient quantities, can stun its victims. Usually that's limited to flying insects, but enough collected can induce sleep in a human or sereia."

Her arms folded over her chest, Lieutenant Benites turned away to preserve Duilio's limited modesty. "Someone walked in here and drugged you, madam?"

Oriana had rolled the blanket back enough that Duilio could slide out. He rose and glared down at the yellow-stained bedding. Then he spotted the black *pareu* she'd brought and donned it. "Everyone stand still. Let me look at things before you disturb them."

Oriana crossed her arms, frustrated. She needed to find the

journal, but Duilio was right. He knew what to look for in this sort of situation, things that could tell them who'd done this. She didn't. So she stayed put, gesturing for Benites to remain where she was as well.

Skirting the pollen sprayed across the floor, Duilio crossed to the window and crouched down to peer at the shutter's latch. "I think, Lieutenant, that the order is reversed. They drugged us and *then* walked in here. I latched these shutters before you returned last night, Oriana."

She still felt queasy. *The journal's gone.* She *knew* it already, even without inspecting Duilio's desk. They had nothing else worth stealing here, nothing worth the exorbitant price of this much *gornava* pollen. *We've lost our best chance of finding my mother's killer.*

Oriana swallowed and forced herself to be calm.

A ring of the doorbells preceded Captain Vas Neves letting herself into the room. She wore her full uniform and even had her rifle with her, as if she slept with one hand on it. Perhaps she did. The captain nodded grimly to Lieutenant Benites, eyes flinty, and then surveyed the mess of the bedding. "What's happened here? Is this a prank?"

Duilio left off his investigation of the windowsill. "Please stay where you are, Captain. I'd like to examine the room before anyone disturbs anything else. Someone pried up this screen's latch from the outside, dusted us with pollen while we slept—apparently to keep us that way—then entered. Note that the pattern of the pollen sprays out from this point, so they had to have blown it in from here. Since there's a guard in the hallway, they simply went back out this way."

Benites cleared her throat. "Actually, Captain, Almeida and I arrived at our stations at five this morning. Costa wasn't at his post."

The captain scowled. "Why wasn't I woken?"

"He told Pinho he needed the water closet," Benites said. "We didn't think it exceptional at the time."

With the limited number of guards they'd brought, they'd known they would be stretched thin. Oriana shook her head. "It probably doesn't matter, Lieutenant. Why would the thief not just go back out the way he came?"

Duilio had crossed to the open desk and now stood holding a small piece of metal between his thumb and index finger. "They broke the lock using a knife, but a piece of the blade snapped off. I'm sorry, Oriana, your mother's journal is gone, along with the book I was reading and my personal journal. It wasn't Costa who did this, Captain."

"How do you know?" the captain asked stiffly.

"If you walk carefully around the edge of the room, you'll see," Duilio said.

The captain's eyes narrowed as she plotted a way around the room where she wouldn't mar the pollen. Oriana followed, trying to step only where the captain did. They stopped at one side of Duilio's desk and followed his pointing finger.

The thief had been insufficiently cautious in the unlit room and misplaced one foot. There on the stone floor was a single yellow-stained footprint, one far too small to be Costa's.

Duilio made a scoffing sound and shook his head. "We were robbed by a child."

Duilio pinched the bridge of his nose as Lieutenant Benites escorted the last of the servants away. They'd adopted this front courtyard as their temporary chancery, a place for local trade representatives and the occasional Portuguese ship captain to visit with them, something humans couldn't do on Quitos. The afternoon sun in the courtyard warmed his bare shoulders. The splashing of the central fountain, normally soothing, served only to remind him that time was passing and the trail was already growing cold.

He set his papers aside, rose from the chair he'd occupied for the last few hours, and swung his arms about before striding quickly to one archway and back to the other. Oriana watched him with sympathetic eyes.

She'd done exceptionally well, for the most part asking the questions he would have. He'd written out everything he wanted followed up, and she or Lieutenant Benites could interview those servants again later. It was frustrating, knowing what he wanted to ask, yet not able to question the women himself. Such a break in custom would signal panic, so he'd complied with the rules and held his tongue.

Lieutenant Benites returned to the courtyard then, her eyes darting between Oriana and him before settling on Oriana. "Madam, that's the last of them. And Captain Vas Neves has just returned with Lady Monteiro."

Oriana's grandmother had taken the captain to talk to some of her neighbors on the beach, hoping to determine whether they'd seen anything unusual. Duilio leaned back against the table he'd been using and crossed his ankles, bangles shifting against each other. He didn't want to sit again for a time, not now that he no longer had to play secretary.

No one had seen Lieutenant Costa since he left his duty post that morning. They'd searched the house top to bottom looking for the missing journal, but also hunting him. The lieutenant hadn't slept in his bed, and his bag and remaining clothes were still in his quarters. How Costa was involved in the theft, Duilio was unsure, but logic insisted that the man's disappearance *had* to be related. His gift, however, was ambiguous when Duilio asked about Costa's guilt, as if the man were involved, but unwittingly. For now they'd left all mention of him out of the discussions with the other guards, hoping they could smooth over his absence when they found him. Only Vas Neves and Benites knew for certain that the lieutenant had abandoned his post.

"It seems clear that the child was in the embassy's luggage," Duilio said. Someone had rifled through Costa's bag, removing most of his garments. That last servant they'd questioned had carried it to Costa's room, but claimed it was very light when she picked it up, despite being a comparatively large bag. Yet the other servant who helped with the unloading—she'd carried the bag from the wagon into the entry hallway of the house—had thought it heavy for its size.

"I agree, sir," Benites said. "Since no one has found Costa's missing uniform pieces, it's unlikely they were removed from the bag in this house."

"The only time the embassy's baggage was out of your sight was while you were on the ferry," Oriana said. "Is that right?"

"Yes, madam."

"Then couldn't his baggage have been emptied there?"

Benites stood at ease, her hands folded behind her back. "We were assured by the ferry's captain that no one was allowed in the hold once the ferry was under way, madam, so I don't think that's the case. I also went down into the hold to watch the porters carry up the bags. I didn't notice any loose uniform pieces lying around."

Duilio had an idea about that. "I think someone else carried Costa's clothes away in *their* luggage."

Oriana's brows drew together. "So they went into the hold, took out some of Costa's clothes, and the child climbed into his luggage? Wouldn't someone have noticed that if the hold was supposed to be closed?"

"I suspect the child was *in* another passenger's luggage to begin with. When the hold was closed he climbed out, picked a piece of embassy baggage—the largest, which was Costa's—emptied out some of the clothes, and placed them in his original hiding place."

"That means the child had an accomplice," Oriana said.

"Who would have been a passenger on the ferry with the advance guard," Benites added.

"Yes, or one of the crew," Duilio said. "It would help if we could question the crew of the ferry to see if any of them noticed anything."

Oriana crossed her arms over her chest. "It should be back to Quitos by this time of day. We can try tomorrow."

That was the best he could hope for. "Could we see the hallway where the bags were left? Then I'd like to look at Costa's bag."

"I'll take you there, sir," Benites said.

They followed the lieutenant out of the sunny courtyard and along the white-plastered hallways of the house. Small tapestries hung at intervals, most depicting scenes of a hunt, old enough to show bows and arrows rather than guns. Not too different from other fine tapestries he'd seen, save that the colors were brighter and, of course, the hunters were sereia—females in pursuit rather than males. At the intersection between the front half of the house and the back half, Oriana caught the eye of a passing servant and asked her to fetch the luggage in question from Costa's quarters. Then they proceeded to the wide entryway of the house with its stone flags. A heavy bronze lamp hung from a chain above their heads, but a rectangular stained-glass window above the dark doors let in enough light that the lamp wasn't needed during daylight hours. Benites opened a door to one side, letting them into a large anteroom that was bare save for a series of shelves that wrapped around its sides.

"So the servants carried the baggage in here first," Duilio said, "and then later to the appropriate rooms?"

"Yes, sir," the lieutenant said.

"And how long did the luggage sit here?"

Benites' lips pursed as she mulled that over. "Two hours at most, sir. The head of staff walked through the assigned quarters with the captain, and then we spoke with Lady Monteiro about the expectations for the males."

That would have taken a while. Duilio went to the threshold of the room and peered along the hallway down which they'd come. He didn't see any servants coming or going in either direction at the moment. He crossed to the main doors, a massive pair made out of a dark wood and bearing carvings that depicted ibexes—the local mountain goats. He'd seen the theme throughout the house, part of the Monteiro family crest. The doors' brass lock could easily be defeated, but the heavy metal bar that swung down to barricade the door provided more security. He glanced toward Oriana, who waited at the anteroom's threshold. "Would your grandmother's servants have locked this?"

"Probably," she said. "I'll ask the head of staff. What are you thinking?"

"The boy would have stayed in the bag until he didn't hear any movement, then climbed out, and hid somewhere in the house. He could have gone outside, but it would have been broad daylight and this side of the house can been seen from the road. Why go outside anyway, when he was already here? I suspect he hid in one of the courtyards or on the roof until the house was quiet, and then slipped to the shore side of the house and broke back in through our window."

"You keep assuming it was a boy," Oriana noted dryly.

"It likely was, madam," Captain Vas Neves interjected. The captain had come along a different hallway from the back of the house. "A member of the household at the other end of the beach— the first house encountered when coming from the harbor, I mean— reported seeing a woman waiting at the edge of the road late last night. Early this morning, she saw a young boy walk along the road and the woman met him there. They went toward the harbor together."

"And you think that was our thief?" Duilio asked.

"For a young boy to walk alone is unusual," Oriana said.

Duilio signed that she was correct. He'd forgotten that boys would be protected here.

"The witness, Lady Guerra, was quite specific," the captain went on. "She noticed the woman because she was wearing a neck clap."

Oriana's nose wrinkled. "Here? On Amado? That *is* odd enough to cause comment."

Duilio shared Oriana's surprise. A neck clap was a leather collar, sometimes placed around the neck of a sereia to place pressure on the gills. It kept them from *calling*, but was reportedly highly uncomfortable. Given the sensitivity of Oriana's gill slits, he didn't doubt that. The only sereia who wore them were local employees of the various embassies—the household staffs. They'd decided not to require them of workers at the Portuguese embassy, one more attempt to show that the Portuguese saw the inhabitants of the islands as equals. Either way, none of the embassies had presences here on Amado, which raised the question of why the woman was still wearing one. If she'd been on the ferry and had worn one there, the crew *would* remember her.

"Could she describe the woman?" Duilio asked.

"Quite clearly," the captain said. "And the boy as well."

Good news. He smiled. "Any idea how old he was?"

"Lady Guerra guessed seven or eight. From what Lady Monteiro said, he should be comparatively easy to find. He was dressed like a local child, but didn't have gills or webbing."

"He was webless?" Oriana asked, brow furrowing again. "But not human?"

"That was the term Lady Guerra used," the captain said with a nod. "*Webless.*"

That could be an insulting term here on the islands, a way of describing someone as too human. Oriana hadn't used the term that way, though. The simpler connotation indicated the person so named literally had no webbing between the fingers. As it was common for males born of a human father and a sereia mother to lack both gills and webbing, their young thief *must* be half human. The boy would still bear the fishlike markings of a sereia on his lower body, so he couldn't pass for human either, not while wearing a *pareu*.

"Can I assume Costa wasn't with the woman and boy?" Duilio asked the captain.

"He was not, sir."

"If the woman and the boy were that remarkable, we should be able to trace them."

"If they took a ferry back to Quitos," the captain said, "we've lost them anyway. We don't have the resources to question people on the main island."

True. The only reason the captain received the cooperation of the neighbors here was that Oriana's grandmother had accompanied her. On Quitos, no one would answer the captain's questions at all. Nor could they go to the police there, not when the item stolen was most likely stolen by the Ministry of Intelligence itself.

Duilio looked at the captain and lieutenant, and then at Oriana with her clenched jaw. She had one fist pressed to her lips, her eyes distracted. She blamed herself for the journal's loss, although it was just as much his fault.

There was one thing he could try, a remote chance. "Captain, first thing in the morning, I'd like you to take a letter to the American embassy."

"Would I not be of more use here, sir?" the captain asked with a frown. "I can question the ferry's crew when they arrive."

"Let's let Benites do that, Captain. I want the Americans to know I'm serious, which is why I prefer to send the head of our military attachment."

The captain inclined her head gravely. "Madam Ambassador, does that meet with your approval?"

Duilio didn't protest the captain's request. She *did* answer to Oriana first.

"What do you mean to do?" Oriana asked him.

In his younger life, he'd studied crime with different police forces across Europe. While in London he'd rescued a boy who'd been taken and held for ransom, not for money but for stakes in a political matter between two countries—the son of an American ambassador. The incident had never been reported by the newspapers or written up by the police, but Duilio hoped his help wasn't forgotten. "I intend to remind the American Foreign Office that they owe me a favor."

CHAPTER 6

Normally Joaquim Tavares would have gone directly to his office at the Massarelos Police Station, but this morning he'd gone to the Ferreira household. It wasn't for the lovely pastry studded with almonds that the cook pressed on him, nor for the friendly chat with the butler. He'd come to see Lady Ferreira's maid instead.

In the back of the house, the modest kitchen was always warm thanks to the large cast-iron stove from which the heavenly scent of baking bread currently drifted. The kitchen maid worked at the far end, preparing fish for luncheon, Joaquim guessed from the grating sound of a scaling knife. Mrs. Cardoza, a large and imposing woman with an equally large heart, rose from the oak servants' table to supervise the girl, leaving Joaquim alone there. Not for long, though, as Miss Felis, Lady Ferreira's elderly maid, came down the steps into the warm kitchen. Her thin frame was draped in black as always, the only hint of color about her being the pale peach threads in her finely embroidered white collar. Joaquim rose to embrace her, worrying over the frail feel of her shoulders. He didn't dare say anything, though, because Felis believed she was made of steel and hated to be seen as infirm.

He and his brother, Cristiano, had moved into this house when Joaquim was only eight years old, taken in by Lady Ferreira when their mother died in childbirth. Lady Ferreira had suspected even then, Joaquim now knew, that he was actually her husband's child, not the son of Joaquim Tavares, the man for whom he'd been named. Even so, she'd always treated him well, like one of her own sons. Felis, old enough to be Lady Ferreira's mother, had become a surrogate grandmother to him. There wasn't much in this household that Felis didn't know.

After a few moments of pleasantries, she sat down at the servants' table, her pack of well-worn cards in her equally well-worn hands. While he waited, she shuffled them and let him cut the deck. Once he'd handed it back, she held the deck out for him to select a card. She set that one facedown and then began laying the remaining cards in three neat piles.

Joaquim pressed his lips together. Normally he would have discussed his worries with Duilio or their cousin Rafael, but Duilio was far away and Rafael had gone to Lisboa to speak with the Jesuit brotherhood there. So he'd come here instead. Since childhood, Felis had been his last line of inquiry. If there was something bothering him, once normal inquiries and even prayer failed to provide guidance, he would turn to her. She was a gentle soul despite her gruff manner. And while there were those who considered reading cards sinful, he had yet to see harm come of anything Felis had done, so he waited patiently while she finished arranging the cards.

Her dark eyes peered up at him, then. "What do you need to know, Filho?"

His nickname within the family, *Filho* simply meant *son*. He'd been named for his father, or more accurately, the man who'd taken responsibility for him and raised him. And while the elder Joaquim Tavares might not have fathered him, he would always hold the place of *father* within Joaquim's heart.

"I had a dream," Joaquim said, "that Duilio needs my help."

Mrs. Cardoza strolled back over to listen, dusting flour from her capable hands onto her apron.

Felis regarded him steadily. "Do you want to know if you should help him?"

Joaquim nearly laughed. *That* had never been in question. He'd always gone to Duilio's aid when needed. "No, I'm going."

Felis nodded sagely, as if she'd expected that answer. "Then what?"

Joaquim licked his lips. "Will Miss Arenias wait for me?"

"She would be a fool not to, Mr. Joaquim," Mrs. Cardoza said, laying a floury hand on his shoulder to reassure him.

He'd have to remember to dust off the back of his jacket after he left. "Thank you," he said, glancing up at the cook. "But I wouldn't blame her. I don't know how long this mission of Duilio's will take."

Felis lifted the solitary card and peered at it. She frowned and laid it back on the table, then picked up one of the piles and began redistributing the cards, flipping some over and leaving others facedown until she had nine cards lying faceup on the table. Her murmurs took on an angry tone.

That doesn't sound good. Joaquim licked his lips. Duilio didn't believe Felis was a true seer. He believed she merely provided a framework for the listener to organize what he already knew about the situation. Joaquim wasn't so sure. She'd always seemed magical to him.

Felis glared at her cards, the corners of her thin lips drawn down in a mighty frown. "You're going to go on a journey."

Since I've already said I was going to help Duilio, that's given.

The old woman fingered the one card *he'd* drawn, the ten of clubs. "You're to go on a journey to visit a relative." She pulled four of the upturned cards to sit next to it, laying the king of spades on the top of that batch. "These all say that you'll be under a cloud, that there will be complications, and that you will come out of this journey changed."

Again, he'd known that. As one of the Ferreira males, he'd

inherited a seer's gift. He'd been told his seer's gift was buried under his inheritance from his mother, the gift of *finding*. That stronger gift served him well in his work for the police, where he usually spent his hours hunting missing people whom other officers couldn't find. But when he slept or meditated, his seer's talent would sometimes emerge, presenting him with dreams or visions of something ahead of him on the road of life. Both his half brother, Duilio, and his cousin Rafael Pinheiro—the bastard son of a bastard son of the Ferreira family—possessed the seer's gift, although Rafael's talent was by far the strongest and most reliable. Joaquim's recent dreams had shown him over and over again traveling to the islands of the sereia and beyond. One thing those dreams carried was a promise of transformation, although of what kind, he didn't know.

He'd never been fond of change.

Felis picked out two more cards, the jack of diamonds and the queen of clubs. "A man and a woman will come to your aid, but that woman will *not* be the woman you love."

"I see. But will Miss Arenias wait for me?"

She pushed the six of clubs toward him. "Soon you will marry."

What? Joaquim glanced up at her. "So Miss Arenias *will* wait for me to return?"

"No," she said softly. "These cards are all tied to your journey, Filho. They say you will marry *before* you return home, while you are on this journey."

His chest tight, Joaquim rose from the table, nearly backing into Mrs. Cardoza. He'd forgotten she was standing behind him. He'd always been sure that Marina Arenias was the one for him. But if Felis was correct, then *he* was the one who wouldn't wait. *How can that be?*

He pinched his nose. He shouldn't have done this. If the prediction Felis made was true, he would rather not have known. Even so, he had to believe that he made his own way in life. No matter what his gift told him about his future, his decisions were *always* his own.

"Thank you for your time, Miss Felis. I have a lot of things to take care of before I go, so I may not see you again for a while."

The old woman gathered her cards and slid them back into their tattered box, her mouth pursed in a worried scowl. Mrs. Cardoza hugged him and promised to bear his farewells on to Cardenas, the butler, and to Lady Ferreira. Then Joaquim took his leave, his nerves rattled.

ILHAS DAS SEREIAS

Duilio sat in the warm afternoon sunlight in the front courtyard. He'd laid out a timeline for every event in the stolen journal's history. He sat back in his chair, pressed his folded hands to his lips, and closed his eyes as he contemplated what was happening.

The ferry captain had proven a fount of information about the thieves who'd taken the journal. The woman, remarkable because she wore a neck clap, had taken the same ferry to Amado that the advance guard had. She'd stayed on the lower deck, so they hadn't seen her. Where she and the boy had gone the next day, taking the journal with them, was still unclear.

Logic told Duilio that the journal was in the hands of the Ministry of Intelligence now, if it hadn't been destroyed outright. He couldn't bring himself to believe it. Every time he asked his gift if the ministry had the journal, it fed him a resounding *no*.

What he couldn't figure out was *why*. His gift never told him that aspect of the future, no matter how important it was. Only yes or no.

He rubbed his hands over his face, got up from his chair, and strode around the courtyard. It was a lovely afternoon, and if he weren't stuck here trying to figure out what had happened, he would have liked to be hiking some of those mountain trails Oriana had told him about. Or swimming. He quit his pacing and leaned with his back against one of the courtyard's warm walls.

The thief could have turned the journal over to the ministry anytime in the past four days. Why hadn't she? His best guess was that she was negotiating with the ministry, possibly for more money, but when asked that, his gift again told him *no*.

He'd tried a different tack, asking whether the theft was related to the Spanish. His gift told him *yes*, but when he asked himself if their thief was a Canary like Iria Serpa, that had seemed wrong. He asked whether she was acting as an agent of the Spanish throne, whether she was working for the Spanish embassy here, whether she was working for the ministry. All were ambiguous, as if all were true, or none. He couldn't make sense of that.

It seemed more and more likely that their investigation needed to be carried to Spain—a place that he, as a member of the ambassadorial mission, couldn't go. He couldn't send Vas Neves or Benites either, not without the Portuguese Foreign Office asking questions they didn't want to answer.

That morning, he'd written a letter to Joaquim, asking for his help. If anyone could find the journal, Joaquim could. But this wasn't Joaquim's problem. His brother had his own life to live, and Duilio didn't want to force Joaquim away from his all-consuming work with the police. Before Lent, Joaquim had written that he intended to ask Marina to marry him. Duilio didn't want to ruin that either.

And there was danger involved; the Spanish weren't fond of witches. Spanish witches were expected to disavow their gifts, leave the country, or be imprisoned. While one couldn't simply look at Joaquim and know he was a witch—save for Inspector Gaspar, of course, who *had* done exactly that—Duilio wouldn't risk his brother's safety by asking him to go there.

So he left the letter in his desk drawer. He had to find someone else.

Oriana sat on the carved bench next to the bedroom door with a small writing table pulled up before it. The sunlight coming in through the east-facing windows was beginning to fade, so she squinted as she plied a soft cloth in an effort to remove ink from under one of her nails. Before her on the table lay the adoption paperwork that would make her a citizen of these islands again. She'd signed on so many lines she'd thought her hand would cramp.

The bells warned her a second before Duilio came into the bedroom. He settled next to her on the bench, and she caught the faint musky seal scent of his skin, warmed from the sunlight in the courtyard. "I've signed these," she said. "Are you sure?"

Shaking his head, Duilio took the cloth from her hand. As her legal advisor, he'd read through the paperwork a couple of times. Despite its being drafted by members of a very different culture, he said the legal terminology was reassuringly similar. He'd asked her grandmother for clarification on several points, and had seemed satisfied with her answers.

It would mean living here most of the time, but they would be able to travel. There was also an expectation that she would step into her grandmother's role as a leader among the top families on the island of Amado. That meant a lifetime of political involvement.

The islands were governed by an oligarchy, with members of all the prominent families serving as a senate. Monteiro was one of the oldest family lines representing Amado in that body. But everyone knew the true power lay in the elders of only five family lines, all of them on Quitos. That concentration of power on Quitos kept the other islands from seizing control of the archipelago.

Until recently Oriana wouldn't have liked the idea of service in the government, but the past few months as ambassador had allowed her to explore her views on political matters. She'd developed aspirations of activism, both on behalf of Northern Portugal, of which she was now a citizen, and the males of these islands. While in Portugal, she'd experienced the constraints under which women there lived. Duilio lived with similar restrictions now, even on Amado, and she didn't want that for him. Or for their children.

His warm eyes met hers. "I understand these documents. I know what they say."

"And will you forgive me for signing them?"

She had nearly refused to marry him for fear that she would have to live out her life pretending to be a human woman. Now *he* would have to spend most of his life in the role of a sereia male. But he merely picked up the papers, secured them with a clip, and took them to the door. "There's nothing to forgive."

The guard outside the door bore the papers away on Duilio's request to Grandmother's head of staff. Duilio came back into the bedroom and locked the door behind him. "Now stop worrying about them. The adoption is the least of our problems."

She sighed and rested her head back against the wall as he told her of his afternoon's musings. The thief's trail only seemed to grow dimmer. Did the woman still have the journal with her? And where did Costa fit in to all this? Duilio's gift seemed confident they'd find the lieutenant alive, but the man had vanished like a mist as well.

After Duilio finished, she asked, "So, did you decide about your letter to Joaquim?"

"Yes," he said. "I'm not going to post it. There has to be someone other than Joaquim we can send to Spain. Besides, he barely speaks Spanish."

They'd chosen not to contact the Portuguese Foreign Office. It wasn't a lack of faith in their own superiors, but instead a distrust of the forbearance of the military. There were too many senior officers waiting for the female military contingent to fail. If they reported the theft of a personal item and the disappearance of an officer to the Portuguese Foreign Office, there would be those in the military who would immediately call for the dissolution of the guard contingent. The women would be thrown out of the army. Given her new awareness of political matters, Oriana suspected that would be a blow to the rights of all women in the country. So she'd decided to keep the matter from the Foreign Office's ears as long as possible. Since the journal was private property, stolen from a private residence, she had no obligation to tell them.

Reporting Costa's absence, however, could only be put off for so long. The other guards had been fed a tale of Costa being on a special mission, although Oriana doubted many of them believed that. Sooner or later they would have to admit he was missing, and charges of desertion of duties would be filed against him.

She turned her mind back to the problem of Spain. Duilio's cousin worked for the new division of the Special Police that handled crimes involving nonhumans and witches. A policeman might be able to collaborate with the police in Spain. "Rafael, perhaps?"

"No, he doesn't speak Spanish at all." Duilio mimicked her pose, closing his eyes. His mouth fell open slightly and his breathing slowed.

She recognized that look. He was talking with his gift, trying to pry loose scraps of information. He had to ask it the right questions to get anything, and even then, sometimes his gift didn't provide the answers he needed. After a few minutes, she began to suspect he'd nodded off, but he abruptly sat up straight, a smile lighting his face.

"What?" she asked.

"I was thinking about those Sundays when Joaquim and Rafael and I would sit in the library, and I was wishing that Joaquim was here now."

"So you want to send the letter after all?"

"There's no need," he said. "Joaquim is coming here anyway."

CHAPTER 7

THE GOLDEN CITY

Late-afternoon light streamed through the northeast-facing windows in the front parlor of the Pereira de Santos home, bathing Lady Ana with a golden glow. The tall and elegant young woman sat at the writing desk next to a potted palm, composing a letter of recommendation for Marina. Not for employment, but to introduce her to a very exclusive seamstress.

Marina's father suddenly insisted on having a dozen new outfits made up for her, both for her work and for social calls, and while Marina knew seamstresses who might alter something ready-made, she hadn't before patronized any who worked the custom trade. It was a daunting prospect, and she welcomed Ana's offer to help with that quest. Ana had an excellent seamstress, one who made her tall frame seem less imposing. Certainly no one would ever call Ana's attire less than elegant. Marina only hoped the seamstress could make her own petite stature seem more substantial.

One of the Pereira de Santos footmen coughed discreetly at the doorway, and Ana gestured for him to allow in her guest. Marina was shocked to see that it was Joaquim. He'd never come to this house before. Not to see *her*, at least.

Marina rose as Joaquim entered the sitting room, and he smiled in her direction.

He wore a brown-checked suit today, not one of his newer ones. He looked out of place in this room filled with its expensive dark velvets and green silk draperies, but he refused to be intimidated by the aristocracy and their fine trappings. He inclined his head toward Lady Ana first. "Miss Pereira de Santos, how lovely to see you."

Marina hid her smile behind her gloved hand. She'd never heard him call anyone *lady* other than Lady Ferreira.

"Inspector," Ana said, meeting his eyes.

Marina knew Ana well enough not to mistake her coolness as dismissive. Ana was exceedingly reserved, earning her the reputation of a wallflower in society. Part of that stemmed from her height, which convinced many young men never to approach her. She stood a finger taller than Joaquim, and *he* was above average. But Ana possessed a finely honed awareness of the character of others, and high standards for those to whom she chose to give her time. So while her stylish morning dress with its severe lines only served to highlight the tattiness of Joaquim's suit, Ana would treat him as if he were the prince himself.

"I'll ask the butler if the mail has arrived," Ana announced, and then walked past Joaquim without a further word.

Joaquim crossed to Marina's side and she craned her neck to gaze up into his face. He was tall, and she definitely was *not*. He stared down at his hands as if they held the answers, and rather predictably, his brown eyes flicked toward *her* hands. Marina held them still, hoping he hadn't noticed she'd been rubbing them together. She often did that when her mind wandered. There was an enduring ache where she'd had the webbing between her fingers removed.

Something has to be wrong. Why else would he have followed her here, to a place he'd never visited before? Why on a Monday morning when he should be at the police station and she would normally have been at work? *How did he even know where to find me?* "What are you doing here?"

"Duilio wrote to me," he said, eyes still lowered. "He needs my help, an investigation. I don't know how long this will take, but I could be gone some time."

Some time? Marina gripped her hands together. "Do you have to go?"

"Yes," he said softly.

Marina wiped a tear from the corner of her eye before it fell. She was not going to cry. He hadn't made her any promises. But she dreaded not seeing him for so long. "Is that all?"

He shook his head then. "I need to tell you something . . ."

Marina glanced up, startled by his hesitant tone. His eyes were shut, his lips pressed together, as if whatever he held in pained him.

"There's something you need to know about me. Something I haven't told you." He took a deep breath, and said, "I'm a bastard."

Marina sat down in the nearest chair, a large armchair in maroon velvet. *What does that mean?*

"I'm actually the son of Alexandre Ferreira, not Joaquim Tavares," he clarified.

That made Duilio Ferreira his brother rather than his cousin. She could see that in Joaquim's face. He and Duilio had the same long straight nose, the same square jaw and wide brows. She'd thought the resemblance between them remarkable for cousins. *This is why Lady Ferreira wants him to move into the Ferreira house. He's Alexandre Ferreira's son and has as much right to share in the family's fortune as Duilio.*

"Does Oriana's husband know that?" she asked.

"Yes," Joaquim admitted, standing next to her chair.

And that meant her older sister knew, yet hadn't mentioned it. *Why not?*

"I don't care." Marina pushed herself out of the chair so he didn't have to lean over so much. "I don't care who your parents were, Joaquim."

He threw a glance up at the ceiling. His lips remained pressed together, though, one of those expressions that reminded her so strongly of Oriana's husband. *Like he's still holding something in.*

How hard had it been for him to say that to her? To admit aloud that he wasn't who people believed him to be? It meant nothing to her—Joaquim was still the same man in her eyes—but clearly it meant a great deal to him. It bothered him, and she wished she knew the reasons for that. But that wasn't what he needed right now. Instead of questioning him further, Marina took his hands in hers. "I will be waiting here when you come back. However long that takes."

He tugged one hand free and cupped her cheek. This close, she could catch the smell of his perspiration and his cologne—a fascinating and very masculine mixture. She laid her hands on his chest. When she gathered her nerve to meet his eyes, he was smiling down at her regretfully. He leaned closer and, fearing he might change his mind, Marina rose on her toes and pressed her lips to his.

His mouth was warm against hers. The hand that had been cupping her cheek slid into her hair as his lips explored hers, softly at first, and then with more urgency. Marina pressed closer, her arms twining about Joaquim's neck.

She had waited so long for him to kiss her that she felt her heart would burst.

One of his hands settled on the small of her back, holding her fast against him. She had never been this close to a man before, not in this way. It was thrilling. He was all heat and strength. He was something she'd never known before, but she wanted more.

But then he pushed her away from him—not hard, just enough to make her stumble back a step or two. Marina stared at him, shocked, but his eyes moved toward the open doorway behind her. She glanced over her shoulder and saw Ana walking back into the room, her attention on a handful of letters she held.

Marina turned quickly to face her, hoping her dress wasn't disarranged or her hair mussed. Her breath was coming too fast. *I hope she doesn't notice.*

Ana placidly looked up from her letters. Her eyes flicked from Marina to Joaquim and back, and her dark brows rose. Then she walked over to her desk and sat down without a single word. She fiddled with papers, opening drawers and hunting a new pen nib, evidently.

Reprieved from an embarrassing discussion, Marina turned back to Joaquim. His breathing sounded stifled, tight, as if he was fighting to control it. *At least I have some effect on him.* "How are you going to get there?"

"I'm taking the yacht."

Yes, the Ferreira family had boats. Her people's islands weren't on maps, and the sereia navy used their magic to divert ships around the islands. It was difficult to get into port there without the government's permission. "How will you find the islands?"

"I'm a witch," he said with an apologetic shrug.

Marina felt her mouth fall open.

"Finding people is what I do," he added. "That's my *gift*, and Duilio's easy for me to find because I know him so well. I'll set my course by my sense of him."

She would have expected him to be a seer. That was what ran in the Ferreira family, wasn't it? But she must be wrong.

"Does that bother you?" he asked cautiously.

"No. Given that I'm not human, I . . ." She wasn't certain where she'd meant that statement to go. Instead she said, "Honestly, Joaquim, I wouldn't care if you were one of the otter folk and had been hiding a tail all along."

He smiled at the ridiculous image, but all too quickly his expression slid back to seriousness.

Marina rubbed her hands together. *How many more secrets does he have? Is it easy for him to find me?* Was that how he'd known where to find her today? She didn't dare press too hard, or he would stop talking altogether. "Are you . . . are you going alone?"

"I'll take João," he said. "The yacht's too big for me to handle alone easily. And I'm out of practice."

Marina caught her lower lip between her teeth. João was the Ferreira family's boatman, and had a beautiful young selkie wife who would surely accompany them. "When do you mean to leave?"

"In the morning. It should be a few days' sailing with good winds."

She'd only traveled between the islands and Northern Portugal once, and that had been an indirect journey aboard a steamer. She had no idea how sailing was different. "Oh."

Joaquim cast a glance over at Ana sitting at her desk, the overseer of their propriety. Then he stepped forward and took Marina's hands in his own. "When I return, we'll talk then?"

She nodded, not certain she could trust her voice. Joaquim wouldn't have come to this decision lightly. He never made *any* decision lightly.

He raised her hands to his lips and kissed them, his brown eyes on hers all the while. That one lock of hair swept across his forehead again. "I'll hold you to that."

Marina felt her cheeks burning, as if he'd said something far more salacious. She let his hands slip away from hers. There was something on his face, though, a faint line between his dark eyebrows or perhaps the set of his lips. Something *was* wrong.

"Be safe, then," he said instead. He walked away, no doubt trying to preserve her reputation in front of Ana or some other upright nonsense like that. Marina heard his voice in the hallway, speaking to the butler as the man let him out the front door. And then she heard the door close. Her heart felt empty.

"Well," Ana said, almost in her ear.

Marina jumped and spun about to face the other young woman. "He's leaving."

One of Ana's slender eyebrows rose, her more usual wordless communication.

"He has to go to the islands. Something about helping . . ." No, she wouldn't reveal Joaquim's secrets to Ana. "Mr. Ferreira asked him to come, and he doesn't know how long he'll be gone."

Ana drew her toward the Brazilian leather couch. Marina sat

on the couch's edge, rubbing her left hand with her right. All she could do now was pray for Joaquim's safe return, yet surely . . .

Ana handed her a square envelope. "This was left for you."

For me? Here? Marina took the envelope gingerly. When she popped loose the wax seal, the envelope opened to reveal a single playing card, the ten of clubs. The sender had scrawled a single sentence on the envelope's flap. *You must give this to Mr. Joaquim.* Marina felt her brow furrowing. "I don't understand."

Ana leaned closer. "Do you know someone who reads cards?"

Marina shook her head. Her people didn't think much of seers of any type.

"If I recall correctly," Ana said, "that's a lucky card. It mitigates the ills of all the other cards in the reading."

Marina wished that were true. She would move the moon and stars to take away whatever was worrying Joaquim if only she could. "But how can I give this to him if he's gone?"

CHAPTER 8

The morning seemed an auspicious one to begin a journey, no matter the ominous predictions Felis had made. The sun shone warmly with no hint of fog. The Douro River sparkled, the dipper birds popped merrily in and out of the water, and even the cries of the gulls overhead seemed cheerful. Joaquim tried to wrap that positive air around himself. He'd hardly slept the previous night, balancing his desire to stay with his need to go. But after hours of wakefulness, he'd packed a bag and headed for the quay where the ship waited.

Deolinda was the Ferreira family's yacht. Commissioned by Duilio's grandfather, it had languished for the last few years, moored with the Ferreira family's smaller boats, the ones they regularly used. Alexandre Ferreira had sailed often, but his eldest son, Alessio, hadn't shared his love for the sea. And while Duilio *did*, he'd always been too busy to take the yacht out. The only time this ship had been away from its moorings recently was when Duilio had taken Oriana to France shortly after their wedding.

But careful maintenance by the family's boatman, João, kept the yacht fit to sail. The lines were all sound and the hull clean. The yacht slipped from its mooring, its small engine chugging away, and shortly thereafter they moved through the mouth of the Douro River and onto the open sea.

Rigging the sails took longer than Joaquim expected. João needed to explain everything to his wife, so Joaquim held his tongue. Aga was a selkie and had only been living among humans for half a year. Things that would be obvious to a child made no sense to her. It was clear, though, that she and João doted on each other. Aga listened to her husband's every word, eyes wide.

She was a beautiful young woman, with a pointed chin and a heart-shaped face that bore a resemblance to Lady Ferreira's. Selkies often had that look about them. Her light brown hair fell over her shoulder in a simple braid and she wore garments that must be João's, altered down for her slender frame. She didn't seem particu-larly clever, but she followed João's instructions perfectly, never set-ting one bare foot amiss on the deck.

"No, like this," João said patiently as he showed Aga how to attach the jib sheet using a soft shackle. He unwrapped the line from the clew and let her try again, smiling when she had it right. "Per-fect. This way it will be easier to loosen it when we need to."

Joaquim turned away, leaving João to explain the rigging. He lacked the young man's patience. And he had other work to do.

He'd always thought his ability to find others was simple intu-ition until the previous fall, when he'd been forced to acknowledge it as witchery by Inspector Gaspar of the Special Police. The man had a special gift of his own, one that allowed him to look at others and *see* what hidden talents they possessed. Gaspar claimed that he rarely forced a witch to acknowledge his or her gift; he'd made an exception in Joaquim's case, since his talent was needed at the time. Despite finding the man likable, Joaquim felt uncomfortable around him even now, months later. He couldn't be sure Gaspar had told him everything, and didn't want to be taken by surprise again.

Now that he knew he had a gift, it was his responsibility to use it wisely.

Joaquim closed his eyes and said a quick prayer, begging for guid-ance. He knew the general direction he had to go to find Duilio—west of Portuguese shores, of course. But when he concentrated, he saw in his mind a faint light, as if his brother held up a lantern in the far distance to guide him.

After fixing that distant point of light in his mind, Joaquim checked the chart against his compass and drew a line straight out from their current position. The islands of the sereia must lie on that line some-where. That course would take them north of Madeira, but he didn't think they would have to go as far as the Azores. It would mean a night on the open ocean, possibly two. He hadn't done that in years, but with João and his wife along, they could split the time on the deck.

The wind caught the sails then, drawing them away from the coast.

"Are we heading the right way?" João called back toward him.

"Yes." Unfortunately, there wasn't any landmark to guide them at all. They were relying completely on his gift to set their course. *Rank idiocy.* But João trusted him, so they kept the ship on the same compass heading throughout the day.

As the hours passed, Joaquim watched the waves under the bright sun with growing unease. It wasn't his meager seer's gift warning him of anything. It was simple discomfort in being so far out at sea. He and Duilio had sailed to Madeira one summer as boys, and it had been as difficult then. He just didn't like leaving home.

Especially now, when he had so much to lose. He would have to hope and pray that Felis had been wrong.

ILHAS DAS SEREIAS

The doorbells leading into the courtyard rang softly, and Duilio saw Captain Vas Neves at the entry archway, waiting to be acknowledged. He waved her in. "Captain, I'm glad you've returned."

She'd been gone since Saturday morning, bearing his letter to the American embassy in the capital. That visit to the main island had also given her time to advise their chief of staff regarding the changed situation and revise orders to her guards there.

She nodded. "I came directly to you, sir, since I have a report on the Americans."

"What did they have to say?"

"The ambassador set her people to investigating immediately," the captain said, "rather than waiting for orders from her superiors." Madam Norton, a clever woman in her midforties, had been American ambassador to these islands for over a decade. She had her own cadre of spies and locals willing to sell her information, an enviable position at the moment. Not only did the Portuguese mission face distrust from locals who feared a Portuguese invasion that would never happen, but they simply hadn't had time to set up a network as the Americans had.

"That's good to know," Duilio said, "but the two Spanish ships left port on schedule this morning, as did one of the English ones."

Vas Neves nodded gravely. "Yes. The ambassador informed me she had people looking into that possibility, sir. Of the woman leaving the islands."

He was glad Madam Norton had that much foresight. He could question the ship captains himself—on the docks, the humans didn't mind a male dredging for information. Unfortunately, he couldn't question the captains who'd already left. "Also good to know," he said anyway.

"She means to send word of what she's learned in a few days, sir."

"Frankly, I'm surprised they're willing to help," Duilio admitted, "so that's just fine. Is there any other news?"

"I've sent the correspondence from the embassy to the ambassador already," Vas Neves said. "I merely wanted to inform you of our interactions with the Americans."

Only the parts that directly concern me. Duilio swallowed his irritation. "Thank you, then, Captain."

The captain nodded again and, before stepping out of the court-yard, said, "Also, the ambassador told me to tell you she's impressed with your . . . audacity. I believe that's the best translation of the phrase she used, which was, admittedly, rather vulgar. I'm not certain she's aware that I speak English."

Duilio grinned at the image of dainty Madam Norton spouting vulgarities. He suspected the American knew more about Vas Neves than he did. With their ample resources, the American Foreign Office had probably had every member of the Portuguese mission investigated before they'd even set foot on Quitos.

He hadn't been sure the Americans would honor an *implied* debt several years old, but he was glad now that he'd taken the chance.

THE OPEN OCEAN

Joaquim sighed as he descended the ladder into the cabin, thinking only of the bunk and a good night's sleep. It had been too long since he'd spent an entire day sailing. In the morning he was going to have sore muscles in spots not often used.

He'd left João and Aga on deck. While the yacht wasn't in the normal shipping lanes, the sea was calm, and they'd put out the sea anchor, they still couldn't afford to take chances. There was almost no moon tonight, and they had no idea where sereia waters began. Fortunately, Aga wouldn't be affected should a sereia attempt to misdirect them away from their course.

Joaquim peeled off his salt-stiffened shirt, then his undershirt, and draped them over the rail. It was dark in the cabin, but he didn't need a lamp. He slipped off his boots and slid under the blankets on the bunk. It was a haven of warmth. After shifting about to find a comfortable position in the small berth, he dragged one pillow about so that he clutched it in his arms, and laid his head on the other.

When he closed his eyes, his earlier cares flooded back. *What is*

Marina doing? Is she thinking of me? He mentally checked his gift, certain he could find Marina even a day's sail away from shore.

Only his sense of her was all wrong.

Joaquim sat up, banging his head on the shelf above the bunk in his haste. He rubbed at his temple and swung his legs over the side of the bunk. Cool air assaulted his bare chest. His eyes had adjusted to the darkness by then. "Marina?"

A cough came from the closet nearest the foot of the bunk. Joaquim rose and opened the door. A hint of light showed him Marina's slim form huddled in the bottom of the closet, arms wrapped about her knees. Her face lifted, revealing reddened eyes.

Stifling the urge to laugh in relief, Joaquim knelt down to help her up. "How long have you been in here?"

"Since before dawn," she whispered, sounding guilty about it. Her small hands shook as they settled on his arms.

Oh God. That was far too long to be hiding in that cramped spot. "Are you hurt?"

"No. I'm fine," she managed. He drew her to her feet, but she slumped against him. "I'm sorry. My . . . my legs are asleep."

Joaquim wrapped his arms about her. *No point in being reserved now.* He helped her toward the bunk. "Here, come sit down with me."

When she sat down on the bunk's edge, he wrapped one arm about her shoulders. Her hands touched on his side, her chilly fingers reminding him that he was only half-clothed. He used his free hand to tug the blanket around both of them. Marina's face pressed against his chest. He wanted to hold her like this all night.

No, he wanted *more.*

He'd intended to propose to her on the first of May. It wouldn't be too far off his schedule to ask her now. He'd wanted their marriage to start off better than this, though. To try to make love to her in this cramped cabin wasn't what he'd planned at all. "Marina, does your father know where you are?"

"Please don't send me back," she whispered. "Please."

She hadn't answered his question. He found her chin and tilted her head up to peer into her eyes. "I won't. Either I will leave you with your sister on the islands, or you'll come with me. But I don't want your father to worry."

She clutched at the blanket. "Ana will tell him."

Miss Ana had something to do with this; that suggested *planning*. "You do know that João and his wife are on the ship as well, don't you?"

"Yes. They were . . . down here, earlier."

Oh dear. João and Aga had come down earlier to nap so they wouldn't fall asleep on the deck. By the hesitant way Marina spoke, Joaquim suspected they'd done more than doze. The cabins were close enough that she would have been able to hear everything that passed between the couple. "Why didn't you tell us you were here earlier?"

Marina sniffed wetly. "I was afraid you would take me back."

And so she'd stayed *in a closet* most of the day. No, she had to have visited the water closet once or twice, but she could have managed that without being noticed. Then again, she could have just sat on his bunk all day. He hadn't come down here at all save to toss his bag atop the chest.

"Are you angry with me?"

Joaquim laughed and drew her closer into his arms. *Now I know why I'll marry before I return home.* A weight lifted from his shoulders, making him almost giddy with relief. "No. I did worry you'd run off with your father's assistant while I was gone."

Her father's assistant was an officious young man, very skilled at his job. But Joaquim hadn't missed that the man showed an interest in Marina.

"Don't be silly. He's seeing one of the maids from the Ferreira house now." Marina drew back and whispered, "I thought this would be romantic."

He fought the urge to laugh again. He had spent the whole day on the deck. The wind had dried his skin, and he must smell of sweat and salt. His hands were roughened by the lines. For her part, she'd evidently been hiding among Erdano's spare garments and carried more than a hint of seal musk. That was *not* romantic, at least not by his definition. And yet he wasn't going to send her away. "Marina, we need to be practical about this."

Her cheek pressed against his bare chest. "You don't want me here?"

Nothing could be further from the truth. His body tightened, not as exhausted as he'd believed, but he was not going to rush this, even if it took every ounce of self-control he had. He located one of her hands under the blanket and drew it to his lips. "I do want you, but as tired as I am, I doubt I could please you. And João might come down that ladder at any moment."

"Oh," she said softly. "I didn't think of that."

Joaquim smiled in the darkness. He wished he could give her that romantic interlude she'd pictured in her mind, but reality didn't favor her chances. He stroked a hand over her hair, his fingers catching on a lock that had come loose from her braid. "Perhaps if we both got a bit of sleep, everything would seem better when we woke."

She sighed dramatically, much like she did everything else. Everything was urgent to her. It reminded him that she was several years younger than him, barely twenty-three. "Here," he said, finding the edge of the sheet. "Lie down."

It took a moment for her to wriggle her way under the sheet, but he lay down next to her, facing her, worked one arm under her head, and drew her closer with the other. She was wearing trousers and a shirt, with no corset. That realization sent another bolt of fire through his groin, but if nothing else, he had ample practice denying that particular urge. He tucked his head atop hers and felt her hand settle on his waist. He could wait a few more hours, he reminded himself, or a few more days. The boat groaned in response to a wave, a strangely reassuring sound.

"I love you, Joaquim," she mumbled in the darkness.

He pressed a kiss to her hair. "I love you too, darling."

"I'm glad you're not angry with me." She sighed and nestled closer.

With her soft hair against his cheek and her body pressed against his, it was going to take him *hours* to get to sleep.

Marina woke tangled in Joaquim's arms, recognizing that only after a panicked instant where she'd dreamed herself entangled in seaweed. But his body was warm and solid. One hand pressed against the small of her back, keeping her close. He smelled of seawater and perspiration.

Not that she smelled any better. The clothes in that closet stank of something acrid, and that scent was all over her now. Her hair must be mussed and she needed to visit the tiny water closet again. And she was thirsty and hungry atop all that. Her careful plan had gone all awry.

But she was still here. *With him.*

Joaquim hadn't taken her back to Portugal. Nor had he told her to take the bed and gone to sleep on the deck as she'd half feared he would. He'd always been so proper and polite with her until the afternoon before. It was as if telling her his secrets had let loose some flood of passion she'd never known he possessed. Perhaps his other reservations about her would fade too.

She slipped out of his arms and off the narrow bed as he slept on. She stared down at him in the darkness, but then the boat rolled on the water and she nearly fell atop him, so she went to visit the tiny water closet before she accidentally woke him. When she returned a few minutes later, she slipped back under the warm blankets and he folded her back into his arms without even waking. His cheek came to rest against hers, stubble pricking her skin. Sereia males rarely had facial hair, so she found the mustaches so common among the men of the Golden City a little off-putting. She hoped Joaquim didn't decide to grow one.

But this was warm and comfortable. It wasn't all she wanted, but it was a good start. She spread her chilled fingers and laid them against his bare chest. He flinched at the cold, but didn't wake. Very softly—so softly that it was no more than a whisper—she began to sing.

Her sister, Oriana, had amazing power when she *called*, one of the reasons her aunts had pushed Oriana to join the Ministry of Intelligence. Oriana could use her *call* to influence humans from a distance, but Marina's magic was far more limited. She could barely draw humans to her at all, not more than a few feet. She had to be touching them to have any true effect.

Even so, she could wrap her meager power around Joaquim to guard him from the magic of other sereia. Headed as they were to the islands, she didn't want him ending up in some other female's grip. She wasn't going to let any other woman have him.

So she hummed a wordless *call*, pouring into it every bit of her longing for him, declaring that he was *hers*, asserting her claim on him. She only hoped her limited powers would be enough to hold him.

CHAPTER 9

Joaquim woke with a start when he heard his name called. He was confused for a split second, unsure what was happening and where he was. He was overwarm, tangled in Marina's arms and the blankets.

He'd never woken in a woman's arms before. It put thoughts in his head that his body . . .

"Mr. Joaquim?" João called down again. "Are you awake?"

Oh, hell and damnation! So much for any lustful ideas his body might have. "Yes," Joaquim yelled back.

Marina blinked up at him blearily. "What?"

"Shhh," he said. "I'll be up in a few minutes, João," he called toward the ladder.

The shadow at the head of the cabin's hatch disappeared. Joaquim let loose a frustrated breath. He had Marina to himself, but the situation wasn't what he wanted.

He'd been thinking of a fine wedding, a small one, with just their families. Perhaps taking her to Sintra and Lisboa in Southern Portugal for a week afterward, down to see the Algarve, or up to the mountains of the Douro River Valley. Instead they were on a cramped yacht, and not alone. Joaquim gazed down at Marina's face.

She still seemed only halfway awake. Her delicate scarred hand came to rest on his chest, and he wrapped his own around it. "I have to go help João," he said. "You can come up on deck if you want."

The corners of her mouth turned down as if she wanted to frown, but she nodded quickly.

What am I supposed to say now? And how was he supposed to escape this bunk? He was pinned next to the hull of the boat. Crawling over her wasn't a graceful option. Joaquim huffed out a sigh, reflecting then that his breath must also be far from perfect. "I need to go up there, Marina. Would you let me past?"

Her cheeks flushed. She jerked her fingers out of his and struggled with the blankets to free herself. But instead of rising to her feet, she overbalanced and slid from the bunk onto the decking with a dismayed cry.

Cursing under his breath, Joaquim swung his feet over the edge. He got out of bed without stepping on her, and then hauled her upright. Her face was red and she looked on the verge of tears again. Leaning down to meet her eyes, Joaquim cupped her cheeks with his hands. "We'll work this out," he promised. "Just be patient with me."

She nodded again wordlessly.

Yes, I've done everything wrong. But he didn't know how to fix it, so he grabbed his portmanteau off the floor, set it on the unmade bunk, and dug out a clean shirt. "I'm going to use the water closet and then head upstairs," he said. "You can join us when you like. Did you bring any clothes with you?"

Marina shook her head, her lower lip enticingly caught between her sharp teeth.

Seeing that, he felt his heart thumping a little harder. For a moment, he actually considered ignoring João. "You're welcome to dig through this and see if anything of mine would work for you. Or I can ask João if you can borrow something of Aga's."

"No, don't do that. I'll just . . ." She made a vague gesture in the direction of his bag.

"Very well, then." He leaned down and pressed a kiss to her cheek, then went off to the water closet before he said anything else stupid.

Marina sat down on the unmade bunk. What she'd wanted to do was urge Joaquim to stay with her, but João and his wife had been on deck all night. That was one thing she'd learned on the English ship she'd been on. Someone had to be on duty at all times, even when the sails were down and the motor quiet.

She considered his bag, so trustingly left open. *Does he have any more secrets?* She could go through his things, find out what was in there. Perhaps there was a journal in which he confessed his love for her. Or perhaps there was a journal in which he *didn't*. Given how poorly things had gone so far, she probably didn't want to know.

But her borrowed garments smelled now, both from the stench in the closet and from a day's worth of sweat. She could wash these when they arrived on the islands, but while she was on this boat, she didn't want to stink. She should have brought a bottle of fragrance.

I'm going to make the best of this, she told herself firmly. There was no excuse for maundering on about a situation she'd created herself. *She* had crept aboard this ship during the night. *She'd* hidden in the closet. It was all her own doing, and she was going to keep her wits about her.

She glanced into the bag and saw a neatly folded pair of linen shirts on top. She picked up one and shook it out. It would be ridiculously long on her, but she exchanged her dirty shirt for the clean one. She picked up the worn garments and laid them aside, set Joaquim's portmanteau on the floor again, and neatly made up the bunk. There was no mirror to check her hair, but she located a comb lying on a shelf near the ladder. That must be Joaquim's. She combed out her tangled hair and braided it.

If she was going to face the morning, she would look tidy while doing so.

Once she'd climbed the ladder to the deck of the ship, she stood still for a moment, blinded by the morning sunshine. The light reflected off the water, making it worse. She shielded her eyes with one hand and looked out over the deck. Joaquim and João were hauling on ropes to raise a third sail—the middle one—that billowed and puffed as it slid up the mast. The ship rolled on the water as that sail belled out. Full sails meant good speed on their way to the islands. Well, she assumed that was what it meant.

This ship had *two* masts, the one toward the front where Joaquim was, and a smaller mast near the back. The sail in the back was already up. Marina spotted a steam pipe protruding from the deck behind the cabin, but it wasn't belching smoke at the moment, so they weren't using the engine now. It was a small steam pipe, nothing like the huge ones on the English steamer she'd traveled on. But she'd heard the engine when the ship had first begun to move on the river the previous morning, so they did use it.

João's young wife, Aga, brushed past Marina where she stood with her back against the cabin. The lovely girl paused and appraised Marina for a second, and then walked on as if she saw nothing surprising about another woman on the ship's deck. Likely Joaquim had warned them about her unforeseen presence. Aga went to the back of the ship and began coiling a rope attached to a huge wet mess of canvas on the deck.

Marina watched all the activity warily. *The wisest thing to do is stay out of the way.*

Once Joaquim and João had finished tying off the third sail, Joaquim came back toward where she stood and eased past her. "I need to check our heading," he said, and then was gone off to the back of the boat.

Chill air came off the water, so Marina wrapped her arms about herself. João climbed up the front mast, his curly hair fluttering in the wind. He tinkered with something up on the top of the mast—a lantern. Joaquim called out something from his spot at the wheel, and the ship began to turn, slowly listing to one side. Not enough to alarm her, but Marina watched as the water came closer . . . and then the ship began to right itself again, the sails fluttering as João scrambled down the mast.

Everyone knew exactly what to do, save her.

Presently the ship was slipping forward again on the wind, and Joaquim called for her to come back and join him. She sidled along the cabin and slipped under the sail's boom to step down into the small spot on the deck where he stood. Aga had spread out the wet canvas, and abandoned it to head toward the front of the ship.

Once the girl was beyond hearing, Marina said, "I didn't know a yacht would be this small."

Joaquim's eyes danced, but he held in his laughter. "This isn't a small yacht."

Marina wrapped her arms about herself. "I've only been on steamers, and they were all bigger than this."

"Hmm. What kind of steamers?"

"Oh, the ferries between the islands, and the freighter I came to Portugal on."

His brows drew together. "How *did* you get from the islands to Portugal? I know there are trading ships, but can you buy passage on one of those?"

"I think so, but taking the ferry to Amado used almost all the money I'd saved up." She licked her upper lip. "I went to the ships that were heading to Portugal and begged them to take me in return for work. An English ship captain took pity on me and let me work in his ship's kitchen on the way here. It was only two weeks, but it was . . ."

It had been *almost* unbearable. The work was hot, endless, and confusing, since she'd never cooked before. She'd burned her delicate hands several times and was always relieved when the time came to wash the pans and dishes. Hot water was tolerable, at least. But the cook—a stout, older woman named Mrs. Davies who could grab a pot of boiling water with her leathery brown hands without flinching—spoke Portuguese. She'd spent the entire two weeks imparting her wisdom about preparing food. She protected Marina from the blandishments of the seamen who came down to eat. And when they reached the Golden City, Mrs. Davies had even told Marina that if she didn't find her father, she was welcome to come back to the ship to work. After all, it was illegal then for a sereia even to enter the Golden City. Marina had been thankful when she found her father quickly. Going back to that hot kitchen hadn't been an appealing option.

"It was?" Joaquim prompted.

She felt her cheeks flush. "It was *difficult*."

That was the wrong thing to say, because his attention focused on her, his brow furrowed with worry. "In what way?" he asked sharply.

She gazed up at his face, perplexed by his tone, and then understood. *He's afraid they mistreated me.* After all, Oriana had been told she'd been *murdered* by the crew of the ship she'd been taken up by. Such things probably did happen. But not to her. "The cook was kind to me," she reassured him, "and watched over me like a mother hen. But I never want to go near a stove again."

The tension in his shoulders eased. "I wish it had been easier for you. That took bravery, boarding a ship full of people you didn't know and coming to Portugal."

Marina shook her head. Oriana would *never* have gone begging to a ship full of humans. She would have stolen a ship and sailed to Portugal herself, or done something else brave and daring. "I just asked, and they helped me."

"Sometimes asking for help is harder than trying to find your own way."

As much as she would like to believe that, she knew better. She'd always been the cowardly one, hiding behind Oriana for protection from her cousins and the other girls at school. Even this—stowing away on Joaquim's ship—while it seemed daring, had been Ana's idea, not hers. *And it hasn't gone well so far.*

Marina let out a sigh and turned her eyes to the sparkling water. She didn't know what she was doing on a ship like this, unlike Aga. She was only in the way.

"Why did it take two weeks?" he asked then. "It shouldn't take more than a few days to reach Portugal."

"We went to England first, then Portugal."

"Ah, now I understand. Will you know when we've reached the edge of sereia territory?" Joaquim asked then, changing the subject. "Will you hear it first?"

Finally an area where I know more than Aga. "Yes. I can warn you when we're close."

"João and I will need to stop our ears."

She hoped the *call* wouldn't have too much effect on Joaquim. He was hers, after all. "The navy's not going to try to convince you to jump overboard. They just want you to sail *elsewhere.* To go around the islands."

His eyes focused inward as he calculated something. "So they'll try to make me change course?"

"Yes. Exactly."

"Then you and Aga can't let us."

"I'll do my best," she said. "And once we pass through the blockade, they'll leave us alone."

At least she hoped that was true.

CHAPTER 10

ⴤⴊ

ILHAS DAS SEREIAS

After a luncheon of shrimp with garlic and herbs, Duilio and her grandmother discussed the implications of Joaquim's imminent arrival. Judging by her grandmother's expression and occasional gestures, she had doubts about Duilio's gift. Oriana hadn't believed in seers herself when she arrived in the Golden City, but Duilio's talent had proven correct too many times to leave any question in her mind. And if she believed that one type of human witch existed, she had to keep an open mind about all of them. If Joaquim found the islands without help, perhaps that would convince her grandmother. Either way, a room had been set aside in the men's hall for Joaquim, next to Costa's empty room.

A discussion that morning with the remaining Portuguese ship captain verified that the woman they were hunting had indeed sought passage off the islands. Wearing human clothing, she'd booked passage for herself and the boy on the Catalan steamer *Confraria*, headed for Barcelona. The captain apparently hadn't realized she was a sereia; he'd been heard to speculate as to why a *human* woman would be on the islands at all. The woman had claimed she wanted to go back to her family in Spain. Since she spoke Spanish—a windfall discovery

for Duilio—the captain accepted her claim even if he doubted its veracity. And since the woman wore gloves, that meant she'd had her
webbing cut away in order to pass more easily as human.

Now they knew where their thieves were headed, and that the
woman spoke Spanish well enough to fool a Catalan captain. Despite
the quibbling of Duilio's gift, it seemed likely that the woman was a
Canary, and two duties that the Canaries performed for Spain were
serving on ships of the Spanish navy and controlling an Unnaturals
prison—a prison for witches and nonhumans—in the city of Lleida.
When their thief reached Barcelona, it would be a simple matter to
take another ship to a naval port or to take a train to Lleida. Either
was equally likely, Duilio held.

"I don't see why the Spanish would want my mother's journal,"
Oriana pointed out.

"Leverage," her grandmother suggested. "If the ministry wants
the information in that journal kept secret, there's value in possessing it. It gives the Spanish something they can negotiate with."

"Why not take it to the Spanish embassy, then?"

Duilio just shook his head. "We don't know that she didn't."

"But your gift says she still has the journal with her."

"True," he admitted, hands spread wide. "I don't believe she
took it to the embassy. I'm simply admitting that it's a *possibility.*"

Her grandmother snorted, and was about to reenter the conversation when one of the young servants came running into the dining
room. The girl's eyes were wide and her hands were knotted in her
pareu. "Madam, I'm sorry to interrupt, but . . ."

Oriana wasn't certain whether the servant spoke to her or to
her grandmother, so she waited until her grandmother gestured for
the girl to continue.

The girl swallowed. "The subminister of Intelligence is at the
door. She told me to tell you that. With guards. *Four* of them."

Oriana rose, her stomach sinking as she did so. The four guards
weren't a good sign. It meant either that her aunt Jovita felt threatened

coming here, or that she intended to take someone away by force. "She must be here to talk to me."

"You've been asking questions," Grandmother said as Duilio helped her to her feet. "That gets around. But we have the upper hand here, so it's better to deal with her now than after you've returned to the capital."

Oriana didn't see how they had the upper hand, but she wasn't going to argue. She took a deep breath, mentally organizing. "Will you stay with me?" she asked Duilio. "To take notes. I don't want to miss anything she says."

Duilio's lips twisted in a brief frown, but he nodded. "I'll go fetch a notebook."

Grandmother Monteiro sent the servant to fetch their guest to the courtyard and turned back to Oriana. "You know her. Would it be easier if I went?"

Oriana licked her lips. Of her three aunts, Jovita was her least favorite. The woman had despised her father's human looks and had constantly chided Oriana's mother for tolerating his unconventional political views. She was quite open in her abhorrence for the human blood so prevalent among the citizens of Amado. And while her mother's other two sisters, Vitoria and Valeria, had worked to convince Oriana to join the Ministry of Intelligence, Jovita had been unsupportive. Oriana had long suspected that the reason she'd been given so little responsibility and so few opportunities in her short career could be explained by her powerful aunt's dislike of her.

Given that her grandmother was a representative of that despised impure populace of Amado, it wouldn't help to have her present during this interview. And while the same might be said of Duilio, Jovita had to know he was human. Provided that he behaved with appropriate decorum, his presence might demonstrate that human males could be respectful of sereia ways. "Why don't you let me handle her alone, Grandmother? That way she can't say you said or did anything disrespectful of the government."

Her grandmother kissed her cheek and left. Oriana headed to the courtyard and entered via the back door, only seconds ahead of Jovita's arrival through the other entrance.

Oriana had seen the woman at a distance a couple of times in the past few months. Her aunt's hair was almost completely gray now but hung down her back in neat curls. She wore a white vest embroidered with blue geometric designs, and her blue *pareu* was tied with a knot that proclaimed her mate dead. Oriana had liked her uncle Ronaldo. Despite being very conventional, he'd been intelligent and kind. Unfortunately, he and Jovita had lived in a separate house, so Oriana hadn't seen him as often as she would have liked.

Pausing on the threshold of the courtyard, Jovita spent a moment appraising Oriana, then stepped onto the carpet. "Ambassador," she said in a cool tone.

"Subminister," Oriana replied, opting for her aunt's professional title. Jovita wasn't as tall as she remembered, a fact to store away.

Jovita surveyed the plastered walls of the courtyard, the small fountain in the center of it, and the dark furnishings. "So you've run home to hide?"

"Our visit here is a temporary retreat," she said. "And a chance for me to speak with my country's representatives here firsthand. The ship captains cannot, of course, come onto Quitos to speak with their ambassador. May I ask the reason for this visit?"

Jovita's eyes narrowed, hands remaining perfectly still. "You're too young to be an ambassador."

Oriana's hands curled into fists, her nails biting into her palms. *Where is Duilio?* He was good at reminding her not to let her temper slip. "I agree, Subminister. My posting was based on my familiarity with the people of these islands rather than experience, and has always been intended to be a temporary one. I will step down as soon as the Foreign Office feels they have an adequately trained replacement. Will you sit?"

Jovita contemplated that offer for a moment, then settled on the nearest chaise. It would put her back to the entry of the courtyard, hinting that she felt she had nothing to fear after all. Oriana settled across from her aunt.

"And when you are replaced," her aunt added, "you'll return here and settle into the resistance, I suppose."

She already knows about the adoption, when the papers were filed in Porto Novo only yesterday morning. That adoption was the only thing that would allow Oriana to settle here. She laid her hands on her knees, careful not to make any gesture that might be misinterpreted. "The resistance?"

"The separatists," her aunt clarified. "I assume you'll lobby for religious tolerance, male suffrage, and everything else that dilutes our people's ways."

Oriana hadn't thought that far ahead. The Foreign Office had promised they would have a replacement trained within two years, but the twenty-one months still left in that span seemed interminably long. "It would be inappropriate for me to take any stance on the government of these islands when my position here is as a representative of the two Portugals."

Her aunt snorted, a sound that came closer to amusement than disapproval. "Is it true, then, that the two countries are moving toward reunification?"

Common knowledge. "Yes. Although there is to be a vote on the subject, the outcome seems inevitable. Reunification would lessen the tax burden on the populace of supporting two bureaucracies, and lays out a path toward a new constitution at the same time."

"And it will combine their military forces."

Oriana didn't flinch. Among the sereia, the continually smoldering fear of invasion by the Portuguese went back hundreds of years. It died off periodically, only to flare up again a handful of seasons later. The banishment of the sereia from the shores of Northern Portugal had stoked that ember into full flame. And while the ban had been terrible for those sereia living in the Golden City, there had never been any real threat to sereia beyond the shores of Northern Portugal. Oriana gave her aunt a level stare. "True, but that does not pose a threat to these islands."

"An ambassador *would* say that."

The bells at the edge of the courtyard rang, and Oriana glanced at the front archway. Duilio stood at the threshold, a tray in his hands. Her grandmother must have caught him and pressed him into service. She gestured for him to enter, and he walked to her side, head bowed, not a single dish clattering.

Her aunt assessed Duilio, starting with his properly downcast eyes and ending up at his well-manicured feet. Given how closely they were being watched, Jovita had surely received thorough reports about him. She had to know he was educated. She would have heard that he wore the Paredes line tattoo rather than the Monteiro one. As such, he was part of the Paredes family and nominally under Jovita's purview, as was Oriana herself. Oriana hoped he kept that fact in mind. She gestured for him to set the tray on the table. "Will you pour?"

He did as bidden, wordlessly pouring out two cups of tea—a fortunate choice, since her aunt had little tolerance for coffee. He handed one to her aunt, who took it with a raised eyebrow, but said nothing. Then he handed a cup to Oriana and stepped back. She gestured for him to take one of the chairs on the side of the courtyard, out of Jovita's line of sight.

Duilio tamely went, tugging a slender notebook from the waist of his *pareu*. He settled facing Oriana, his expression carefully neutral.

Oriana took a sip of her tea, wishing it was something stronger—she recognized the variety grown on Quitos. "So, may I ask the reason for this visit, Subminister?"

Jovita set aside her cup. She crossed her legs and tapped the nails of one hand on the arm of the chaise as if contemplating scratching Oriana's eyes out with them. "You have set a handful of my agents into a furor. I would like to know why."

"A personal item was stolen from me, and we've been hunting for it. How can that be considered provoking your agents?"

Jovita's eyes narrowed. "What was stolen?"

Oriana swallowed. "I assume you already know the answer to that question."

"Do you think I would spend my afternoon traveling out to this damned island if I knew?"

Jovita *had* come here herself when it was clear she had spies on the island. Oriana wasn't sure what that meant, but there wasn't any point in lying about the theft. "My mother's journal. It was stolen from our bedroom while we slept. Someone blew *gornava* pollen into the room—a large amount of it."

Her aunt's brows rose. She recognized how expensive that much pollen would have been. "They slipped past your guards?"

"We believe we brought the thief to the house with us," Oriana admitted. "One of the pieces of luggage was tampered with in the hold of the ferry that brought us over. A small child was placed in the luggage, and once the luggage was carried into the household, the child slipped out and hid until nightfall."

"That seems like a desperate effort," Jovita said. "What was in Lygia's journal that would make them resort to such a plan?"

This must be what she's after. She wants to know how much I read, or how much Grandmother did. "I don't know. It was stolen on our first night here, not long after my grandmother handed it over to me. Something inside was worth arranging that theft. What did my mother know?"

Jovita regarded her silently, her face and still hands giving away nothing.

"Was it worth murdering her for?" Oriana added.

Jaw clenched, Jovita rose. "Watch what you say, girl. You may have some protection out here, but making unsubstantiated claims back on Quitos will get you killed. Do you understand me?"

Oriana rose and inclined her head slowly. "I understand very well, Subminister."

"No doubt your foolish father has set you on this path," Jovita said with a dismissive swipe of her hand. "It was all I could do to keep the ministry from having him executed. If you press this non-sense, I cannot promise to *protect* you, family or not."

That wasn't the way Oriana had expected this conversation to go. "They wanted to execute him?"

"Your father supposedly implied complicity on the part of the minister at the time."

And Jovita had stopped his execution? "You never liked him. Why interfere on his behalf?"

"I may not have agreed with Lygia's choice of mate, but I know what is due to my line. He's part of my family." She cast a cynical eye over Oriana and then, nostrils flaring, turned toward the chair where Duilio still sat. "Escort me out, boy."

Duilio had already decided that Jovita Paredes was one of the hardest women he'd ever seen. She might stab him on the way to the front door, and he doubted she would stop to watch him fall. But he wasn't going to refuse her request. It would be unthinkable for a sereia male to refuse anything to the head of his line. *Within limits.*

In appropriate silence, he led Oriana's aunt to the house's main door. When he reached to open the door for her, she stopped him, sharp nails pricking his wrist. "Look at me, young man."

Duilio raised his eyes, getting his first full look at her face. He'd known that Oriana strongly resembled her mother. Clearly that ex-tended to her aunt as well. Her aunt's eyes were larger than a hu-man's, but not so much so that it was startling, as he'd seen among some sereia. Nor did she have the silvery sheen to her face that the purest family lines had. He could still see a hint of red in her hair, much like the burgundy streaks in Oriana's. The subminister shared

Oriana's height and strong build, and despite her age, she was a strik-ing woman.

"The younger generation doesn't respect our customs any longer," she said.

Every generation believes that. As her comment didn't seem to require a response, he didn't bother.

"They don't understand the meaning of service."

One of his eyebrows drifted upward, but he said nothing. That was service with a capital S. This was one of the aunts who'd told Oriana she was never meant to have a mate, that she was destined to serve her people instead. Since sereia females outnumbered males—almost two to one—many females couldn't win a mate. Duilio sus-pected that the myth that those females were destined to live out a life of service instead had developed out of convenience. Easier to send those females out to serve in their navy, directing ships around their islands with their *calls*, to work in the gold mines, or into the fields to tend the produce others ate and the tea that provided the bulk of their exports. The sereia who worked the docks, the fishing ships, and the factories that produced the linen and cotton worn here; they were the *unmated*. It irritated him, primarily because that was the life Oriana's aunts had envisioned for her and her sister.

Jovita let go of his arm. "I don't approve of Oriana's choice of a mate . . ."

He inclined his head, a mere acknowledgment.

". . . but as I understand you're the one who rescued her from the execution site, I can understand that she feels indebted to you. I am as well. I didn't know if Braz could get anyone to help her. I am relieved he managed to do so."

She was the one who sent word about Oriana's attempted execu-tion? Duilio wasn't sure if he should believe that. The information had come by official mail to the sereia ambassador back in the Golden City, Braz Alvaro, brother of the Paredes women and Oriana's uncle. Thus the same government who'd condemned Oriana had also tried to save her. Could that have been the doing of the subminister of Intelligence herself? That had to have been a dangerous step for her to take, defying the actions of the ministry. "If you sent word to him, then I am grateful," Duilio said cautiously. "I didn't know where to look for her."

"Clearly the gods wished her to be saved. In that I was their implement, as were you."

That fatalistic way of thinking supported whatever course Jovita Paredes had chosen to take. She'd sent word—a deed that some might consider acting against her own government—with the belief that if Oriana lived, her action was merely part of the gods' plan. If Oriana had died, that outcome would have been the gods' will as well. Then again, Duilio knew plenty of humans who used the same logic to justify their actions, so the sereia weren't alone in that attitude. "Oriana tells me the leviathan that intervened was a sign of the gods' will."

Jovita's shoulders straightened slightly. "Leviathan?"

Yes, that surprised her. The leviathan was one aspect of Oriana's rescue of which very few people had heard. Once Duilio and Joaquim had unchained Oriana and carried her aboard their sailboat, a ship attempted to stop them. Far larger than their little sailboat, the steam corvette would have quickly overtaken them, but a leviathan attacked it. The creature broke off the corvette's bowsprit, forcing the ship to give up the pursuit. Leviathans were typically shy creatures that preferred deep waters, so its unexpected intervention had been most startling. And as the sereia held that leviathans acted only on the will of the sea gods, it bolstered Oriana's belief that she'd been spared so she could one day find her mother's killer. "It attacked the ship that tried to prevent us from rescuing Oriana," Duilio explained. "We would have died that night had it not appeared."

Jovita eyes narrowed. "A ship tried to stop you?"

She was repeating him, a trick he used when plying others for information. Her quizzical tone seemed genuine, as if she truly didn't know the details of the incident, but Duilio didn't know her well enough to evaluate her acting skills. He took a chance. "Yes. The sailors demanded that we hand her over. When we ran they attempted to overtake us."

"What manner of ship?" she asked cautiously.

"A steam corvette," he said. "Human sailors. They didn't make landing in any Portuguese port after the incident—a missing bowsprit would have been remarked—but we finally learned that the ship limped into Ferrol, a Spanish port. That ship *knew* Oriana was on that island that night. They'd come hunting her, just as we had."

The corner of Jovita's mouth pinched in, but she merely gestured for him to open the door. She stopped on the threshold and peered at him, brows drawn together. "Is it true that you carry a gun?"

Duilio felt heat creeping up his chest, burning in his cheeks. He usually wore his Webley-Wilkinson revolver strapped to his thigh, hidden under his *pareu*. He should have expected that she would have heard about the embarrassing incident. He took a deep breath and let it go. "Yes."

"Interesting." She swept past, and Duilio watched as she stepped into a closed carriage. Her guards climbed into a second carriage, an open one, and the two vehicles slowly pulled out of the drive.

Duilio shut the door and closed his eyes. Jovita's surprise about the leviathan had seemed genuine, but he doubted she would have been able to climb to such a high position in the Ministry of Intelligence if she couldn't lie convincingly. Even so, the idea that the unidentified ship had known Oriana was there and had come specifically for her—*that* had disturbed Jovita. He needed to spend some time mulling that over, but later, after he'd discussed it with Oriana.

He turned back toward the courtyard and spotted Lieutenant Benites standing off to one side in an alcove, at ease, with one hand on her pistol. She must have taken that position in case the subminister's guards tried to enter the house. Corporal Almeida watched from the opposite hallway, her rifle in her hands and her narrow face pale. She didn't look as sanguine as Benites about the possibility of taking on four sereia guards.

"It's fine," he said to them both. "They're gone."

Almeida slung her rifle over her shoulder then and stood at ease as well.

"They wouldn't have gotten past the door, sir," Benites said. "Captain's on the roof with her rifles. She would have dropped them long before they reached the house."

"I have to agree." Four guards wouldn't be enough to defeat a marksman like Vas Neves. He thanked the two guards and headed back to the courtyard, where he found Oriana pacing.

The stiffness in her shoulders eased when she saw him unscathed. "Was she rude to you?"

"Not terribly," he said. "She doesn't approve of me, but that isn't a surprise."

Oriana came and set one hand on his waist. "I warned you."

"She did, however, thank me for bringing you back from that island."

Oriana stepped back, a line between her brows.

"She said she wasn't certain the ambassador could do anything to help you." When Oriana continued to look confounded, he recounted most of his conversation with her aunt. "She could have been lying," he finished. "I don't know her as well as you do, so I hesitate to make that judgment."

"I don't know her all that well either," Oriana admitted softly.

"What we need," Duilio said, "is to determine whether she was actually the one to send the message to your uncle Braz about your execution."

"Or if she actually did keep my father from being executed as she claimed," Oriana agreed. "Unfortunately, we don't have any spies within the ministry."

That *was* a problem.

CHAPTER 11

THE OPEN OCEAN

Marina had quickly grown bored with watching the water and skies, although Joaquim could tell she was trying not to *seem* bored. Sailing could be that way. Despite her disgust for stoves, she'd gone below and put together a hot lunch of cod with potato and onions that was far better than the cold meals of bread and *chouriço* Joaquim had managed the previous day. She'd talked with Aga over their meal and listened intently to João's idea for starting a business carrying tourists up and down the Douro River Valley.

But otherwise she'd stayed at his side, keeping his mind occupied. Truthfully, though, his mind had been occupied with her even when she was away from his side. After João and Aga went below to nap, Marina asked questions about the ship and sailing, neither of them mentioning what was on *his* mind, if not on hers.

If we're traveling together, we should be married. He'd waited a decade for her to come into his life. Now that he'd let himself kiss her, he wasn't sure he would hold off bedding her. And he didn't think she would refuse him should he ask.

Marina's people didn't have the same expectations as humans. According to Duilio, their idea of marriage was a verbal agreement, not sanctioned by any of their mysterious gods; the man simply moved into the home of the woman's family. No ceremony at all. He didn't know how Marina felt about that, and couldn't find a way to broach the topic that wouldn't sound as if he found her people's customs inferior.

She'd been sitting in silence for some time, merely watching the sails, when he saw her shade her eyes to look up. A seagull floated above the masts, hunting for food, no doubt.

"We must be close to land," Joaquim said.

"The outer islands are just piles of rock in the ocean." Marina tilted her head. "I don't hear anything yet."

His experience with the *call* of a sereia was limited. He'd once heard Oriana *calling*, luring Maraval's henchmen into the water to save Duilio's life. With his ears stuffed with wool, Joaquim hadn't felt much. The second time, however, had nearly been his death. He'd been so fixated on reaching the sereia who *called* him, Iria Serpa, that he paid no heed to the woman's husband slipping up behind him with a knife. If Oriana hadn't shot the man, he'd be dead.

"They're not trying to hurt us, right?"

"They shouldn't be," Marina said.

He nodded, feeling a prickle of apprehension anyway. Even though he was a witch himself, he still found magic disturbing.

They waited, listening to the wind in the sails, the increasing squawks of gulls, and the creak of wood from the ship as it rolled on the swells. Marina tilted her head sharply. "I hear it now."

Joaquim blinked. If there was a sereia's song on the air, it wasn't affecting him. *Not yet.* "I need to go below for a moment. To get the cotton."

He checked the wheel and then headed around toward the cabin. He still couldn't hear anything—perhaps he was supposed to *feel* it instead—but just as he turned to step down onto the ladder, he saw João about to climb up. He stood back from the hatch to let the young man come out on deck.

Once João's head was above the deck, he asked, "Have you checked the course, Mr. Joaquim?"

Oh, Mother of God. "We talked about this earlier, João," Joaquim said, exasperation creeping into his voice. "We're still on course. You're hearing the blockade."

Joaquim still couldn't hear it himself, but he could feel it tugging at his will. He recognized that touch of magic now, but didn't feel the compulsion to obey that João evidently did. The magic brushed past his skin, like fog or smoke.

Brows drawn together, João climbed out onto the deck. "What are you talking about, sir? I don't hear anything."

Neither do I, come to think of it. If João was responding to a sereia's call, shouldn't they be able to hear the sereia in question? Joaquim turned his eyes on Marina. "Why can't we hear it?"

João tried to push past him on the narrow deck to get back to the wheel. Joaquim blocked him, earning a mulish look from João.

"I can hear her," Marina said to them both. "You'll hear it in a moment."

Joaquim moved between João and the rail, blocking his path. "João, just go below and fetch that cotton we set out earlier."

"We need to change course," João insisted, punctuating that with a shove.

Joaquim took a step back, surprised. João was usually an easy-going young man. "You're not thinking straight."

João answered that with a swipe of one fist, and Joaquim didn't hesitate. He leaned out of the way of the punch and answered with a cut to João's chin. The young man's head snapped back and he crumpled toward the deck. Aga, halfway up the steps, grimaced at Joaquim and made an angry sound, halfway between a grunt and a scream.

Joaquim blinked, too startled to respond. He'd certainly never heard Lady Ferreira make a sound like that.

"Aga, the sereia at the blockade are calling him," Marina inserted quickly. "We need to keep him from listening to them. Can you go get that cotton?"

Aga turned swiftly, her braid spinning out behind her. The sound of her feet hitting the floor below hinted that she'd simply jumped down. After only a couple of seconds, she emerged from the cabin, cotton in one closed first and a coiled line over her shoulder.

Marina reached out to take the cotton from her and knelt next to João. The young man's eyes fluttered open. He shook his head and touched a hand to his reddened jaw, groaning. Marina rolled up a small ball of cotton and proceeded to stuff it in João's ear as if he were a child. For her part, Aga stood on the deck with her arms folded over her chest, watching Marina with narrowed eyes.

Her task done, Marina rose and stood next to Aga. "Do you think we need to tie him up?"

For a moment they gazed down at the still-dazed João. Then Aga knelt down next to her husband and began running loops of line about his chest to secure him to the railing.

Joaquim watching her work, a knot of worry in his stomach. Apparently neither of the women thought it necessary to tie him to the railing.

The ethereal sound of a sereia's *call* brushed his ears, but the magic didn't latch on to him.

Why not?

CHAPTER 12

THE OPEN OCEAN

Marina waited until Aga had João securely tied before turning to Joaquim. He stood at the rail a few feet away, arms folded over his chest and jaw clenched. "Are you . . ."

"I'm fine, it appears," he said. "I can hear it, but it's not bothering me. Not like it did him." His eyes met hers, a thin line between his brows as if he wondered why that was the case.

Marina licked her lips. "I—"

A shout from nearby saved her from having to explain. Marina went to the rail and glanced over. There, to the aft, was a small naval vessel. It was single-masted, but she could hear an engine pushing the boat to keep up with the much faster *Deolinda*.

The call came again from a sailor using a bullhorn. It was more distinct this time, a request for them to drop their sails and prepare to be boarded. Marina looked back at Joaquim. "They'll put a pilot aboard. That's the only way we'll be allowed closer to the islands."

He nodded once and gestured for Aga to take the end of the main boom while he headed to the mast. After a moment of his fiddling with a rope, the sail began to slide down the mast while Aga furled it with quick and clever hands.

Marina sighed. *Once again, I'm of no use.* She waited as Joaquim and Aga lowered the other sails. João tugged at his bindings, the scowl back on his face. Clearly the blockade was still affecting him.

The ship slowed and the smaller vessel came alongside. Once Joaquim pointed the rope ladder out, Marina flipped it overboard. A moment later, a sailor in a tan *pareu* and vest stood on the *Deolinda's* deck—the pilot who would take them into harbor. She surveyed João's bound form with amusement. An older woman, she had a touch of gray in the brown hair twisted into a tight knot atop her head. She was career navy, a fact given away by the webbing missing from either side of her index finger. That allowed her to handle a firearm yet preserved the webbing between her other fingers so she wouldn't be water-blind.

She turned to Joaquim and yelled, "Why are you crossing our territorial boundary?"

Apparently she believed his ears were stuffed. Joaquim looked startled, as if unsure how to respond.

"We're on our way to Amado," Marina answered instead. She adopted the firm tone she used with her father's clients, her *business* voice. "We're to meet with the Portuguese ambassador there."

The sailor cast an appraising eye over her, one eyebrow lifted. Marina knew what the woman must see—a smallish human woman, dressed in borrowed clothes. "Embassies are all on Quitos," the woman protested.

Marina lifted her chin. "The Portuguese ambassador and her mate are currently on a retreat to Amado, to visit with the ambassador's grandmother. *My* grandmother. Her house is on Cartas Bay, so we don't even need to enter the harbor at Porto Novo."

"Ah," the sailor said, eyes sliding back toward Joaquim. He remained silent, but was clearly following the conversation. "Now I understand. That one's yours."

Marina crossed her arms over her chest, feeling Joaquim's eyes on her. "Yes."

The sailor grinned. "The gods favored you, little one. Human or not, he'll make pretty daughters."

Marina felt a flush creeping up her cheeks. *Will the woman never stop talking?* "Could we get back under way? We'd like to reach the bay before sunset."

"Fine," the sailor said briskly. "I've got some paperwork you'll need to fill out, and then we'll set sail again."

Marina sighed inwardly. *There's always paperwork.*

One of the sailors had boarded the ship to act as pilot. She'd leered at him and João both, but Joaquim held his tongue. Among Marina's people he was expected to be quiet, wasn't he? Marina dealt with the woman firmly—surprising him, he had to admit—and soon they were passing the harbor of a rocky island.

After an hour or so, the *calling* that had itched at the back of his mind ceased, and he realized they'd reached the far side of the magical blockade. Joaquim let loose a breath. He hadn't realized how much it had nagged at him until that moment. João looked far worse, slumping against his ropes. After Aga conferred with Marina, she went and freed him. The young man seemed unnerved, but quickly got to his feet and took stock of their location. He came over to Joaquim's side and apologized for his earlier actions, eyeing the pilot warily the whole while. But his attention was soon drawn away as they sailed past the breakwaters of a large port.

Joaquim stared. The nearest pier in the harbor was busy with bare-chested men with silvery legs bared by tucking up their wraps. They labored alongside the sailors unloading the English ships docked there. From a distance it seemed very chaotic, although in Joaquim's experience, most cargo exchanges happened in an orderly fashion, no matter the outer appearance. But as they eased past the harbor, he realized he'd been fooled by one aspect: those weren't bare-chested *men* out working the freight. They were women, or rather, *sereia*.

Duilio had told him the women on the islands often went scantily

clad, but for some reason he'd expected they would alter that custom
when working with human sailors. The sailor piloting the *Deolinda*
wore a vest, after all. But apparently on the docks that didn't apply.

Marina grew up dressed like that.

He hadn't put his limited knowledge of the sereia's customs together with her. She seemed so proper and modest that he couldn't
imagine her doing such a thing. Surely when she'd been on that English ship, around English sailors, she'd dressed more like she did now.

Joaquim shot a quick glance at her as they sailed into a bay with
a beach. She peered out toward the sands, one hand held up to shield
her eyes from the sun. Months ago, he would never have believed her
a sereia if she hadn't told him. She seemed completely human, with
human ideals and morals. What had that effort to fit in cost her? When
she'd arrived in Portugal, she had her webbing cut away to protect
her safety. He knew that her hands often ached with ghost pain from
her missing webbing. And even now she wore his shirt with the neck
buttoned to the top to keep anyone from seeing her gill slits.

Does she regret that? Why have we never talked about that?

"Over there," she said, pointing toward the shore.

The mountains marched away from that bay in all directions,
but Joaquim could see a few houses built there. Children played at
one spot on the beach, and at the far edge of the bay, a single figure
stood waiting. It was Duilio, dressed in native garb. Farther back on
the sands, two Portuguese soldiers waited, his guards.

The pilot relinquished the wheel as the ship moved farther into
the bay, and then they were busy with the anchor and sails, and he
didn't have time to worry any longer.

CHAPTER 13

ILHAS DAS SEREIAS

Duilio stood on the beach, his bare feet on the sand, as he watched the *Deolinda* striking sails. Another small boat had followed them into the bay, a patrol boat. A pilot boarded every incoming ship to guide them the final distance into Amado's harbor. When Duilio lifted his looking glass, he saw a sereia woman in a tan *pareu* and vest climb down the *Deolinda*'s ladder and jump to the deck of the small boat. After a moment that boat began moving away.

Once the ship was anchored and all the sails furled, he saw the dory being lowered to the water. He turned back to the two guards who'd accompanied him to the beach. "Time to send for Lady Monteiro."

Corporal Pinho headed back up toward the house, floundering in spots. His boots weren't as well suited to the sand as Duilio's bare feet.

Duilio turned his looking glass back to the ship and nearly laughed in surprise. Joaquim had already clambered down to the dory. For a second Duilio thought Aga was following him, but quickly realized it wasn't the selkie girl climbing down that ladder. It was another girl dressed in men's garb, her hair darker than Aga's. *Why did my gift not warn me of that?*

Duilio returned to watching as Aga handed a single piece of luggage down to Joaquim. He set it on a thwart, settled at the oars, and began rowing the distance from the edge of the bay to shore.

"Is this your brother after all?" Grandmother Monteiro called from the house's deck.

"Yes, Grandmother," Duilio called back. "And he's brought a surprise for you."

D uilio stood on the beach waiting, arms folded over his tattooed chest. Now that he'd gotten close enough, Joaquim could see Duilio hadn't had his hair cut in some time. And yes, he had cosmetics about his eyes. He looked perfectly comfortable, though, as if he'd worn this garb his entire life. That was Duilio's chief talent, greater than his seer's gift—he could make himself at home anywhere.

Joaquim tossed him the painter and clambered out of the boat into the water. Together they pulled the dory up onto the beach, and then Joaquim threw his arms about Duilio.

Duilio laughed and pounded him on the back. "God, it is good to see you."

Joaquim drew away to look at him. "You too."

Duilio's eyes slid past him, fixing on the boat's rather bedraggled occupant. "And you brought Marina?"

Feeling guilty, Joaquim went back to help her out of the boat. She'd waited for him to do so, although she could have managed by herself. Then again, he liked helping her. He lifted her into his arms and conveyed her to the sand without dumping her in the water. And when her shoes touched the beach, she smiled up at him brilliantly. Yes, that made it worthwhile.

She shifted to face Duilio, brushed her hands down her borrowed shirt, and licked her lips nervously before holding out a hand to him. "It's good to see you, Mr. Ferreira."

Duilio grinned and shook her hand firmly. "And you as well,

Miss Arenias." He turned to Joaquim, one hand lifted to shield his eyes. "Is João out on the yacht? I only see Aga."

Joaquim swallowed. Did Marina expect him to paint his eyes like that? "Yes, he reacted badly at the blockade, so Aga ordered him to stay below while the pilot was aboard."

Duilio's eyebrows drew together, but he didn't ask the obvious question, the one that had been bothering Joaquim since they'd crossed the blockade. "Good decision," Duilio said instead. "I won't worry about the yacht being at anchor there, then. Let's go up to the house."

Joaquim grabbed his portmanteau out of the dory and, reaching one hand to grasp Marina's, followed Duilio up the beach toward a sprawling house that faced the ocean. "Is that your grandmother's house?"

Marina nodded. "Yes, I lived here when I was a girl, until I was twelve."

With white plastered walls and red tiles on the rooftop, it looked little different than a house in one of the fishing villages on the Portuguese coast. Heavy wooden shutters stood open at the moment, allowing sea air into the house. The house was as huge as it had looked from the bay, and the distance between each of the houses on this beach spoke of land ownership as well. Marina must be from a wealthier family than he'd realized.

Duilio walked up the steps to a wooden deck. An old woman dressed in a black skirt and jacket with gold embroidery running down the plackets waited at the large center doorway. She held her arms wide. Marina's hand slid out of Joaquim's and she ran to throw her arms around her grandmother.

"You're going to need to prostrate yourself to her in a moment," Duilio whispered in Joaquim's ear.

Prostrate? Marina pulled out of her grandmother's arms and demonstrated just that, dropping to her knees and bowing her head to her grandmother's feet. He could do that. Probably. The old woman reached down to touch the top of her head, and Marina pushed her-self back up to her feet. Then she turned and looked for him. Duilio took the portmanteau from Joaquim and added, "You address her as 'Honored Grandmother' until she tells you otherwise."

Forewarned, Joaquim walked to Marina's side.

"And who is this, child?" the old woman asked.

Marina glanced at Joaquim, her brow furrowed, and he grasped her problem. *How is she supposed to introduce me?*

"Is this the young man you're courting?" her grandmother prompted.

That *she* was courting? Joaquim had forgotten that aspect of Duilio's courtship—among the sereia, the women did the courting, not the men.

"Yes, Grandmother," Marina said quickly. "This is Joaquim Ta-vares."

Joaquim realized that was his cue. He dropped to his knees and did his best to bow down gracefully. Duilio doubtless did this far better. He probably practiced. The woman's hand touched the top of his head, so Joaquim rose awkwardly, cheeks flushed.

"Welcome to the house of Monteiro, child," she said gravely.

"Thank you, Honored Grandmother." He'd gotten that correct, it seemed, because she beamed at him.

"Do I understand correctly, that you're Duilio's younger brother?"

"Yes, Honored Grandmother." It was still odd to say it aloud.

"Just call me Grandmother," she suggested. "Now, let's go inside and get you both settled."

And with that, all the formalities were over. Joaquim followed the others through the main doorway and down a white hallway. He leaned over to ask Marina, "Why isn't your sister here?"

"She's not head of the household," Marina whispered back. "She won't greet visitors unless they're *her* visitors."

They went through the large doors into a courtyard with a foun-tain in the center. The floor was tiled with dark stone, probably quar-ried in the mountains rising above them. Two young women met them there, apparently servants. Both wore blue-pattered skirts and went as bare-chested as the women working the docks. Joaquim averted his eyes, noting that Duilio didn't even flinch. He must be accustomed to this. The first servant gestured for Marina to follow her, but the other motioned for Joaquim to head down a different hallway. Fortunately, Duilio accompanied him.

The servant showed him a room that was clearly a bedroom, although there wasn't a bed. Duilio followed him inside and closed the door, then crossed the room to open the shutters, letting in the sea air. "What was she thinking," he said, "not calling you her mate?"

"It would be a lie," Joaquim said, taken aback. "I'm not . . . sharing her bed."

Duilio folded his arms over his bare chest and leaned back against the wall. He seemed a strangely savage visitor with his tattoo and jewelry and painted eyes. Joaquim had to remind himself that *he* was the one out of the ordinary in this place.

"What is she doing here with you, then?" Duilio asked.

Joaquim set his bag on a wooden bench that stood near the door. "She hid away on the ship. In the closet in the cabin. I didn't find her until we were a full day out at sea. Are you even going to ask why I'm here?"

Duilio grinned. "Very well, why are you here, brother?"

"You wrote a letter," he said, "asking me to come."

"I never sent it," Duilio pointed out.

Joaquim raked a hand through his hair. "I know that, but you're going to show it to me."

"I plan to." Duilio gestured toward a cluster of shelves set along that wall. "The pillows and blankets you can arrange however you want, but you need to replace them on the wall in the morning. There's a dressing area back there," he added, pointing, "plus a bath. You can put your bag in there and clean up. You probably have time to nap before dinner. I'll come to wake you, just to be certain."

"Do I have to wear a skirt?" Joaquim asked, gesturing toward Duilio's strange attire.

"*Pareu*," Duilio corrected in an amused tone. "And no, I don't think Grandmother will be upset if you wear trousers. I keep this up . . ." He made a gesture that swept from his painted eyes to his gold ankle bangles. ". . . to bolster Oriana's standing here. You don't have to."

"Thank God," Joaquim said gustily. "What do I do about Marina?"

Duilio shrugged eloquently. "You've been seeing her for six months. If you haven't decided that yet, brother, I'm not going to interfere."

"Fine, be an ass." Joaquim pinched the bridge of his nose. "Are we going to discuss why I'm here?"

Duilio gestured toward the dressing area again. "Later. Get cleaned up, take a nap, and after dinner we can do this one time with everyone present. I'll get the letter and leave it on the bench for you to look at when you've napped."

A nap sounded terribly seductive at the moment, and a bath would be truly welcome.

Duilio pushed away from the wall and laid one hand on Joaquim's shoulder. "And after dinner you and I can have a nice private talk."

Joaquim watched Duilio let himself out, and went to contemplate the auspiciously familiar-looking faucet in the bathing area.

Marina sat down on the bench in her guest room with a groan. They'd taken Joaquim off to the males' wing, which meant she wasn't supposed to talk to him unless he was chaperoned. Surely Grandmother didn't mean to hold her to that. Then again, her grandmother probably still thought of her as twelve years old. She puffed out her cheeks. She was twenty-three now, and whom she courted was her own business.

A quick shake of the bells warned her before her door opened and Oriana stepped inside. Marina ran to embrace her. "I've missed you so much!"

Oriana stepped back, a fond smile on her face. "I missed you too. But how did you end up here? We were expecting Joaquim, not you."

Marina heard the reproach in her voice. "I hid in his boat. I didn't want him to leave me behind. And he would have," she added. "He meant to leave me in the city while he sailed off to help you."

Oriana's lips pressed together in an expression she'd stolen from her husband. She was holding something inside. "Did you let Father know you were going?"

"Yes." Marina gazed at her sister, trying to place what had changed. Oriana wore a black vest embroidered in rose and gold over her *pareu*. That would save Joaquim from embarrassment if nothing else. She'd grown her nails out and filed them to points, and the bangles on her ankles and her bracelets were all rose gold. Then Marina noticed how the *pareu* was secured at Oriana's hips, with five folds rather than the traditional three. "You're pregnant?"

"Yes," Oriana said with a secretive smile. "We haven't told Father yet."

Which was why Marina hadn't heard it herself. Their father could keep a secret endlessly, but he would have told her if he knew this. "Um, how long until you have the baby?"

"About six months," Oriana said. "Now, what do you intend to do about Joaquim?"

She threw up her hands. "Nothing, since he's locked away in the men's hall."

"I've never known the rules to stop you," Oriana said mildly.

Marina stole a glance at her sister's face. There was no point in announcing it if she did decide to break the rules and sneak into the men's quarters. She changed the subject. "So, what does your husband want Joaquim to do?"

"It's about Mother," Oriana said. "Something you don't know.

Father chose not to tell you. He didn't tell me either, not until I pushed him."

"What?"

Oriana took a deep breath. "Mother didn't die of food poisoning. She was murdered."

Marina gaped at her. "*What?*"

"Mother was murdered," Oriana repeated. "Father didn't know until the very week he was exiled. Do you remember we went to visit our aunts on Quitos that summer?"

"Yes," she managed, thoughts in a whirl. How could they have kept this secret from her?

"Father found Mother's journal hidden under the floorboards in their room. In it, she wrote about something being wrong with a new recruit to the intelligence ministry. She was going to go speak with that person's superior that day, but she died first."

Marina felt her hands curl into fists. "Who? What person?"

"The woman who jumped off the palace rooftop back in the Golden City."

The woman who killed the prince the previous fall? "But I thought she was a Canary. What would she have to do with Mother?"

"She was also an agent of the Ministry of Intelligence." Oriana paused, waiting for her to take that in. "She said to me once that I look like Mother. She had to have known her."

"And you think she killed Mother." Marina wrapped her arms about herself, chilled all the way through now. "I'm glad she's dead, then."

"The problem is that someone in the ministry was protecting her. They were aiding in her plan to assassinate the prince. They condoned her actions, including her efforts to kill me. And Father was exiled because he was asking questions about what Mother wrote in her journal."

All this time she'd thought he'd been exiled for his unpopular political beliefs. That had been common in those days. "Why didn't Father ever tell me?"

"Because he was concerned you might run off and do something about it," Oriana said. "That's part of the reason Duilio and I came to Grandmother's house. She had Mother's journal here, and we came to retrieve it."

"Does it say who that woman was working with?"

Oriana held her hands wide. "It was stolen from this house before I read it."

"Stolen?"

"Yes. That's what we intended to ask Joaquim to find. We hoped that if he could find the thief, we would learn who wanted the journal badly enough to send someone here to steal it. That's our only way to find out who's responsible for Mother's death."

Marina folded her arms over her chest. "Then I'm going with him."

CHAPTER 14

Joaquim felt far better after bathing and taking a nap. Once he'd stepped outside his room, though, he realized he didn't know where he was. Where exactly would he find Marina? Or Duilio, for that matter.

He closed his eyes and garnered a reassuring sense of Duilio. And Marina had been taken somewhere near Duilio, but that seemed to be in a different part of the big house. He couldn't walk through the walls to reach them, so he traced his steps back until he saw an arch that led onto the courtyard with the fountain. He stopped and peered at the rooftops, hoping to get an idea of the layout of the house.

The house continued back from the courtyard, and acquired a second floor at one point. There were arches on each side of the court-yard, leading off onto other hallways, so he walked straight back and ended up in a second courtyard, this one populated with a handful of wooden chaises with colorfully embroidered pillows. The comfortable furnishings suggested that they spent more time in this room, while the front courtyard seemed more formal.

"Would you like me to show you around the house?" Marina asked from the archway to the left. "I'm not supposed to, but . . . well, I think Grandmother wouldn't mind if I bent the rules."

Her appearance took his breath away. Marina's brown hair was pulled high atop her head with two pearl combs, and it trailed in curls down her back. She wore a black skirt that came almost to her ankles but left her silvery feet bare. Over that, she wore only a blue vest held together in front by a brooch, leaving an inch of skin exposed between it and the skirt. Her arms were uncovered as well, and on her neck he could see the narrow lines of her gill slits. In Portugal, a man generally didn't see this much of a lady's skin unless she was his wife—or if she had a similar relationship. His mouth went dry.

Was this the true Marina Arenias? Was this how she *preferred* to dress? He took a careful breath and hoped he sounded normal. "I would like that."

She stepped down into the courtyard, closer to him. "This is where we spend evenings. And mornings as well, sometimes. Like a sitting room back in Portugal."

"What if it rains?" he asked.

"We go inside," she said in an exasperated tone. "There are a pair of sitting rooms and a dining hall. Plus, Grandmother has a large library."

He'd meant that to be a rhetorical question, but clearly she hadn't heard it that way. "Do you miss it here?"

Her eyes rose to meet his and she seemed about to answer, but paused. "Some things," she said after a moment. "I miss how comfortable this house is. I miss the sea and the beach and sleeping out on the terrace at night. Mostly I miss being a child."

"But?"

"But I don't miss dressing like this. I've gotten accustomed to my dresses and my shoes and . . ."

Oddly, that reassured him. *I don't want other men to see her dressed this way. No, I don't want her to be the sort of woman who likes to dress this way.*

He felt his cheeks heat with shame. It was a horribly judgmental thought, particularly since he'd always considered himself fair-minded toward others. That sort of thought had led to centuries of humans labeling the sereia as more lascivious than other peoples. He knew Marina better than that. How she was dressed should not affect his opinion of her.

"How could you not be more comfortable without shoes?" he finally asked.

Marina flushed. "It's fine not to wear shoes in my apartment, but I feel like you're staring at my feet now."

Joaquim shook his head. "If I were to stare," he admitted, "it would not be at your feet."

"I have lovely feet," she protested incongruously. "Everyone says so."

He dutifully turned his eyes down toward her feet. They were attractive, although he wasn't certain what made them so. They weren't tiny, nor did she have high delicate arches, but the scale pattern of her skin made them seem shapely. He wanted to touch them now, something he'd never thought about feet before. Perhaps the feet were important here, a strange contrast with their apparent nonchalance about a woman's breasts. "I have to agree," he said. "Your feet are lovely. Do you resent that I haven't noticed before?"

"You haven't seen my feet before today," she said softly.

He hadn't, but that wasn't what he actually meant. He stepped closer. "Do you resent that I've . . . always treated you like you're human?"

He hadn't, actually. At first he'd been taken aback when he learned she was nonhuman. Duilio's lack of concern over the same attribute in his own wife had reassured Joaquim, but Oriana and Marina were very different women. He was occasionally surprised that they were sisters.

Marina shook her head. "I like being human. No one expects anything of me there."

"What do you mean?"

She folded her hands together. "My mother's family are politicians and spies, and I never wanted that for myself. It would be horrible. I'm a runt, and no one would ever take me seriously. I'm not sure what I do want, but at least in Portugal, I have more choices. It's . . . easier."

Runt? Did she actually believe that of herself? Joaquim found himself staring at her, trying to figure out how she'd deceived him into thinking her self-confident.

There was a delicate cough behind Marina, and her white-haired grandmother stepped into the courtyard. "You are small, child," the old woman pronounced in a stern voice, "but you are not a runt. You take after your mother's father, who was very clever, I'm told, even if short."

Marina's gaze dropped to her feet again.

Joaquim hadn't realized it before, but Marina did seem to be small for one of her people's women. Oriana stood a full hand taller, or more. Marina's grandmother and the servants he'd seen so far were almost as tall, and the women at the harbor had been large and strong enough for him to initially mistake them for men.

"Now, before you descend into further self-deprecation," her grandmother said, "we're about to have dinner served. Why don't you bring your sweetheart back to the dining hall?" With that the old woman turned back into the hallway and disappeared from his sight.

Eyes downcast, Marina gestured for Joaquim to follow her.

He grabbed her hand to keep her from slipping away. "Marina, will you marry me?"

Her wide eyes finally rose to meet his. The moment stretched in silence until she finally asked, "Why now?"

His stomach went cold. *I thought she would say yes. Without question.* "I planned to ask you on the first of May, after lunch." His words rushed together, spilling out. "We were going to visit the gardens at the Palácio de Cristal, remember? I meant to buy you a fine pearl ring. I already have one picked out. I asked your father's permission last Wednesday night, but I couldn't ask you until I'd told you the truth about myself. And then I had to come here, and didn't know when I'd be back. Then we were on the ship, and it just wasn't the right time, and I don't know if I'm allowed to ask you *here*, so—"

He didn't finish whatever rambling statement he'd been about to make. Marina threw her arms about his neck, rising on her toes to do so. "Yes. I don't need a fine ring or anything like that."

He suddenly felt warm all over, as if the sun had come from behind the clouds. He held her waist to steady her, all too aware of the bare flesh under his fingers, and the lightly clad body pressed against his chest. "Marina, I want everything to be perfect for you."

She drew back, shaking her head. "I don't need *perfect*, Joaquim. If we're married before we leave, no one will say anything about our traveling together. Grandmother can have the priest come here, if you're willing. He'd marry us right away if she told him to."

Ah yes, this is the island that's partly Christian. "Are you sure?"

"Absolutely." Her jaw firmed. "I won't let you change your mind either."

Not that I want to. "Shall we go tell your grandmother?"

Marina stepped out of his grasp, a calculating expression flitting across her features. "No."

It was his turn to shake his head. "Why not?"

"We need to tell her the other way around. If we tell her you've accepted *my* courtship, then . . ." She flushed again.

And he suddenly grasped what she meant, even if she couldn't quite say it. That would mean they were already married. Joaquim licked his lips, feeling his breath go short.

If they followed her plan, tonight would be their wedding night.

How the hell am I supposed to make it through dinner with that on my mind?

Marina hadn't forgotten the rules of etiquette used here. And while Duilio clearly knew when to pass platters and about talking out of turn, Joaquim didn't. He spoke to her a couple of times without being addressed before realizing that was forbidden. He didn't know how to signal to the servants that he'd finished—or not finished—a course. Marina found herself gesturing to them in his stead after they took away his plate when he hadn't had a spoonful of his soup yet. Her grandmother took it in stride, but if this were another woman's table, he might have been asked to go eat with the children until he learned his manners.

After the meal, Duilio escorted him out to the second court-yard, possibly to smooth his ruffled nerves. Marina didn't know if she would have been comfortable speaking out in front of Joaquim. "He's accepted my courtship, Grandmother. I wanted you to know."

Oriana smiled, but didn't comment, leaving this between them. Her grandmother patted Marina's hand gently. "It was only a matter of time, wasn't it, child?"

"Yes, Grandmother."

"Do you have his mother's blessing?"

Marina's mouth fell open. She hadn't thought of that.

Oriana stepped in, saving her. "Joaquim's mother is dead, Grandmother, but Lady Ferreira is his foster mother, and I can as-sure you she approves of the match."

Her grandmother gestured her acceptance. "And how long are you planning on staying?"

Marina shot a glance at Oriana. They hadn't discussed that yet.

"We're expecting to hear from the Americans tomorrow," Ori-ana said promptly, "so they need to stay for that at a minimum. Why don't we take this into the courtyard? Joaquim will also need to hear it. If nothing else, it could be helpful to have a fresh perspective on our information."

So they headed that way, Oriana stopping at the door to ask a servant there to fetch two of the guards to join them. They entered the back courtyard where Duilio and Joaquim had already taken two of the wooden chairs. Her grandmother gestured for them to sit, and a moment later two of the guards arrived, an older woman with hard eyes and a stocky younger woman. Judging by their uniforms, they must be the officers of the Portuguese guard—the *female* officers.

Marina eyed them curiously. It wouldn't be her choice to be a soldier, not any more than she'd want to be a spy. These women must be more like sereia than she was herself. Since she'd arrived in Portugal, she always conformed to human society's expectations, even if she didn't truly believe they were right. It had been *easy*. These women had to be very determined. She suspected they put up with terrible ridicule—perhaps worse—back home.

Oriana came to stand behind her grandmother's chair. "On the first night we were here, not quite two weeks ago, someone broke into our bedroom and stole Mother's journal."

She relayed the details they'd dug up so far, a tale of two unlikely thieves. Marina scowled as she puzzled over the missing parts. "If you'd just arrived," Marina said when there was a pause in the story, "how did they know you would have the journal in your bedroom? And how did the boy know which room you'd be in?"

"Good questions," Duilio answered. "As to the second, we suspect someone who knew the layout of the house informed them, which means either someone on our embassy staff, or anyone who's ever visited this house before. We were given the best guest room. As to your first question, we don't know. They could have simply taken a chance."

"A seer could have told them you would have the journal," Joaquim said.

Duilio shrugged. "A good seer, I suppose. More likely they could have predicted that the boy's quest would be successful. It's interesting to note, though, that the boy was probably illiterate, since he stole every book I had in my desk, including my personal journal, which had only a handful of pages filled."

"Is there any chance the boy was after *your* books and not the journal?" Marina asked.

"It's *possible*," Duilio said, "but there doesn't seem to be much motive for stealing the old Haggard novel I was reading. When Oriana and I looked at the journal, it included a hidden cipher, but we didn't have time to decipher that to see what it said."

Marina licked her lips, her mouth dry. Her mother had always liked puzzles. On occasion her father's office handled confidential materials that were encrypted, and she'd done some of the deciphering work. It was tedious, but she could do it. "We have to get it back."

"Which is where you come in," Duilio said to Joaquim. "Our information is that the woman who stole it is headed to Barcelona, but we don't know where she'll go from there."

"Two sereia should be easy to track in Barcelona," Joaquim said cautiously.

"No," Oriana said. "The woman's had her webbing cut and the boy is webless. In human clothes, they can both pass as human."

"Webless?" Joaquim repeated.

Oriana explained that to Joaquim, and Marina could almost feel his eyes on her. They'd never discussed that topic—what their children might be like. Perhaps he'd just assumed they would be human. Or had he even thought about children?

"We're hoping the Americans have turned up something more helpful," Duilio added. "They have far more resources than we do here. They're sending someone tomorrow afternoon to hand over what information they've found."

Marina shook her head. "Why would the Americans care?"

"They owed me a favor," Duilio said with a dismissive shrug. "I suggest revisiting this in the morning, since it's almost dark. Joaquim can help us find Costa then."

Joaquim nodded quickly, and Marina realized that Duilio intended for him to use his gift of finding to locate the lost man.

Duilio rose. "A good night's sleep is the best counsel, isn't it?"

Apparently that was the end of their meeting. Marina rose along with the others, uncertain where all this left her. Duilio drew Joaquim away in the direction of the males' hall. Joaquim mouthed something at her that she didn't grasp. And then he was gone.

Oriana spoke to the two guard officers a moment longer, and then walked with Grandmother out of the courtyard, leaving Marina alone there. She threw up her hands in disgust. What was she supposed to do now?

CHAPTER 15

"Are you going to read me a lecture?" Joaquim asked once they reached his bedroom.

He dreaded the idea of having this sort of talk with Duilio. While not anywhere near as promiscuous as Alessio had been, Duilio had been experienced with women when Oriana came into his life. Joaquim wasn't. Yes, there *had* been a few girls before he went to seminary, but he'd always taken his relationships with women far more seriously than had any of his brothers.

"I only want to keep you from making an ass of yourself," Duilio said. "Oriana says you've accepted Marina's courtship, which means you're expected to share her bed now."

"I am aware of that," Joaquim said, the tips of his ears burning.

"I have one thing to warn you about." Duilio folded his arms across his chest.

Joaquim grabbed his bag off the bench. "I know she has sharp teeth."

Duilio chuckled. "Yes, something to keep in mind, but that wasn't it. I'm relatively certain she's a virgin, Joaquim."

Why on earth would he say that? Annoyed, Joaquim yanked his garments off the shelves in the dressing area and began cramming them into his bag. "And therefore I must be gentle. I understand the concept."

"Wrong assumption," Duilio said in his most patient tone. "Sereia females do not possess a maidenhead, the cause of numerous misunderstandings about them throughout history."

Joaquim dropped his last linen shirt in the bag's open mouth and turned to look at his brother. "And you were afraid I would misunderstand, and say something hurtful."

Duilio folded his arms over his chest. "No, I know you better. You wouldn't say a word, but you would fret over it endlessly."

Joaquim closed up the bag. He had never questioned Marina about her experience—or lack of experience—with men. He hadn't *wanted* to know. But his reluctance to inquire about her past had led to the quandary he'd been facing all day. "I've just realized that I know almost nothing about her. I've been courting her for six months, and I've never asked. Not the right questions, at least."

Duilio clapped one hand to Joaquim's shoulder. "It will take years before you truly know her. And then she will change, or you will, and you must learn again. People grow. Experience makes them do so. Oriana and I aren't the same two people who arrived here three months ago, and certainly not who we were on the day we married."

Joaquim regarded him steadily, wondering how Duilio had changed. He was more than simply *older*. He seemed more serious now. He would be a father soon, and that would change him further. And Oriana, who had begun their journey together as a woman who'd lost almost everything, had gained a regal confidence that Joaquim had only glimpsed in her before. "Has it been hard on the two of you, being here?"

"Yes, but if nothing else, it makes us rely on each other more."

Joaquim let out a huff. "I feel like everything has spun out of my control. Everything is happening too quickly, and not . . . how I planned. I prefer my life to be planned."

"I know you do," Duilio said. "And you can get back on that yacht and return to the Golden City tomorrow morning. You can go back to your apartment and back to work at the police station. You can have every day the same and keep everything perfectly serene. You don't have to do any of this."

He means that. Duilio would let him off the hook, let him go home to his regular life.

But he'd decided to come to Duilio's aid. This was his doing, not Duilio's, and he was responsible for the path ahead of him. If he was honest with himself, he felt less nervous about following that journal to Spain than he did about the night ahead of him. "Why didn't you send that letter to me?"

Duilio chuckled. "Because you have your own life, beyond help-ing Oriana and me settle the affairs of her family. And my gift told me you were soon to marry, so I didn't send it."

Yes, that sounded like Duilio. He would try to fix everything him-self. Joaquim sighed. "I dreamed that, ten years ago when I was still considering the priesthood. I dreamed of cramped quarters, heading for Spain, Marina with me. I just didn't know it was prophetic then."

He hadn't known who the woman in his dreams was. He hadn't even been aware she was a real person. He'd realized instead that his desire for a wife and family was stronger than any avocation he felt for the priesthood. He'd had other doubts, but that was the main reason he'd left seminary and joined the police. It hadn't been until the day he met Marina—and recognized her as the woman from his dreams—that he'd understood he was a seer. And that knowledge had changed everything.

"I am choosing this, Duilio," he finally said. "I am choosing to marry her, even if it's not how I planned. I am choosing to go to Spain."

"Then I'll pray for your safety every day," Duilio said.

Joaquim nearly laughed. Duilio was one of the least devout peo-ple he knew. "Thank you," he said anyway.

Marina sat on the bench near her door, waiting. Would Joaquim come to her? Surely he could find her.

Or perhaps she should go find him.

She pushed herself off the bench and began pacing the length of the room. With everything else that was going on, perhaps he was distracted from joining her. Her hands had started to ache, and she rubbed the fingers of one with the other. But then a knock came at her door, something only a human would do. She ran to the door and drew it partially open.

Joaquim stood outside, his bag in one hand. "Are you going to let me in?"

Marina grabbed his free hand, dragged him inside, and shut the door behind him.

He dropped the bag onto the floor. Then he stepped close enough to wrap his arms around her. "If I understand correctly, we're married now. Is that right?"

Since he'd accepted her offer, he was her mate. It wasn't precisely the same, but she wasn't going to argue. "Yes," she managed.

"And tomorrow, the priest's visit is just a formality."

"Yes," she whispered again. "It's not, but it is."

His eyebrows drew together. "Would you rather wait?"

She shook her head rapidly. She should be taking control of the situation now. She should order him to do as she wished. But she couldn't bring herself to do it. Her nerve wasn't sufficient to tell Joaquim what she wanted him to do.

"Will you kiss me?" he asked instead.

Marina stretched up to reach his lips and pressed a chaste kiss on his lips. This was one of the worst parts of being short.

Joaquim laughed under his breath. "Wait."

He put his hands on her waist, lifted her, and set her on the bench by the door. It was ridiculous, because now she was taller than him, but she could see his face without craning her neck upward.

"Is that better?" When she nodded, he gazed up at her face. "Are you nervous?"

"I don't know what to do," she admitted. "I mean, in general, I do . . . but not specifically."

He reached up and removed the pearl combs from her hair, sending her curls tumbling down around her face. "Were these your mother's?"

She nodded, surprised he remembered, and almost said that, but then his hands slid from her waist to the brooch securing her vest. That must have mystified the servants, but when she'd dressed she'd discovered that she had grown unaccustomed to baring her breasts, so she'd begged Oriana for something to hold the vest closed.

Joaquim lifted his eyes to hers again. "May I?"

She nodded again, unable to find any words.

Joaquim removed the brooch and dropped it atop his bag. He turned back to her, reaching up to push the vest from her shoulders, but paused, regarding her solemnly. "You do understand, don't you, that it might take some practice to get this right?"

"Right?"

"You don't expect me to be . . . very experienced at this, do you? I'm not."

Human men were promiscuous. She'd always been told that. "Never?"

He smiled up at her, one corner of his lips twisting wryly. "There were a few girls when I was younger, but I've known I wanted to marry you since I was eighteen."

"Since you were eighteen? How?"

"I am a Ferreira," he said, "so I do have a touch of the seer's gift as well. Even if I didn't know your name, I'd dreamed of you. I knew your face. Why involve myself with any other woman? It would have been like adultery."

And adultery was something Joaquim would never find acceptable. Marina felt warm all over. She'd been terribly nervous only a moment before, but that had passed. "I'm sure we'll figure this out."

Joaquim pushed the vest from her shoulders. Then his hands had returned to her waist. He leaned forward and pressed his lips to her collarbone. His hands slid upward until they touched her breasts.

For a moment he simply held his hands there, cupping her. Then his hands stroked her flesh, as lightly as a feather.

Marina drew a shaky breath. "Joaquim . . ."

"Wait." He tugged her closer and his lips touched her breast.

Marina's knees went weak, but Joaquim's hand slid around her back, pressing her closer against him. His tongue circled her nipple, sending a cascade of strange and unfamiliar sensations through her body. If she'd ever thought her small breasts lacking, she didn't now. "Joaquim . . ."

He drew far enough away to look at her. "What do you want me to do?"

Everything. She wanted him to touch her everywhere. She wanted to touch him. "I want you to undress," she decided. "And then I'll show you my stripe."

He stepped back, a slow smile spreading across his handsome face. "That sounds like a good idea."

Joaquim awoke in the middle of the night, although he wasn't certain how late. They'd left one of the lamps burning. Marina dozed, one leg draped across his thighs and her head resting on his chest. He eased away from her carefully.

With the shutters closed, the room was warm and she'd pushed away the blanket he'd drawn over them before he drifted off to sleep. The lamp sputtered and, trying not to disturb Marina, he rose awkwardly from the bed. Once on his feet, he stared down at his wife. She was absolutely lovely, and absolutely not human. A swath of iridescent black ran down the center of her back, widening from between her shoulder blades to its widest across her buttocks, and tapering down to a point again at each heel. It looked exotic, but felt no different under his fingers than the skin covering the rest of her body. From what he'd heard after dinner, their children would carry that same coloration.

He went and blew out the lamp that had been sputtering,

plunging the room into darkness. He went to open the inner shutters of the windows, letting in a soft breath of sea air and a pale hint of moonlight. He stood there for a moment, smelling the tang of salt on the breeze and the indescribable scent of a seashore.

When he glanced back at the bed, he saw that Marina had risen, one of the blankets clutched about her in belated modesty. She came to his side and peered out across the beach.

He wrapped one arm about her and drew her closer. "If I ask you to stay behind here when I go after the thief, will you?"

She laid her head against his shoulder. "No."

"I thought not." She had as much at stake as he did in this hunt for the journal. This was about *her* family. But he'd needed to ask. He hated the thought of her in danger.

"You barely speak Spanish," she said.

"I speak Spanish," he protested.

She laughed softly. "No, you don't. I've heard your Spanish."

She's right. He understood Spanish well enough when it was spoken to him. It was *answering* in Spanish that gave him trouble. "I speak Catalan."

"And therefore we should go together," she said. "You will talk to the Catalans and I will talk to everyone else."

He couldn't argue with that logic. "When we're in Spain, you mustn't be caught unclothed."

"I've lived in the Golden City for years. I know what to do." She clutched her blanket with one hand, but lifted the other, presenting him with a playing card. "Here. I was told to give this to you."

He took the card and peered at it in the dim light. It came from Miss Felis' deck, the ten of clubs, the card she'd had him draw himself. "How did you end up with this?"

"Someone sent it to the Pereira de Santos house, to me. The note said I needed to give it to you."

Joaquim smiled to himself. Miss Felis wouldn't have approved of Marina's *method*, but he could see her sending that order. "I won-der why."

"Ana said that this card is lucky. It mitigates all the other ills in the reading."

He could see Marina's face tilted up toward his. Yes, his plans might have all gone awry, but her presence here rendered the untidy unraveling of his plans insignificant. Having her at his side would surely mitigate any ill that came his way on this journey. He stroked her cheek with his thumb. "I think Ana was right."

He leaned down and kissed her gently, trying to memorize the feel of her lips against his, the touch of her cool fingers against his chest, the warmth her touch sent cascading through his body.

"Among my people," she whispered, "it's customary for the woman to make all the demands."

From the way she'd cocked her head, he felt sure she was blush-ing. "What?"

"When a woman wants her mate," she said, "she demands that he provide for her pleasure."

That sounded *exactly* like something her people would say. "I see."

She laid one hand on his bared chest again. "So please me."

While he wasn't certain how well he'd done the first time, he was more than willing to give it another try.

CHAPTER 16

Joaquim found himself nodding off again as Duilio rowed back to the shore. They'd gone out after breakfast to the yacht to update João and Aga on their plans. João had used that chance to present his idea of using the *Deolinda* to ferry tourists up the Douro, a proposal Duilio pronounced promising. The yacht was rarely used and due for refitting anyway. They left a beaming João with instructions to present the idea to Lady Ferreira, who was currently managing her son's business affairs.

"Want to talk about it?" Duilio had asked. That was all. Duilio hadn't pried into his night with his new wife, hadn't tried to embarrass him. That was one of Duilio's best qualities. He talked a great deal, often about *nothing*, but he knew when to let a subject alone.

In truth, Joaquim didn't want to talk about it. Not because he didn't want Duilio to know about what had, in his judgment, gone rather well. He wanted to keep it to himself. He wanted to *treasure* it. He wanted time to think over his changed relationship with Marina. So instead they drew the dory onto the beach in companionable silence, and Duilio took him to see Lieutenant Costa's quarters, one room over from the room Joaquim had initially inhabited.

Everything had been left untouched. The missing lieutenant had laid out his bedding, but hadn't slept on it that night. His bag sat on a heavy chair, opened up but not emptied. Duilio walked over to it and put one hand in the bag. He stuck a couple of fingers through a discreet slit along one of the bag's seams. "This is where our little thief was hiding. He cut this so he could look out."

Joaquim appraised the bag. The size was adequate for a child of seven or eight. "How many uniforms did the guards bring with them?"

"I've no idea," Duilio said. "Most of Costa's gear is missing, though. I'd guess he didn't bother to unpack because of that."

"Or he was planning to leave?"

"Possibly. We won't know until we locate him."

Of anything in the room, the remaining articles of clothing would have the closest ties to the young man. Joaquim reached into the bag and picked out one item—a ribbed silk undershirt. "What can you tell me about him?"

"Twenty-five or -six. From a wealthy family in Lisboa. Youngest son, I think. He and I didn't talk a great deal. You'd do better to ask one of the other guards, or Lieutenant Benites."

"Were they lovers?"

Duilio's eyebrows drew together momentarily. "Oh, you mean Costa and Benites?" He chuckled. "No. They worked together peace-ably enough. Benites did half his job, though. Costa's been struggling for the last month or so. Unable to sleep. Very unfocused."

That wasn't a good quality in a guard who likely stood hours on duty. Joaquim gazed down at the shirt in his hands. The shirt was well made, off the rack, but pricey. Neatly folded, but it had proba-bly come from the laundry that way. Joaquim closed his eyes and tried to get a sense of the shirt's absent owner.

His mind provided a strange split image, one of the lieutenant being close by, and a second shadow far away.

Joaquim opened his eyes and peered down at the shirt again. Why had he seen two answers? He glanced out through the small open bit of screen. This room didn't look out over the beach but toward the mountain ridge around which the ship had sailed. "I'm facing east, aren't I? Toward the harbor? And home?"

"Yes," Duilio said.

"I'm getting two images from this. One is close, on this beach, I think."

Duilio's jaw clenched. "He's on the beach? Is he dead?"

Joaquim pinched the bridge of his nose. He had never had any training in doing this, and his talent was as much a mystery to him as it had been six months ago. "I think if he was dead I wouldn't see him at all."

"Why don't we step outside?" Duilio said. "You can point out which direction to look."

Joaquim followed Duilio through the halls to the deck that overlooked the beach. After taking another moment to orient himself, he repeated his mental search and pointed. "In that house," he said, "or along a straight line with it. I'm sure he's alive."

Duilio puffed out his cheeks as he gazed at the house to which Joaquim was pointing. "That's the Guerra home. Grandmother already questioned the head of that household."

"That's where you should look. Can we not just walk over there?"

Duilio gave him an expression of exaggerated shock. "Two males, intruding on another woman's household? No, that wouldn't work out well."

Joaquim had to bow to his greater knowledge of the culture here. "So, what do we do?"

"We wait until Oriana and Grandmother can make a respectful call on the home."

"Wait? That's all you can do?"

"The Guerra family is almost as politically influential as the Monteiros. If we go over there and demand that they produce Costa, they'll refuse."

Joaquim closed his eyes and concentrated again, checking his sense of the lieutenant. "I'm sure he's there."

"*Damnation.*" Duilio ran a hand through his hair. "Unfortunately, much of our information about the thieves came from them. The Guerra household, I mean, so Costa must have been involved."

Joaquim didn't protest Duilio's profanity. Instead he followed that second shadowy presence his gift had tracked, far to the east. So far that he couldn't guess the distance, similar to his sense of Duilio two mornings ago on the ship. "I think the boy was touching this shirt," he said to Duilio. "I've captured a sense of him just from this."

Joaquim opened his eyes to find Duilio regarding him quizzically. He glanced down at the silk garment in his hand. His mother had never even admitted she had a gift. And he had no idea to whom he could go for training, although once he returned to the Golden City, he was going to do his best to find someone to teach him. If he could do *this*—pick up a sense of the boy from an item he'd touched—he'd bypassed far too many opportunities to locate missing people in the past. He owed it to them to learn his gift better.

Marina and Oriana had returned from a trip to the harbor with new garments for Marina to wear, a trio of dark skirts and shirtwaists with embroidery around the neck and placket and cuffs. The islands were apparently known for their excellent embroidery. Joaquim couldn't help smiling at Marina's obvious relief in having something more *proper* to wear, even if it wasn't the most fashionable garb.

The priest—a serious man of middling years—joined them for lunch. Interestingly he was deaf and had to watch their lips to understand what they were saying. At last the Jesuits had discovered a way not to lose their priests to sereia magic.

They gathered in the front courtyard, and Joaquim faced the man squarely, responding properly when required during the ceremony. Afterward the others left Joaquim and Marina alone with only the tinkling of the fountain and the cries of the gulls.

Joaquim gazed down at his new wife, who flushed and smiled softly. Being married in the eyes of the Church had been terribly important to him just a few days ago. It *was* still important to him, but little had actually changed with those words. The agreement between them the previous day, this ceremony, and the one that would follow eventually in their parish church back in the Golden City: they were merely the formalization of their union. His marriage to her, that was in his heart.

Before he had a chance to tell her that, though, one of the servants rang the bells at the edge of the courtyard. "Lady Monteiro has sent me to tell you a guest has arrived—the visitor from the American embassy. She would like you to join them in the back courtyard."

Marina took Joaquim's hand. He let her draw him along the halls until they entered the other courtyard, the one with all the chairs and pillows.

Their visitor walked in just as Joaquim sat down at Marina's side. He rose when the woman entered only to wonder if that was done here. *Perhaps the women rise when a man enters.* Unfortunately, Duilio stood against the plastered wall, so Joaquim couldn't use his actions for guidance.

Their visitor was a slender, dark-haired woman not quite Lady Ferreira's age, with delicate features and a demure attitude portrayed in her stance that was completely belied by her coolly calculating eyes. She wore a white lace-trimmed gown that displayed her figure well, and carried a parasol in one gloved hand. She nodded her head to Oriana first, then to her grandmother. "Madam Ambassador, Lady Monteiro."

"You are welcome in my home, Ambassador Norton," Grandmother said.

Aha! This was the American ambassador herself, not one of her people. Joaquim gave her a sharper perusal, curious that a mere theft demanded her personal attention.

"I am grateful, Lady Monteiro," the American said with a slight bow. "Please forgive me, but I am unable to prostrate myself appropriately in my people's native clothing."

"And yet you chose to wear it," Grandmother pointed out.

The American inclined her head, as if granting that point. "Unfortunately, my government lacks the grasp of the situation here that the Portuguese so clearly possess. If I were to, as Mr. Kipling calls it, 'go native,' my government would believe my mind had turned and recall me."

They reminded Joaquim of circling cats, trying to decide whether to fight. Or perhaps they were merely taking the measure of each other. Grandmother Monteiro's white hair and kindly face hid the mind of a shrewd politician. The American, on the other hand, struck Joaquim as hardened, an adventurer.

"May I introduce you, Madam Ambassador," Oriana said, "to my sister, Marina, and her husband, Joaquim Tavares? He is with the police in the Golden City, and they'll be tracking the thief to her destination."

The ambassador smiled up at Joaquim, who was still standing. "Inspector Tavares, I am pleased to meet you," she said in a low, melodic voice. She turned to Marina. "And you as well, Mrs. Tavares. Congratulations on your marriage."

Joaquim stole a quick glance at Duilio, who shrugged. The ambassador hadn't been told his rank. The woman must have very good sources of information. After a few more pleasantries, they settled, the ambassador sitting almost knee to knee with Oriana. The ambassador flicked a glance over her shoulder and, spotting Captain Vas Neves kneeling at the edge of the roof, gave her a smart salute.

"I'm glad you're taking precautions," the ambassador said to Oriana. "You may be young, but I can see you understand there's something odd about this situation, something higher powers may find . . . awkward. Now, shall we get down to business? My presence here *will* be remarked, so the less time I take, the better."

"Yes, since you came yourself," Oriana noted. "Why, madam?"

"Officially, I'm here to pay my respects. I'm planning to spend the afternoon shopping at the harbor, as I'm preparing gifts to send to my nieces in New Jersey. I could buy them garments on Quitos, but they'd never be able to wear a *pareu* back home." She opened up her handbag, produced a photograph, and handed it to Oriana. "Here are your thieves, as seen early Tuesday morning on the docks of Porto Novo."

Oriana angled the photograph and from behind her, Joaquim got a clear look at it. On the bustling dock, a woman in a dark shirtwaist and skirt stood with one hand on the shoulder of a young boy wearing oversized trousers, a shirt with the sleeves rolled up, and a tweed cap. His face was turned away, but the woman's was clearly visible. She had large dark eyes, dark hair pulled back in the requisite chignon, and pale skin. She looked frightened. *Hunted*, Joaquim reckoned.

Madam Norton continued, speaking to Oriana. "I beg your pardon for making you wait, but on seeing this photograph, I realized the situation is more complicated than I'd previously guessed."

"How so?"

The ambassador pointed at the picture. "She's dead."

Oriana's eyes lifted. "Someone killed her?"

"Your government did," Madam Norton said coolly. "About a decade ago."

Joaquim glanced over at Duilio. He stood against one wall, his eyes closed. He was trying to get his gift to give him an answer, anything that could verify that claim.

"How is that possible?" Oriana asked.

"That she died years ago yet this photograph was taken of her only Tuesday? I don't know yet. However, I can tell you a bit about her. Her name is—or was—Leandra Rocha. When I first arrived here, she worked in the American embassy on Quitos. She was one of the household staff, in charge of the maids, only twenty-four then."

Oriana's brows drew together. "Was she a native of Quitos?"

"As far as I could tell," Madam Norton said. "But tell me, when you were a spy in Northern Portugal, did they know you weren't native to their shores?"

"Very few did," Oriana said with an inclination of her head as if awarding the older woman a point. "Then you don't know for whom she was working."

Madam Norton smiled slyly. "My government has, especially in the past few years, acted in ways that prompt other nations to fear we have expansionist ideas. Therefore, I wouldn't have been surprised to learn that every member of the household staff was a spy for one government or another. Given Leandra's familiarity with the locale, I assumed she worked for your Ministry of Intelligence."

"And how did she end up dead?"

"She was arrested. Grabbed while out at the market, thrown in prison, and then handed over for execution. Left to die of dehydration on some tiny island. Traditional execution, I'm told."

Her eyes locked with Oriana's. She obviously knew Oriana had nearly died that way. Joaquim watched them. *What is the ambassador daring her to say? Or ask, perhaps?*

"Do you have any idea why they arrested her?" Oriana asked after a moment.

"Yes," Madam Norton said. "After a couple of months, she became friendly with me. I often sought her advice concerning local customs. Simple things: how to address elders, what manner of gift to give, what restaurant had the best food. I don't believe she ever revealed anything of a vital nature to me, but in the game of adventure, trust is dangerous. It is possible that she was taken up because of her interactions with me. I felt responsible for her death."

"And now you know she's not dead after all."

Madam Norton absently twirled her closed parasol. "Yes. When showed this photograph, our people watching the Spanish embassy recognized her. They saw her leaving the embassy with the boy Thursday morning. They don't recall seeing either before that, so they must not have come and gone from the embassy grounds often. But it leads me to question whether she was an agent of Spain all along."

"You might check with anyone who was there concurrent with her," Oriana suggested. "If someone noted that she had stripes on her thighs—perhaps if they'd caught her bathing—that would reveal she was a Canary rather than a sereia. They have different markings than we do, and a dorsal fin, although that can be removed."

"A dorsal fin? How interesting." The ambassador sat back, a speculative gleam in her eyes. "I will ask about that."

"Is it possible this is someone who merely looks like her?" Joaquim asked. "It has been a decade, after all."

The ambassador turned to him. "We keep photographs of all staff on file, Inspector. When compared against the old photograph, there's no doubt. It's either her or her twin, and I understand that twins are exceedingly rare among sereia."

Joaquim glanced down at the photograph again. The woman on the docks—Leandra Rocha—didn't seem like a hardened spy. Appearances were often deceiving, though.

"Our inquiries about Leandra Rocha haven't gotten very far, but my investigator ran across something interesting. She's not the only one who's been asking about Leandra. Several people she talked to mentioned having been quizzed about Leandra recently, within the last two months, by someone they assumed was a member of the Ministry of Intelligence. My woman there, though, says there's not any record of an agent with that name."

"Who?" Oriana asked.

"Inês Palmeira," the ambassador said. "She was, by the way, also asking questions about you, Madam Paredes, and several other women."

Oriana sat back, her expression unreadable. "I see."

"An oddity," Madam Norton said with a wave of her hand, "but worth mentioning."

"What about the boy?" Duilio asked. "Do you know who he is?"

"I'm afraid not. As I said, our people hadn't noticed him before."

Oriana leaned forward. "Have you heard whether she turned the missing book over to the Ministry of Intelligence? Or to the Spanish embassy?"

"My sources say neither," Madam Norton said. "Given the current hornet's nest of activity over at the Spanish embassy, I don't think they have your book. They sent out most of their staff to hunt Leandra. I suspect she took that book with her."

"To Spain?" Duilio asked.

Madam Norton tilted her head to gaze at him. "Yes, I heard you were on the docks asking questions, Mr. Ferreira. While the Spanish were searching for Leandra Rocha, she was in hiding somewhere in Porto Novo. She booked passage on the *Confraria*, which sailed for Barcelona two days ago. It should arrive there within the next day or so, and my people will be watching for her to disembark with the boy."

Joaquim rubbed a hand over his face. It would take *them* more than just two days to reach Barcelona. Leandra had at least three or four days' lead on them.

"How did you get word to Barcelona so quickly?" Oriana asked.

The ambassador smiled coyly. "We have our ways."

That meant the woman wasn't going to tell them. But it also hinted that information could pass between the islands and Barcelona with reasonable speed. While there were cables that allowed telegraphs to cross the Atlantic, there weren't any laid to the Ilhas das Sereias. Joaquim suspected they used a less scientific method of communication instead. The Americans had always been more daring in their use of magical devices than most European countries.

"Your representatives?" Joaquim asked. "Will I be able to meet with them there?"

"Yes, Inspector. The consulate general will have a man keep an eye on Leandra. Their direction in Barcelona, right on the harbor." She withdrew a card from her reticule and handed it over to Oriana. "If you find her, I am willing to offer aid, should she need it. Any

American embassy or consulate can protect her. If nothing else, I want to know what happened . . . whether she was betrayed, or she betrayed us. Either way, we were on friendly terms. I don't like people hurting my friends."

"We will keep that in mind," Oriana said.

The ambassador hefted her dainty umbrella as if preparing to leave, but then set its point on the ground again. "As you know, my people recently fought a war with the Spanish, a war that was disastrous for them. Our intelligence personnel in the country found it very strange, because the actions of certain government officials seemed to be, shall we say, not in the best interest of the country. The women of these islands don't interact with human men as frequently as the sirenas in Spain."

Joaquim wasn't sure where she was going with this.

Oriana shifted on her chair. "We refer to them as Canaries."

"They do not refer to themselves as such," the ambassador said. "I'm sure that in your training, Madam Paredes, you were taught to use your *call* more subtly. To influence gently, to get your own way."

Oriana licked her lips. "I was."

The ambassador turned to regard Joaquim. "Imagine, then, an entire population of sirenas using their *calls* subtly, to twist and turn human men about their fingers, to act in whatever way they demand. *That* is what our agents in Spain believe they observed. On too many occasions, men of power pushed the country into damaging circumstances. Often those men had a wife or mistress of questionable lineage, one who can be traced back to the area around Lleida."

Lleida was where the Unnaturals Prison was located, Joaquim recalled, where supposedly the Canaries ruled. "Your government thinks the Canaries pushed the country into the war?"

"There *is* evidence that a sirena—a Canary, as you say—planted an explosive device on the hull of one of our ships in Cuba, the action that sparked the war. However, I suspect their influence was felt in more subtle ways, touting the country's honor, the strength of their navy. In the end, that proved an illusion that cost Spain dearly."

Joaquim rolled that possibility around in his mind, managing not to glance at Marina as he did so. The idea that a group of women could be manipulating the government of an entire country seemed far-fetched. Then again, they only needed to influence the *right* people, and they had magic to help accomplish that. So long as they were discreet, they might succeed. If that was the case, then Spain had made a terrible mistake in bringing the Canaries onto Spanish soil. "Has the Spanish government looked into it?"

"Our people believe the situation expanded greatly during the reign of Queen Isabella. The sirenas purportedly share many of the former queen's reactionary leanings, and she allowed many of them to *leave* the prison to help foster her intrigues, not taking into account that they might have plans of their own."

"But Queen Isabella abdicated long ago, did she not?" Duilio asked.

"Yes, after she was exiled to France, in 1870. She continues to meddle in affairs of the Spanish state, though, from a distance. The Spanish government was made aware of our concerns about the sirenas a few years ago. My understanding is that agents of the Spanish government are investigating the problem."

"So the Canaries are behind the theft of the journal," Oriana said, "and the Spanish are their pawns in this, rather than the other way around?"

The ambassador smiled sweetly. "My point, Madam Paredes, is that while the government of Spain as a whole may not be interested in that journal, any individual man in the government *must* be suspected of being in the sirenas' thrall. Their army, their navy, their police: any of them may be working for the sirenas. So be very cautious whom you trust."

Although she'd begun that speech looking at Oriana, she finished it with her eyes squarely on Joaquim. Then she rose, lifting her dainty parasol. "I'll keep pressing over on Quitos, and advise my people in Barcelona of anything I find out. Good luck, Inspector, Mrs. Tavares."

She exchanged a ritual leave-taking with Grandmother Monteiro and headed to the door of the sitting room, but stopped at the threshold. She glanced over her shoulder. "Is that charming yacht anchored in the bay yours?"

She looked at *him* when she asked, so Joaquim answered, "It belongs to my family."

"By now I'm certain the Spanish mission knows what your ship looks like." Her head cocked to one side. "As I'm not entirely certain there's not a sirena among *them*, I'd take the train."

And with that ominous pronouncement, she swept out of the courtyard.

CHAPTER 17

Oriana watched the ambassador leave, escorted by a servant. Her grandmother sat again, a signal for them all to do so, so Oriana complied, her mind still reeling.

They had discussed whether the Canaries themselves might be behind the plot that killed the prince of Northern Portugal—and Oriana's mother—but hadn't believed the idea viable since the Canaries were all held in the Unnaturals Prison in Lleida. The Americans, however, didn't believe they *were*. That the Canaries might be acting *outside* the prison and the navy—twisting the minds of powerful men to suit their purposes—was worrisome. Especially since she didn't know what their purposes were.

The question of Leandra Rocha's execution was equally troublesome. *What did Leandra Rocha do to deserve execution? Or had there been an execution at all?*

Perhaps the alleged execution was instead a cover for the Spanish extracting a Canary spy from the islands. Someone within the ministry *was* working with them—of that they were certain—so it would have been a simple matter to arrange. They could disseminate the story of an execution to hide Leandra's disappearance.

And if that was the case, how did that relate to her own attempted execution?

The ship that had come after her had fled to a Spanish port after the leviathan damaged it. Had they believed her a Canary agent?

Would they have taken *her* to Spain? Or slit her throat and dumped her overboard when they discovered that she wasn't a Canary?

"I like her," Grandmother Monteiro pronounced, apparently speaking of Ambassador Norton. "She has promise."

Oriana smiled at that faint praise. "She's given us a name for our thief and the information that the Spanish embassy was involved, although possibly against their national interests. It seems definite that this Leandra Rocha is a Canary, working on their behalf rather than Spain's . . . or the ministry's."

"It *would* explain why she didn't take the journal back to Quitos," Joaquim offered. "The Canaries must want it for leverage in future interactions." He rubbed one hand over his face.

He'd probably not had a full night's sleep, Oriana realized. And they'd already had this discussion a dozen times over the last few days, trying to force together pieces of a puzzle that didn't quite fit. Oriana knew from past investigations that the pieces would all make sense when looked at from the other end, but for now their questions simply led to more questions.

"Who is the boy, do you think?" Duilio asked abruptly, peering over her shoulder at the photograph on the table. "Her son?"

"He could be," Oriana said. "He would have been born after she left here. Given that he's webless, he had a human father. That would be more likely in Spain than here."

Duilio picked up the photograph and handed it to Joaquim. "He's important. Find *him*. You have a sense of him. He'll lead you to her."

Oriana recognized how he'd used that word—*important*. His gift often warned him of people who would be pivotal in his life. Apparently the boy was one of them.

Her grandmother held out a hand and Oriana went to help her rise. "Now, I know the four of you have plans to make. And I, I'm afraid, must find a diplomatic way to accuse my friend Lady Guerra of lying."

That should prove a delicate matter, not only because of their friendship, but because if Oriana recalled correctly, Lady Guerra's mate had come from the powerful Palmeira family on Quitos. The Inês Palmeira who'd been questioning others about Leandra could very well be their neighbor's daughter.

In light of the ambassador's revelations, Duilio dragged Joaquim to the main sitting room inside, hoping to have a private discussion. He wanted to be sure that Joaquim grasped the danger he faced in Spain. The male guards had suffered through three difficult months, giving Duilio ample experience as he watched them fend off the constant barrage of sereia magic on Quitos.

"I've got a box of wax earplugs I can give you," he began as Joaquim settled in a chair across from him. "They're more effective than cotton or wool. If you're going up against the Canaries, you may have to wear them all the time. I'd work out some hand signals with Marina as well."

Joaquim's brow furrowed. "When we crossed the blockade at the edge of sereia waters, it didn't bother me. João went crazy and his wife ended up tying him to the railing, but I didn't react. I could *feel* the magic, Duilio, but it just slipped past me."

Duilio pressed his lips together. He had a very good idea of what had happened.

"I've felt a *call* before, Duilio," Joaquim added after a second. "I reacted then."

He huffed out a breath. "Remember how the ambassador talked about a sereia using their *call* more subtly? There's a way for a sereia to guard a human male against other sereia. They call it wrapping a hand around his heart."

Joaquim pinched the bridge of his nose. "You think Marina did that to me?"

"I cannot think of any other reason you wouldn't react to the blockade." Joaquim didn't like magic, Duilio knew. He had an egalitarian turn of mind, and disliked anything that bestowed an unfair advantage, whether it was money, nobility, or magic. That Marina had evidently used her magic on him had to bother him. "On the plus side," Duilio said, "you don't have to wear earplugs the whole time you're in Spain. You should be grateful to her. She was protecting you."

Joaquim frowned. "She didn't ask."

Duilio crossed his arms over his chest. "When you planned to leave the Golden City, did you give her the option of coming with you?"

"Of course not. I don't know how dangerous this will be. I don't want her hurt."

"You didn't ask, though, did you? You were trying to protect her, and gave her no choice. How is that different?"

Flushing, Joaquim turned his head to gaze at a tapestry on the sitting room wall.

"You're married to her," Duilio said. "Trust that she has your best interests at heart."

"I do," Joaquim said with an aggrieved sigh.

"But you're still annoyed."

"Has Oriana ever done that to you?"

"No," Duilio admitted, "but I'm half selkie, so I'm partially immune to the *call* of other sereia. You don't have that advantage."

Joaquim just shook his head.

Duilio rose and went to a desk near the door and dug out a handful of hand-pressed stationery and his fountain pen. "Very well. You should sail to Lisboa rather than home," he began. "That will save you a day. The *Sud Expresso* travels from Lisboa to Madrid overnight, but not every day. I can't remember which days. You'd best book into a hotel in case you have to stay overnight in Lisboa. I recommend the Hotel Avenida Palace. It's new and clean and stands next to the train station in Lisboa's downtown."

Dragged out of his sulk by the need for information, Joaquim sat up. "I don't have funds with me for a fancy hotel."

"You're listed on my account at the Bank of Portugal. Since this trip is to help Oriana and me, we should pay for it. I suggest making a large withdrawal while you're in Lisboa, although that would mean staying until Monday night." It was unlikely they would reach Lisboa until Saturday, or Sunday at the latest.

"Why am I on your account?" Joaquim asked.

Duilio patted his shoulder. "You're my legal heir. Also, I'd hoped you would move into the house on the Street of Flowers. You'll need access to those funds to keep the servants paid and the house repaired. It's shocking how much a place like that costs to maintain."

Joaquim blinked at him. "Your legal heir?"

Joaquim had been for years now; Duilio had simply never informed him. But he knew Joaquim would take care of his mother should anything happen to him. "If Oriana and I live here most of the time, that house will stand empty when Mother remarries, which is a waste."

Joaquim rubbed a hand over his face, shaking his head. "I'll consider it."

Duilio knew better than to press Joaquim further, so they moved on to the fascinating topic of train schedules.

CHAPTER 18

FRIDAY, 24 APRIL 1903; ILHAS DAS SEREIAS

Duilio clapped one hand to Joaquim's shoulder. "Be careful."

The morning had dawned clear and cool, so Duilio wore a light coat over his *pareu*. He hadn't painted his eyes, though, which made him look more like the Duilio that Joaquim knew. Together they stood next to the rowboat while Marina was exchanging farewells with her sister and grandmother up on the deck.

"Will we see each other anytime soon?" Joaquim asked.

Duilio closed his eyes, but then shook his head. "I don't know. I wish I could tell you that this would be a simple matter, but I'm not sanguine about that."

Joaquim stole another glance at Marina. "I know I'll get home. I know she'll arrive there with me. I've dreamed of us together in too many instances that haven't come true yet."

They were simple things, dreams of the two of them walking in the park, dreams of dinner at the table in the Ferreira house. If other dreams had come true, surely those must as well. He clutched that idea to his heart, and Duilio didn't argue. That was reassuring. And Felis hadn't said he wouldn't return; she'd only said it would be a difficult journey. He laid one hand over the pocket of his jacket that held the playing card Marina had brought him. He had to believe her presence would make everything bearable.

Joaquim waited for Marina to join him in the dory, and then they were on their way, Duilio growing smaller on the beach with each stroke of the oars.

Lady Guerra was welcoming enough, but Oriana could immediately see the older woman was nervous at this second visit. Given the grim set of her jaw, she was prepared for a fight. She cupped her hands together as if afraid to sign anything, as if she might let something slip.

Oriana had become accustomed to other officials behaving in that manner back in the capital, but she didn't like to think of a potential neighbor that way. And once she came to live here, the lady *would* be her neighbor. The Guerra family had owned a house here on Cartas Bay as long as the Monteiro family had.

The lady bade them settle in a sitting room rather than her courtyard, a welcome choice given the chill in the air that hinted rain would be coming later. Like in the Monteiro household, the furnishings of the sitting room were made of dark wood, carved in a martial spearhead design. The crest of the Guerra family hung on one white wall, a tapestry of bright colors against blue: two warriors, each clutching a spear in her webbed hands. It was a reminder of a long-past time when the fear of invasion meant that armed sereia watched every beach.

"Have you found the child who stole into your house?" the lady began as she sat, trying to steer the conversation where she wanted.

Grandmother Monteiro nodded. "We're tracking him down even now," she said. "Your information was very helpful to us."

"One of the effects of increasing age," the lady said. "I wake in the early hours and cannot sleep. I wouldn't have seen the boy otherwise."

The woman fell two decades short of her grandmother's age. "Or the woman who joined him?" Oriana asked.

"No," Lady Guerra said. "It was *dawn* when I saw her with him. They headed toward the harbor."

"Did you actually see them yourself?" Oriana asked. "Or was it someone else within your household?"

The lady paused just a second too long. "Why would I say that I saw them if I did not?"

That was *not* an answer.

"Your daughter lives on Quitos, I think," Grandmother Monteiro inserted. "Inês, is it not?"

A rhetorical question—her grandmother knew everything about all her neighbors. Oriana sat back in her chair and let her grandmother take control, mulling over her memories of Lady Guerra's daughter.

Inês was close to Marina in age. The two had been friends growing up, living on the same beach as they did. Oriana recalled the younger woman as headstrong and clever, always leading Marina into one kind of trouble or another. But she'd always taken responsibility for her odd starts and had never betrayed Marina. It had been years since Oriana had seen Inês, not since her father's exile ten years ago. The girl would be twenty-three or four by now, grown up. But if she lived on Quitos, she wouldn't have been on Amado when Costa disappeared, would she?

"I thought she went to live with her cousin's family there," Grandmother said. "Where does she work now?"

Lady Guerra shook her head. "I do not know. Since her cousin's death, she hasn't been the same."

"I didn't know," Oriana said, trying to recall if she'd met that cousin. "What happened?"

Lady Guerra shifted uncomfortably. "It's hard to get details here, but three years ago Safira was accused of treason. Inês refused to believe it. It has made her difficult, capricious. I often do not know what to think of what she does. She cannot seem to hold a position anywhere now, and . . ." She laid her hands over her face, bowing forward.

Oriana's mouth had gone dry. She wanted to shake Lady Guerra until she told her everything. How did Duilio manage to talk all the way around an issue that concerned him without losing his temper? Trying to think the way he would, Oriana forced herself to sit still, focus on the matter at hand, and wait for her grandmother to deal with the woman.

Grandmother Monteiro crossed to Lady Guerra's side and laid one hand on her shoulder. "Inês is young. The young make foolhardy decisions."

Lady Guerra laid her hands in her lap and raised her eyes. "Yes, they do. I do not know what she's involved herself in. Inês would not tell me. She feared for my safety. But that woman slept in our outer court that night, and the next morning I saw her leaving with the boy."

"What about the young man? The Portuguese? Was he here as well?"

Lady Guerra exhaled deeply, eyes closing. "I did not know he was here, not until this morning. It is my own disgrace that I deceived you, but that part was done unknowing."

Was here meant Costa was gone now. Oriana bit down her frustration.

"And where did they go?" Grandmother said patiently.

"I do not know," Lady Guerra repeated. "I could not believe Inês had done such a thing, stealing a male from another household. It was bad enough that she told me I must lie about the woman who came here, but then to discover she'd stolen a male without his mother's consent or yours. We argued, bitterly. In the end, she left, taking him with her."

And Costa had sat meekly by as all this happened?

"Did you speak with him?" Oriana asked.

"Young Julio? Yes," the lady said. "He said he had no choice, that he was to be sent back to Portugal soon, and Inês would not let him go."

Lieutenant Costa was so firmly *Lieutenant Costa* in Oriana's mind that it seemed bizarre to hear him referred to by his given name.

Here on the islands males were customarily addressed so. Costa would have to become accustomed to that.

But if he'd been presented to Lady Guerra as Inês' mate—which appeared to be the case—then that made his status as such legally binding. Inês now determined where he went and what he would do. Oriana tapped her nails on the arm of the chair she occupied, frustrated with both of them and their terrible timing in their flight.

"Lady Guerra," she began, "Costa . . . uh, Julio . . . was in a position of responsibility within our embassy. By going with Inês, he has failed his family. He will be treated as a deserter. If we can find them, he might still be able to quit the position in an honorable fashion and preserve his mother's good name." She *hoped* they could arrange that. It would also help preserve the standing of the entire guard contingent. "Do you have any idea where they went? Perhaps to your mountain house?"

For a moment, Lady Guerra sat still, her chin firm. "If it would spare his mother, I would gladly tell you, but I do not know."

"May we visit your mountain house to determine if they're there?"

The lady rose and sent for one of her servants. "I will give you a key. And if you find them there, bring them back."

That was the least of what Oriana planned to do to them. She waited until her grandmother and the lady exchanged information about the mountain house and then, after the servant brought the keys, parting pleasantries. Her teeth on edge, Oriana paused as they were leaving. She asked the question, even though she felt sure of the answer. "Tell me, what happened to Inês' cousin Safira?"

Lady Guerra's chin quivered. "She was executed, left to die on one of the Ilhas de Morte."

CHAPTER 19

SATURDAY, 25 APRIL 1903; LISBOA

They dropped anchor off Cascais, and once Joaquim had everything loaded onto the dory, Marina climbed down. He and João began rowing toward the stretch of sandy shore.

Marina smiled at Joaquim when he caught her eye. She wasn't wearing a hat, and the wind had teased one strand of hair loose from her bun, but her face glowed with pleasure, which he was glad to see.

The trip from the islands back to Portugal had been far easier than their outward voyage. The sun had been warmer, and Marina had spent most of her time talking with him. This time they'd talked about important things rather than simply passing the time. They had discussed his gift of finding, along with his minimal talent as a seer. She'd told him more about her childhood and her family. His worry that he didn't know her had faded, replaced now with the strange realization that getting to know his wife would be an adventure.

They rowed past an ancient citadel, through the many small craft moored in Cascais Bay, and finally up to the beach, its pale sands gleaming in the sunlight. Children ran along the small stretch of shore, and adults reclined on lounges and chairs, enjoying the fresh sea air. They angled the boat toward the base of the stone pier, farther from the crowds. João shipped his oar, jumped over the side of the dory, and drew it onto the sand. Joaquim slipped off his shoes and joined the younger man. Once they'd beached the boat, Joaquim lifted Marina out and onto the shore. She waited while he carried their two bags back. Joaquim shook the younger man's hand and left him with a wish for smooth sailing back to the Golden City.

Marina had picked up her bag and pinned on her hat, and now stood taking in the lovely buildings that stood near the small beach. Joaquim wasn't sure whether he was looking at very large houses or small palaces, their style quite different than the Golden City's stern mansions, with fanciful turrets and an occasional steepled tower.

"It's beautiful," Marina breathed, her eyes wide.

"I thought your people believed that Lisboa is cursed," he pointed out.

She watched him as he picked up his bag and walked to her side. "I'm a Christian, Joaquim. I don't believe in the sea gods and their curse on the city."

They took the steps leading up to the seawall and, at the top, a portly gentleman pointed them in the direction of the train that would take them into Lisboa proper. A few minutes later they were aboard, Marina on the outside so she could watch the scenery along the coastline. The train carried them to the Sodre Quay in Lisboa itself, and from there it was only a short walk to the Praça do Comércio.

The plaza was part of the magnificent downtown, all built after the earthquake that destroyed much of Lisboa. A statue of the first prince of Southern Portugal mounted on a horse stood on a high pedestal in the center of the plaza. Joaquim let Marina gape at the huge square with its arcade of arches and numerous cafés and restaurants where people enjoyed leisurely afternoon repasts under the shade of large umbrellas. Then he took her hand again. "Let's go. Duilio says if we go through the main arch and straight on, we'll find the hotel."

They walked through the central archway and into the downtown area with its straight streets and elegant buildings, all very modern. Not far away they emerged into another huge square with a wide avenue down the middle. People strolled along the avenue, others drove along in open carriages, and occasionally a young man would speed past on a bicycle. The sidewalks formed mosaics in black and white that were art in themselves.

Joaquim had seen photographs of Lisboa before, but they clearly did not do justice to the city's beauty. *I must bring Marina back here for a visit one day.*

His admiration was tinged with jealousy, though. Lisboa boasted of its beauty and modernity, the wide new streets and neoclassical buildings. The whole city had electricity now, and telephones supposedly abounded. The Golden City, stifled for two decades by Prince Fabricio's determination not to modernize his capital, was seen as backward by comparison. The epidemic of plague in 1899 hadn't helped the Golden City's reputation either. Joaquim wished that he could have Lisboa's modernity for *his* city, although not at the price of the earthquake and tidal wave that had swept away old Lisboa to make this new city possible.

He sighed at such morose thinking. *I can't change what's past.*

Looking up, he saw that they'd reached the hotel. The Hotel Avenida Palace, with its understated columns and dark roof, was indeed right next to the train station and, like everything else, was *new*. It was also intimidating, dressed as they were. Joaquim had pulled on a coat over his salt-laden shirt and thought he looked presentable, although not wealthy enough for this hotel. Marina had chosen the plainest of the garments purchased back on the island, with only a discreet line of embroidery about the collar of her shirtwaist. Even so, the pair of them still looked as if they had wandered in from the countryside.

But no sooner had they walked under the rust-colored drapes adorning the hotel's lobby door than an officious-looking clerk came bustling up to them and told a porter to take their bags. "We've been expecting your arrival, Inspector, Mrs. Tavares," he said, nodding in Marina's direction. "Your room is ready, and . . ."

"You've been expecting us?" Joaquim asked.

The clerk's bushy eyebrows drew together. "Yes, sir. The captain came down and made all the arrangements on Lady Ferreira's behalf. Your baggage is waiting in your room, and your tickets for Barcelona are in the hotel's safe, along with a letter of credit to the Bank of Barcelona. And we have called ahead and booked you a room there in the new Hotel Colón on the Plaça de Catalunya."

Joaquim shook his head in amazement. Before he'd left the Golden City, he wouldn't have been able to predict he was coming to Lisboa, that he would have Marina with him, or that Barcelona was their ultimate destination. But unlike him and Duilio, their cousin Rafael had full access to his seer's gift and had been training in its use with the Jesuit Brotherhood here in Lisboa on and off for the past several months. Joaquim shot a glance at Marina. "Rafael," he said. "Rafael must have come down to arrange this."

"Yes, Captain Pinheiro," the clerk agreed. "He's stayed with us several times before. Now, shall I have a porter show you up to your room?"

So, despite their shabby attire, a few minutes later they were ensconced on the fourth floor with a view of the Rossio Square below. Save for the bed, the furnishings were in the rococo style. Lovely, although too elaborate for Joaquim's tastes. Best of all, three pieces of luggage waited for them in the closet on ornate wooden stands—two bags for Marina and one for him. "There's a note from Ana in mine," Marina said, her eyes flitting across the slip of stationery that she held. "Captain Pinheiro came on Thursday and asked her to pack a couple of bags for me. Does he often do things like that?"

"He's quite astonishing," Joaquim admitted absently. Rafael must have packed his for him, which made him question how his cousin had gotten into his flat, but he didn't find a note from Rafael in his bag. He supposed he would have to do without Rafael's explanation.

Marina exclaimed over Ana's thoughtfulness. In addition to her Portuguese passport, Ana had packed a novel for her, one that

Joaquim hadn't read yet either—*The City and the Mountains*. It would be nice to have something to read on the train. After perusing the clothing her friend had packed and pronouncing it more than satisfactory, Marina crossed to the windows and held back the golden drapes to gaze out over the square below. Joaquim followed, looking over her shoulder and admiring the greenery planted there, trees and spring flowers and even palms. "We need to make a list of all the things we want to see here," he suggested, "and when we come back, we can see them all."

Marina smiled up at him. "We'll see."

He wasn't good at taking time away from work. He usually felt guilty if he did. Apparently she knew that. It was just one of the things that would have to change. He needed to make time for his wife and, eventually, their children. This trip was the first time he'd left his work in another officer's hands—Gustavo Mendes, who'd once been employed in the Ferreira house as a footman. Gustavo had a sharp mind, though, and was eager to prove himself. Joaquim had faith that Gustavo could handle the work.

"What shall we do, then?" Marina asked.

It was still early afternoon, and Rafael's foresight had saved them running about to secure funds and more clothing. They'd eaten lunch aboard the boat, so he wasn't particularly hungry. "I know that you'd like to explore, but to be honest, I wouldn't mind a nap in a bed that wasn't moving. And a bath. And a clean change of clothes."

Her eyes slid toward the wide bed with its marquetry head-board and brocaded spread. "Definitely a nap first, then."

Ilhas das Sereias

O riana fit the key into the lock and pushed the door open. They had made better time than expected, and had reached Lady Guerra's house in the mountains in the late afternoon. There was still light. Instead of waiting until morning, they'd chosen to venture inside to determine whether the clandestine lovers were there. Captain Vas Neves insisted on going first, her pistol drawn, while the rest of them waited outside. A few moments later the captain returned, sliding her pistol back into the red sash about her waist. "There's no one here. Not now, at least."

Oriana turned her gaze on Duilio, who shook his head. "Can you tell if they *were* here?"

The captain's jaw flexed. "I believe so. I'll show you."

They followed the captain inside the house. It was darker, built for withstanding the worst winters and heavy storms, so it lacked the courtyards and terraces that a beach house usually had. Heavy braided rugs lined the hallways, and dark furnishings completed the chilly feel of the place. But in the kitchens the captain showed them lamps that looked to have been lit quite recently. In one of the bedrooms, the mattress pad still lay on the floor.

"They moved," Duilio said quietly to Oriana. "Sometime between yesterday afternoon and this moment. My gift couldn't predict *when* they would flee. That's why I didn't know if they would be here."

Oriana cast a vexed look at him. "Where are they now?"

He just regarded her with brows raised. "*Where* is not one of the questions I can answer. That's Joaquim's purview."

She huffed out a breath. "How long do you think they've been gone?"

"Judging by the fact that the lamps are cool, I'd say not within the last few hours. But later than this morning, because I asked myself then."

"Inês had to have known this would be the first place we looked. The question is, where would she go from here? Where would she take him to hide?"

"You're assuming that Inês is making the decisions," Duilio felt obligated to point out. "Costa could be."

Oriana laid her steepled hands against her lips. "I don't know Costa well," she allowed after a moment, "but it's possible. If you were in his place, where would you go?"

"To Portugal," he said without pause. "I would run home to Lisboa on the next ship and beg my parents to give me enough money to get to Brazil." Brazil had no problem with sereia, and greater acceptance of mixed marriages.

"So we're up here in the mountains," she snapped, "while they could be slipping away."

Duilio held up his hands. "When I talked to the captain of the Portuguese ships in harbor last week, I took care of that. If Costa— or Inês—tries to buy passage, they'll refuse."

Oriana nodded. She blew out a vexed breath anyway. "I suppose we've wasted our time, then."

LISBOA

Marina found the city enchanting, what little of it they saw. They'd dined at a restaurant across from the hotel, where they sat outside to watch the traffic pass by. Then Joaquim strolled with her up and down the avenue, past numerous shops that looked enticing, but were all closed since it was late. They finally ended up back at the hotel so they could retrieve their bags and the tickets from the hotel's safe. They walked the short distance to the train station and took a train there to the station at Santa Apolonia. There the *Sud Expresso* was allowing passengers to board, so after they gave the conductor their tickets, their steward directed them to their compartment.

Both bunks had already been turned out for them, and a bottle of port and chocolates lay on the table next to the pillows of the lower one. Like the hotel, the first-class compartment was a luxury that Joaquim likely found uncomfortable. She suspected if she weren't with him, he would have exchanged the tickets for third class and sat up all night. Once their bags were properly stowed, she sat next to him on the lower bunk and stroked that lock of hair back from his forehead. "It was kind of Lady Ferreira to pay for these tickets."

"She wants us to move into the house on the Street of Flowers. Duilio says the same."

"It makes sense," she said, relieved that she wouldn't have to convince him. "A house does better when someone is there to care for it. And you were raised there, weren't you?"

"My bedroom is exactly how it was when I moved out, as if she was waiting for me to move back in someday. I've liked having a place of my own."

"We don't have to do it," she said. "We can stay in your place."

He shook his head. "It would be foolish. There's hardly enough room for two. What would happen when we have children?"

She didn't think he expected an answer. "My father wants to train me to take over his business," she offered instead.

That made him look up. "He does?"

She folded her arms over her chest. "Do you not think a woman could do so?"

His jaw clenched as if he realized he'd stepped into trouble. "Don't forget, darling," he said, "I was raised by a woman who was very involved in business. The reason I expressed surprise is that I can't imagine *you* wanting to pursue that."

She let out a deep breath. "I'm not sure I want it either. Our families have expectations of us, and it's hard to know what the right choice is."

"Surely it's not something he needs you to answer now," Joaquim said.

"No, it's just that he wants me to learn all the parts of his business, not just the conversion of files I'm doing currently. Learning about the investment and banking and management. That takes years. I don't mind the work. I'm just not certain that's what I want. I don't know if I have any . . . passion for it."

"I've always had a passion for what I do," he said. "Perhaps that's because of my gift. I don't know."

While she might be good with numbers, a trait inherited from both parents, that wasn't the same as running a business. Joaquim remained silent for a while, which made her wonder where his mind had gone. Clearly *away* from their previous discussion. She ran her hand through his hair. It was annoyingly straight, so she couldn't twine it about her fingers. Perhaps she could convince him to grow it longer as his brother had done.

When Joaquim spoke, his voice came softly. "I have family in Catalonia."

Family? Marina sat back. "Have you ever mentioned that to me before?"

"No," he said. "I've never told *anyone*."

Her mind spun. How like Joaquim to hold in a secret like that until moments before the train began moving. But if he had a secret, she wasn't going to get it out of him until he was ready.

"My mother's grandmother is still alive," he added. "The only one left of my mother's family."

Joaquim was nearly thirty. Marina didn't know how old his mother had been when he was born, but his mother's grandmother had to be older than her own grandmother. "How old is she?"

"In her eighties," Joaquim said softly.

"Do you want to meet her?"

"I don't know. She's not actually in Barcelona. She lives outside Terrassa, in the wine country. There's a train that goes there."

"How do you know that?"

"I made inquiries," he admitted, "years ago. Father doesn't know."

By *Father* he meant the elder Joaquim Tavares, not Alexandre Ferreira. She doubted he would ever comfortably call Ferreira his father, even if he had learned to call Duilio his brother.

"We could go there," she said, "and meet her, once we've found what we're looking for." If he'd made inquiries, Joaquim must be curious about the old woman.

He gazed toward the window with its drawn shade. "Thirty years ago, her granddaughter—a gentlewoman—was sold on the docks of Barcelona like a common whore. Did her grandmother do anything to prevent it? Did she ever lift a finger to help my mother?"

There was no emotion in those whispered words, but she recognized the pain beneath them. His mother had died when he was eight, just as hers had. She couldn't picture her mother's face any longer; she didn't know if Joaquim could recall his mother's. That didn't make either woman less important in their memories.

"Surely she didn't know," Marina pointed out gently. Barcelona was a large city, and one young woman could easily become lost there.

"It's not that far," Joaquim said flatly. "Her husband was dead, and her granddaughter was her only living relative."

Marina laid her hands over his. "Perhaps she didn't know where her granddaughter was or how to find her."

He sighed heavily again. "Inspector Gaspar tells me that this gift always passes down through the maternal line. In other words, I had to have gotten it from my mother, who in turn got it from hers."

"And she from her mother," Marina surmised. "Perhaps there was nothing she could do."

"She's wealthy," Joaquim said with a short laugh. "She has power. By all accounts she delights in trifling in every small issue in the town."

Had he been thinking of this since the moment he first heard their destination was Barcelona? It felt as though she never knew where his mind actually was, not like Oriana and Duilio, who seemed to think so much alike. Joaquim held things inside, hidden from everyone. If she were talking to Oriana, she would press harder, but that didn't work with Joaquim. He would only go silent. "How do you know all this about her?"

The train lurched and its whistle blew, a warning that they

were almost under way. Joaquim glanced at her. "Do you want to go to the dining car? For a glass of wine before bedtime?"

It was a desperate attempt to change the subject. Marina glanced at the bottle of port the steward had left for them, but Joaquim wasn't fond of the drink. Too sweet for his taste. "I think that would be nice."

So they made their way down to the dining car, as finely appointed as any restaurant back home. Other passengers crowded the car, some having dessert and a drink while others were merely talking. Joaquim drew her to a table near the car's doors, away from the chatter. Marina didn't bring up the subject of his great-grandmother. Instead he told her what he knew of Barcelona and its troublesome politics, and once they'd had a glass of wine, they headed back toward the front of the train to their compartment.

As they walked along the corridor, she tried again. "I think we should go meet your great-grandmother."

He gazed back at her, his jaw clenched, but said nothing.

"I'm not going to start a fight over this," she added. "I'm merely informing you of what I think. If you do not go, you *will* regret it."

Joaquim took out the key and set it into the lock. "I will keep that in mind, darling. I promise."

He swung the door open and stopped only half a step into the compartment. With one hand, he gestured for Marina to wait. Over his shoulder, he said, "Someone's gone through our luggage."

CHAPTER 20

Joaquim twisted a lock of Marina's hair about his finger. He hadn't slept well, and not for pleasurable reasons. The bed was comfortable enough, but the jerking motions of the train, very different than that of the ship on the water, had jarred him awake time and time again. And each time he would lie awake afterward, worrying.

Whoever had moved his bag had been discreet and made an effort to get everything back in place, but they'd left a few signs: his bag had been turned around, the stack of white shirts put back in the wrong order, with a soiled shirt between two clean ones, and a bit of his tooth powder spilled into his kit. He always made an extra effort to secure that tooth powder, since the cap was faulty. Unfortunately, Marina didn't pack as carefully as he did, and therefore hadn't been able to tell him whether anything of hers was disordered.

It was possible that the steward who'd turned down their beds had done it. It was the most likely explanation, although he'd turned down the beds before they went to the dining car. But given their mission, Joaquim was reluctant to trust in simple avarice. At least the conductor still had their passports. He would hate to be trapped in Spain without proof that he was Portuguese.

"We're going to miss Mass," Marina said, startling him.

He hadn't realized she was awake. The train began to rattle around a curve, causing her body to roll closer against his side. "I'm afraid so."

She shifted onto her side and smiled lazily at him. "I went for years without attending a Mass when I lived with my aunts on Quitos."

"They wouldn't let you go?"

She laughed shortly. "There are no churches on Quitos. Christianity is not allowed there. My aunts tried very hard to force me to drop my beliefs. They were hateful about it sometimes, both my aunts and my cousins. Oriana tried to protect me, but she couldn't stand between me and them all the time."

"But Oriana's not Christian herself."

"No. I think in some ways that's because she was angry with our father, so she reverted to our mother's beliefs."

He could understand that. "But your grandmother is Christian, like your father?"

Marina propped herself up on one elbow. "More or less. Father is far more devout now that he lives in Portugal. On Amado, one can be Christian on Sunday and not on all the other days of the week. You can go into some houses and you'll find that their statues have been turned to face the wall or a cloth laid over them, as if by hiding the face of the Virgin, their actions remain veiled from her eyes."

He didn't recall seeing a statue in the house of Marina's grandmother, but he hadn't seen the whole house. Perhaps there was a prayer niche hidden somewhere along those airy white halls. It was hard to imagine Marina's kindly grandmother hiding anything.

But everyone had truths that they wanted to believe were hidden.

I'm not all that different, am I? He was still uncertain whether he wanted others to know he was a witch, even if it was the truth. It had been difficult to tell Duilio and Rafael, who were family and would never walk away from him. It had been doubly hard to tell Marina, who *could* have turned away. If he gave in to Rafael's urgings and moved over to the new division of the Special Police—the one dedicated to investigating crimes against, or committed by, witches and nonhumans—everyone would know why he was there. They would know he was brought over from the regular police specifically because he was a witch.

He didn't want others to know he was a bastard either. Part of that came from wanting to protect his mother's reputation and keep from hurting his father, the elder Joaquim Tavares. If he moved into the Ferreira house on the Street of Flowers, it could be seen as an admission of his bastardy. That was simply another truth he was hiding.

There were always valid reasons to hide the truth. Because of the ban on nonhumans in the Golden City, the family had hidden the fact that Lady Ferreira was a selkie for his entire life. *But I don't have a reason like that. I just don't want to hurt my father's feelings. And he already has to know the truth, doesn't he?*

"Where have you gone?" Marina asked softly.

Joaquim gazed up at his wife, so determined to love him no matter what he was. He was the most fortunate of men to be here with her, even when they were heading into a country where they could both be imprisoned. Even while he had so many doubts. She truly was the thing that mitigated all his other worries.

And since a sliver of light now crept beneath the compartment's drawn shades, they would soon need to dress and head down to the dining car for breakfast. So Joaquim decided to take advantage of their early wakefulness. He lifted one of her delicate, scarred hands and brought it to his lips. "You do know that I love you, don't you?"

Marina smiled broadly, then leaned down to kiss him, her dark curls falling about him and hiding them within a world where only they two existed, and it didn't matter who they were. Only that they belonged to each other.

ILHAS DAS SEREIAS

This would someday be their house, so Duilio walked the halls of Lady Monteiro's mountain house, trying to familiarize himself with the layout. The guards were loading the carriage to head back down to the beach house, and thus he had a few moments alone. He stepped out onto a small balcony on the second floor, its stone balustrade providing a place to lean. He had a commanding view of the mountains rising behind the home and of the valley spreading below.

His looking glass showed him that some pale spots up on the side of the mountain were actually ibexes, their thick curving horns identifying them as the same ones shown in the tapestries in the Monteiro house on the beach. He wasn't certain, but he suspected they were Portuguese ibexes, a breed grown terribly rare in his homeland. He would have to send back home for a book on mountain fauna to verify that. If it was true, it would be interesting to learn how they had ended up here on these islands. He'd been told that the sereia island of Capraria, in particular, was swarming with the creatures.

"Are you ready?" Oriana asked from behind him.

He sighed. "I wish we could stay. It's beautiful."

She came and peered up at the mountainside. "We should head back to the beach house. If nothing else, the Americans might have news."

He turned back to survey the valley below. The Guerra house was visible from where he stood, as well as a dozen others, half shrouded in trees. "They're here somewhere," he said. "In one of these houses. I suspect they broke into one. One where they could watch us but stay hidden."

"I thought they were going to try to book passage off the island."

"Not yet," he said. "They're waiting to see what we do." He felt sure of that now, a situation that his gift found promising.

She gazed out over the valley below. "Do you know which house?"

"It doesn't matter. If they're watching us, they'll move as soon as they see us coming. In this terrain, they can stay hidden almost indefinitely. We'll have to lay a trap instead."

"What are you suggesting?

"Where's the nearest home that will take guests?"

"About five miles down the road," she said cautiously.

"I think we should leave here, making it easy for anyone to see us. Then when we hit some overgrown spot in the road, you and I slip out of the carriage and make our way back to the Guerra house through the woods. Once they think we're gone, they'll go back there."

Oriana frowned, but didn't reject the plan immediately. "We bring the captain as well. I want the odds in our favor."

Oriana reached up to grasp Duilio's hand, and he helped her over a rocky ledge. She clutched his elbow for a moment, catching her breath. Steep slopes were not her forte. Almeida was some distance up the slope from them already. Vas Neves brought up the end of their train, her rifle in her hands as if an assassin might jump out of a tree at any moment. The woman was vexingly tireless.

"How much farther, do you think?" Oriana whispered into Duilio's ear.

"Do you need to rest?"

Oriana shook her head. Captain Vas Neves had argued against her coming. While it was primarily on the grounds that she was the ambassador and shouldn't be putting herself in harm's way, the captain's secondary concern was that she would slow them down. Oriana didn't want to prove the captain right.

Yet they wouldn't be able to capture Inês without another sereia present, not without shaming Inês terribly. Duilio might be her deputy, but for a male to arrest a female went against all her people's customs. Oriana was grateful that the captain relented. She could no more afford to alienate the captain of her guard than she could a member of the Guerra family.

Almeida slipped down the slope toward them, making surprisingly little noise. Most of the guard contingent was composed of city dwellers, but the corporal came from the countryside in the Douro River Valley, and had spent much of her childhood hunting to keep her younger siblings fed. She knew how to move quietly in the woods. She stopped next to Duilio, and softly said, "We're almost on the house. Saw movement inside. Couldn't identify the person, though."

Vas Neves had caught up with them. She used a branch to pull herself up onto the rock ledge. "Almeida, head around the back of the house, cut off any escape that way. The ambassador and I will make entry through the front door. That leaves you to prevent any escape along the road, Mr. Ferreira."

Duilio nodded once, accustomed by now to taking orders.

"We can't guarantee that they're alone," Vas Neves added grimly. "If you see a Spanish uniform, shoot. If it's a choice between Costa escaping and shooting him, Ambassador, what are your orders?"

The army had rules about shooting one of its own, didn't it? Oriana gazed into the captain's hard eyes and knew she would do it. Costa's weeklong flight had jeopardized not only the contingent's reputation, but the future of all women who might want to serve in the Portuguese army. "I don't want him dead," Oriana said firmly, "and I'd rather you not shoot him at all if you can avoid it."

Vas Neves lifted her chin toward Almeida, and the corporal slipped silently away in the direction from which she'd come. Once Almeida was out of earshot, Vas Neves turned back to Oriana. "Ambassador, the question might have been shocking, but we have to consider the option that Guerra is working for the Spanish and has control of Costa. Costa could be coerced into assassinating you. Because of that, we must treat him like an enemy agent until we know that's not the case."

Oriana shook her head. She'd assumed the wrong motive for the query. "You're correct, of course, Captain."

"If you'll follow along behind me, madam," the captain said. "And, Mr. Ferreira, if you'll guard our backs."

While Oriana had focused on the captain, Duilio had drawn his revolver from its holster. She lifted her chin and followed in the captain's footsteps, grateful they didn't have far to go.

Duilio waited back at the gate, among the rhododendrons that bloomed at the property's entrance. He kept out of the line of sight of the house's windows, wishing Oriana could do the same; she and the captain walked directly up to the house's front door. He had no idea where Almeida was, but suspected the corporal didn't mean to be seen. He had a new respect for the young woman. He'd sounded like half a herd of sheep while working his way through the trees.

From his vantage point, he saw the captain take something from Oriana's hand—likely the key to the house—and a moment later, the captain strode into the house, pistol at the ready. Oriana walked in behind her. He waited, his breath held.

On the side of the house, a window swung open, and he saw Costa clamber out. His black *pareu* caught on the window's frame, and he had to jerk it free. Duilio chuckled. As he watched, Costa turned back to help a woman step down from the window, and the two ran toward the back of the property.

Duilio nearly went after them, but the report of a rifle sounded. Dirt sprayed up not far ahead of the escaping pair's feet, followed by a screech from the woman. Costa grabbed her hand and dragged her in the opposite direction, right toward Duilio. Duilio shrank back into the cover of the tree. *I'm only going to get one chance at this.*

It seemed to take a long time, but Costa and the Guerra woman finally reached the pathway leading off the property. Duilio tucked his revolver in the waist of his *pareu*. Costa led the woman now, her breathing ragged. He glanced back over his shoulder just as he drew even with the trees where Duilio waited.

"Costa!" Duilio jumped out, fists up.

Costa's head snapped around, and before the young man actually came to a halt, Duilio landed a hard right to his chin. Already off balance, Costa fell to the ground, landing on his backside. The woman rounded on Duilio, her sharp teeth bared. Duilio drew his revolver, but trained it on Costa, and the woman went still.

Costa gazed up at him, blue eyes wide with despair.

"The way I understand it," Duilio said, "is that I can talk to you, Costa, but not her. So this is simple. If she attacks me, I'll shoot you."

"Run, Inês," Costa said very quietly.

The woman drew herself up to her full height and crossed her arms over her bare chest. "I demand to speak with your mate."

Because she won't lower herself to deal with me. Duilio took a deep breath. Out of the corner of his eye, he saw Oriana and Vas Neves emerging from the house. He turned back to Costa. "Tell her that can be arranged."

MADRID

Marina stared up at the magnificent steel and glass roof of the train station that rose overhead. She'd waited alone with their bags for half an hour now if the nearest clock was accurate. People hurried past or waited like her, an ebb and flow determined by the arrival and departure of the trains, although she suspected that the platforms would be far busier than this were it any other day of the week.

She watched her fellow passengers, noting an unusual suitcase here, a striking outfit there. One woman walked past wearing a navy skirt and a blue-and-white-striped shirtwaist that Marina particularly liked. She would have to suggest that to the seamstress back in the Golden City. Most passengers scarcely glanced *her* way. She was merely one woman dressed in her Sunday best, waiting.

Joaquim sat on the far side of the station where he could see her. He was watching for anyone who might be watching her, a traveler who might have followed them from Lisboa and gone through their luggage. It could have been anyone on that train, even one of the stewards. Given the ambassador's warning about men being under the spell of the Canaries, Marina understood the reason for Joaquim's caution.

But traveling across Iberia took money. If someone had followed them from the islands—or just from Lisboa—they had invested a great deal of money already.

Joaquim came striding toward her then, his handsome face lighting with a smile. When he reached her side, he bowed over her gloved hand. "I cannot believe a lady so lovely is waiting for me. I've kept thinking that as I watched you." He leaned against the wall next to her. "I didn't see anyone watching you. Not overtly anyway."

"Well, that's good to know."

"Our train leaves in half an hour," he added. "Shall we go settle in?"

They'd switched trains at Medina del Campo and were doing so here in Madrid as well, but they were in a first-class compartment the rest of the way to Barcelona. So they made their way to the proper platform and found their compartment on the train. It wasn't as fine as the night train's compartment, but clean and private. Once the train rattled out of Madrid, they sat in silence, watching the arid-looking Spanish countryside slip by.

Marina couldn't imagine living here, so far from the sea. While the countryside had its own kind of beauty, her gills ached just thinking about it. What must it be like for the Canaries, forced to live in Spain? Had they, over the centuries, become accustomed to the dry air?

After a time she pulled the shade closed and turned up the gaslight in the compartment, earning a quizzical look from Joaquim. "It all looks the same out there," she said.

"The locals would probably disagree. I think it's rather pretty."

Marina shook her head. Joaquim was determined to find the best side of everything, but he didn't have to worry about his gills drying out. "Shall I read?"

He leaned back against the wooden paneling of the compartment wall. "For now."

So she spent the remainder of the morning reading from the novel Ana had packed for her, regaling Joaquim with the droll tale of the wealthy hero's chaotic yet empty life in Paris.

CHAPTER 21

ILHAS DAS SEREIAS

When Oriana had left Amado, Inês Guerra was a gawky twelve or thirteen. She'd matured past her awkwardness. She was as tall as Oriana herself now, although slimmer and strikingly beautiful. Her curling flaxen hair had darkened to a golden shade, and she wore it loose to emphasize her youth. She wore the bright blue of the Guerra line, a *pareu* with gold and orange embroidery at the hem.

Duilio escorted the fleeing lovers back into the main hall of the Guerra house. Inês was clearly angry, but she'd always been given to high drama. Lieutenant Costa stood a couple of feet behind her, wearing only a black *pareu*. He bore the winglike mark of the Guerra line across his chest, but Oriana assumed it was painted. He wouldn't have had time to heal from a tattoo yet, would he? He was trying to maintain a defiant expression, but seemed far more intimidated than Inês. The swelling forming on the left side of his chin made him look a bit pathetic.

Oriana met the other woman's eyes steadily, and saw that Inês knew quite well who had the upper hand. She gestured for the young woman to sit in a heavy wooden chair, and settled across from her in its mate. Duilio came to stand behind her, just as Costa stood behind Inês' chair. "Does your mother know you're here, Inês?"

Inês' chin lifted. "No."

Oriana signaled that she needed to think. In truth, she wanted Inês to squirm for a moment. She surveyed Inês, taking in her lovely face, her tall and strong frame. "Why Costa?" she asked bluntly. "You could likely have had any male on this island. Your family is well connected and you appear to be healthy. Why choose a human male for your lover? Why a member of my household?"

As she'd expected, Inês' jaw clenched at her use of the term *lover*. It carried the implication that Costa wasn't actually her mate. Not yet.

"I love him," Inês said.

Standing behind Inês' chair, Costa actually blushed.

"Did you *call* him?" Oriana asked. "Did he have any choice in this?"

Costa impressed Oriana by not speaking out of turn. He'd clearly learned from the past few months watching Duilio hold his tongue. Perhaps he would adapt.

"No," Inês said. "I did *call* him out to the beach that morning, but nothing more than seeking his presence, I swear. He has his own mind."

Oriana looked at Costa's face, permissible since he was part of *her* household no matter what the tattoo claimed. He hadn't misunderstood that last question, one she'd asked out of concern for him. He nodded once, which reassured her. There was hope, then, that they could untangle this mess. "Then we won't force him away from you, but we want answers before we commit to helping you out of this situation."

Inês blinked, as if surprised that they might help them. "I had no right to take him, I know," she said. "Not without his mother's permission, or yours."

"Then why not court him properly?"

"I wanted to," Inês insisted. "When I learned he was coming here, to your grandmother's house, I abandoned my job at the Spanish embassy and took the ferry here. I planned to approach you to ask permission, but on the morning after he arrived, he came to me on the beach and told me something had happened to his luggage. I realized the boy must have hidden in *his* bag, of all the terrible luck. I knew Julio would be blamed for the theft and sent back to Portugal. I couldn't allow that."

There was a great deal of information in that passionately delivered speech. "You knew about the theft?"

Inês drew herself up. "The boy is a thief, and he'd been in the Monteiro house, so he stole *something*. I couldn't let Julio be blamed. He needed my protection."

Oriana didn't look at Costa's face. Most Portuguese men would flinch at being referred to in such a way by a woman. But the relationship between Inês and Costa—Julio, she reminded herself—was their business. Perhaps he *wanted* her protection. If he was willing to defer to her regularly, their relationship might work out well. "And how did you know that the boy was in the house?"

"I was going out to the beach to see if I could find Julio not long after four. I saw the boy coming out of the shadows of your grandmother's house toward the beach. He met the woman there, and they hid in one of my mother's courtyards until dawn. Of all the places to pick," she finished ruefully.

That was a coincidence? Oriana felt her jaw clench. This was the time when she needed a Truthsayer, a witch who could parse out the truth of a speaker's claims. Perhaps she should include a recommendation to hire one in her next report to the Foreign Office. "It never occurred to you to confront them? Or to come to us and report the theft so we could confront them?"

Inês folded her arms over her chest. "I'd been working at the Spanish embassy. I knew you wouldn't believe me. But I told my mother to tell you about them."

She'd talked her mother into lying about the woman and boy, a backward way of getting their description back to the Portuguese. It was a strange choice, but hinted that Inês wasn't completely against them. "How did you know the boy was a thief?"

"Everyone at the embassy knew it," she said with a graceful shrug.

Oriana regarded Inês silently, trying to decide what trouble spot in her story needed attention first. She finally decided she should start at the beginning. "How did you meet Costa?"

Inês took a deep breath. "Madam Davila paid me extra to suborn one of your guards. I could hardly turn her down without her growing suspicious of me."

Madam Davila was the wife of the Spanish ambassador, and many felt she held the true power at that embassy, not her often-ailing husband. "Does she know you're Amadean?"

Inês shook her head. "No. I used my father's line name, Palmeira."

"So you accepted Madam Davila's charge?" Oriana prompted.

"Yes. I watched the guards for a few days and I picked Julio. I liked the way he smiled."

Costa flushed again.

Oriana couldn't fault Inês' logic. She'd always admired Duilio's smiles. She pressed on. "Where have you been meeting him?"

"At the park where the human men are allowed to walk."

A small park was located between the embassy compounds, fenced so that only embassy personnel would enter—the one place they could get fresh air and exercise when not on duty. But there were sereia who loitered nearby to watch the spectacle of human males parading about . . . or to taunt them with their *calls*.

"At night?" Oriana asked, wondering if the lieutenant had ever had bad dreams as he'd told the captain. More likely he wasn't sleeping at all.

"Yes," Inês admitted.

"How did he get off embassy grounds to meet you?"

Inês shrugged.

Oriana suspected Duilio would have to get that out of Costa privately. Costa had erred in slipping out at night to meet a local woman, and later in running away with her rather than facing any accusations made against him. Inês made the mistake of assuming Costa would be blamed and also that she wouldn't be believed. But Madam Davila's misstep was the source of this; she'd chosen the wrong employee to spy on the Portuguese soldiers. She'd chosen an Amadean, a woman who might look on a human male as a potential mate rather than a simple target for seduction.

Oriana sat back in the chair, laying one hand on each arm. "I am willing to help you gain the approval of Costa's family and therefore mine. We can transport you both to Portugal to seek them out, with the assurance that Costa won't be jailed for desertion, if you are willing to meet certain conditions."

Inês glanced up at Costa's face. She understood, then, that he could be *imprisoned* for desertion of duties. She looked back to Oriana. "What do you want in return?"

"At this moment? Information."

"And what happens to us?"

"Costa will resume his duties until he returns to Portugal. You will be allowed to stay at my grandmother's house as a guest of the mission. When he goes back to Portugal, you will go with him and seek his family's permission to marry. He will resign his position with the military. Then you will both be free to return here."

"And he won't be charged?" Inês asked cautiously.

"Not so long as we can claim his absence for the past week was an effort to track *you*."

Inês sat back, mouth agape. "That's ridiculous."

Oriana tapped her nails on the arm of the chair, and then recalled that her aunt Jovita had done the same thing when vexed. She stilled her fingers. "Not at all. Only his captain and Lieutenant Benites knew he didn't have permission to leave. They are, I believe, willing to support that ridiculous premise to safeguard the overall reputation of the mission. For all the others know, Costa's been on a special assignment all this time."

That wasn't strictly the truth. All the guards *suspected* Costa's defection, but since the captain and Benites had kept quiet, they couldn't prove he'd left without orders.

Inês sat back in her chair, eyes narrowed.

"Or are you suggesting it's ridiculous," Oriana continued, "because he couldn't possibly have found you if he was trying?"

Inês fumed, but couldn't affirm that in Costa's presence. "We'll take your offer," she said firmly. "Now, what do you want to know?"

D uilio caught Costa's eye and nodded toward the far archway. Costa glanced down at Inês and gestured discreetly toward the door. She nodded, granting her permission, so he followed Duilio from the main hall. Duilio waited until they'd gotten into a hallway before asking, "Do you miss trousers yet?"

Costa returned a perplexed look. "How did you know?"

"It's the one thing I miss. I could go bare-chested and without shoes daily, but there are days I wish trousers were acceptable here."

"Inês says I should start a new fashion."

What an unusual thing for Inês to say. Duilio wondered if she meant that, or if she'd merely said it to appease Costa. He opened the door that led to one of the sitting rooms, shooed the lieutenant inside, and closed the door. "Who was helping you get off embassy grounds at night?"

Costa went pale. "We're not prisoners there, sir. It wasn't illegal. And if you want the others to keep silent about my absence, I have to return that discretion."

He hadn't expected Costa to have worked that out. Perhaps he'd underestimated the young man's intelligence. "How long have you been meeting with her?"

Costa flushed again. "Almost two months, sir. Not every day, but regularly."

There was definitely someone closemouthed among the guards to have held that secret for him. Duilio suspected Corporal Pinho. He and Costa were on good terms. "And you left with her willingly that morning?"

"Yes. I knew that if something had been stolen, I would be suspected, sir. Because of what happened with my luggage."

Duilio gazed at Costa. "Do you not want to return to Portugal? You're willing to stay here the rest of your life instead?"

Costa's shoulders squared. "I'm not clever like you, sir, but I'm not stupid. I'm the last of five sons. Most of the money will go to my eldest brother to keep the estate running. I barely recall speaking to my father as a child, and my mother died when I was too young to remember her. There's not much waiting for me back there. Given these last few months, I doubt I have an illustrious military career ahead of me."

Looked at that way, it had to have been a simple decision. "You are, essentially, a fortune hunter."

Costa didn't deny it, mouth in a thin line. "It was a practical choice, sir."

He didn't claim that he loved Inês, but when Duilio had been holding a gun on him, Costa told her to run, to leave him to face his fate. Even if Costa hadn't said as much, he must care for her. "You understand that life here will be very different?"

"I have watched you, sir, for the last three months. I've seen how different it is."

Duilio wanted to point out that he had a very tolerant wife, and also the protection of a handful of guards on most occasions. Then again, Costa had been there during the embarrassing incident in the marketplace, so he knew there could be very awkward moments. "Is your mother's mother still alive? To give her approval."

"My grandmother? Yes," Costa said. "And no matter what my father says, she's fond of me and will agree. I know she will."

"You've given that some thought."

"We were hoping to travel to Portugal to ask," Costa said, frustration creeping into his tone, "but when we spoke to the Portuguese captain in harbor, he wouldn't take us as passengers. I suspect that was your doing, sir."

"I'm afraid so, Lieutenant."

"Then why help us now?"

Duilio smiled at Costa, wanting to set the younger man at ease. "The Guerra family and the Monteiro family are neighbors. I would rather get along. You help us substantiate the claim that you were on a special mission, and we'll help you clear your conscience."

Oriana turned back to Inês once the men were gone. "I want to talk about what happened *before* Costa. Why have you been asking questions about me?"

Inês scowled. "You're supposed to be dead, executed, but three months ago you turned up alive. I needed to know why."

"Because of your cousin?"

"If you're alive," she said with a quick shake of her head, "then Safira could be."

Oriana tapped her fingernails on the arm's chair. "How did you come to *that* conclusion?"

"About six months ago a woman approached me with questions about my cousin—her position in the ministry and her execution. When I pressed, the woman told me she investigated all executions, a routine matter for the ministry, and asked if I'd known any of the others she was investigating. It seemed strange, so I decided to investigate myself. Before her arrest, the ministry had Safira working at the Spanish embassy, so I found a position there."

"Why not go to the ministry itself?"

Inês wrapped her hands together, betraying anxiety. "The executed women were all in the ministry, like you, like Safira. All had talent but were never placed in positions of responsibility. All had powerful family members inside the ministry, but that didn't make any difference. It didn't help their careers. It was as if they were held back. Then they were charged and executed."

Oriana thought back on her two years in the Golden City. The trajectory of the career path Inês described was quite familiar. "And what happened to that woman, the one who was asking questions?"

"I don't know," Inês said.

"Do you believe she was from the Ministry of Intelligence, as she claimed?"

Inês sat still, her lips pursed. She tapped her index finger and thumb together, a sign either that she was about to lie or that she was afraid to answer. "She had too much information to be anything other than ministry, but it sounded more like she was investigating them—the ministry—questioning the motives behind the executions."

"As you did," Oriana pointed out.

"True. I suspect one part of the ministry is investigating another. The questions started after *you* were left on the Ilhas de Morte. You were the first agent on foreign soil to be accused of treason. That means you were the only one under the foreign intelligence wing. I think someone within the ministry—in that department—took exception to your execution and started an inquiry."

"Any idea who?"

Inês licked her lips nervously. "If I were to guess, I would point to Jovita Paredes."

Her aunt *had* moved to save her when she'd been left to die, hadn't she? The timeline was beginning to make sense. "Did you learn anything about the other women?"

"Not much," Inês admitted. "I've lost my position with the Spanish now, so I don't know how to find out what happened to my cousin. I still pray every day that she's alive somewhere, and that she'll return."

"You gave up finding out your cousin's fate?"

"I had to," Inês said, her shoulders squaring. "For Julio."

Oriana touched her chin, acceptance without belief.

Inês' nostrils flared. "Have you never been in love?"

Oriana licked her lips. She had obeyed orders until her execution. She had left Duilio's comfortable home, even knowing she was in love with him. And she had bent her orders as far as she could so that she could avenge a friend's death. But she had, in the end, *followed her orders*, and had nearly died for that loyalty.

"The woman who was with the boy?" Oriana asked, changing tacks. "What can you tell me about her?"

Inês shrugged. "She was at the Spanish embassy, but I only caught a glimpse of her once. She was sequestered, locked in a room."

That seemed needlessly cruel. "Locked up? Why?"

"She's ill. Gill rot, I think. No one wanted to talk to her."

Oriana gestured for Inês to wait as she thought that through. *Gill rot* was the common name for tuberculosis on the islands. For sereia the disease usually attacked the gills and air bladders before the lungs. Leandra might have been wearing a neck clap to keep from infecting others. That also would explain why Leandra had slept in the Guerra courtyard instead of trying to find a room at an inn. "So you didn't know her name—Leandra Rocha?"

The young woman's mouth formed an O of surprise. "I know that name," she whispered. "She was on the list. One of the early ones, I think."

The list that the mysterious agent of the ministry had presented to her. Oriana wasn't surprised. "She worked at the American embassy, not the Spanish, but she was executed like me . . . and your cousin."

Inês sat for a moment, one slender hand laid over her mouth. "I wrote most of the names down," she said after a moment, "in my journal. It's at my mother's house. I can tell you other names."

That *could* be helpful. "What can you tell me about the boy?"

Inês shook herself out of her daze. "Uh . . . he and the woman—Leandra, you said—arrived at the embassy about a week before we came to Amado. When I saw them together, I had the impression that they were mother and son, but I can't be sure. The boy was kept in the office with the secretaries so they could watch him. They said not to leave things about because he was a thief."

The boy had certainly stolen from them. "Was he ill, like Leandra?"

"Not that I could tell."

"Did you hear any name for him?"

"They called him Jandro," she said, pronouncing the name in the Spanish way. "Uh . . . Alejandro Ferrera."

Oriana held up one hand. It took only a split second for her to make the connection—Alejandro Ferrera was the Spanish version of Alexandre Ferreira, the name of Duilio's father. That could *not* be a coincidence.

⚘

CHAPTER 22

They'd arrived in Barcelona late Sunday night because of some trouble with the train—they'd had to replace an engine near Zaragosa. But once the train arrived at the station, a hotel omnibus had whisked them through the still-crowded streets to the Hotel Colón where their reserved room waited. The hotel was almost as opulent as the one in Lisboa, and they'd been given a room on the second floor that would look out over the plaza. Joaquim had the impression that the desk clerk knew they'd recently married.

In the morning they ate at the hotel's restaurant, a long room with white tablecloths and courteous staff. Despite the elegance of the dining car on the train, Joaquim decided he preferred this place specifically because it *wasn't* moving. So they ate their breakfast and planned what steps they would take first.

The American consulate general in Barcelona was right on the harbor, and while Joaquim's Catalan was rusty, the cabdriver pulled his horses to a stop at the appropriate building, so he must have made his desire clear enough. Once he'd paid the driver, he led Marina up the steps.

The guards asked his business, but as soon as he'd given his name, they sent him on through to speak with a secretary, proving that Madam Norton was as good as her word. The secretary, a stern-looking young man with spectacles and chaotic hair, led them on, the scent of cigarette smoke drifting from his garments.

"A liaison has been assigned to your case, Inspector," he said, taking them along a dim hallway toward the back of the building, away from the water. He knocked on a door with a paper label that read BENJAMIN PINTER. "Benjy's a good fellow. He'll set you right, whatever it is."

Another young man, this one rounded with ruddy cheeks and dark hair, answered the door. He eyed Joaquim and cast a worried glance at Marina, but thanked the bespectacled man and quickly ushered them into his office.

Joaquim introduced himself and Marina, and refrained from rolling his eyes as the young man bowed over Marina's gloved hand and pretended to kiss her knuckles. "You can call me Benjy," he said in Catalan. "Or Pinter, whichever suits you."

Joaquim eyed Pinter as the man sat behind his plain desk again. His office wasn't much different than Joaquim's, but this one was tucked away in the back, meaning that Pinter was either very much a secret or utterly unimportant. Given the tatty state of Pinter's charcoal suit and the dusty hat that sat atop his file cabinet, Joaquim suspected it was the latter.

"Madam Norton told us your people here would be looking out for a woman coming from the islands," Joaquim began. "Have you spotted her?"

Pinter nodded. "Yes, Inspector. We spotted the woman, Leandra Rocha, the moment she stepped off the ship onto the docks here."

Joaquim glanced over at Marina, wondering how much of that she'd caught. Marina spoke Spanish, which was not the same as speaking Catalan. She nodded at him, which meant she'd understood enough. He doubted she'd caught that the man phrased his news in the past tense. He turned back to Pinter. "Have you lost her?"

"Not sure," Pinter admitted with a grimace. He ran a hand through his dark hair. "A member of the Paris mission took over that job. Unfortunately, he hasn't reported in for a day now. We don't know if he's somewhere where he cannot make contact, or if he's gotten into trouble."

"A member of the Paris embassy? Why?"

Pinter took a careful breath. "He outranked me, and wouldn't tell me why. A specialist, I'm afraid."

"Specialist?"

"A foreign service specialist. This fellow handles affairs with *special* people."

Since his cousin worked in a division of the police whose purview included special people, Joaquim had a good idea what Pinter meant by that. "Such as the sereia?"

"There *is* a division that focuses on interactions with witches and nonhuman individuals," Pinter confirmed. "She would qualify as being of interest to his branch."

Had Madam Norton contacted this gentleman from the Paris office? Because it didn't seem as though the Barcelona office had invited his interference. And did that mean someone in the American embassy considered this affair to be of greater importance than they'd thought? Paris wasn't as far as Lisboa, but not a negligible distance either. Joaquim caught himself chewing his lower lip. "So, what happens now?"

"We were going to turn the pursuit over to you, Inspector, but she's out of my hands now."

Joaquim rubbed a hand down his face. "To your knowledge, did she contact anyone? Did she hand over the journal she's carrying?"

"She headed into the old city," Pinter said, "and met up with a local lawbreaker, a sort of master pickpocket. He gave her a place to stay in the tightest part of the old city. I can't know if she still had the book in question. My mission was only to watch her, not to make contact."

"And this new person? The specialist from Paris? Did he make contact with her?"

Pinter didn't answer, but the way his lips twisted in disapproval told Joaquim the specialist *had* made contact with Leandra Rocha, or planned to, against orders. To do that, he must have a motive. "So he knew her."

The young man's mouth opened. It was fortunate he wasn't a spy, because he'd be terrible as one. "I didn't say that," Pinter protested.

Joaquim glanced at Marina, who was politely paying attention whether she understood them or not. In Portuguese, he told her, "I think our American ambassador left something out."

"Are you surprised?" she asked in turn.

"No, I suppose not." Privately, Duilio had expressed some doubts about Madam Norton. Not that her aid hadn't been vital so far. Instead Duilio questioned her motives. Mere curiosity about the fate of a former employee didn't seem a strong enough motive to help them as much as she had. Joaquim turned back to Pinter, wondering how much Pinter had caught of what he'd said. Portuguese wasn't all that distant a cousin of Catalan and Spanish. "So, what role are your people taking in this now? Now you've misplaced my quarry and inserted one of your own people into the situation."

"I'll give you what I do have," Pinter said, wiping his forehead with a handkerchief. "But until I hear from the other agent involved, I can't tell you any more."

Joaquim watched him closely. "And will you do so when you hear?"

"Madam Norton asked us to cooperate, Inspector," Pinter insisted. "I *am* trying to do so."

The poor man was caught between two of his superiors, an uncomfortable position that Joaquim had been in himself from time to time. "Very well. We're at the Hotel Colón, on the Plaça de Catalunya. You can leave word for me there." Joaquim rose, noting that Marina was giving him a speaking look. He took her hand and set it on his arm to lead her out of the office. But he stopped on the threshold and turned about. "What about the boy?"

Pinter seemed surprised. "We were only told to follow the woman. Once she'd gotten rid of him, we didn't worry about him any longer."

Joaquim's mouth went dry. "Got rid of him?"

"I assumed she'd rented him or had a similar arrangement, because she left him where she stayed the very night she arrived. Where he went from there, I can't tell you."

The boy was *webless*, half sereia, no ordinary boy off the street, but Pinter clearly didn't know that. Madam Norton must have neglected to forward that information.

No, Joaquim doubted the omission was a matter of neglect. The woman was too crafty to forget a pertinent detail like that, so it had been intentional. "Where exactly did Leandra Rocha go that first night?"

"To a den of thieves within the old city's walls, a place I certainly would not have been able to enter. The boy didn't leave with her, though. Children like that run rampant in the poorer parts of the city."

There were poor children everywhere, in every city. They very often fell into a life of theft and begging, if not worse, often working to fill someone else's pockets. But this boy was *important*. Duilio had told him so.

"We'll find the boy, then, and if you figure out what your man has done with Leandra Rocha, please send word."

Marina kept one eye on Joaquim as he sat on a bench in the midst of the crowded walkways. In his hands he held an undershirt taken from the luggage in which the boy had hidden back on the islands. An odd thing to carry about, so he'd concealed it in a paper bag borrowed from the hotel's concierge.

They'd followed Joaquim's sense of the boy to an area in the old part of town, inside the ancient walls, and had ended up on a wide bricked walkway lined with plane trees. Pedestrians milled about, shopping and visiting cafés for coffee and a late breakfast of bread rubbed with olive oil and tomatoes, even though it was nearer time for lunch in her opinion.

Joaquim had warned her this was a place where tourists abounded, even this early in the year, so she should guard her handbag against pickpockets. That had, however, only increased his certainty that they would find the boy here. One thing they *did* know about the boy was that he was a thief, and this was exactly the sort of place where they could count on finding one—the Rambla. So Marina waited near a stand where an old crone sold flowers, once again watching other people stream by.

Joaquim's head turned toward the harbor, almost as if the boy was in his sight. Then, eyes wide with surprise, he turned to look over his shoulder at *her*.

What? Marina glanced down and saw that a boy stood against the wall, right next to her. She stifled a gasp. She recognized that shirt and cap from the photograph Joaquim had in his keeping.

The boy swept off his cap and pressed it into her free hand. Marina clutched the thing without thinking; there was something hard within. Without so much as a glance up at her, the boy settled at her side, one foot propped against the wall. His face was downcast, as if he were sulking.

A second later Marina realized why. A large man in a blue and red uniform with brass buttons, a tall black hat atop his head, came jogging down the street, his dark eyes scanning the people that crowded the stalls and shop fronts and cafés. Marina surreptitiously opened her handbag and stuffed the boy's cap inside, praying that it didn't contain lice. *Thank heavens Ana packed my largest bag.* She reached out her hand to the boy. "Come along."

The boy huffed out a long-suffering breath. But he slipped a small, dirty hand into her gloved one. She led him to the flower seller's stall and made a show of perusing the lady's wares. Taking her lead, Joaquim came and joined them. As the uniformed man approached, Joaquim purchased a bunch of pink roses, turned to the boy, and said, "Carry these for your mother."

"Flowers?" the boy complained in Portuguese, the pronunciation only slightly different from the Spanish, but noticeable.

Apparently the boy spoke their language. Marina held his hand and thanked him fulsomely. He let out another dramatic groan, but clutched the flowers close anyway.

The man in red and blue was almost on them, so Marina tugged her handkerchief out of her sleeve and knelt down to make a show of dabbing dirt from the boy's nose. Hopefully that would prevent the man from getting a good look at him.

But that was when she got *her* first look at the boy's face. Her heart nearly stopped.

CHAPTER 23

ILHAS DAS SEREIAS

Duilio dressed in his shortest *pareu*, the one that came only to midthigh. It was one he wore only when going down to the beach to swim, although it was early in the morning for that. But the wife of the Spanish ambassador had come to call and she was notoriously prudish. If anything would put her off her guard and provoke her to make mistakes, it was a display of bare skin. Unfortunately, that meant he had to leave his revolver in the bedroom.

He double-checked the paint about his eyes and made sure his overlong hair wasn't too disordered, then turned to Oriana. "Good enough?"

She ran a hand across his tattooed chest. "You look lovely."

He rolled his eyes. She always told him that. "Let's get this over with."

They had returned to the house on the beach the previous evening, Costa and Inês Guerra with them. The lovers were now settled in the guest quarters, and Duilio's best guess was that Vas Neves had spent a couple of hours giving the lieutenant a severe dressing-down.

Since Inês' information confirmed that Madam Davila was neck-deep in this chaos, the woman's visit was timely. So Duilio followed

Oriana along the hallways to the courtyard where the ambassador's wife waited for them.

Grandmother Monteiro hadn't dignified the woman's presence by joining them; thus only two of the guards were there, the captain out of deference to the *office* of the Spanish ambassador. A rare smile lifted one corner of Captain Vas Neves' lips when she spotted Duilio. She knew exactly why he was dressed as he was. Costa stood at her side, back in his Portuguese uniform. Reddish bruising marked his jaw, but most of the swelling had passed. Since they'd both been there for the incident in the market, Duilio wasn't shocking either of the guards with his attire.

Madam Davila waited in the center of the sunny courtyard. She must be baking alive in all the layers of fabric she wore. She had on a dark blue suit with beige lace showing on her high collar and spilling from the cuffs of her sleeves. She cast a startled glance at Duilio's mostly bared legs and quickly averted her face.

She glanced up again when Oriana entered the courtyard, and vexation flickered across her features. Oriana had chosen to eschew any vest. Apparently the ambassador's wife was no more comfortable being confronted with Oriana's bare breasts than she was with Duilio's thighs. As long as her husband had been ambassador here, Duilio would have thought she'd become accustomed to near nudity by now.

Ignoring the woman's reaction, Oriana ran through the customary greetings and inquired politely after Ambassador Davila. The ambassador was suffering from gout, his wife claimed, which Duilio considered just as good an excuse as any other. For all intents and purposes, Madam Davila *was* the Spanish ambassador in his stead.

The woman's dark eyes flicked downward, taking in Duilio's legs again, and returned to Oriana's face. Madam Davila lifted her narrow nose in the air. "I see that you're still playing at being a native, Madam Ambassador."

"Playing?" Oriana smiled. "I was raised here, Madam Davila, in this very house, so this garb is quite natural for me. We were about to go down to the beach for a swim though, so you did catch us in less formal attire."

It wasn't a secret, so Madam Davila knew Oriana had been raised here. Instead she was commenting on their clothing to cover her discomfort. Duilio moved behind Oriana and leaned against the wall, crossing one ankle over the other. He folded his arms to display his armbands better.

"To what do we owe the honor of your visit today, Madam Davila?" Oriana asked.

"We don't usually share information about our native staff, but it's come to my attention that one of our domestics recently came to this island."

An interesting tack to take. The unnamed member of the domestic staff had to be either Leandra Rocha or Inês.

"Why would one of your household come here?" Oriana asked innocently, hands folded.

"We aren't certain," Madam Davila said. "But now we can't find any trace of her."

"Surely you can replace her," Oriana noted. "If she wished to leave your employ, that's her concern, isn't it?"

Madam Davila plucked at the leaves of one of the plants next to the fountain. Her glove, a delicate netting one, snagged on a leaf and she jerked it away. "If it were that simple, I wouldn't have troubled you. But when she fled, she took a young boy with her, the son of one of the young women who work in our offices."

"I'm surprised you haven't contacted the government on Quitos, then," Oriana said. "Why would this domestic steal another woman's child?"

"We've speculated that she's delusional and believes he is her child," Madam Davila said, waving one lace-obscured hand. "It's hard to be certain why until we can find her and question her."

Now that was a hastily concocted story if ever he'd heard one; they'd resorted to claiming madness. Madam Davila's story was weak.

"I fail to see how *we* can help you," Oriana observed.

"There is one aspect of this that you should know," the woman said, her eyes fixing on Oriana's bare feet. "The boy is almost eight years old. Clever, with dark hair and dark eyes."

The ambassador's wife lowered her lovely face then, as if embarrassed. "His mother named him Alejandro Ferrera," she added, "and his resemblance to you is quite marked, Mr. Ferreira."

Aha! So Inês had heard the boy's name correctly after all. Duilio had given some thought to the probable timing of the boy's birth. Nine years ago Alexandre Ferreira had been in Spain, selling off the family's businesses in Barcelona. That would put him in the right place at about the right time.

His bastard uncle, Rafael's father, Paolo Silva, had once warned Duilio that he had *two* bastard brothers. Duilio's gift had told him then that he'd eventually learn it was true. He'd been waiting some time for that day to arrive.

"As you can see," Madam Davila continued with ill-concealed spite, "this does concern you, Madam Ambassador. Or rather it concerns Mr. Ferreira."

Duilio gave Madam Davila what he hoped was his best smile. "My father's unfortunate behavior while away from home was known to the whole family, I'm afraid. My mother even raised one of my half brothers alongside me. And now to learn I have another brother? I would love to meet young Alejandro."

Madam Davila must have expected dismay. She didn't look pleased. And that made his day all the better. She left shortly after that, with Oriana's generous promise that should Leandra show up, they would immediately send word. Not a difficult promise to make, since they knew Leandra was in Spain.

"Why would she come all the way out here?" Oriana mused after the woman was gone.

"I'm sure she has spies watching the house," Duilio said. "I'd bet the watcher recognized Inês and sent off a report immediately.

All of that might have been an attempt to learn what Inês told us." He glanced at Costa, who shrugged. "Or she could have intended to prompt us to look for Alejandro."

"He's in Barcelona, isn't he?" Oriana pointed out.

"Perhaps . . ." Duilio ran his fingers through his overlong hair. "I'd like to send a message to the Americans. Ask whether they can forward the boy's name to Joaquim. It may help him locate Alejandro."

"Do you think the Americans would do that for us?" Oriana asked.

"The ambassador very much wants to find Leandra," Duilio said, "so I believe she will."

Benites and Almeida were dispatched within the hour via ferry to Quitos. It would be interesting to find out how long it would take to get news of their new brother to Joaquim.

Barcelona

Joaquim sat across the table from the boy, watching as he consumed an apple he'd stolen from some vendor on the Rambla. They'd strolled along the wide avenue back to the plaza and the hotel, avoiding the eyes of the blue-and-red-uniformed men. Once at the hotel, they'd ordered a lunch to be brought up and made their way back to their room, the very image of a family planning to rest after a morning of sightseeing.

It was eerie how much the boy resembled a younger version of himself.

Many years ago, Lady Ferreira had gathered all her boys to take a picture. She still had that photograph in a silver frame in her room, Joaquim knew. He'd been twelve and Duilio thirteen. Erdano had been a terribly restless fifteen, Alessio fourteen, and Cristiano only four. Shortly after that Alessio had begun teasing him about being a bastard. In hindsight Joaquim realized that Alessio had looked at the photograph and *guessed* the truth about him. In it, he and Duilio sat side by side. They'd looked almost like twins.

The boy sitting at the table could have made them a set of triplets. He was younger than the boys in that photograph, yet the Ferreira stamp that showed on Joaquim's face—and Duilio's and Rafael's—already showed on this boy's. His jaw hadn't formed, but he had the wide brow they all shared. His eyebrows arched exactly like Joaquim's own.

Joaquim guessed the boy's age as seven or eight, although he might be small for his age. He was thin, and the reverence with which he'd consumed his stolen apple suggested familiarity with hunger. But if he was around eight, that meant he would have been conceived when Duilio was twenty-one and still at Coimbra. Joaquim didn't think Rafael had ever been to Spain at all, and he'd been in seminary at that time himself. No, if this child had Ferreira blood, he'd gotten it through Alexandre Ferreira.

Joaquim waited until the boy finished eating his apple, core and all. "Will you tell me your name?"

The boy's dark eyes flicked toward Marina where she sat on the far side of the table. "Jandro," he said, pronouncing the j in the Spanish way. "Alejandro."

And that clinched the matter; Alejandro was the Spanish form of Alexandre.

"We went down to the Rambla to find you," Joaquim said to him. "But you found us first. Were you looking for us?"

Alejandro glanced at Marina again, and nodded.

"Do you know who we are?"

The boy's lips twisted. For a moment he seemed disinclined to answer, but his eyes crept toward Marina once more.

"Do you know me?" she asked gently. "Who I am?"

"You're going to be my new mother."

Marina's mouth fell open.

So the boy had the seer's gift as well. The only way he could have recognized Marina was if he'd seen her in dreams or visions. Joaquim tapped his finger on the table to get the boy's attention, buying time for Marina to regain her calm. "What about *your* mother, Alejandro? Leandra, right? Where is she?"

"She didn't tell me where she was going," Alejandro said. "She left me with Capitan Captaire."

That translated roughly as the *chief beggar*. But he hadn't denied that Leandra Rocha was his mother, even if she'd left him behind. "Forever? Or does she mean to come back for you?"

The boy's mouth twisted downward again. He shrugged. "She said if she didn't to go to the Golden City."

An odd order to give a boy so young. *Is this boy clever enough to make his way across Iberia alone?* "How? Do you have money to go there?"

"Capitan has it. He owes her, so he says he'll send me."

Honor among thieves? It did exist. "What will you do in the Golden City?"

"I'm supposed to find my family."

Joaquim was fairly certain who that family was. "The Ferreira family?" he asked, just to be sure.

The boy nodded. "They call me Ferrera, but my name's Ferreira. That's why the Vilaró taught me Portuguese, so I'll sound right there."

Leandra Rocha had a mission that required she leave her son behind. She'd arranged for a caretaker to transport him to his father's family if she didn't return. She'd made preparations in case she died. "Who is the Vilaró?"

"He's in the prison," Alejandro said. "In the very bottom. The other prisoners leave me alone because they're scared of him."

Joaquim licked his lips, his stomach sinking. "You live in the prison?"

"I did," the boy said, matter-of-factly, as if it were normal for a child to be raised inside a prison. "Mother told me never to go back there."

Joaquim tried not to react, but nausea welled in his stomach. He had no doubt this boy was exactly who he seemed, a son of Alexandre Ferreira and a woman carelessly left behind.

He had a *brother* who'd been raised in a prison.

He'd held a grudge for some time against his dead father for refusing to acknowledge him. Alexandre Ferreira had always avoided being in the same house as Joaquim, and even if he hadn't realized the man was his father, Joaquim had felt shunned anyway. He hadn't complained of the man's behavior, not even to Duilio, but he'd *resented* it.

Despite that, he'd had a good life and a loving father in the elder Joaquim Tavares. He'd had food and clothing and never worried for his safety. He'd had brothers who fought with him, but respected him anyway.

Alejandro had none of that. He'd been raised in a prison, and spoke of it so flatly that it must never have occurred to him to resent that fact. At the moment, Joaquim resented Alexandre Ferreira enough for both of them. He took a deep breath, forcing down his twisting stomach.

"Do you know your father's name?" he asked the boy.

"It was Alexandre," the boy answered. "He had ships and lived in the Golden City."

"Alexandre Ferreira was my father too. That makes you my brother."

The boy's mouth made a round O. Not surprise, but epiphany, as if some missing piece of a puzzle had fallen into place. "That's why I'm supposed to live with you."

It was telling that Alejandro had identified Marina so easily as his new mother, yet didn't call Joaquim his new father. Somehow the boy's gift had recognized that he was a brother instead.

A knock came at the door, a welcome distraction. When Marina jumped up to answer it, Joaquim raised a hand to forestall her and went himself to be sure it was safe. He opened the door only a sliver and saw that a waiter had arrived, so he allowed the man to bring in their lunch and handed him a couple of pesetas as he left. Joaquim locked the door behind him.

Marina took over, moving the food to the small round table near the balcony doors where the boy already sat. They had a basket of the local tomato-rubbed bread, soup with pasta and rice accompanied by sausage, and coffee with almond biscuits. Joaquim picked up his cup of coffee first, hoping it would help clear his mind.

After removing her gloves, Marina laid out utensils for the boy and placed a large chunk of the sausage on his plate with his bowl of soup. The boy's eyes lifted to hers, almost as if he didn't grasp that she'd set it there for him. "That's yours," she said to him. "I know you just ate, but it never hurts to have a full stomach."

"Makes you slow," he said. "Mossos are looking for me."

"The men in the blue and red?" she asked. "Are they police?"

"Mossos d'Esquadra," Joaquim offered. He recognized the name if not the uniforms. "The provincial police for Barcelona. Are they looking for you because of the apple?"

A shake of the head. "They want to take me back to the prison."

Marina's jaw clenched. "Well, you're safe here. You can take a nap afterward. We'll keep the door locked. No one will take you back to that prison. I promise."

Alejandro watched silently as she sat in the chair next to him, laid out her napkin, and sliced up her portion of the sausage to put it in her soup. The boy began cutting up the sausage just as Marina had done, demonstrating that he understood either table manners or mimicry. Joaquim suspected it was a mixture of the two. Belatedly, he joined them at the table.

"Your hands are cut," the boy said, eyes on Marina's scarred fingers. "Like my mother's."

"Sometimes that has to be done," Marina said. She talked to Alejandro at intervals during the meal, trying to determine what the boy liked. Most of his answers were vague, making Joaquim suspect the boy had never given much thought to his own preferences. He ate everything placed before him, finishing up with the almond biscuits that Joaquim neglected to eat with his coffee.

With a full stomach, Alejandro seemed about to nod off, so Joaquim led the boy into the bedroom. The boy went willingly enough and, after removing his worn shoes, curled up atop their coverlet. "We'll be in the sitting room," Joaquim said, and pulled a spare blanket over the boy's thin form. "I have to go out for a bit, but Marina won't leave you."

Alejandro didn't respond. Perhaps he was already asleep.

Joaquim left him there and quietly closed the bedroom door behind him. Marina watched him with wide eyes. "What do we do?" she whispered.

"I'm not going to leave him here," he said. "We have to keep him with us. I don't . . ."

Just because he'd found a brother he hadn't known he had, that didn't mean their quest to find the journal—and Alejandro's mother—was over. But it changed everything.

How could they protect the boy here? He was not going to hand the boy off to some local nursemaid's care. He didn't know whom he could trust, and Alejandro was at risk of imprisonment merely for being half sereia. He *could* place both Marina and the boy on a train back to Portugal immediately, but if he suggested it, Marina would balk. And he couldn't be certain they would be safe heading back alone anyway.

"I need to send a telegram," he said to Marina. "I'll let Lady Ferreira know . . ." *Know what? That I've found another of her husband's bastards?* "I'll figure out what to tell her on the way to the telegraph office," he finished weakly.

He hoped that was the case.

CHAPTER 24

BARCELONA

After double-checking to be sure that the door was still locked, Marina went to the balcony and stepped outside to let the breeze clear her mind. The plaza below was crowded, busy with people crossing its paths, heading in every direction. A tram moved by, and she saw a wagon selling something from its bed. Pigeons fluttered like clouds from one spot to another. Marina leaned over the fancifully curved wrought-iron railing and peered in either direction in hope of seeing Joaquim.

He'd been gone a long time, and she didn't like that. If Joaquim was caught by the Mossos d'Esquadra, they couldn't prove he was a witch. That afforded him some protection out on the street. Like her, though, Alejandro could be exposed by the simple act of tugging up his trouser leg high enough to reveal scale-patterned skin. And that alone could get him hauled back to the prison.

She knew very little about the Unnaturals Prison at Lleida. The Canaries could use their *calls* to control the prisoners, and therefore managed the prison for the Spanish government. The other prisoners were the purported undesirables of Spain: nonhumans and those witches who wouldn't disavow their powers. There were many kinds of witches, but she knew of very few types of nonhumans. Selkies, sereia, and otter folk lived on the sea for the most part. There were the great fairies, but they were reportedly almost extinct, and all manner of lesser fey, but they hid themselves from humans. She wasn't certain what existed beyond those, but a prison like that could not have been a safe place for a child.

According to what Oriana had told her while on Amado, there was another, more frightening aspect to that place. The duo who'd killed the prince of Northern Portugal, Dr. Serpa and a healer, Father Salazar, had also come from that prison. Dr. Serpa had been experimenting on the prisoners with the healer's help—experiments that involved transplanting parts from one person to another. They had been trying to see if they could give a normal person a nonhuman's special abilities—the same surgery they'd tried on the prince of Northern Portugal the previous fall. None of their patients had survived. Father Salazar had been defrocked when his order found out, but since he was already in the prison, he simply remained there.

Marina hoped that Alejandro had stayed well clear of that poisonous duo. She'd nearly become one of their victims herself in the Golden City. With Joaquim's help, she'd escaped their efforts to find a sereia to experiment on, but one of her closest friends hadn't, and had died.

She heard a cough in the room behind her, and turned to see that Alejandro had woken. He stood next to the table, gazing down at the note she'd left there—a list of questions she wanted to ask him. His hair was rumpled, angling up on one side, and his expression seemed bewildered. Had it frightened him to wake up in a strange place? "Alejandro, why don't you come here? There's a lovely view."

He hesitated but came to stand next to her. She reached over to smooth down his hair, only to be dismayed when he flinched away. "Your hair is mussed," she explained.

He quickly ran his own hands through it, settling it back into a semblance of order. His eyes surveyed the plaza below them, but he said nothing. At least from this vantage point she could see the top of his head. It didn't look as though he had lice, a small mercy.

"Did you read that paper on the table?" she asked him.

He shook his head. "I don't know how."

Hadn't Duilio said he suspected the thief was illiterate? Marina couldn't recall a time when she hadn't known how to read. "Would you like to learn?"

After a moment he shrugged.

She wasn't certain what that meant, so she tried something else. "I know that most boys hate being told this, but I think it's time for you to have a bath."

At least he didn't ask what a bath was.

Joaquim came out of the small shop on the Passieg de Gracia with a wrapped bundle under his arm. The hotel's concierge had sent him there, citing it as a place where he could replace some of the garments that had been in the bag of his nephew's that went missing on the train. That was the best way to explain the sudden addition of Alejandro to their party. Alejandro would be his sister's son, come to stay with them because his mother was ill and couldn't care for him.

Joaquim stopped in the lobby and placed a telephone call to the American consulate only to learn that they'd *still* not found Leandra Rocha and their missing man from Paris. He considered trying to find the woman as he'd done with the boy, but he didn't know very much about her. If Alejandro had something of his mother's, that might work, but Joaquim wasn't certain. For the moment, it seemed he was destined to wait on the Americans, especially annoying when he didn't understand their motives.

He went upstairs to their room and knocked on the door to warn Marina before he unlocked it. She wilted when he stepped inside and came to throw her arms about him. "What took so long?"

"I had to place a telephone call and send a wire and go to a store," he said.

"You told me you were sending a telegram, not the others."

"I apologize," he said, taking in her worried look. "Is Alejandro still asleep?"

Marina took a deep breath. "No, he's taking a bath."

Now that was surprising. "How did you convince him to do that?"

"I doubt it occurred to him he had any choice," she said. "I think he's accustomed to doing as he's told."

Joaquim sighed. Had Alejandro ever had much choice in his life? He would suggest that the next time the boy needed to bathe, he should be told he *could* refuse, but that would make their lives unnecessarily complicated. He handed Marina the bundle from the store. "I had to estimate his size, but I bought a pair of clean outfits for him. Trousers, shirts, suspenders. I should have thought to take his shoes to find a match, but we can probably get a new pair for him later."

Marina caught her lower lip between her teeth. "His feet are probably wider than a human's. It would be better for him to have custom-made."

That would take time they didn't have. "Noted."

"There is one thing," she said as she untied the bundle. "When he undressed to get in the bath, there were no stripes on his legs, no sign of a dorsal fin."

So his mother was definitely a sereia, not a Canary. "Someone other than his mother taught him Portuguese," Joaquim said. "If she came from your islands, wouldn't she have raised him speaking her language?"

Marina's shoulders slumped. "I suppose. It just seemed odd."

One more puzzle piece that doesn't fit.

ILHAS DAS SEREIAS

Duilio had been the first to see the soldier approaching on horseback, one in Portuguese uniform. So Oriana waited on the drive in front of the beach house, squinting in the late-afternoon sun. *Why would one of the soldiers be in such a hurry as to rent a horse?*

Captain Vas Neves stood with her. As the horse came galloping down the road, they could see the rider was Corporal Almeida, who had gone just that morning to Quitos with Benites to speak with the Americans. The horse slowed, and as Almeida neared, the captain grabbed the horse's headstall.

Face flushed, Almeida swung one leg over the horse's bare withers and slid down to the ground. She drew the reins over the creature's head and held them as it snorted and blew. "Madam," she began with a nod in Oriana's direction. "Captain. I've ridden ahead of the main group, but they should start arriving in a few hours."

Oriana cast a glance at Duilio and turned back to the corporal. "Main group?"

The corporal faced her squarely. "Yes, madam. Not long after we handed that message over to the Americans, our embassy was contacted and given two hours to clear out. Since there's nowhere on Quitos that will take humans, the lieutenant and your chief of staff agreed we should come here."

"Clear out?" Oriana asked, beginning to feel like a parrot.

"Start at the beginning, Corporal," Duilio said, coming closer. "Who gave the order to leave the embassy?"

"Subminister Paredes," Almeida said. "She came to the embassy herself and informed us it was for our safety."

Oriana pinched the bridge of her nose. What was going through her aunt's head? She wasn't even certain such an order was legal. Could a single government subminister order out an entire ambassadorial mission? Didn't an expulsion order have to come via the oligarchy itself, or from their Foreign Office? And why so fast? Two hours was ridiculously short notice. While she had no doubt her guard contingent was handling this with aplomb, all the secretaries and clerks and typists were likely terrified.

"Did she say anything else?" Duilio asked. "Are we being *ex-pelled?*"

"No, Mr. Ferreira, she didn't use those words. The lieutenant made the call to evacuate, though, based on the warning. The Brazilians were already clearing out when the subminister got to us, so we gave it credence. She went from us directly to the Americans. If there was official paperwork, it came after I left."

"She told *all* the embassies to clear out?" Oriana asked. That was a sign of trouble. All the missions' personnel would have to ferry over to Amado. And while there were a few hotels in Porto Novo, there was certainly not room for that many.

"I was with the first group to get across, madam, so I don't know. Benites sent me immediately to inform you, and the Brazilian ambassador was kind enough to leave one of his people behind at the ferry so I could get here sooner."

The Brazilian mission was the smallest, an informal arrangement with a minimal guard. The English, Spanish, and Americans would all have far more people crossing over to Amado. Oriana touched a finger to her temple, needing a moment to think this over.

There were ships in harbor: one Portuguese, a handful of English, a Brazilian, and two American. The embassy staffs, if they couldn't find lodging, could prevail on the captains of those ships for protection. The Spanish currently didn't have that option.

"Did you see the English moving? Or the Spanish?" she asked the corporal.

"The subminister seemed to be going along the row of embassies, madam, so notification of the English would have fallen after the Americans, and the Spanish last. But there were already soldiers moving in by the time I was off embassy grounds, so the English would have known something was happening."

Vas Neves shook her head. "Corporal, *what* soldiers?"

"Sorry, Captain," Almeida said, flushing. "Sereia soldiers. Navy, since they wore khaki skirts. Lieutenant Benites will be able to tell you more when she arrives."

First things first: water, food, and lodging. Duilio gestured for Oriana's attention. "I'm going to take the boys—"

"Sir," Vas Neves protested.

Duilio spread his hands wide in apology. "Excuse me. I'd like to take the remaining *male* guards up to the harbor and meet our people. The chief of staff will be bringing our files, and I'd like to find a safe place to put them."

As much as she would like to be at the harbor too, just to hear their news faster, Oriana knew she would be more useful at the house, organizing. Benites would have more solid information when she eventually arrived. Along with the full complement of guards. And a dozen clerical workers and the chief of staff. *Where am I supposed to put all those people?*

And why were they being booted out of their own embassy on such short notice?

Many citizens on Quitos felt the same as her aunt, that the human stain on the islands was destroying their people. She only hoped that the massing of troops near the embassies wasn't the start of a complete purge of foreigners. That would be the worst possible way to end her tenure as ambassador.

CHAPTER 25

Alejandro hadn't run off in the night, as Marina had halfway expected. In the morning he'd been in his bed in the sitting area, feigning sleep. When she'd told him to get up and get dressed, he acted as if that was an order. He had a disconcerting tendency to do as told and a disregard for his own privacy that made her suspect he'd learned never to protest anything.

He hadn't given them many answers the previous evening, and they hadn't wanted to press him too hard. He had nothing of his mother's that Joaquim could use to find her. He *had* seen the journal; his mother still had it in her possession when she left him. He didn't know who, if anyone, had hired them to steal the book. He didn't know Iria Serpa and hadn't ever met Dr. Serpa or Father Salazar. As for his situation at the prison, he'd been born there, had lived his whole life there until he and his mother went to the islands. He didn't like to talk about it, Marina could tell.

He also never asked questions, which she found odd. He didn't ask Joaquim anything about his family in Portugal. He didn't ask why they were in Spain hunting his mother. He didn't ask how long they would stay or where they would go. He didn't complain either. He

donned the new clothing that Joaquim had purchased, never commenting on the fact that his sleeves were too long.

His old garments were nearly worn out, some of the grime so embedded that Marina didn't think it would ever come out. She folded
each piece as neatly as possible to have the hotel staff launder them.
The key rattled in the door, and Joaquim came back in. His eyes went
to the small bed against one wall, and then he looked at her, one eyebrow raised.

"I sent him into the dressing room to make himself presentable,"
she said.

"Ah." Joaquim shook his head, looking bemused by their new
responsibility. They'd lain abed late into the night, trying to decide
what to do with the boy. *Whispering*, because they worried he
would overhear them. "I placed a call to the consulate again. They
had a message from Duilio. It turns out they'd discovered Alejandro's name and that he must be related to Duilio and me."

"We already knew that," she said.

"Yes, but he couldn't have known that we knew. But the message was sent yesterday, so it's helpful to know the Americans can
get word from the islands to Barcelona that quickly."

"Can they send word back?"

"That, they didn't tell me. Also, they've not found the man
from Paris or Leandra herself."

Marina sighed, unable to hide her frustration. "The Americans
seem to have fouled up everything."

"Yes, this fellow from Paris has done more harm than good." He
came over and wrapped his arms around her from behind, briefly
resting his chin atop her head. "Since they have nothing for us, what
would you think of going to Terrassa this morning?"

They'd discussed that possibility during the night, for the first
time since he'd mentioned his great-grandmother on the train. "We'll
have to bring Alejandro along."

"Do you mind?"

She turned to face him. "No. Let's go."

Out of the corner of one eye, she saw that Alejandro stood in the door of the bedroom, his new cap in his hand. She went and knelt down in front of him. "After breakfast we plan to visit a relative of Joaquim's. Would you mind that?"

He shrugged, not much of an answer.

"The people who are supposed to find your mother still haven't done so, but as soon as we return, I promise we'll start looking for her too."

Alejandro nodded, so she rose and offered her hand. "We're going to go down to the restaurant and have breakfast there."

He wordlessly put his hand in hers. Clearly, food was important to him.

ILHAS DAS SEREIAS

The guards were camped out on the beach, most acting content to be there. Grandmother Monteiro had borrowed several canvas pavilions that offered cover from the sun and protection should it rain. The members of the clerical staff were all lodged inside the house itself, most sleeping on the terraces at night.

Their previous visitor had returned. Madam Norton had rented most of a hotel in Porto Novo for her staff. She'd driven out early to join them for a late breakfast and to inform them that their message to Joaquim had been sent despite the precipitous evacuation of the ambassadorial missions. "I'm sure you realize, Mr. Ferreira, the sereia government doesn't give a damn what we consider a reasonable action to take against a foreign embassy."

"I do," Duilio admitted. "I merely point out that their Foreign Office, limited as it is, had to know a rushed evacuation would be looked upon with a jaundiced eye."

Madam Norton smiled down into her cup of coffee. She was

attired in far more casual garb today, a white shirtwaist with a beige-striped skirt. It made him suspect that clothing had been low on her list of priorities when choosing what to carry out of the embassy. What had she chosen to take instead?

Their own chief of staff had packed most of the paperwork deemed sensitive into locked cases and put them in a heavily guarded wagon. Once ferried across to Amado, those cases were transported directly to the Portuguese steam freighter *Tesouro* and placed in its hold. The chief of staff and the remaining male guards—minus Costa—were stationed on the ship with that cache. Duilio had been taken aback by how much so-called sensitive material they'd accumulated in only three months. The Americans, with their years of work here, could not possibly have transported everything important.

"While I would like to say I'm concerned for the safety of the Spanish," Madam Norton added, "I admit to being rather blasé about their situation."

Their situation. During the exodus of the various embassies, one notable fact had become clear. The Spanish embassy compound wasn't being evacuated. In fact, the military personnel who'd been seen massing nearby had moved to surround the wrought-iron and stone walls of the Spanish compound, a row of sereia naval sentries outside the Spanish guard posts. The Spanish guards were keeping them out, but the sereia were keeping the Spanish *in*.

Madam Norton leaned back in her chair. "You've been here on Amado less than two weeks, Madam Paredes. You've been visited by two ambassadors—I'm calling Madam Davila an ambassador because we both know that's what she is despite her husband's title. The subminister of intelligence, who also happens to be your aunt, has come to see you, and now that subminister is holding the Spanish embassy hostage with the navy's help. I must say, I've been here more than a decade and have never provoked the evacuation of the embassies. For someone so young, that's an impressive feat."

Duilio kept his grin under control. Oriana preferred not to draw attention. It was an aspect of politics she was learning to *tolerate*, but he didn't think she'd ever choose the spotlight. Certainly not this way.

"As for your queries about Subminister Paredes," Madam Norton said, "my source inside the ministry says that it was indeed the subminister who sent a notice to Ambassador Alvaro in Northern Portugal about your near execution. One of her coworkers recalled it, since the subminister was agitated enough on that occasion to be remarked upon."

"Thank you, madam," Oriana said.

Duilio tucked away the fact that the American ambassador had a source inside the ministry itself for later consideration. What the agent had found, though, meant that Jovita Paredes *had* moved directly to save Oriana's life. That moved Jovita into the role of potential ally.

"She hasn't been able to locate any records old enough to verify anything about your father, though," the ambassador continued.

"Ten years is a long time," Oriana said.

"I agree." Madam Norton tugged on her plain cotton gloves and gathered her parasol and handbag. "Now, I must return to the hotel. If you find out anything else about Leandra, will you let me know?"

With their promise—they could hardly refuse when the woman had gone so far to help them—the ambassador made her stately way out.

TERRASSA

Joaquim straightened his tie. He rubbed the top of each shoe against the back of the opposing pant leg. He should have asked Duilio about this, or Rafael. His own limited seer's abilities had never told him anything about seeking out his great-grandmother.

He'd always wanted to know why his mother's life turned out the way it had. He'd hired an investigator in Barcelona who'd traced his mother's difficulties back to her grandmother. His mother's mother,

Mereia Quintana, had married an unapproved suitor, Emilio Castillo, a scion of the minor gentry from the north. Her mother had refused to speak to her ever again, and Mereia had died when Joaquim's mother, Rosa, was born.

Joaquim knew little of his mother's early life; she had died when *he* was only eight. When Rosa was a young woman, Emilio Castillo had sold his daughter to Alexandre Ferreira like a piece of chattel. Joaquim's investigator had said it was widely known that Castillo had gambling debts, but Joaquim didn't care *why* the man had sold his daughter. It was criminal of him to have done it at all, a betrayal of the trust a child should be able to have in her own father.

He gazed down at the top of Alejandro's head. The boy had fallen asleep next to him on the bench, his head lolling against Joaquim's side with the train's motion. His cap had come off and now lay on Joaquim's leg. The boy had slept a great deal in the last two days. That might have something to do with being able to eat his fill and having a safe place to sleep.

Joaquim didn't know what he was going to do when they found Leandra Rocha. She was the boy's mother. While Joaquim recognized her right to keep her son to herself, she'd already made plans for Alejandro's disposition, which involved turning the boy over to the Ferreira family. For the moment, that was Joaquim. But when they found her, would she demand him back? And would he fight her to keep the boy?

He was beginning to suspect that Marina wouldn't let him do anything less.

What had Alexandre Ferreira done for this son of his? Had he known that Alejandro existed? *I'll probably never find the answer to that.* But he could amend Alexandre Ferreira's negligence, just as the elder Joaquim Tavares had once done by raising a son he knew not to be his own. Joaquim set his arm about the boy's shoulders, only to withdraw it when Alejandro jerked awake, eyes wide.

"It's only me," Joaquim said. "I didn't mean to startle you."

Wordlessly, Alejandro settled back on the bench. He snatched up his cap and put it on his head again, then leaned forward to gaze out the window. The train was passing over a narrow river and rumbling the last of the distance into the town of Terrassa. It was by far the smallest town they'd visited, although since the station was north of the town, Joaquim suspected they weren't seeing much of Terrassa itself.

The station wasn't grand, although new, a building of white brick with arches that led to the street before it. They walked to where drivers waited and quickly found one willing to take them out to the Quintana Estate for the right number of pesetas. Joaquim helped Marina up into the carriage, let Alejandro scramble up on his own, and a moment later they were on the move again. The open carriage allowed them to view the edge of the town, but the horses went at a good clip and they were out on a country lane in only a couple of minutes. Alejandro watched the countryside pass without comment, although the first time he saw a vineyard, he turned his head to view the rows of vines as they passed.

"Is it a large estate?" Marina asked Joaquim.

"I'm not certain. The man who investigated it for me gave me the size in a unit called *jornal*, which means nothing to me." He wouldn't have grasped the size if it was explained in hectares either. He'd lived in a city all his life, where land measurements were irrelevant. "She's a marquesa, so I would expect it to be large."

Marina's eyes went wide. She glanced down at her costume, a plain white shirtwaist and a twilled brown skirt, and in a plaintive voice said, "You didn't tell me that before."

"That she's a marquesa?"

"Yes, you failed to mention it."

Joaquim glanced at the back of the driver's head. Was the man listening to them? Or would he plead the oft-claimed Spanish inability to comprehend Portuguese? "I didn't think of it," he said. "But I told you my mother was a gentlewoman, didn't I?"

"Yes," she snapped, waving a horsefly away from her face. "But you treat all women like they're gentlewomen. I thought you were being polite."

He glanced at Alejandro, who just shrugged, so he turned back to Marina. He stared at her face as the carriage continued to bounce along the dirt road. "Are you offended that I didn't tell you? Or that I have a nobleman somewhere back in my lineage?"

"That you didn't tell me," she said in a milder tone.

He turned his gaze in the other direction, trying to figure out how to answer that. Vines marched in careful rows on low trellises, the fresh green of early summer. He turned back to her. She was rubbing her hands together as if they ached. She always did that when upset, and he hated that he'd overset her. "I didn't mean to, Marina. It didn't occur to me that it mattered."

"Because you're so adamantly republican that you don't want to be related to anyone with noble blood?"

He opened his mouth but closed it before the protest could come out. He *was* adamantly republican, although no one had ever said as much to his face before. Not even Duilio. She wasn't going to let this go, was she? "I tend to be wary of people with titles."

"Is that why you feel bad taking the Ferreiras' money for this trip?"

That wasn't the same thing at all, was it? "I don't feel it's my money."

"So you don't feel entitled to your father's fortune, but you think others should?" Her eyes flicked toward Alejandro as she said it, and he recalled his insistence in their late-night conversation that the boy deserved to have a portion of the family's fortune, no matter what his birth. Marina hadn't pointed out the fallacy in his argument then, and he hadn't seen it for himself. Now that she'd said something, it made a shambles of his logic.

The driver turned his carriage off the main road onto a smaller one that paralleled a stream, cedars growing up on the far bank and hiding the vines that climbed up the hills in neat rows. After a short distance, they reached a pair of splendid gates of sand-colored stone and wrought iron. The gates stood open, so the driver took the carriage on through toward an old house with plastered walls and a tiled roof that was brown with lichen rather than the clay red Joaquim knew from the Golden City. It was more like a farmhouse than a manor, but the size of it was stunning, with outbuildings and wings all running together in his view.

Another wall separated the house itself from the drive. The driver stopped and let them down, promising he'd stay to take them back to the town. They entered through that gate onto a wide terrace that surrounded the house. Ivy climbed the walls, local cactus stood in urns and planters near the stairs, and two large fan palms flanked the green-tiled steps that led up to the house. Marina clutched Alejandro's hand while trying to brush off her skirts with her free hand. Joaquim waited until she finished and picked up her handbag from the stone walkway, then led her to the house. She walked up the steep steps to a heavy-looking door.

Joaquim rapped smartly with his knuckles. No one answered, and after a moment, he raised his hand to knock again, but the door was opened by a stout gray-haired man who must be the butler. The old man squinted at them. "How may I help you?"

"We've come to speak with the marquesa." Joaquim didn't have any calling cards like the ones Duilio carried, so he settled for giving the butler his name. The butler allowed them inside but directed them to wait in the parlor while he determined whether the lady was home to callers.

Joaquim hoped she was. How annoying it would be to come all this way only to be ignored.

CHAPTER 26

TERRASSA

Marina held on to Alejandro's hand. She didn't *think* the boy would steal anything, but the parlor was cluttered with porcelain trinkets. *Only imagine if he snatches something that belongs to Joaquim's great-grandmother.* It would not be an auspicious introduction.

The room was crowded with ancient furnishings, shawls and throws covering aging fabrics and torn upholstery. Marina ran her fingers over the arm of the blue upholstered couch in the center of the room and tugged the ivory throw over to cover a rip. A cigarette or cigar burn marred the old Persian rug on the floor, the rug's original colors faded by the sunlight into drab tans.

It wasn't the home of a poor person, an owner who couldn't afford to replace things. No, this was the home of someone so set in his ways that he refused to change anything, even when it fell into disrepair. It reminded Marina of the house of one of her father's clients she'd visited last year to drop off and pick up paperwork. The client was wealthy, but aged and infirm. He hadn't wanted to spend time refurbishing a house he could barely enjoy.

Near the door was a prayer niche, the Virgin standing within with her pale marble hands outstretched. Marina tugged Alejandro over so she could look at it. A Bible lay opened out atop the kneeler's shelf, open to the Psalms, perhaps a source of solace to the marquesa. Marina ran her finger down the page, trying to guess what the woman had been reading. When she drew it away, dust clung to her glove.

Joaquim paced back and forth behind the couch, arms folded over his chest. He would stop periodically, place his fist against his lips, and then resume his pacing.

Evidently the marquesa didn't mind keeping guests waiting.

Alejandro didn't complain. Not that she expected he would. Most boys would have, but not him. She finally suggested that he sit in a chair where he could look out a window. Then she wandered about the room, stopping to peruse the books stacked on one of the tables. She neatly folded the shawl laid over the back of a leather chair. She was tempted to use the corner of it to wipe dust from the mantelpiece, but resisted. The windows could use a good cleaning as well. She came back to where Alejandro sat and gazed out at the terraced vineyards. It was a beautiful view, despite the cobwebs in the corner of the window frame.

Apparently some male cousin of the marquesa's husband would inherit all this. If life were fair, Marina reflected, Joaquim would inherit this place with its lovely views. Then again, he would never accept it if it were offered to him. He didn't even want to move into the Ferreira house, even though it would stand empty after Lady Ferreira married.

He didn't think he *deserved* such things.

She stole a glance at him. He was still pacing back and forth, his expression worried. "How long has it been?"

He drew out his watch and checked. "Half an hour now."

Marina shook her head. This delay was intentional. If the woman was struggling to ready herself, she would have sent a servant with her apologies. Much longer and they would miss the return train to Barcelona. "How long do we intend to wait?"

Joaquim licked his lips. "Would you mind giving it another quarter hour?"

The delay annoyed her. If a client had kept her father waiting like this, he wouldn't be pleased, but Father handled their money, which made him important to them. Joaquim was more accustomed to being kept waiting. Nobles didn't like associating with the police, and considered them beneath their notice.

Tapping in the hallway alerted her a moment before the marquesa shoved the door open. It banged against the wall. The marquesa was a wizened creature, bent and leaning over an ivory-handled cane. She wore mourning, a dress in heavy black silk perhaps a decade out of fashion. A jet and ivory brooch adorned the high collar that framed her pale face and thinning white hair. Instead of looking frail, she looked fierce.

"What right do you have to come here?" the old woman snapped in a voice that wasn't frail at all. "Why do you think you can come and disturb me?"

The woman spoke to Joaquim, so Marina kept her mouth shut. She stepped in front of Alejandro, as if she could protect him from the old woman's spite by keeping him out of sight.

"My name is Joaquim Tavares." Joaquim inclined his head respectfully toward the old woman. "And this is my wife, Marina."

Marina bobbed a curtsy, but the old woman didn't even glance in her direction.

"You didn't answer my question, young man." The marquesa tottered toward the leather chair and sat down in it. She set her cane against the chair's high back and laid her withered hands on the chair's arms as if it were a throne. "Why are you disturbing me?"

Joaquim held his hands folded like a penitent. "I live in Portugal, but my mother was born here in Catalonia. She was Rosa Castillo i Quintana, your granddaughter."

That sparked no hint of interest in the old woman's hard eyes. "What of it?"

Marina rubbed her hands together. She wanted to shake the old woman, but this was Joaquim's fight.

His dark eyes narrowed. "I only wished to introduce myself to you."

"You've done so," the marquesa said, waving one hand. "You can leave now."

Joaquim took a slow breath, but Marina could see his clenched jaw. "I also have a younger brother," he added, "recently graduated from the university at Coimbra."

The woman glared up at him. "Do you think I don't know who you are? You are a policeman and your brother is a builder of boats. If I wanted to contact you, I could have at any time. I chose not to acknowledge your mother, nor will I do so with her children, not even the one who isn't a bastard."

Marina hadn't caught all those words, but that last comment had been clear. Before she thought better of it, Marina snapped, "Do not insult my husband."

That had come out in Portuguese, but the Catalan must be close enough that the old woman understood. She glared at Marina for the first time. Her face had fine bones, hinting that she would have been handsome when young. "Why not? It's true, isn't it?"

Marina bit back her reply. Clearly the woman wanted a fight.

The marquesa turned back to Joaquim, waving dismissively in Marina's direction. "And who is this common girl you've taken for a wife? If you hoped to raise your station in life, you could have done far better."

A smile spread across Joaquim's face. Marina wasn't fooled by the expression. He was furious now. "I married for love, madam, not to . . . raise my station."

"Ha! My daughter married for love, and what became of her? Dead before she was twenty."

Joaquim shook his head. "Then why did you not take in my mother? Did you wish to punish her because you were angry with her mother?"

"My daughter chose to marry outside our kind," the marquesa said. "Why should I take in that man's child?"

"Is kindness beyond your experience?" Joaquim asked softly.

Marina guessed they were past trying to earn the woman's goodwill.

The marquesa harrumphed and grabbed her cane, leaning forward as if she might swat Joaquim with it. "The world has never been kind to me."

"You knew my mother was mistreated, yet did nothing about it," Joaquim said. "She was your only grandchild. How could you hold her mother's faults against her?"

The woman pushed herself back to her feet. Joaquim, unable to help himself, moved forward to help her rise, but stepped back when she swung her cane at his shins. "You know nothing of my daughter's betrayal. You know nothing of who you are." And then she spotted Alejandro, still obediently sitting in his chair. "And who is this? Your bastard? I know you haven't been married long enough to have a child."

Marina's breath went short. Her jaw hurt from holding in the words that threatened to spill out of her mouth. Apparently the attack angered Joaquim as well. "Alejandro is my foster son," he snapped.

"Don't give me that," the old woman returned, pointing a gnarled finger. "My eyes still work, and that boy looks too much like you to be anything else."

Marina watched as Joaquim struggled to answer civilly.

"Alejandro is my half brother," Joaquim managed. "Since our father is dead, I intend to raise him as my son."

With that the marquesa turned her back on Joaquim and tottered out of the room, her cane crashing angrily against the wooden floor. Joaquim turned to Marina, his face pale and his jaw set. "I have my answer now, don't I?"

She came around the couch and put her arms about him. He rested his cheek against her hair. "I'm so sorry," she whispered against his waistcoat, wishing now she hadn't pushed him to come.

"Did you understand all that?"

"I missed a few words," Marina admitted. "But I got the general idea."

He took a deep breath. "Let's go home."

She knew what he meant. Not Portugal, but the hotel. He just wanted to be somewhere where they could be alone. "It's good we asked the driver to wait."

Alejandro said nothing as they made their way back out to the carriage, but once they'd settled onto the seat, he peered up at Marina. "She isn't nice."

Marina ignored Joaquim's clenched jaw. Alejandro would have caught most of what the old woman had said to Joaquim . . . and what she'd said about *him*. "I know she wasn't, but perhaps she doesn't feel well today. Since she's older than us, we have to try to be respectful anyway."

Alejandro regarded her doubtfully, his eyebrows raised.

"Try," she repeated softly.

Joaquim shook his head. "It's hard to believe she would treat her daughter that way just because she married a Spaniard."

Marina wrapped an arm about Alejandro's shoulders and was glad when he didn't flinch away. "It's never just one thing. Families have convoluted reasons for why they act the way they do. They have all manner of expectations to be failed and feelings to be hurt."

Joaquim squeezed her hand. "Remind me, when we have children, never to let something turn me away from one of them. If I say something foolish, remind me of how I feel today."

It was comforting that he was thinking in terms of the future. "I won't forget."

BARCELONA

They left the train station in Barcelona and stopped to eat before heading back to the hotel, but when they finally got there, they had news. The young man from the American embassy had left a message. Joaquim took the sealed note from the desk clerk and when they reached their room, he stopped only to drop his hat on the entryway table before he opened the envelope.

"What does it say?" Marina asked.

Joaquim read down to the bottom of the note. "Mr. Pinter would like us to come to the consulate again. Apparently the missing American turned up at a hospital last night."

"The one who came from Paris?"

He tossed the note on the bed and let out a breath in frustration. The Americans were helping, but this particular gentleman had been nothing but problematic. "Yes. I have a strong feeling this man's lost Leandra as well. We just have to hope he has some information for us."

After freshening up, they headed back to the consulate. This time Pinter met them just inside the consulate's outer doorway. He eyed Alejandro and expressed surprise that they'd located him, although not that they'd kept him. He must have read the message the embassy had forwarded from Duilio, claiming Alejandro as a member of the Ferreira family.

Pinter led them up to the second floor of the building rather than the back hallway they'd visited before. The guard outside the door agreed to keep an eye on Alejandro. Marina seemed reluctant, but since this involved Alejandro's mother, she agreed that it might be better for them to hear any news first and then tell the boy. So after producing a chair for him, the guard led them into the bright room behind Pinter and then left, closing the door.

On a white-draped bed lay a man with longish blond hair that brushed his shoulders. A dark stain splattered across the front of his expensive linen shirt, dried blood from his swollen nose. A cut over one eyelid had been stitched closed. He held a damp towel to one side of his jaw, but that didn't hide the bruising there. A suit jacket that looked to be of silk and wool lay over a chair next to the door, ripped up the back where someone had evidently grabbed the skirt of it. Whatever he'd been doing before he landed in a hospital last night, it had involved a fight.

"This is William Adler," Pinter said. "He's a specialist at the Paris embassy, and has an interesting tale to tell you, Inspector Tavares."

The man in the bed turned his eyes toward Joaquim. One showed red at the corner. "You're the Portuguese we've been waiting for?"

The man spoke Portuguese. Joaquim felt the tightness in his shoulders ease, out of relief that he wasn't going to have to work to understand him. He'd expected Spanish or English. "Yes, I am."

"And who exactly sent you?"

"The Portuguese ambassador to the Ilhas das Sereias. Your ambassador there gave us her blessing, more or less, although she didn't mention you, Mr. Adler."

"She didn't know I was coming here." He dropped his head back against the pillow. "So you work for the Foreign Office in Portugal? Which one? Northern or Southern?"

"Neither. I'm a police inspector from Northern Portugal, and although we have our prince's permission to pursue this, it's not an official inquiry."

He pointed at Marina then. "And who is she?"

Marina glanced at Joaquim.

"My wife," Joaquim said, choosing the path of least information. For some reason, Pinter hadn't handed over that detail to Adler, hinting at a lack of trust.

"You brought your wife along?" Adler started to laugh, but coughed instead. He grasped his side with his free hand and grimaced. "Cracked ribs," he choked out after a moment. "Send her home, man. These people don't hesitate to hit women."

Joaquim didn't intend to let that happen to Marina. "Which people?"

"They were Mossos," Adler said, "but this wasn't any normal police matter, not about her being sereia. Leandra wouldn't tell me why they came for her."

Joaquim drew over a chair for Marina and one for himself. "Why don't we start at the beginning? Why did you come here in the first place?"

"My aunt contacted me to ask some questions about Leandra—about whether she had stripes on her legs, of all things—and then told me she was alive," Adler said.

Yet another thing the ambassador hadn't mentioned—that she was Adler's *aunt*. She'd contacted the man in Paris, and he'd rushed here to find Leandra. "Your aunt is Madam Norton?" he asked to be sure. "The American ambassador?"

"Yes," Adler said.

"But she didn't send you here?"

Adler flushed. "No, but how could I have stayed away?"

Had the man abandoned his post to come to Barcelona? "Let's go back further," Joaquim said. "How do you know Leandra in the first place?"

"I met her when I visited my aunt on the islands, about ten years ago."

"And?"

"And the day before we were to take ship to America, she was arrested by their government. A few days later we heard she'd been sentenced to execution."

That was not what Ambassador Norton had claimed. "Why was Leandra going to America with you?"

Adler gave him a bloody-eyed stare. "Because she was in love with me, you dolt."

They'd suspected the American ambassador was holding back information. She should have told them that Adler and Leandra had been planning to run away together. "For all I know she was going to go to work for your American navy," Joaquim pointed out. "You didn't specify, so I needed to hear you say it."

Adler looked away. "Now I believe you're a policeman."

Joaquim ignored the dry comment. "After you heard she was to be executed, what did you do?"

"We were scrambling to figure out exactly what happened. My aunt didn't have grounds to file any protest, and to be frank, the sereia government wouldn't have cared if she had. They have such a tight grip on their people that no one would interfere, and the press there wouldn't dare print a word about such things."

Joaquim glanced at Marina again. She nodded, confirming Adler's guesses. Joaquim turned back to the American. "When you knew Leandra back on the islands," Joaquim asked, "did she tell you whether she was working for the Ministry of Intelligence?"

"She was," Adler said. "But she wanted to get away from them."

"Why?"

"They were asking her to do things she didn't want to do. They wanted her to cut her hands."

Cut her hands meant having the webbing between her fingers removed. Joaquim resisted the urge to glance at Marina's gloved hands. "And she was refusing?"

"Yes," Adler said, an ugly expression flitting across his features. The anger in the man's tone was unmistakable. "It's been done since, and not particularly well."

"So she wasn't cooperating with the ministry's demands?"

"No." Adler sighed. "That wasn't why they arrested her, though. They must have learned she was planning on running away with me."

Madam Norton had claimed Leandra was picked up for being overly friendly with *her*. "Did your aunt know about your relationship with Leandra?"

"No. Not until afterward."

That could explain the disparity between their statements. It was possible both Americans believed they were responsible for Leandra's arrest. It was also possible neither actually was. "And you heard nothing about Leandra in the time following her execution?"

"Nothing. My aunt sent me home after that. I was stationed in Lisboa for a couple of years, and then I was shipped to the Paris office," Adler said. "But when I saw her on the street Sunday, I had no doubt. It was my Leandra."

The time he'd spent on the islands and Lisboa explained his excellent Portuguese. But now they'd gotten back to the topic of Barcelona. "And you decided to approach her?"

"I had to know," Adler said, shaking his head. "The office here was told to monitor her, but I had to know if she needed help. She looked so tired and worn. I had to do something."

Joaquim kept his eyes on Adler's face. Every instinct told him that the man was sincere in wanting to help Leandra, but he wasn't a Truthsayer. "What did she tell you?"

Adler spread his hands wide. "She wouldn't tell me anything. She said the Mossos were coming for her, and if I interfered, they would kill me."

CHAPTER 27

Marina kept her mouth closed while Joaquim asked question after question. The man on the bed answered dutifully, although he became agitated at times. She would bet money that the man *had* been in love with Leandra. Not just infatuation, but as much in love as she and Joaquim were. That would explain his rushing to Barcelona, even ten years later.

According to Adler, Leandra had refused to tell him why she'd been arrested, what had become of her afterward, or what she was doing in Barcelona. Instead, she'd tried to get Adler to leave her.

But then Mossos arrived. Two of them took her away without a fight while two others asked Adler questions, beating him to determine his veracity. That was the source of his current injuries. "They threw her into a carriage and left me there," Adler finished.

Marina rubbed her hands together. They had to have taken Leandra back to the prison at Lleida. That was the only thing that made sense.

"Very well," Joaquim said. "Did you see the boy at all?"

"The boy who was supposed to be with her? No."

Marina held her temper in check. Adler sounded dismissive, as if Alejandro's fate held no importance. How dare he?

"What about a book?" Joaquim pressed. "Did she have the book with her, the one she stole on the islands?"

Adler paused for a long moment. "She didn't say anything about the book," he finally said. "The Mossos searched her clothing and emptied out her handbag. That must be what they were looking for."

Joaquim's lips pursed, as if he were holding in some comment.

Marina leaned closer. By that morning, Leandra no longer had the journal. She'd told Adler that the Mossos were coming, yet she hadn't had the item they so clearly wanted. They'd assumed this was about the journal, that Leandra was taking it back to whoever had hired her. The fact that Leandra had done something with the journal, hidden it perhaps, suggested a completely different explanation. "When she said the Mossos were coming, did she mean they had a *planned* meeting?"

Adler turned an affronted expression on her. "What are you suggesting?"

Joaquim's dark eyes slid toward hers and he nodded slightly, so Marina pressed the issue. "When you found her, Alejandro was already separated from her, as was the book, apparently. I think she stashed the boy and the book somewhere, contacted the people she was working for, and then waited in that park until they came for her. So she's protecting Alejandro and holding back the book. She must be using it for blackmail."

Adler's brow rumpled, but Marina didn't see surprise on his face. Had he already guessed that?

"The next logical question," Joaquim inserted, "is what she wants in return for the book."

"Money?" Marina supplied, already knowing that wasn't the answer.

"I don't think so." Joaquim turned toward her as if they were alone in the room. "She would have sold the journal back to the Portuguese if that were the case. Or to the Ministry of Intelligence on the islands."

Marina nodded. Whatever it was that Leandra wanted, none of them had it. What *was* this about?

"So your job is just to find this book?" Adler asked. "Is Leandra's safety incidental?"

"Not at all," Joaquim said, turning back to him. "While we want the journal back, what we actually need to know is who arranged for it to be stolen, and why. That's something I don't think we can answer without finding Leandra."

"Then I'll do my best to help you get her back," Adler promised.

Marina had her doubts. Adler had already defied his own orders. She thought he was too blinded by either his feelings for Leandra or his perceived guilt over her fate to be completely honest with them.

Apparently Pinter recognized that as well. "Mr. Adler, I must remind you that your superiors have ordered you to return to the embassy in Paris as soon as you're out of that bed."

Joaquim rose from his chair and extended a hand to help Marina up. "We'll be heading back to the Colón," he said to Pinter.

"I'll send a message for you if I hear anything further," Pinter promised.

"Thank you, then, for your cooperation. I'll be sure to tell Prince Raimundo of your people's help in this matter."

With that Joaquim led her from the room. The guard outside the door pointed to where Alejandro now stood next to a window, watching pigeons squabbling on the balcony. Marina went to him. "We're ready to leave now, Alejandro."

He nodded solemnly and held up his hand for her to take. "Did the man know where my mother is?"

"No, I'm afraid not."

Alejandro took one last look at the pigeons, the corners of his mouth turned down, and then followed Marina from the embassy.

"Nothing?" Marina sat curled in a chair next to the balcony windows of their hotel room, arms wrapped around her tucked-up knees.

Joaquim didn't know how long she'd been watching him. Outside, the sky had gone dark. She'd passed much of the time after dinner reading to Alejandro from the novel Ana had packed for her. It wasn't the best choice of book for a young boy, but it was the only one she had with her. She'd also written out the letters of the alphabet for him. He recognized most of them, so Joaquim suspected Alejandro would have an easy time learning to read.

While they'd been so industrious, Joaquim had been lying on the bed, trying to get a feel in his mind for where Leandra's captors had taken her, but his gift refused to supply an answer. Although the Mossos who'd taken her must work for the Canaries, he couldn't be sure whether they would have taken Leandra to the prison in Lleida or held her in Barcelona in the hope that she'd tell them where the journal was. His gift wasn't helping with that. He just didn't have much grasp of who Leandra was. "How long have I been lying here?"

"Long enough," Marina said. "I finished my book. Did you learn anything?"

He pushed himself into a sitting position. He could still hear traffic in the plaza below and music from a café nearby. "No. If I knew more about her I might be able to find her, but . . . I don't know what she wants. There doesn't seem to be anything I can latch on to."

Marina came to sit next to him on the bed, her back against the headboard. "You know what I think? Adler's still in love with her."

"After ten years?" Joaquim said doubtfully. "I don't know. Does a man stay in love that long with a woman he believes dead? With her memory?"

She touched his cheek with her scarred fingers, her hand bearing the scent of rosewater. "You said you waited for me for ten years, and you didn't even know I was real."

"But you were in my future, not my past," he pointed out.

"It's hard to let go of the past. And . . ." She contemplated the closed door to the sitting room.

"And?"

She met his eyes. "She might have her hand about his heart."

"I assume you mean that figuratively," he said, recalling his discussion with Duilio that last night on the islands. Was she finally going to confess that she'd used her magic on him?

"A sereia can . . ." Marina licked her lips. "She can *call* a specific male, if he's human, and bind his heart to hers. It supposedly lasts a long time."

Joaquim pressed his lips together. *Think before you speak.* "And what effect does that have on him?"

"Mainly that he won't be susceptible to another sereia's *call*." Her eyes were wide in her pale face, her eyebrows drawn tight.

"Is that why the sereia at the blockade didn't affect me? Because you did that to me?"

"On the boat," she whispered ruefully. "I didn't want one of the women on the islands to steal you away from me." She toyed with one of the buttons on his shirt. "Are you angry?"

From her hesitant tone, she feared that. "I know you didn't mean any harm."

She let go a breath she'd been holding, and her shoulders relaxed. "I shouldn't have done it without asking," she admitted. "But I was worried."

He tangled his fingers into her hair, seeking the pins that held her braid tight. "Does it feel the same as hearing a *call*?"

She reached up to pull out the pins herself. "No. It's more . . . subtle. My talent is weak, but this is the sort of thing I'm particularly good at. I can affect men if I'm close, although touching is better. I never do it, though. You run the risk of them figuring it out and becoming angry." When her braid tumbled free, she began to unravel it.

His fingers itched to touch her hair. "Angry?"

"It's a suggestion, that's all. If a man is strong-minded, he can shrug it off, and then you're within arm's reach of a man who suspects you've toyed with him, even if he doesn't know how."

"Suggesting what?" he whispered.

She shrugged. "When I wanted to go to Portugal, I could have convinced the captain of the English ship that he needed to help me. I didn't, but I could have."

"Could you make Adler talk?"

She considered for a moment. "If I was desperate I might try. But otherwise it's risky."

"Will you show me?" he asked.

She blushed. "You want me to do that?"

The previous night they'd lain in this bed, only talking, afraid to touch each other for fear Alejandro would overhear them. He'd heard men at the police station gripe that once they had children, privacy was hard to come by. Joaquim hadn't expected *that* problem less than a week into their marriage. "Would Alejandro notice if you were very, very quiet?"

Marina shook her head. "It's not that. If I'm *calling* you, *he* shouldn't hear it. It's just no one ever asks me to use my talent. Because I don't have much, I mean."

He found himself gazing at her lips. "Didn't we have the same discussion about your breasts on the train?"

That must be the right thing to say. She threw back her head and laughed softly. Joaquim shifted to lift her onto his lap, and she cupped her hands about his cheeks and kissed him. He tangled his fingers into her loosened hair, drawing her curls forward to frame her face, catching the scent of roses again, and her skin. But he pulled back. "You never needed to worry about losing me, darling. Never."

She smiled, her nimble fingers on his shirt's buttons. "Help me take this off."

He could do that. He dropped his suspenders, tackled his cuffs, and then slipped off his shirt while she tugged at his undershirt. When he sat bare-chested before her, she laid one hand over his heart and began to hum, eyes demurely lowered.

Joaquim closed his eyes, concentrating on her voice. There was a tune buried in her humming but not one he knew. It sounded strange, foreign. He was breathing in time with it. Or she was humming in time with his breathing. He wasn't sure which. It was as if she was becoming a part of him, sinking into his mind, his psyche. Or perhaps it was the other way around, and he was becoming part of her. He felt her magic wrapping around him like smoke, just as he had felt the sereia's *call* at the blockade, but this didn't slip away. It cradled him in its grip.

He opened his eyes, gazing down at her lowered features as if he were seeing her for the first time. There were still things about her he didn't know, so many secrets they'd not explored. None of that mattered. They had chosen this, both of them, chosen to belong together, choosing each other above all others who might come between them. And it didn't matter that he was human and she wasn't, or that he was a bastard and she wasn't. They'd chosen each other despite all that. Or perhaps even because of it.

He touched her cheek with the back of one finger. "I love you."

Her eyes lifted. "Do you trust me?"

It wasn't lost on him that he didn't feel the need to ask her the same. She demonstrated her trust in him on a regular basis. He was larger than she was, easily able to overpower her if he felt threatened. The only advantage she had over him was her *call*. "Yes. You may do whatever you want to me. Ask whatever you want."

She slid her arms about his neck and kissed him. "Make love with me, then."

Joaquim wrapped his arms about her and bore her back to the bed. "Just be very quiet."

CHAPTER 28

Marina peered at her face in the mirror. She did look tired, but she expected that. She'd lost track of the days of the month and was now terribly grateful that Ana had packed her bag with such foresight, including supplies for her monthly. There was even a paper envelope with a dozen aspirin tablets in it. Ana had thought of everything.

A knock at the bathroom door made her start in surprise. She dabbed some cool water on her face and set the hand towel aside. "Come in."

Joaquim smiled at her. "Are you ready to go?"

Evidently even Alejandro was dressed and presentable before she was. She picked up her hat and followed Joaquim into the sitting room. The boy wore his old trousers—which fit better than the ones Joaquim had purchased—and a clean plaid shirt. He held his new cap in his hands as if he'd been waiting for a while now. He followed dutifully when they headed toward the door.

Is there anything he does because he wants to? Marina had a sudden urge to take the boy to a shop that sold nothing but toys and make him pick one out. He would probably do so if she ordered him to. She felt a surge of anger against Leandra for letting her son be raised in a place like a prison.

Joaquim's hand was raised to turn the door latch when a knock sounded. He gestured for them to step back and cautiously opened it himself. Mr. Pinter stood in the hallway, his hat clutched in his hands.

"Ah, Inspector Tavares," he said, "I'm glad I caught you before you left."

"Won't you come in?" Joaquim set his hat back on the table. He opened the door wider to allow Pinter inside and shut the door after him.

Pinter's eyes swept the room, taking in the small empty bed in the sitting area for Alejandro and then Alejandro himself. Marina ignored the roiling of her stomach. She was suddenly hungry. "What brings you here, Mr. Pinter?"

"We've lost Mr. Adler," the young man announced without preamble. "I'm to ask that if you run across Adler in your investigations, you'd please report that information back to us." He sounded vexed.

"How exactly did you lose him?" Joaquim asked.

Pinter ran his fingers through his rumpled hair. "He slipped out of the consulate during the night. We don't know how he got past the guards."

Mr. Adler was beginning to be more interesting by the moment. Clearly he didn't want to go back to Paris, but fleeing the consulate was an interesting choice. Marina glanced over at Joaquim, who didn't look at all surprised by this turn of events.

"Did he bribe one of the guards?" Joaquim asked.

"They deny it, of course," Pinter said.

"Of course." Joaquim sighed. "We'll keep an eye out for your missing man."

Pinter picked up his hat. "We would appreciate being kept apprised of anything you learn on this case. It appears that Ambassador Norton has more than an academic interest in this, so we're keen to follow up."

Joaquim opened the door for the young man. He would like to understand Madam Norton's interest in this case himself. "I will keep that in mind."

Pinter tipped his hat to her and slipped out the door.

Marina waited until the sound of the man's footsteps faded, then glanced at Alejandro before whispering, "Where do you think Adler went?"

Joaquim laughed shortly. "Didn't you catch it yesterday?" he whispered in return.

She shook her head. "Whatever you're thinking, I missed it."

"Adler said that Leandra didn't *tell* him anything about the journal."

Marina pressed her lips together. "Oh. He never said he didn't *know* about it."

"He wants to trade the book for Leandra's safety, and he knows where it is," Joaquim said with a grin. "In his position for the Paris embassy, he's a specialist, accustomed to working with Truthsayers. You can lie to a Truthsayer by wording your answers very carefully. The way he answered that question was only a denial of having discussed the book with Leandra. I think she hid it somewhere, and he saw her do so."

"So if we find *him*, we'll have the journal."

Alejandro watched them whispering together, his brow rumpled.

"I have a pretty good feel for Adler now," Joaquim said, "and I'm sure I can find *him*."

Marina picked up her hat again and gestured for Alejandro to join them by the door. "Why don't we get some food? I'm starving and you'll do better after you have some food in your stomach."

Joaquim shook his head. "I should try to find Adler first."

Marina pinned her hat on firmly. She wasn't going to let Joaquim sacrifice his health for this quest, Alejandro needed to eat, and she was truly quite hungry this morning. "No. We eat first. No argument."

And to her surprise, he gave in.

Joaquim was glad Marina had bullied him into eating. She clearly wasn't feeling her best, and in all honesty, he'd forgotten that Alejandro needed to eat as well. He wasn't accustomed to making his decisions based on having others about him at breakfast time, a meal he often skipped in his hurry to reach the police station. Another habit he would have to amend.

He managed to be decent company for the meal despite his desire to get about his task. He convinced Alejandro to talk about whether or not he'd had any favorite toys. It turned out that the boy liked football, a game some of the prisoners from Barcelona occasionally played in the prison courtyard. Because his cousin Rafael played the game, Joaquim knew something about it. So he talked about that while the boy consumed a croissant and a roll with cheese. The topic held the boy's interest, which was a step in the right direction, and Joaquim promised to take him to a game whenever they got back to the Golden City.

Once they'd finished their coffee, they took their cups back up to the bar and walked out onto the plaza, hunting a spot where he could contemplate Adler's location. They located a bench in the plaza and he sat while Marina and Alejandro continued to walk about. Pigeons, believing he intended to feed them, gathered about his feet in surprising numbers. Joaquim ignored their squabbling and fluttering and closed his eyes.

What did he know about Adler? Career diplomat, specializing in *special* people. Judging by his clothes, from a family with money. Able to speak several languages, willing to lie to preserve his advantage. No, Adler hadn't lied; he'd omitted the truth. Fell in love at a young age and a decade later pursued the woman to Spain immediately when he learned she still lived. Injured, but pursuing her despite that.

When Joaquim held his recollections of Adler in his mind, he had a sense that the man was to the north of him, and not too far. He opened his eyes and saw Marina and the boy walking toward him. "I've found Adler," he said, rising and sending the pigeons flapping away.

Marina waited until the sound of wings died out. "Where?"

Joaquim offered her his arm. "I don't think it's far."

He pointed discreetly and they walked along the pathway through the plaza and onto the wide Passeig de Gracia, the avenue crowded with shops and restaurants. People hurried past on either side under the rows of plane trees, heading to work or out on errands. His sense of Adler didn't waver, though, firmly pulling him along. "I'd bet we're looking for a bookstore."

Marina nearly stopped on the sidewalk. "A bookstore?"

"Think about it," he said. "If you want to hide a book somewhere safe but where no one will notice it, why not a bookstore? Or a library would work too, but given the street, I think a store is more likely."

Only a couple of minutes later, his supposition was proven correct. His gift led him to a large bookstore set on the corner of two streets, in the ground floor of a new building with balconies above. Tearing her eyes away from the wrought-iron work on the balcony—which seemed to be designed to look like vines—Marina peered through the store's glass window. "I don't see Adler."

"He's in there," Joaquim said. "I can feel him."

She glanced back at him. "Do we go in?"

"I think so," Joaquim said. "We're not a threat to him." He held open the door and followed them inside. Books were stacked on tall shelves, both freestanding and set against the walls, making a maze of the store. Alejandro gaped at the shelves of books as if he'd never imagined such a place could exist. He'd probably never seen a bookstore—or a library—before. *I should find a book for Marina to read to him while we're here, a story better suited to a boy's tastes.*

The store had few customers so early, so Joaquim suspected the proprietor would have an eye on them, particularly as they'd brought a child in with them. Joaquim gestured for Marina to take Alejandro in one direction while he followed his sense of Adler along the far wall. He peered between each row as he went, and finally saw the blond head he was hunting. William Adler was crouched down, fingering his way through the shelves of books there.

"Have you found it yet?" Joaquim asked quietly.

Adler jerked and abruptly fell to his rump. Grimacing, he clutched his injured ribs. "What are you doing here, Tavares?"

"Looking for the journal," Joaquim said. "Same as you." He crouched down and peered at the shelf Adler had been perusing. The books on that set of shelves were all old, secondhand. Many of them were worn enough that the lettering on their spines had long since disappeared. Judging by the half dozen books lying on the floor, Adler had been opening each one to check it.

"How did you find me?" Adler asked.

Joaquim picked a book off the floor while Adler shifted himself into a more comfortable position. "I've never seen the journal either."

Marina rounded the nearest shelf. She shot a glance back toward the front of the store and came to where they waited, towing Alejandro with her. "What are we doing?"

Joaquim held up the book in his hand. "Could you pick out the journal just by looking at it?"

Marina caught her lower lip between her teeth and shook her head. Oriana *had* described the journal for them, but there were thousands of books here.

"Why don't you keep an eye out for the proprietor, then, and we'll search through these books?" Joaquim didn't wait for her to answer, but turned back to Adler. "Was she hiding it here when you decided to talk to her?"

Adler's back was pressed against the narrow span of wall between two sets of shelves, his long legs folded up awkwardly in the small space. Against his pale skin, his bruises stood out more lividly now, and his shoulder-length blond hair looked uncombed. He wheezed out, "How did you know?"

"I'm a police investigator. I'm accustomed to people hiding the truth from me." Joaquim pulled the first batch of books off the lowest shelf, set them on the floor, and began opening them individually. When he saw that the page was printed rather than handwritten, he set it back on the shelf and picked up the next. "You phrased your answers to my questions very carefully, Mr. Adler. You were trying not to lie, yet you didn't want to admit you knew something about the book. Can I assume you're searching for it in order to offer it in exchange it for Leandra's safety?"

"Yes," Adler said after a pause.

The man wasn't a very good liar. Joaquim didn't know what he was lying about now, but that answer had fallen flat. "You understand she's not trying to secure her own safety, don't you? Or young Alejandro's? They were both free a few days ago. If she let them take her, then there's something else at stake."

Adler's pale eyes met his.

Joaquim had finally worked through the books from the first shelf and moved up to the second. "So you did figure that out."

"She lied to me about it, I think," Adler said.

Marina leaned back, glancing toward the front of the store, but then she relaxed again.

Joaquim looked back at Adler. "What is she fighting for? Why risk herself?"

Adler's lips pressed together in a grim line, his eyes dropping to the lowest level of shelves.

"My book's right there," Alejandro said abruptly, pointing toward a shelf two over from where they were looking.

"Which one?" Marina let him steer her toward the book. She drew it out of the shelves and peered at the cover. *The Mines of Solomon*, it said in Portuguese. "This is your book?"

Alejandro nodded. "My mother was reading it to me."

Marina gave the book a puzzled glance but handed it down to Joaquim. Then she reached for the book that had been standing next to it, a leather book bound with red thread. She opened the book and glanced down at the open page. Then she stole another peek at the front of the store, quickly opened her large handbag, and stuck the book inside. She directed a guilty glance at Alejandro. "We're not supposed to steal, but this journal is my mother's. I'm only taking it back."

The look the boy gave her was almost comical. Clearly he recognized that as sophistry.

Adler's pale eyes fixed on Marina, angry now. He probably would have risen and snatched the journal from her if not for his cracked ribs. "Your mother's? Who do you work for?"

Marina gazed down at him, not intimidated by his expression. "I work at my father's offices in the Golden City—Monteiro and Company. My mother, however, worked for the ministry on the islands. That journal is the reason she was murdered."

Adler started trying to push himself into a standing position. Joaquim took pity on the man and wrapped an arm about his shoulders to help him to his feet. Adler leaned against the wall for a moment, trying to catch his breath. "They're willing to kill to get that back. What the hell is in it?"

"Details about a conspiracy, we think. It's encrypted, so we won't know until it's deciphered."

Adler shook his head, lip curling.

Marina peered back in the direction of the front door. "The proprietor is coming."

Joaquim hefted the book Alejandro had claimed. He nearly laughed when he opened it and saw a bookplate inside from the Ferreira family library back in the Golden City. It was indeed Haggard's *The Mines of Solomon*, the very copy he and Duilio had both read when it was first translated into Portuguese more than fifteen years ago. Duilio *had* mentioned that the thief had taken all the books in his room that night.

The proprietor, no doubt curious where his clientele had gone, came around the corner and saw all of them there. "May I help you?" he asked in Catalan, his eyes creeping toward Alejandro.

"I'd like to purchase this book." Joaquim closed Duilio's stolen book and handed it over.

"Most excellent." The shop owner headed back toward the front of the shop.

Joaquim followed. As he'd hoped, Marina and Alejandro headed for the door to wait for him outside. Adler followed, although he didn't look happy about it. A couple of minutes later Joaquim joined them on the sidewalk, his new—or old—acquisition in hand.

Marina looked vexed, so he wondered what Adler could have said to her. "Why don't we head back to the hotel? We can sort things out there in private."

Fortunately, the hotel wasn't much farther than the restaurant, so they reached it quickly enough. Once upstairs, Adler vented his frustration. "You can't just keep the book."

"It's my mother's journal," Marina snapped back, "stolen from my sister's house. Why should you have any right to it at all?"

"I need it," Adler said. "*She* needs it. If you take it back to Portugal with you, she'll have nothing to negotiate with."

"And what is she hoping to get in trade for the journal?" Joaquim asked him again.

Adler scowled at him. His eyes slid toward Alejandro, resentment there, although Joaquim couldn't imagine why. Then he realized that Adler saw the boy as *another man's child.* Evidently Adler wasn't as kind as the elder Joaquim Tavares had been to Joaquim himself.

Joaquim tried for a conciliatory tone. "You said you think she lied to you?"

Adler didn't look any happier, and jerked his head toward Alejandro. "Not in front of him."

Joaquim cast a glance toward Marina, who didn't look pleased. She held out her hand for Alejandro anyway. She picked up the newly purchased novel, led the boy back to the bedroom, and closed the door.

Joaquim turned back to Adler. "What do you think she lied about?"

Adler sat down in one of the leather chairs and stretched his long legs out. He touched his ribs and groaned. "When Leandra was supposedly executed, she was with child. My child."

Joaquim was certain Alejandro was not that child. If Leandra had borne Adler's child, it would have been nine or so by now. Besides, Alejandro's parentage was all too plain.

"When my aunt contacted me with questions about Leandra, she mentioned there was a boy with her. My aunt said he was too young and that she was looking into it. She wanted me to *wait* until she had more answers."

And Adler had resented that. "You didn't do so."

"No. I couldn't, so I came to see for myself. Leandra told me that the boy was some other man's son, not to worry about him." He took a deeper breath and then grimaced. "Then she told me she was plucked off that island—the one where they left her to die—by a ship. The sailors beat and raped her into submission. She barely survived."

Joaquim felt as if the whole world had shifted, and he was nauseated with the motion. The day before, he hadn't asked Adler how Leandra had escaped her execution. The news that a ship had taken her from the Ilhas de Morte told Joaquim how she'd gotten to Spain. It could not have been her choice, not given what Adler just said. It sounded more as though she'd been carried into slavery.

He sank down into a chair across from Adler's. As a police officer, he'd seen terrible things, heard terrible things, but he'd never gotten to the point where they didn't bother him, especially when women or children were involved. "She lost the child."

Adler laughed harshly. "It wasn't until I was lying in that bed that I realized she *hadn't* said that. She never actually said she lost the child. She merely wanted me to go away, not to interfere. But I see it now. My child has to be alive still. That's why Leandra let them take her back to the prison."

That *would* give Leandra a reason to return to the prison. It made her actions more plausible. And it also offered an explanation as to why Madam Norton had been so helpful. She wanted to know the fate of the child. It was a family matter. Just as he was willing to interceded for Alejandro—a boy he'd just met—Norton wished to help her nephew's child. Joaquim had no idea what he would feel in Adler's place.

They'd assumed that Leandra was an agent of the Canaries. Given her actions, bearing the journal to Catalonia, it had seemed the logical conclusion. A very different interpretation of her actions rested in Joaquim's mind now. Leandra Rocha was the *victim* in all this, and the theft of the journal—an article valuable enough to the Ministry of Intelligence to make it a bargaining chip—could be a desperate attempt to gain freedom not only for Alejandro but also another child, Adler's child.

Leandra had been left chained on an island to die, but ended up on a ship instead. Joaquim had a very clear idea of what that ship would look like, a steam corvette with dark sails and a mermaid figurehead. It would have lain in wait until the sailors were certain that Leandra was too weak to fight them, and then the ship would have come to the island and taken her away.

What had happened to Leandra in the ten years between her supposed execution and her reappearance in the Spanish embassy? He'd been angry about the way she'd allowed Alejandro to be raised, but what if she'd had no choice in the matter? Alejandro had been born in that prison; Leandra might never even have held him in her arms.

"Mr. Adler, if you'll stay here," he said, rising from the chair.

"I'm too exhausted to go anywhere, I promise," Adler said, waving one hand vaguely.

Joaquim went into the bedroom and pulled the door closed. Marina sat on the bed, Alejandro next to her as she read from the middle of the book. Her eyes lifted and her voice fell silent.

"I need to ask Alejandro a couple of questions."

She marked the place in the book with her finger. "What is it?"

Joaquim came closer. "Alejandro, do you have a brother at the prison?"

The boy's dark eyes seemed worried, but he shook his head.

"A sister?" he tried.

Alejandro shrugged in response.

"Did your mother tell you not to tell me you have a sister?"

The boy's eyes darted about as he decided how to answer that, which was answer enough. He was an unusually reticent child, and Joaquim suspected that came naturally. But Alejandro was also *holding back*. How much did he know that he hadn't told them because he'd been told not to do so? "It's fine, Alejandro, you don't need to answer."

The tension on the boy's features eased.

How far could he push Alejandro without breaking the boy's trust? He didn't want the boy to hate him, but he needed answers.

He sat down on the edge of the bed. "Alejandro, is your mother the only one?"

Alejandro's eyes shifted to one side, hunting the answer on the coverlet. Then he shook his head.

"The only what?" Marina asked softly.

"You recall that when Duilio and I rescued your sister from the Ilhas de Morte, a ship tried to overtake us? I think the same thing happened to Leandra, only there was no one there to save her. Those men turned her over either to the Spanish government or to the Canaries. To someone who's been controlling her ever since because she has children who can be threatened to ensure her compliance."

Marina had paled. "You think there were others besides Oriana and Leandra?"

That he should be tied to two incidents ten years apart seemed unlikely. It was far more plausible that he knew of two incidents out of *many*. "I would lay odds that there were."

Marina's eyes glistened with tears. She got up off the bed and walked quickly to the bathroom. Joaquim looked to Alejandro. "At the prison, if you did something wrong, would they hurt your mother?"

After a moment, the boy nodded. Joaquim suspected the bargain went the other way as well, with punishment for his mother's actions being taking out on the boy. That was why she'd left him behind in Barcelona. As long as Alejandro was safe, even in the dubious care of a beggar king, Leandra had freedom to act.

Marina emerged from the bathroom, her eyes reddened but composed now. "If Leandra Rocha needs the journal to buy the freedom of her child, we should let her have it."

When weighing the safety of a child against solving a murder ten years past, Joaquim was inclined to agree. Leandra's daughter had to take priority, even if it meant they never discovered who'd ordered the murder of Marina's mother. And if there were others like Leandra, then any information she had could help free them. "I'll go talk to Adler."

He opened the door to the sitting room but stopped on the threshold, cursing himself for a trusting fool.

Marina's handbag stood open, and Adler was gone.

So much for the man's promise.

ILHAS DAS SEREIAS

Duilio puffed out his cheeks as Captain Vas Neves lectured Oriana again regarding her safety. It was a waste of breath. Oriana had made up her mind.

They'd spent the entire morning in the dining room, hashing

out the information that Ambassador Norton had passed to them the day before, along with every other piece of intelligence they'd gathered. The captain, along with Benites and Costa, represented the guard contingent in this, although Costa had remained silent throughout the meeting. They were concerned with the mission it-self, whereas Duilio and Oriana considered this a chance to make political headway with the government of the islands.

For her part, Inês sided with Oriana—perhaps the reason that Costa chose not to speak out. Although Inês had no information about the missing journal, she had retrieved her own personal jour-nal from her mother's house. It proved a fascinating source of infor-mation about the Spanish embassy and Madam Davila.

According to her notes, Madam Davila was fanatically devout and had even spoken of bringing Christianity to Quitos. Oriana snorted when Inês revealed that last tidbit, since the teachings of Christianity were not the best match for a female-dominated society, even the Virgin-centered version practiced on Amado. Madam Davila also required the domestic workers in the embassy to wear what she considered appropri-ately modest garb, a plain shirtwaist and skirt that matched the ones in the photograph of Leandra Rocha taken on the docks.

Another interesting tidbit was that the Spanish embassy never did business with the ships that came from Catalonia, as if Catalan captains could not be trusted to be loyal to Spain. Nationalism was a potent force in Catalonia. That made Leandra Rocha's choice of the Catalan ship as transport back to Spain a telling one. Since that captain would not have been in contact with the embassy, a day or two might have passed before Madam Davila discovered that Lean-dra had left the island.

Inês continued to pore through her journal as they talked, one pointed nail skimming along the pages, her brow furrowed. Then she looked up. "I found it!"

"Found what?" Oriana asked, latching on to the distraction from the captain's lecture.

"The woman's name," she said. "Evangelista. She told me her name was Lorena Evangelista."

Duilio felt his own brow furrowing. "This is the woman you thought worked for the ministry. The one who was investigating the executions, right?"

Inês cast a brief startled expression his way, surprised he'd spoken out of turn. Then she took a deep breath and answered him anyway. "Yes. I wrote her name down because it was unusual."

Names like Evangelista or Anjos or Santos were unusual here. They were distinctively Christian, although it didn't follow that the bearer of the name would be as well. "Did you know anyone in the ministry with that name?" he asked Oriana.

She shook her head. "No, but since I intend to ask about her, it helps to have her name."

Vas Neves shook her head slowly, but apparently had given up arguing.

CHAPTER 29

BARCELONA

Joaquim tracked his sense of Adler along the Rambla, still seething.
He was annoyed mostly with himself, since he'd been the one who'd
trusted Adler alone. The man clearly thought nothing of breaking a
promise. Joaquim had no doubt he could get the journal back from him
without a fight. He could knock Adler over with a pillow right now.
Marina followed, though, clutching Alejandro's hand, and Joaquim
wasn't sure *she* wouldn't resort to violence against the American.

They hadn't gone far down the street when he felt he was close.
Sure enough, Adler sat on a bench, one hand pressed to his ribs.
Joaquim walked up behind him and set one hand on the man's shoul-
der. "Give me the book."

Adler didn't argue. He must know he was too weak to do this
alone. He withdrew the journal from inside his coat and handed it
over. Joaquim flipped it open and glanced at the familiar writing, just
to be certain. Marina caught up to him, her jaw clenched. Joaquim
passed her the book and she quickly stashed it inside her handbag.

Then he saw that Alejandro was watching something behind
them on the boulevard. Joaquim followed his gaze. Three of the red-
and-blue-uniformed police stood under the striped awning of a store

that sold cigars and cigarettes, peering down at a sheaf of papers. One glanced up and pointed directly at Alejandro. Joaquim stepped in front of the boy, hoping to block their view, but two of the Mossos, one thin and one stout, immediately began jogging toward him.

Joaquim shoved Alejandro backward. "Get back to the hotel."

Alejandro didn't argue. Hand atop his cap, he took off running, although heading farther down the street, *away* from the hotel. One of the Mossos glared at Joaquim, but the thin man took off after Alejandro, and after a split second of indecision, the other chased the boy as well.

"Stay here," Joaquim told Marina quickly. He ran after them. He was not going to let them get a hand on Alejandro.

The stout man stopped and threw a poorly aimed blow at Joaquim's head. Joaquim stepped under that wild swing and punched the man in the stomach as hard as he could.

In the corner of his vision, he saw Alejandro dash down a side street. The thin man slipped on a puddle as he rounded the corner but managed to stay on his feet. Abandoning the gasping heavyset man, Joaquim chased them and rounded the corner only a dozen yards behind Alejandro's pursuer. He jumped over the puddle and discovered that the side street he'd gone down opened out into another plaza where tables waited for lunchtime diners. Alejandro sprinted directly across the square, losing some of his lead. The man almost had him when Alejandro doubled back around the fountain and dashed toward one side of the square where a handful of tourists were lingering over their coffee.

Joaquim pushed himself after them, aware he was breathing heavily. *Damn, I need to run more often.*

The boy reached the tables and darted between them. The thin man shoved his way through, knocking over a couple of chairs and setting a group of tourists abuzz, cursing in what sounded like German. Joaquim avoided them, following as Alejandro slipped through the arches at the edge of the square. The boy fled down along the darker hallway, and then dropped to the ground. He rolled under the wreckage of an old fruit vendor's stand, pushed open the door of the building behind it, and disappeared inside. The thin man shoved the damaged cart out of his way and followed.

When Joaquim reached that door, he jogged inside only to find a cramped place that must have housed a restaurant. Alejandro was nowhere in sight, but the thin man was. He faced Joaquim, the expression on his narrow face murderous. "Who are you?" he asked in Spanish. "Why are you interfering with the queen's business?"

Joaquim paused for a second, wondering if he'd heard that right. Spain had a king, not a queen, didn't it? He stopped a dozen feet inside the room, breath puffing in and out. "What do you want with the boy?" he managed in his workmanlike Spanish.

"He's the queen's property," the thin man spat out. "I'm taking him back." His eyes narrowed as he surveyed Joaquim's features. "You're the Portuguese, aren't you?"

Joaquim didn't see any point in answering. He heard a sound at the door and cast a glance that way in time to spot Adler stepping over the threshold, wheezing horribly and clutching his side. *Amazing. The man is trying to help.*

Joaquim turned back to the thin man. "No child is property."

"That child isn't human," he said with a laugh. "It's a half-breed. A toy, no more."

Joaquim huffed out an angry breath. If this man believed that of Alejandro because he was half sereia, he would feel the same about any child Joaquim might father himself. "That boy is . . ."

The sound of a scuffle at the doorway made him spin about. Adler struggled in the grasp of the heavyset man, eyes wide in panic. Then he cried out and slumped to the ground, clutching his side.

The heavyset man loomed over Adler, a bloodstained knife in his hands. "Well, what have we here?"

Oh, hell and damnation. Joaquim weighed his chances. He had no idea where Alejandro had gone. The thin man would be easier to take, but the heavy man was at the only exit he could see. If he made it out to the square, he could call for help and get Adler out of here.

Joaquim ran for the door, but the heavyset man slammed it shut before he reached it. He swung his knife at Joaquim, and Joaquim tumbled back over Adler's prone body. Then his pursuer was atop him, breath hot in his face.

"I know who you are," the man said smugly, settling his weight more firmly across Joaquim's chest. "No wonder you're chasing the boy."

With his arms pinned underneath him, he couldn't even take a swing at the man.

"You're Alejandro Ferrera," the man said with a laugh. "Thought you'd be older. Not what they'd pay for your boy, but I suspect there's a decent reward for you too."

Joaquim nearly choked. *They think I'm my father.* "I'm not who you think I am."

But the thin man had reached them. He produced a flask and handkerchief from his pocket and proceeded to douse the cloth with the contents.

Joaquim struggled against his captor's weight. "The American consulate general knows—"

The thin man knelt and pressed the cloth firmly over his mouth. The heavy man got off his chest, letting him breathe, but what he could breathe only made his head spin.

I need a watch.

Marina had no idea how long Joaquim and Adler had been gone. Or where they'd gone.

They should have discussed this possibility, how long she should wait for him if they were separated. Eventually she would just go back to the hotel. That was one place where he would know to find her. He'd told Alejandro to go there. *How long should I wait?*

She eyed the small café across the street where people were stopping for coffee, but not for lunch yet. The first thing after Joaquim returned, she was going to purchase a watch. It didn't have to be a nice watch.

She sat there on the bench under the plane trees, watching the pedestrians streaming by on their way from one business engagement to another. A few cast glances her way, perhaps thinking she was lost. Marina took a few deep breaths and concentrated on appearing as if she belonged there.

Then someone in the passing traffic caught her eye. Marina's mouth went dry as she watched a tall woman pass in front of the café. The woman herself wasn't distinctive, but her blue-and-white-striped shirtwaist was. Marina remembered sitting in the train station at Madrid and thinking she should have her new seamstress make up one like that. Had it been the same woman?

A clammy hand touched hers and she almost cried out before she caught herself. She glanced down to see Alejandro sliding onto the bench next to her, breathing hard. His damp fingers wrapped around her palm. "Alejandro? What happened?"

"I ran through the Romero Building, into the halls behind it." He shook his head. For the first time since she'd met him, he looked upset, his eyebrows drawn tight with worry. "The Mosso stabbed the blond man and I ran out the back. I shouldn't have left him."

Her breath stilled and she swallowed, urgency suddenly filling her. Alejandro had left Joaquim somewhere, and Adler had been stabbed. "Show me where."

He nodded, his small jaw firming. She wished she had a disguise for him, since she was taking him back to wherever his pursuers had gone. "Where's your cap?"

"I dropped it."

"We'll get you another one later," she said as she rose. "Just hold on to my hand and look like you belong with me."

They ambled along the crowded street. Alejandro tugged on her hand when they reached a side street and whispered, "That way."

The side street quickly spilled them out into a square, four buildings surrounding the court with a gallery of arches on each side. There was no other way out of the square that she could see.

The boy led her under a row of arches and peered across the wide plaza where people were gathered to eat and talk under the shade of large umbrellas. Marina realized he was checking for his pursuers before they went any farther. "Is it safe?"

After a second's hesitation, he nodded. He drew her along the corridor, turned the corner, and led her along that side of the square. Most of the doors that led inside the building were closed up, but one stood ajar, a ruined cart or wagon standing beside it.

Alejandro led her past the broken cart and peered inside the door. "He's still there."

Marina looked past him, thinking he meant Joaquim. Instead she saw Adler slumped on the dusty floor, blood pooled about his side. She pressed her fist to her mouth to stifle a cry of horror. *That's too much blood, isn't it?* She crossed herself, knelt next to him, set her handbag to one side, and turned him over onto his back. He grunted when his side hit the floor, and his head rolled senselessly.

But he was still alive. "Alejandro, are there police out in the square? We have to get him to a hospital."

He shook his head, his eyes sliding toward the open door. "You don't want *them*."

No, she didn't, but she couldn't leave Adler here to die, and she didn't have time to take a cab all the way to the American embassy. "Um . . . try to find one of the restaurant owners instead."

Alejandro frowned. "I'll get one."

He disappeared out the door before she could remind him to be cautious. He probably knew that better than she did. Marina laid one hand across Adler's forehead. His forehead was clammy and cold, but his eyes fluttered open and he moaned. "We're getting help," she said. "You have to hold on."

His lips moved, but she couldn't make out what he was saying.

"Say it again," she begged, leaning closer.

"They took him," Adler whispered.

CHAPTER 30

ILHAS DAS SEREIAS

"Madam, let me say one last time that this is foolhardy."

They were almost at the Quitos jetty. Oriana had watched the island approaching with trepidation in her stomach. She was gambling not only with her own life, but that of Duilio and Vas Neves as well. *And* that of her unborn child. Unfortunately, Duilio's gift wasn't offering an answer as to whether they'd walk out of the capital alive. Oriana turned to Captain Vas Neves, who stood on the ferry's deck, her face grim. "I know. I'd say there's a fifty percent chance this isn't going to end well."

Duilio shook his head. "That's a fifty percent chance of it succeeding."

"I can add," she pointed out.

"Wouldn't that be subtraction?"

She cast him a dry look. "I'm also moderately proficient with that."

As the ferry nestled up to the pier and the sailors began setting the mooring lines, he smiled and signed acceptance without belief, vexing her. He always chose her most anxious moments to joke, resorting to nonsense when he wanted to ease her worry. Or perhaps he truly doubted her mathematical skills.

He wore a very formal *pareu* today, the black linen one that almost reached his feet. She'd chosen a brocaded *pareu* in loden green, worn along with a pale green vest—one of her favorites—hoping that the choice would bolster her nerves. She'd left off most of her jewelry, picking only one piece, a gold armband studded with aquamarines that had belonged to her mother. She hadn't even worn her usual hair combs, and felt exposed without their hidden blades.

They waited as the other passengers debarked, following at the tail end of that queue. Fortunately, there were still carriages for hire waiting. As she moved to hail one, a closed carriage approached, bypassing the line. The driver gazed down at her. "Ambassador Paredes?"

She shielded her eyes with one hand to peer up at the driver. "Yes?"

"I'm to take you into the city."

The door of the carriage opened and a woman stepped down. *She* wore the uniform of the navy, khaki *pareu* with a matching vest. An older woman and, judging by the rings on her webless index finger, an officer of high rank, the equal of Captain Vas Neves.

Oriana knew her aunt had spies on Amado. It was impressive, though, that news of their arrival on the ferry had preceded them. Maybe there was a telegraph cable laid on the ocean floor between the islands. It wouldn't be that difficult.

The naval officer gestured for Oriana to climb up into the carriage, then waited politely as Duilio and Captain Vas Neves followed. Then she climbed up with them and sat next to the captain, facing backward. She eyed Vas Neves speculatively as the carriage began to roll. "I understood that human women were too frail to serve in their military."

Vas Neves regarded her with one gray eyebrow raised. Not confrontational. It was more a look of respect from one soldier to another. "I am certainly not, nor are my guards."

The naval officer gave her a grim smile. "Good to know."

Oriana watched the streets pass outside the carriage's windows. They were in a hurry, the horse moving along at a surprising clip. On the streets, life moved on at a normal pace, as if nothing was wrong. The outside world didn't concern most people on this island.

"You have not asked, Ambassador," the naval officer said, "why the navy is involved in what seems to be an affair of the ministry."

Oriana looked to her. "The ministry's judgment regarding the state of foreign affairs influences the navy's actions, so it's wise for the navy to assure themselves that the ministry is accurate."

"Very good," the officer said, as if to a schoolgirl. "Do the Portuguese have plans to invade our islands?"

"No," Oriana said firmly. "We are in the process of molding two countries back into one. We have neither the time nor the inclination for war. What we need is trade."

"So you must say," the officer opined. "However, as we are about to lose our trade with Spain, the return of the Portuguese to our shores *is* fortunate."

"Lose your trade with Spain?" Oriana said, hoping the officer would expand on that.

"Yes. Madam Davila currently sits in our prison and the remaining members of the Spanish mission are being questioned before being expelled."

The arrest of an ambassador's wife shocked her. It took a moment for Oriana to come up with an appropriate response. "On what charges are you holding her, may I ask?"

"Canaries are forbidden on these islands, Ambassador. Her mere presence is a violation of our treaty with Spain."

Oriana glanced over at Duilio. His eyebrows rose, as if he shared her surprise. It was one thing for there to be a Canary spy among the embassy staff, but Madam Davila herself? "How did you know that she's not human?"

The officer simply smiled.

Apparently Madam Norton had been correct about a Canary

among the Spanish mission's personnel after all. The navy wouldn't have taken Madam Davila into custody without proof she was a Canary, not unless they were willing to risk the wrath of Spain. But Madam Norton had also noted that the government here didn't give a damn about reasonable actions against a foreign embassy. Then again, once they had Madam Davila in custody, it would have been a simple matter to determine whether she had the ventral stripes on her thighs that sereia lacked.

"It turns out the Spanish have brought in a handful of Canary agents over the last few decades. Instead of trying to disrupt the government," the officer continued, "the Canaries have been concentrating on infiltrating the press. Can you guess their intent?"

Oriana sat very still, hands on her lap. "To spread the notion that Portugal is on the verge of invading?"

"Very good," the officer said with a nasty smile. "An odd tactic, but surprisingly effective. We've arrested several of the spies, as Madam Davila has proven talkative."

Oriana swallowed, hoping they weren't saying that about *her* in a couple of days.

They'd reached the section of the city that housed many government buildings, neat stacks of no more than two stories with little embellishment on the gray walls, perhaps a conscious attempt not to look like the Portuguese architecture common on Amado. The headquarters of the Ministry of Intelligence had a triangular pediment on each end, similar to Greek temples Oriana had seen in photographs. Most of the activities of the ministry took place far from here, but the highest officers could be found within.

The naval officer walked them up the steps and inside, her expression impassive, leaving Oriana uncertain whether she would be heard out, or whether she was walking to her execution. A heavyset woman with hard eyes and gray hair greeted them once they'd walked up the stairs into the building.

"They're here to meet with Minister Paredes," the officer informed the secretary, even though they'd never said that.

A prickle went down Oriana's spine. Duilio hadn't reacted, but she was sure he'd caught that. Her aunt was *Subminister* Paredes . . . or had been the last time Oriana spoke with her.

"You'll need to stay here with me," the officer said to Vas Neves. They'd expected that. The secretary walked next to Oriana and Duilio, leading them down a gray stone hallway. A moment later they were ushered into a large and ornate office where her aunt Jovita presided over a handful of minor functionaries, bidding them off on small tasks, most to seek out paperwork for her. Their escort bade them remain at the entryway to the large office, so they both waited under a large tapestry that probably depicted a scene of their people's glorious past. Unfortunately, neither of them could see it from where they stood.

After her aunt had dispatched the last of her lackeys, most of whom spared them only the quickest glance on the way out of the office, Jovita turned annoyed eyes on them. "I don't have time for you today," she snapped.

No, whatever was going on here, it didn't look leisurely. "We have information," Oriana began, "that we felt necessary to bring to your attention."

"I don't need information," Jovita said bluntly. "I need evidence. Close the door."

Oriana did as bidden.

"Now, what do you want of me?"

"I have more information than I did last time we spoke, Subminister."

"*Acting* Minister, I'm afraid," Jovita said. "My predecessor is currently under arrest, forcing me into a position I don't have time for."

"Minister Raposo is under arrest? Does that have something to do with the arrest of Madam Davila?"

Her aunt leaned back against her desk, arms crossed over her chest. "It will come out eventually, so yes."

"If I may ask, what evidence did you have to arrest Madam Davila?"

"Worried for yourself, are you?" Jovita asked.

Oriana drew a calming breath. "It's a reasonable concern."

Jovita snorted. "A photograph fell into our hands yesterday morning of the woman stepping out of her bath. Adequate proof that the Spanish mission was harboring a Canary spy."

Yes, that would be seen as grounds to search the embassy and detain its personnel. "What was your source?"

"One of my people working in the American embassy. The photograph had just been developed, and fell rather conveniently into her hands."

The implication being that the Americans had *fed* the information to the ministry. "I see."

"Yes, there's little love lost between Norton and Davila. Davila had gone that morning to visit you on Amado, so we waited until she returned. We had to move quickly, so as to capture her before she left again. After her arrest, Madam Davila implicated Minister Raposo, who was also imprisoned last night pending investigation. We didn't have evidence yet, but those involved seem more than willing to turn on each other. At this point, my office is having trouble keeping up with the numerous confessions. We would, however, like more substantial evidence before proceeding with trials, especially evidence that tells us something about where this conspiracy started."

"You have someone seeking that evidence, don't you? The agent who's been collecting information about the executions for the last six months, Lorena Evangelista."

Jovita cast an exasperated look her direction. "Yes, I hired her not long after your supposed execution. She's from Capraria and has no ties to anyone in the ministry. I thought it would help to have an outside perspective. Unfortunately, all she's been able to collect is hearsay."

Capraria was one of the outer islands, one that sided more with Amado than Quitos in political matters. "Well, I have one piece of evidence for you that may help," Oriana said. "But first I would like you to answer a few questions for me."

"I'll consider it," her aunt said slowly.

That was as good as she was going to get. Oriana took a deep breath. "When my mother died, did you see her body?"

Her aunt shot her a disturbed glance. "This is about Lygia?"

"Did *you*—not Valeria or Vitoria—identify my mother's body after she died?"

Her aunt's strong jaw clenched. "As head of the Paredes line, I did."

"And her body was recognizable?"

"Yes. I wouldn't have signed the paperwork otherwise."

Oriana felt some of the tightness slip from her shoulders. One of her worst fears had been that her mother had ended up where Leandra Rocha had. "What about Marina's body? Did you also see hers?"

Jovita's jaw clenched again. "No. I'm aware it wasn't her body you were shown. I didn't learn that until over a year later. You'd already been assigned to Northern Portugal by then."

"Is it customary for members of the ministry to produce disfigured bodies whenever they wish to deceive grieving family members?"

"Not to my knowledge," her aunt said. "But one thing I've learned as subminister is that there are factions within any group."

Oriana wished she had the ability to weigh the truth in her aunt's words, like a Truthsayer. "Why did you not think I would make a good spy?"

"A spy has to see her mission as all important. You, on the other hand, question the validity of everything, like your mother. You were cooperative enough, I heard, at first, but I knew that once you got your land legs you would start debating every order."

Oriana licked her lips. She *had* been obedient at first. Isabel's death had been the breaking point for her, when the ministry's orders had ceased to make sense. That was when she'd decided to leave the ministry. And when she'd become expendable. "A woman known as either Maria Melo or Iria Serpa showed up in the Golden City. Do you know either of those names?"

Her aunt took a deep breath. "I won't answer that question."

"When I met her in the city," Oriana said, "she said something odd to me. She said that I had Mother's look about me, and that Mother didn't know how to play the game either. I will never forget those words."

Her aunt sat back, folding her hands over her stomach. "You think she was responsible for Lygia's death?"

"Yes, directly or by some other agent's hand. I was present at this woman's death. Despite being an agent of the ministry, she had the markings of a Canary. Prince Raimundo's men took photographs for me." Duilio handed Oriana his notebook, and she took out one of the precious photographs from that night, showing a woman's body partially wrapped in a bloodstained sheet, her skirts drawn up high enough for the photographer to capture the image of her striped thighs—the skipjack markings that indicated Canary bloodlines, the same markings that had given away Madam Davila's identity. "She leapt from the roof at the palace, so her back was mangled, but the doctor who examined the body said there were scars that could have come from the removal of a dorsal fin."

Her aunt's lips pressed in a thin line, but she said nothing.

"When she died, this Iria left behind documents indicating that the assassination of Prince Fabricio was planned by the government here on the islands, by the Ministry of Intelligence."

"If that's the case," her aunt said, spine stiffening, "why has Northern Portugal not demanded retribution?"

"Because Prince Raimundo believed *me* when I said she didn't represent our people."

Now her aunt looked truly concerned. "And if you hadn't been there?"

"If she'd succeeded in getting rid of me beforehand? The islands might now be at war. With Northern Portugal at a minimum, and possibly Southern Portugal. The English would be bound by their ancient treaty with Portugal, and I think the Americans want the goodwill of the Portuguese more than they want trade with these islands. Tell me, to whom would the government have turned for support?"

"The Spanish, of course."

"Marina and her husband are currently in Spain, looking for Leandra Rocha, the woman who stole my mother's journal. You'll find her name on Evangelista's list as well. Her testimony might offer that proof you seek, as would that of any other survivor." Oriana didn't know how much of Leandra Rocha's recent movements Jovita was aware of, so she laid it all out before her, including the information that the boy, likely Leandra's son, was Duilio's half brother.

"If this is all true," Jovita said, "what makes you think I'm not involved?"

That had been the dangerous question all along. Duilio signaled to Oriana that his gift considered the situation safe, though. "I'm very aware this may be a mistake," Oriana said to her aunt, "but you've always been honest with me, even if you didn't like me."

"You are family." Jovita sighed gustily, her face weary. "Madam Davila already admitted to us that the women supposedly executed are being transported to Spain, one every six months."

Oriana felt hollow inside, but it wasn't too much of a surprise. "Why was anyone being given to the Spanish? Has Madam Davila admitted that yet?"

"A trade," Jovita snapped. "Apparently the Canaries' numbers are low and most of them are involved in controlling certain individuals in the Spanish government. They've been using these stolen women to serve on Spanish ships in their stead, to enforce their will in their prison, and, I'm afraid, to bear the next generation who will one day replace them."

Oriana felt ill. That could have been her fate if Duilio and

Joaquim had not rescued her. "And if the Spanish succeeded in taking over the islands?"

"The conspirators here represent all the major lines in the ministry. In return for their collaboration, they would have a place in government when the Spanish came to take over. They sold their own daughters into slavery for a promise of power. No woman should ever betray her family."

Her aunt believed that. The family line was all important.

Jovita sighed heavily, and added, "Valeria and Vitoria are among them. They denied knowledge of Lygia's murder, but have both admitted they allowed you to be executed under false charges of treason. They hoped that by giving *you* to the Spanish, they wouldn't have to turn over their own daughters one day."

Oriana laid one hand over her belly, feeling the slight swell there. She didn't know what she would have done in her aunts' place. She hoped to the gods she never faced such a question.

Jovita's gaze locked with Oriana's for a long moment. "Iria was right, by the way. You do have your mother's look."

Oriana bowed her head to acknowledge the compliment.

"She was wrong, though, about the other. It was never the case that Lygia didn't know how the game was played. Your mother simply refused to violate her principles. I believe you've also inherited that trait."

Oriana wasn't certain whether that was a compliment or a warning. "Thank you," she said anyway.

Jovita looked away, picked up a stack of papers, and began flipping through them as if anxious to return to her work. "The Spanish embassy will be completely cleared in a day or so. I didn't have enough personnel I trusted to clear all the embassies, which is why we simply forced the others out. But the navy has since agreed to supervise the investigation of the foreign missions, so your people can start moving back in as soon as tomorrow. They will, however, each be interviewed and cleared to ensure that the Canaries haven't slipped in another agent."

Oriana signed her acceptance of those terms. Fortunately, it would be a simple matter to prove the humanity of her personnel—they only had to display their human feet.

Jovita crossed her arms over her chest. "Would you, if needed, be willing to testify in the trials?"

That would make her more of a target, but she had to do it. Her mother had surely given her life trying to prevent this. She could help put an end to it and bring the collaborators to justice. Oriana glanced back at Duilio, and when he signed agreement, she said, "Yes."

"This . . . series of revelations has shaken the oligarchy. When it gets into the press, we may see repercussions against the families in power."

Oriana couldn't hide her surprise. "It's going to be allowed into the newspapers?"

"Yes," Jovita said gravely. "It's frankly the best way to protect any witnesses who do come forward. And as long as I'm alive, I mean to ensure that these people will not escape what they've done."

Oriana hoped her aunt lived a long life, then.

CHAPTER 31

BARCELONA

Marina laid one hand over her mouth, kneeling on the floor next to Adler's unmoving form. She closed her eyes. *Be calm,* she reminded herself. *Be calm.*

She had to help Adler first. She wasn't a healer. She had no idea what to do with injuries, but once aboard the English ship there had been an incident with a seaman stabbed by another in the dining room. The cook had ordered one of the other men to hold a clean towel against the wound until the ship's surgeon got there. Marina surveyed Adler's clothes. Blood stained the left side of his coat, near the floor. He must have been lying atop the injury before she'd turned him onto his back. She clambered around to that side and drew his coat back, exposing a bloodied shirt. The wound was clearly visible from this angle, a deep cut between two ribs. She took off her gloves, dug a handkerchief out of her handbag, and pressed the handkerchief against the cut.

Adler groaned again when she did so. She had to be causing him pain, but that meant he was alive. She could only hope this was the right thing to do.

She looked up when voices sounded outside, echoing in the corridor under the arches. A moment later, two large men with aprons pushed the door wider open. They spoke quickly to each other in Catalan, and one immediately left. The other came to Marina's side. "Is this your husband, madam?"

At least she was moderately certain he'd asked her that. "I'm sorry, I don't speak Catalan," she said in Spanish. "He's not my husband. Mr. Adler is with the American consulate general."

"An American?"

Thank heavens he spoke Spanish. "Yes. He was with my husband, and two men set on them." She could hardly admit that *police* had taken her husband, or the man in the apron would simply walk away. "Mr. Adler told me they took my husband, but I . . . I don't know why they would take him."

"Is your husband American also?" the officer asked.

"No, we're Portuguese."

A man in a black coat came jogging through the door. He surveyed the abandoned restaurant quickly, knelt next to her, and gestured for her to remove her hand. Marina edged back while he peeled away the now-bloody handkerchief. He took one look at the wound, replaced the handkerchief, and rattled off a sentence that she didn't catch. *German*, she guessed, a language in which she only had a few words.

"Do you speak Spanish?" she asked instead.

"Only a little," the man answered. "I am a doctor. Who is this man?"

"William Adler," she supplied. "He's American. He needs a hospital."

"There's one . . . not far, where I am a visitor. I will take him there."

"I *must* find my husband," she insisted. "I must go."

The doctor patted her arm. "Go. go."

Grabbing her handbag first, Marina pushed herself to her feet and headed for the door just as a pair of policemen came dashing into the old restaurant with the man in the apron in pursuit. They weren't the same officers she'd seen before on the Rambla, a fortunate thing. She averted her face and eased past them. *Where has Alejandro gone?* If anyone knew where the police had taken Joaquim, she suspected it was him.

She stepped out from under the gallery of arches into the bright sunlight of the square. Although a few people had gathered around the entry of the old restaurant, most of the plaza's inhabitants sat chatting and drinking as if nothing were wrong. Anger surged through her for a moment, only to flow away and leave her weary. She wanted to cry but didn't have time.

I'll go back to that bench. If Alejandro had run off, perhaps he would go back there. Then again, Joaquim had told him to go back to the hotel. She took a deep breath, gathering her wits. Then she turned and marched across the square back to the entry through which she'd come. There, leaning against one wall, Alejandro waited, his cap in his hand.

Well, at least he'd found his cap. That was one problem she didn't have to solve now. She held out a hand and he set his in it. They came out onto the Rambla, and she immediately turned toward the hotel, walking as fast as she could without dragging Alejandro.

"I'm not going to run away," Alejandro said, a hint of exasperation in his voice. "You could let go."

Marina realized she'd been squeezing his hand in hers and turned him loose. "I'm sorry, Alejandro. I'm upset. Do you know where they took Joaquim?"

"To the prison," Alejandro said without hesitation.

She leaned down closer to him. "Why do they want to take you back there?"

He shrugged.

"Because they need you to make your mother do what they want?" When he nodded, she asked, "But what about your sister? Can't they use her to make your mother do things?"

"She's a girl," Alejandro said. "They don't hurt the girls."

Marina almost stumbled. There weren't just two children at that prison, Alejandro and his sister. There were *girls*. "Only the boys, right?"

"Boys aren't important," he said.

And that meant there were other boys as well. Marina felt the urge to cry return, prickling at the back of her throat. *Botheration!* She hated it when she got weepy. "Well, that's not true, Alejandro. Boys are just as important as girls."

"Not to the sirenas," he said.

They were nearing another pair of police. Alejandro stuck his thumb in his mouth and turned his face toward her skirts, clearly mimicking someone he'd seen before. Marina didn't speak again until they were far past the two men in red and blue. They walked out into the square, and she paused before making up her mind. "I need to go to the American consulate general, to tell them Mr. Adler has been hurt. I have to do that."

The boy looked up at her, eyes narrowed. "It's not your fault, is it?"

"No, but it's the right thing to do." She wondered if he grasped that Adler must be the father of his sister. It likely wasn't important to Alejandro, though, not if he'd been taught that males weren't important, a very sereia attitude.

She led Alejandro over to the cab line near the tram tracks and hailed a cab, suddenly grateful for Joaquim's insistence that they divide up their funds. If he'd carried all the money, she wouldn't have anything. She helped Alejandro up and then called instructions to the driver.

Alejandro remained silent as the cab carried them out toward the harbor. When they arrived at the consulate general, they stepped down and she wrangled for a moment with the driver. He spoke in Catalan and she answered in Spanish. He thought because she was a woman and foreign, he could charge her more money than was reasonable. She finally gave him the same amount Joaquim had paid the drivers on their previous visits and walked on toward the guards at the doors. Familiar with her by now, they let her in without a fuss.

"Please wait here," a secretary said.

As Marina rubbed her fingertips against her left temple, trying to stave off a nascent headache, she spotted Mr. Pinter hurrying down the hallway toward her.

He peered at her from behind his spectacles. "Mrs. Tavares?"

She gestured for him to walk some distance from the desk where they might speak without being overheard. "We met with Mr. Adler on the Rambla this morning. A couple of Mossos set on him and my husband. Mr. Adler was stabbed, and he told me my husband was taken. I don't know where."

Mr. Pinter blinked rapidly. "Adler was stabbed?"

"Yes. I think the police—other officers—conveyed him to the hospital near there."

Mr. Pinter ran a hand through his dark hair. "I'll find Adler. Now, what was that about your husband?"

She took a deep breath to calm herself. "Mr. Adler said the men had taken him. I don't know where or why. Alejandro thinks the prison in Lleida."

"Were you not there during this assault?"

"No," she admitted. "They were all chasing the boy. I'm not particularly fleet of foot, so I stayed behind. When they didn't come back, I went to find them, but only found Mr. Adler."

"These men," Pinter said, drawing a small notebook out of a pocket, "can you describe them?"

She sighed. "They were Mossos. One was heavyset, average height, thirtyish, dark complexion. The other was taller, but thin with a narrow face. Younger as well. That's about all I can tell you. I didn't get much of a look at them."

Pinter pushed his spectacles back up his nose. "That's more of a description than most people would give me. Do you have any idea why they took your husband?"

Her headache was getting the better of her now, making her snappish. "No. Is there anything the consul can do to help?"

His shoulders slumped. "It might be better to go to the Portuguese consulate and have them start making inquiries, since your husband's not an American."

She didn't know enough about consulates and embassies to have any idea if that was true. But they hadn't visited the Portuguese consulate here because they'd been trying not to pull the Foreign Office into this. Marina looked at Pinter and had the sudden urge to touch him, to use her meager *call* to force him to help her.

She closed her eyes for a moment. Pinter seemed to be a good man, and she had to believe he would be helpful without her interfering with his mind. "Please, is there nothing else you can do?"

Pinter nodded. "We can't make official inquiries, Mrs. Tavares, but I'll get some guards out looking for him, and check the hospitals while I'm looking for Adler. I'll let you know what I find."

It wasn't much, but it was more help than she'd had a few minutes ago. "Thank you, Mr. Pinter. I am grateful."

"I'll go take care of that now, Mrs. Tavares. I'll come to your hotel when I have news."

Marina watched him stride away. She'd done the proper thing and advised Adler's people of his injury. Now she was expected to go back to the hotel and wait. "We need to get back to the hotel," she said to Alejandro, "and then you and I need to have a talk."

The carriage dropped Duilio and Oriana at a whitewashed hotel only a short distance from the harbor of Porto Novo. The two-story building had a long ell on each side, leading off the main street. One entire arm of the building had been commandeered by the American mission as their temporary headquarters. American guards stood in the hallways, the colors of their uniforms similar to the Portuguese, but with white belts and caps. Unlike the Portuguese, the guards were men. Reportedly they kept their ears plugged with wax at all times, communicating primarily with a hand language developed for the deaf. One stepped to block their path. "Your business?"

Oriana spoke very little English, so Duilio answered for her. "The Portuguese ambassador and her deputy to speak with Madam Norton."

The guard carefully watched Duilio's lips as he spoke, much as the priest did. *Lip-reading.* The young man asked them to stay in place and waved over another guard. With a series of intricate hand gestures, he silently repeated their request and the second guard strode down the hallway to deliver their message. A moment later, that guard returned and escorted them down the hallway. He reached the last room, opened the door, and ushered them inside.

In the hotel's finest sitting room, Madam Norton ruled over a table covered with papers, a young woman in a smart suit with her. "Mr. Ferreira, Madam Paredes, how can I help you today?"

"We've just returned from a visit with Minister Paredes," Oriana began, "where among other things she informed us that Madam Davila has been arrested. Something to do with a conveniently placed photograph."

Duilio hadn't expected Madam Norton to deny it, but was surprised by the smirk that touched the woman's lips.

Madam Norton held up a hand to signal for her to wait and then asked her aide to leave the room. The young woman gathered up a sheaf of papers and hustled out, closing the door firmly behind her. The ambassador turned back to them. "If there's one thing I know, it's the importance of who possesses a photograph. I don't like when my friends are hurt. As Madam Davila's people are behind what happened to Leandra, I have no qualms over a little espionage."

Duilio reminded himself never to cross the woman.

Oriana went on to summarize her meeting with Jovita Paredes, focusing on what Madam Davila had revealed and the Canary plan to take over the islands by provoking a war between the sereia and Portugal.

Madam Norton didn't look particularly surprised. "Well, that explains quite a few things. Spanish domination of these islands would provide the Canaries with an endless supply of new blood to fill out their numbers. They might eventually control the entirety of Iberia." She sat back in her chair and laced her fingers over one knee. "I left out a few details about Leandra's history at our embassy."

Duilio wondered if they were about to learn the true reason behind the woman's eagerness to aid them.

She told them of a nephew's visit and his subsequent near elope-ment with Leandra. "It now sounds as if neither my friendship with her nor William's attempt to take her abroad provoked her arrest. She would have been accused regardless of her actions."

"Yes," Oriana said.

"Unfortunately, my nephew shares my tenacity. When he learned Leandra was still alive, he made his way to Barcelona. He's been inter-fering in the investigation, I'm afraid. He ended up in the hospital and says that Leandra has been taken up by the police there."

"When?"

"Monday morning. William was taken to the consulate general there, but he slipped away from them again this morning. We *can* get information quickly, Ambassador Paredes, but we have about a day's lag time."

"But you can still get information to them there tonight, right?" Duilio asked.

Madam Norton peered at the clock on the mantel. "We still have time. Why don't you follow me, and we'll try to get your news to Barcelona?"

She rose and led them from the temporary office, back up the hotel hallway, and to another room. She knocked on the door and waited. After a couple of seconds, an older woman in blue opened the door. "We have a pair of soldiers on loan from the army's signal corps," the ambassador said with a glance back at Oriana.

Inside the room, a second young woman in uniform—not the same uniform as the guards in the hallway, but a brighter blue jacket and skirt—sat at a table. A golden device was affixed to her right arm, a mechanical arm built over her own. Silver gears formed the joints, large ones at the shoulder, shrinking down to the most delicate clockwork at the tips of her fingers. The pen in her hand was an integral part of the apparatus, fixed to the mechanical hand, and the delicate gears whirred with each movement of her metal-encased fingers.

An older woman stood near her, feeding notes onto an easel in the seated woman's line of vision, as the younger woman slowly transcribed those notes in large letters on the blank paper before her. Her delicate features were blank as she copied out the words in a trance-like state.

"We only have a few minutes left in our window," the ambassador said to Duilio. She stepped over to the table and wrote a note on a clean sheet of paper and handed it to the standing woman, who quickly perused it and nodded.

"Thank you, Sergeant," the ambassador said to the standing woman, and then shooed Duilio and Oriana back into the hallway. Once the door was shut, she asked, "Are you familiar with the concept of automatic writing? Where a writer jots down words that come into her mind from elsewhere?"

"I heard of it in England," Duilio said.

"Pseudoscience," the ambassador returned. "However, when the concept became popular a couple of decades ago, our army's signal corps decided to develop their own, more scientific, version. It's quite useful when a mission is in an area that has no telegraph or on a ship at sea. I suspect radio wave technology will soon make this obsolete."

Lowering the risk of admitting to the Portuguese that they'd developed it, Duilio guessed. "Where does the message go from here?"

"Fort Myers, in Virginia," the ambassador answered. "The receiver is an identical device, manned by another of the writers there."

No doubt the devices, like most magical devices he'd seen before, were fueled by blood. "Can anyone use those?"

The ambassador smiled. "On this end, yes. Not on the other end. The receivers—the soldiers at Fort Myers who man the other end around the clock—must have natural receptivity, something the signal corps hasn't yet been able to quantify. Simple witchery, if you ask me. But each distant office reaches out to them on a schedule so we're not overrunning each other's messages. That turns into a mess and no one's information gets through."

"So there's only one receiver?"

"At any moment, yes." The ambassador led them back to her temporary chancery. "Fort Myers will forward the information to Barcelona for us. While it's not instantaneous, it's far faster than a pigeon."

"And not vulnerable to hawks," Duilio agreed, mulling over the constraints of having only one receiver. "Can you receive messages this way?"

"Unfortunately not," she said, "which is why my information is a day old. For us to get messages *from* Barcelona, we have to wait on the damned pigeons."

CHAPTER 32

BARCELONA

Marina went through their baggage while Alejandro finished the last of his lunch. She wasn't certain whether she could access the Ferreira family's funds at the bank. The letter of credit for the Bank of Barcelona had Joaquim's name on it, not hers. But Joaquim had hidden some of his cash in the inner pocket of his bag. There, tucked between the bills, she found the playing card she'd given him. She peered at it, her throat tight. She wasn't superstitious enough to believe he'd been taken because he'd not had it with him.

Not quite, but it crossed her mind anyway.

Shaking her head at her foolishness, she slipped the card into her passport to ensure that she didn't lose it. She would just have to find Joaquim and give him the card again. She took the remaining money and divided it between her luggage and her handbag.

Then she settled at the table across from Alejandro and watched him as he consumed a second *coca*, a small piece of bread with meat and tomato sauce on it. Even as late as they were for lunch, she didn't think she could eat anything. The boy eyed her warily.

Whom else can I ask? She knew she shouldn't force a child to deal with her problems, but she didn't know where else to turn. If

Alejandro was a seer at all, he might give her some guidance. She took a breath. "Will my husband come back?"

He glanced up at her, then shook his head no.

Marina laid her hand over her mouth, holding in the sobs that threatened to well out. She calmed herself and folded her hands together in her lap, where Alejandro couldn't see her rubbing at the missing webbing. "You know things, don't you? Things you're not supposed to tell me, right?"

Alejandro regarded her with his brows drawn together dramatically, but didn't answer.

She leaned closer. "Alejandro, did you know they were going to take Joaquim?"

The boy shifted on his chair, but still didn't answer, eyes fixed on a corner of a table.

She wasn't going to threaten him. It sounded as if his whole life had been one threat after another. But she could use anything he knew to better build her plan to find Joaquim, and she wanted the best plan she could construct before . . .

She could *not* be the first person to realize that. His mother surely knew he had a seer's gift. "Alejandro," she asked gently, "is there a plan?"

His lips pursed then, as if he wasn't sure how he should answer.

"You don't need to tell me what the plan is," she said. "I only need to know if there is one."

He nodded slowly.

"Your mother's plan?" When he shook his head, she pressed further. "Whose, then?"

"The Vilaró's," he said.

The prisoner who lived at the bottom of the prison who'd taught him Portuguese? "Was Joaquim being taken to the prison part of his plan?"

"He's supposed to find the key. I didn't know the Mossos would take him."

How else would Joaquim end up in a prison? Marina felt a stab of anger, but shook her head to drive it away. Alejandro was only a child. "The key?"

"The key for the Vilaró's chains. No one knows where it is."

And they need a finder to locate it. Marina slumped in the chair, but sat up straight again when she realized she was setting a bad example. "The key's in the prison, though, right? Will the Vilaró free him if he finds the key? And your mother?"

"All of them," the boy said. "The Vilaró's going to break the prison."

Joaquim woke with a horrendous headache and a throbbing in his right arm. He opened his eyes, but the world around him was dim. When he tried to push up onto his elbows to get a better look, a stab of pain from his arm made him flinch. Nausea surged through him and he set his left hand atop his stomach to get the sensation under control. He closed his eyes and breathed deeply for a moment.

"So you're awake," a feminine voice said. "Best lie still until the effects of the chloroform wear off. You've been under for several hours."

He opened his eyes to see a shadowy form standing over him. Not close enough for him to touch her. "Where am I?"

"Prison," the woman said. "In my infirmary."

"In Lleida? I'm at the Unnaturals Prison?"

The woman chuckled. "You are in Lleida, but you're not at the main prison. You're in the Morra."

His head was spinning again. "The what?"

But whatever the woman had to say was lost as he slid back into unconsciousness.

Marina had spent part of the afternoon reading to Alejandro from the book he'd claimed as his own. The story followed a man in Africa as he and a group of other men sought out a gold mine, guided by a map left behind by an old Portuguese explorer. Not having read the first half of the novel, Marina could make little sense of it, but she read anyway, desperate to have something to distract her from the waiting. And Alejandro liked the book better than the one she'd read to him before.

When a knock came at the sitting room door, she jumped up and ran to answer. Mr. Pinter waited outside, his tired hat clutched in his hands. "Mrs. Tavares, I don't have much news, but I wanted to let you know that Mr. Adler is safely in the hospital."

"Will he live?"

"He might," Pinter said. "The stab wound caused his lung to collapse. We'll have a better idea in the morning whether he'll make it."

Marina crossed herself and said a quick prayer of thanks. Even if she didn't like Adler, she didn't want him dead. "Have you heard anything from the guards looking for my husband?"

"No, Mrs. Tavares. The Mossos claim there were no orders to apprehend the boy. Someone must have paid the officers to look for him. Paid them on the side, if you know what I mean."

Well, they'd been warned that the Canaries had probably suborned men all over the country. "Thank you for checking, Mr. Pinter."

"I'd advise you to wait here until your husband returns so we can keep you in touch with your people back on the islands." Pinter withdrew a sealed envelope. "This was sent to your husband, but I feel safe handing it over to you."

Marina took the envelope and thanked him. "Can you send word to them, and tell them my husband has been taken prisoner?"

"I can," he said, "although any message will take a day at a minimum to reach them."

"Could you please do so anyway?"

"I'll do so as soon as possible, Mrs. Tavares. If Adler pulls through, he'll owe his life to you for going to his aid." Mr. Pinter tilted his head in a mock bow, donned his hat, and headed off down the hallway.

Marina locked the door. She'd listened to his advice to stay at the hotel without protest, but she wouldn't follow it. She couldn't simply wait here and do nothing, even if she had Alejandro's assurance that this unknown prisoner would free her husband. She couldn't afford to rely on the man's plan.

Alejandro wasn't in the sitting area any longer, so Marina crossed to the bedroom and peered inside. Alejandro had curled up atop the bed, and seeing him there, she wondered whether she was growing too attached to him. She'd always wanted to have children. And she wouldn't mind taking care of them, despite her people's belief that it was males' work. She didn't know why Alejandro had called her his *new* mother, but it was going to break her heart when Leandra came to take him back.

Sighing, she drew the bedroom door mostly closed and returned to the table to open the envelope that Mr. Pinter had given her. The words were taken from a telegram, she guessed, and translated into Spanish here in Barcelona. *LR one of twenty-four.*

Marina rubbed her temples, suddenly grasping what the message meant. They'd already figured out there were others beyond Leandra, other sereia stolen from the islands. Alejandro had verified that. But twenty-four?

She couldn't sit here and do nothing. And there was one thing she could do tonight to help solve this puzzle. Marina dug her mother's journal out of her handbag and passed the time looking through it. Not reading the words, but studying the capitalization as Duilio had suggested. Apparently, Leandra had worked on that as well, following the same clues. She'd circled each of the capitalized letters and, farther back in the unused pages of the journal, painstakingly recorded each one, four entire pages of letters that meant nothing.

Outside, the sky had grown dusky, red where the sun was setting. If it *was* a cipher, all Marina had to do was determine what each letter stood for. If she counted how many times each letter was used, then the one that appeared most often could usually be exchanged for A. The second would be E, and then O, S, and R should follow in turn. If she could figure *those* out, the rest might fall into place. So she sat and counted letters, making lists on the hotel stationery. Once she had those, she copied out the first half page on a piece of stationery with ample space around the letters. Then she wrote her first guesses under the corresponding letters.

After staring at those jumbled letters for a time, she pinched her nose. She wasn't focusing well. She got up and went to stare out the window into the darkness, out over the plaza where people hurried past. On the edge of the city in the direction of the sea, she could see the mountain. Montjuic, Joaquim had called it, where the remains of an old castle stood. A storm was creeping over the ridge toward the city, gray and gloomy skies that suited her mood. Lightning flashed in a spectacular display.

"Are you watching the people?" Alejandro had come up behind her. Shoeless, the boy hadn't made a sound.

"I'm watching the storm come in," she said honestly.

He yawned widely. "I don't like storms."

"Most of the time they're harmless," she said.

The boy shrugged. Marina had decided that was his standard response when he had nothing more to say. She rubbed her aching back. "How often did you get to see your mother at the prison?"

"Once a month." He puffed out his cheeks. "Then they sent us to the islands, so I got to spend whole days with her." He sounded wistful.

"Was that nice?"

His head tilted. "She was tired a lot. She's sick."

He hadn't said *yes*. "Bad?"

"She's going to go away," the boy said in a matter-of-fact voice. "She said so."

Does he understand what he just said? Marina swallowed. Given that he'd been raised in a prison, people had probably left his life before, never to return. "I'm sure she doesn't want to."

"My mother loves me," he said defiantly.

She wasn't quite sure why he'd said that. "What is your sister's name?"

"Liliana," he said in a sulky tone. "She's mean."

Marina had only one sister, who'd been very protective of her, but the same couldn't be said of her older cousins. They'd been as mean as crabs. "Does she look like you?"

His lips pursed. "No. She's blond and all pale. She always calls me webless."

Liliana must take after Adler in appearance. "She does sound mean. I used to be called webless all the time, and I hated it."

He looked up at her then. "You're not webless."

"No. They used to call me that because I'm small. And I blush."

"I'm small too," he said.

"Well, you'll get taller eventually," she said firmly. "Neither of your brothers is short."

"Brothers?" Alejandro asked, his expression wary.

Of course, he only knows about Joaquim. "When you took the book from the house on the island," she added, "do you remember there was a man sleeping in that room? That was Duilio, your other brother, Joaquim's brother."

His brow rumpled. "I didn't want to steal from him. I had to."

"He knows that." Marina set her hands on the boy's shoulders. "They want to help you and your mother, and they know you've both had to do things you didn't want."

He nodded, his eyes downcast.

She suspected she'd just made a huge understatement. "Tomorrow morning, I'd like to take a train again. Will that hurt the plan?"

"We *have* to go."

Interesting. She reached out to brush a lock of hair back from Alejandro's forehead, but he flinched away. She tried again, more slowly, and brushed the hair from the boy's forehead, then laid her hand against his cheek. "I'm not going to hit you. Not ever."

"I know," he said quietly.

Was that something he foreknew? Or was he just giving her the answer he thought she wanted? In a way she was relieved he was here. If she didn't have him to look after, she would be out of her mind with worry over Joaquim. Alejandro served as an excellent distraction.

CHAPTER 33

Joaquim woke again, rising out of dreams of confused images. He lay on a hard bed, narrow and smelling of musty old stone. His head ached, his right arm felt tight and confined, and there was something about his left wrist. He lifted his left arm to look at it, only to have it jerk to a stop after only a few inches.

His left hand was cuffed to the iron frame of the bed.

"*Shit*," he said under his breath.

He wasn't given to cussing. Not aloud, at least. So he lifted his free arm to cross himself contritely and saw a bandage wrapped about his right wrist. He stared at it dully, wondering where it had come from. He didn't recall injuring that arm, but it felt tight and achy. "Marina?"

A dark form came closer to him, a woman bearing a lamp—definitely not his wife. She dragged a chair closer and set her lamp on a table beyond his reach. She turned the lamp up, and for the first time Joaquim got a good view of his location.

The ceiling above him was stone. The walls were stone. The room had only a trio of narrow beds and the single small table. Joaquim turned his head to one side to take in his captor. A woman of middle years with dark hair going gray, she wore the garb of a nurse, a tidy white apron and cap over a somber black dress. She regarded him with curiosity in her hazel eyes. "How are you feeling, Mr. Ferreira?"

Joaquim chuckled, but that quickly turned into a cough. The woman helped him sit up and held a tin cup to his lips. The water soothed his throat. He hadn't realized it was so dry. He took the cup in his free hand and quickly downed the remaining water. "I'm not Alexandre Ferreira."

She smiled gently. "Of course not, but they don't know that. What is your name?"

Her accent sounded Andalusian, not Castilian. "Joaquim Tavares. Where am I?"

"I suspect you don't recall much. You're in Lleida, in the Morra."

Lleida was the town with the prison, but that last word sounded suspiciously like death. "What's the Morra?"

She sighed. "It's a separate prison, an old one built in the cellars of the town hall itself. The sirenas keep special prisoners here."

Special? He looked at his companion more closely. The hair pulled back from her face had a wiry curl to it, and her wide cheekbones gave her an exotic look. He would put her age between forty and fifty. "Are you a prisoner as well?"

"Yes," the woman said. "I'm called Prieto. I'm the healer here."

He glanced down at his bandaged wrist. "What happened to me?"

"They branded you, I'm afraid," she said, "while you were drugged. That's why you can't remember."

Branded? He tugged at the bandage with his cuffed hand, setting off another wave of pain.

"Stop," she ordered in a voice of authority. "You'll tear the wound."

He went still. "Why would they . . . ?"

She unbuttoned her white sleeve and showed him her right forearm. An old scar marked her arm just above the wrist, pale against her dark skin—a B. "So that all know my sin," she said. "*Bruja.*"

That was close enough to the Portuguese word that he recognized it. They had marked him as a *witch*? He wished Marina was here to help him with his execrable Spanish, and then unwished it. He didn't want her here. "How do they know I'm a witch?"

"Alejandro is a witch, so you must be."

He nearly choked again—oh yes, they'd assumed Alejandro was his son. "I've never even seen his mother."

She gazed at him levelly. "Yes, I know. But there's an incredible likeness between you and the boy, especially around the eyes. And you were defending him from the Mossos. What else were they to assume? Don't rub," the woman said. "You'll disturb the poultice and tear the skin."

He realized he'd set his fingers over the aching spot on his wrist. He jerked them away. "Thank you for reminding me, Miss Prieto."

"You are leverage," she said in answer to his question. "As they do not have Alejandro to force Leandra's obedience, they will use you."

He hadn't quite caught all those words, but inferred their meaning from context. It didn't bode well for him. Being used as leverage couldn't be pleasant. "Is Leandra here? In this prison?"

"Yes. I'm not sure if she will leave it alive this time, but you will. You're here for a purpose."

"A purpose?"

She nodded. "When they discover that Leandra truly doesn't know you, they'll take you to the main prison. You'll receive more instructions there."

"Instructions?" He heard footsteps on the stone of the dark hallway outside. "What does that mean?"

She leaned closer and whispered, "Please forgive us, but we are desperate."

"Prieto!" A guard dressed in a gray uniform stood outside the bars. "Piedad's waiting on you."

The healer rose and gazed down at Joaquim. "One of the guards will unchain you so you can use the chamber pot," she said loudly enough to be heard in the hallway. "Don't make a mess of my infirmary."

With that she left, locking the door behind her. Joaquim regarded those iron bars, mind whirling. What was happening here? If he was to receive instructions, then surely they had a plan for him. That meant they'd known *he* would be captured in Alejandro's place.

He stared up at the stone ceiling. What had become of Alejandro? And Adler? What was Marina doing? Was she safe? Joaquim closed his eyes to fight back bitter tears. He was cowardly, being more concerned for his own fate than his wife's. How could he not have thought of her first?

He covered his face with his hand and prayed that God would protect her through this trial. He felt better afterward, that first flush of anguish eased.

He hoped she would think to send a telegram to Lady Ferreira. His foster mother would, no doubt, swoop down and retrieve Marina from Barcelona. Or the American consulate general could help her. He doubted they could get him out of a Spanish prison, but they could instruct Marina in how to get home safely. Even the Portuguese consulate could do that for her.

Marina was resourceful, even if she doubted her courage. She had found a way to escape the islands and find her father in Portugal. She'd made a new life for herself. Even the day he'd met her, she'd been fighting the man who'd attacked her. She would figure out what to do.

And he would figure out a way out of this place.

Or perhaps, sooner or later, justice would prevail.

He nearly laughed at that thought. *It so often does not.*

A burly guard appeared at the door, unlocked it, and set his lamp inside. He looked at Joaquim and hefted a set of keys. "I'm going to unlock your manacle so you can piss. You try anything, I'll shoot you. Understand?"

———

Marina had spent a mostly sleepless night. She had *tried* to sleep. She wasn't doing Joaquim any good by tossing and turning. But sleep had eluded her, so she'd tugged and pulled at the maze of problems that surrounded her.

She'd dismissed the idea of going to the police. The Portuguese consulate wouldn't be any more help than the Americans, she suspected. They would urge her to return to the Golden City. Mr. Adler was in the hospital and wasn't in any shape to be helpful either. And while Pinter did have guards out collecting information, she wasn't going to wait for results.

Marina picked the smallest of their bags and in it placed only two outfits and as few toiletries as possible, as well as Alejandro's spare clothing. She moved all but a handful of the paper money to her luggage and, after a moment's consideration, Alejandro's book as well. It might add weight, but it pleased Alejandro.

"Where are we going?" Alejandro asked from the doorway to the bathroom.

"We're going back to Terrassa," she said.

He didn't argue. He came and sat on the bed while she finished packing.

"Will she help us?" Marina asked. "The marquesa?"

Alejandro's eyes took on a faraway look that reminded her of Joaquim when he was trying to find someone. "Maybe. Not sure."

Well, that meant the woman *might*. Marina had to figure out the right way to get the marquesa to do her bidding. She could touch the old woman, but her *call* didn't work as well on females, and thus might only annoy the marquesa. No, she had to find some other way to persuade the woman to help Joaquim. "We'll stop and get some breakfast at the station," she said to Alejandro. "Will that be soon enough?"

He nodded, so she put her mother's journal on top of the bag's contents and closed it up. Then she and Alejandro left the hotel room, locking the door firmly behind them. The room was paid up for a couple of weeks, so it should still be theirs when they returned. She closed her eyes and said a quick prayer that it wouldn't take that long.

The telegraph office was close to the hotel, so they walked there first. She sent a short message to Lady Ferreira stating that Joaquim was in trouble and that she would send more information later. She hoped that by the time *later* came, she'd have more to say. Then they headed back toward the line of cabs waiting patiently at the edge of the Plaça de Catalunya. One of the drivers caught her eye and she drew Alejandro in that direction, but a hand on her arm stopped her.

Startled, Marina jerked away, putting Alejandro behind her.

The woman who'd touched her stood with hands held wide now. "I mean no harm, Miss Arenias."

The woman might not be wearing that same shirtwaist Marina had admired before, but she recognized the woman's narrow face now. It was the woman she'd seen earlier, both in Barcelona and at the train station at Madrid. But she hadn't used the name Arenias in either of those places. A prickle of fear spread down Marina's spine. "What do you want?"

"I was hired by Jovita Paredes to watch over your safety. I've been following you since you left the islands."

Marina reached behind her blindly and Alejandro's hand slid into hers. "Why?"

"I'm here to collect evidence, not to interfere with you, but when I saw your mate was taken, I knew I had to offer my aid. I can't help find him—that's beyond my assignment—but if you need to get anything back to the islands, I can see that it reaches there safely."

Marina thought of the journal in her bag with its encrypted message. She hadn't worked out the whole cipher yet, and wanted to finish it herself. On the other hand, if she handed it over, she could concentrate her whole effort on finding her husband.

But she didn't know if she could trust anyone her aunt had hired. "I'll consider it."

The woman seemed disappointed, but didn't argue. "I'm at the Gran Hotel on the Rambla del Centro," she said, "if you need my help, come there."

Marina regarded her silently for a moment, fixing that face in her memory. "I may do that," she said, and quickly drew Alejandro to the waiting cab. Once they'd settled, she glanced back, but the woman had already gone on her way.

Unnerved, Marina kept Alejandro's hand in hers until they were safely seated on the train. He warily eyed the other passengers in the car, and then settled back with his arms across his chest. There weren't any others sitting close enough to them to overhear, so Marina decided to pry more information out of the boy. "Will you tell me about the Vilaró?"

Alejandro's mouth pursed. "He was nice to me. I gave him my bread."

"Why?"

"You're supposed to give him bread."

Perhaps the Canaries weren't feeding him, and Alejandro had been slipping him food. "Why is he in the prison? Is he a witch?"

As the train lurched into motion, Alejandro shook his head. "He's a fairy."

He'd delivered that in a perfectly serious tone. About all she knew of fairies was that they were rare now, and kept their distance from humans. Beyond that? In stories, they granted wishes to sailors who pulled stones out of fishes' bellies or made princesses out of scullery maids. To be honest, she'd never given them much thought, as she'd never expected to meet one.

There were people who didn't believe sereia existed. Given, her people's islands were the last free colony of sereia known, but there were the Canaries, and stories about other sereia throughout the world. Unfortunately, most of the smaller groups of sereia hadn't had enough males to breed true and eventually died off. Their children by human mates had, over the generations, become more and more human until the very traits that made them sereia bred out. That was one reason the oligarchy on Quitos was so adamantly against allowing humans on the island. Quitos was seen as *pure*.

"Alejandro, how many Canaries are at the prison?"

He gave her a strange look.

Marina wished she could shake answers out of him. Either it was a question he wasn't supposed to answer, or . . . she'd asked the wrong question.

She opened the bag of meat pies she'd purchased outside the train station. They weren't the kind she was accustomed to, more like a circle of soft bread folded in half over the stuffing. They smelled tasty anyway. She handed one wrapped in paper to Alejandro, and he immediately stuffed half into his mouth.

Once he'd eaten two of the pies, she tried again. "The women who run the prison. How many are there?"

He shrugged. "Twenty?"

The prison, especially one that held other prisoners, couldn't be large enough to hold a whole population, but the Canaries were spread across Spain now, if the American ambassador's information was correct. Even so, twenty was *negligible*. "Does that include your mother?" When he shook his head, she asked, "And the other women like your mother? The ones who spoke Portuguese. How many of them?"

His eyes closed as he calculated. "Eight? Not sure."

Had there been twenty-four at one point? She doubted Alejandro knew the answer to that. "Why are you not sure?"

"Some want to stay there. My mother doesn't count them."

Marina sat back, rubbing one hand with the other. If there had been twenty-four, some must have defected to support the Canaries. That seemed to put Leandra in the minority. "Alejandro, do you know how your mother got to Barcelona? Back before you were born, I mean."

He took another bite of his meat pie. "The Vilaró said she escaped. She took Liliana and ran away when Liliana was just a baby. Capitan Captaire helped her. Or she helped him. I'm not sure."

So Leandra had been trying to escape for years, but many of the others didn't feel that way. After all, had the islands done anything to save them? They must feel abandoned and betrayed. And if she guessed correctly, they had children to protect, children who might be hurt if they did try to escape. She glanced over at Alejandro again. What would *she* do if someone threatened him?

CHAPTER 34

LLEIDA

Joaquim didn't know how long he'd waited in that cell before footsteps on the stone outside warned him of more visitors. This time it was *two* guards. Either was large enough to take him on his own, so when they stepped into his cell, he didn't bother to try to fight. *Better to save my energy.*

One of the guards unchained him from the bed, and the other stepped behind him and dropped a hood over his head.

"Let's go meet a new friend," he said, and shoved Joaquim in the direction of the door.

Joaquim walked, unable to see, but guided by the grasp of the first guard on his left arm. The mask was unnecessary—once he'd been somewhere he could *always* find it again. But they thought he was a seer, not a finder. Once out of the cell, they pushed him along a stone hallway, turned down another, and then another after a moment.

The guard dragged Joaquim to a stop, keeping a tight grasp on his arm. He yanked off the hood, and Joaquim blinked a moment in the lamplight until his eyes adjusted.

Inside a cell stood two women, elegantly garbed—a young one all in white, and the other, a graying matron, in a charcoal suit with black accents. A third woman sat in a chair, her arms bound behind her. That was Leandra Rocha, without a doubt. Joaquim recognized her narrow face and tired eyes. She didn't seem frightened, though, as she had in that photograph. Instead her eyes stared off into an empty corner of the cell, the very image of exhaustion.

She still wore the garb she'd had on in the photograph. Her shirtwaist was spattered with blood, mostly dried to a sickly brown, and one eye was swollen almost shut. Her white shirt collar had been pulled down to expose a neck that looked as if it had been savaged by a wild dog in the past. It took Joaquim a moment to realize that her gills had been cut out, leaving hideous scars. The neck clap she'd worn on the islands had hidden that. He swallowed, his stomach turning. That had to have been Dr. Serpa's work. *What did they do to her?*

"Do you see who we've found for you, Leandra?" the white-garbed woman asked in a sweet voice with a Castilian lisp. She was young, no older than Marina, her straight hair pulled back neatly from a lovely face. Her white shirtwaist and skirt made her look pure and innocent. It brought to mind the garb of a religious novice, though, rather than a debutante. "It's Alejandro's father," she added, "come to visit you."

She gestured sharply, and the guards pushed Joaquim down onto another chair, where he faced Leandra. One jerked his arms behind him and proceeded to tie them, the rope tight across the bandages on Joaquim's burned forearm. He hissed with renewed pain.

Leandra gazed at him with resignation, and lifted her eyes to face the white-garbed girl. "Piedad, he isn't Alejandro's father. I don't know where you got him, but he's about thirty years too young."

Joaquim took a deep breath. This wasn't going to go well for him. "I've seen a photograph of this woman before," he agreed, "but that's all."

The young woman in the white dress—Piedad—walked over to a small table and donned a glove. As she approached him, Joaquim saw it was more of a gauntlet, metal plating the back. She raised her hand and backhanded him across his face, hard enough that his vision went black for a second. Then he realized his eyes were closed. He fought for a moment to get them to open. He blinked rapidly as the pain subsided. He'd been hit harder by Alessio as a boy, but he was moderately sure she'd just broken his nose. And the metal had cut his face in at least one spot. Blood trickled down one side of his jaw and pooled hot on his upper lip. He waited a moment until the blood trickled into his mouth, and then sputtered out a breath, splattering Piedad's white garb with red.

Her chilly metal-encased fingers stroked the side of his face. Then she wiped her hand down the front of her shirtwaist, leaving streaks of his blood behind. "You're the Portuguese who's come looking for Leandra. If you're not the boy's father, then why?"

Does it matter what I tell her? "I was sent for the book, not her. I hoped the boy could lead me to it."

Leandra gazed at him, a guarded expression on her tired face.

Piedad laid her hand under his chin. "And what have you done with the book?"

"I don't have it," Joaquim said. "The boy didn't know where it was."

She leaned closer and smiled for the first time, revealing teeth that had been filed down to points. The sight sent a chill down Joaquim's spine. "Try again," she said.

"The boy didn't know where it was," Joaquim repeated. He swallowed, tasting blood. *The journal is fourteen years old. Why do they need it so badly?*

Piedad abruptly turned back to Leandra. "So, tell me, Leandra, where's the book?"

Leandra gazed across at him but didn't answer.

After a moment of silence, Piedad turned back and struck Joaquim across the face again. Better prepared this time, he swayed with the motion, but still felt his teeth rattle.

"Are you sure you don't want to tell me?" Piedad asked, hand poised to strike Joaquim again.

When Leandra didn't answer, another blow fell, and then another.

Joaquim spat out blood. His collar felt wet with blood now, warm and sticky.

"She hasn't flinched," the woman in gray said from behind him. "She doesn't know him. Don't ruin his pretty face for nothing."

Feeling dizzy, Joaquim figured his pretty face was probably already ruined.

"I want answers," his tormentor insisted.

"Try something else," the unseen woman said firmly.

"Yes, Reyna," Piedad said. She turned to look over Joaquim's shoulder, toward the guards in the cell's doorway. "Bring *her* in."

Joaquim heard the guards moving out of the cell. They weren't gone long before he heard them returning, a high-pitched voice protesting. That voice belonged to a pretty young girl with curling flaxen hair, a girl not much older than Alejandro, but taller and better fed. One of the guards had his hand wrapped about her upper arm as he dragged her to stand between Joaquim and Leandra. The girl took in the scene with frightened disdain.

"Do you know why you're here, Liliana?" the unseen woman—Reyna—asked.

The girl shrugged dismissively. "That woman's done something wrong again."

Joaquim felt a twinge of sorrow for Leandra. The girl had surely been trained to act that way, but it must sting, particularly considering all her mother had endured for her sake.

"What happens when she does something wrong?"

The girl tugged but wasn't strong enough to escape the guard's grasp.

Joaquim licked blood from his lips. Were they actually going to hurt her?

Piedad slipped off the gauntlet and dropped it on the floor. She moved to the girl's side. "Usually I have your brother, but not today."

And before Joaquim could protest, she backhanded the girl.

Liliana screamed, her dark eyes wide with shock. Her cry sent chills down Joaquim's spine; she already showed a hint of a sereia's power. Free hand pressed to the side of her face, she huddled toward the guard who held her captive.

Piedad turned toward Leandra. "Now let us try again. Where is the book?"

"Stop this," Joaquim said before she could strike the terrified girl again. *What can I claim that won't make us expendable?* "She doesn't know. Not any longer."

But that caught Piedad's attention. "And do you?"

"The Americans have it. They're planning on using it to trade for prisoners."

Leandra's shoulders slumped. She couldn't know whether he was telling the truth, but his claim sounded plausible.

One of Piedad's fingernails pricked under his chin, forcing his chin up. "Which prisoners?"

"Leandra and the girl, I think. I doubt they know you have me."

Piedad's eyes narrowed. "And why would the Americans want them?"

"Because that girl is William Adler's daughter, and therefore an American citizen." He had no idea if that last part was true, but he suspected they wouldn't know either.

The girl cast a horrified glance at him, mouth agape, making Joaquim wonder if she'd ever heard her father's name before. "I'm not webless," she protested.

Ah, she's upset that she's half human. How could she not have known?

"Yes, you are," Piedad said nastily. "Your mother always had poor taste."

"Enough, Piedad," the older woman said. "We have our answer. There's no point in damaging them further."

"Yes, Reyna," Piedad said dutifully. She gestured toward the guard holding Liliana's arm and he dragged her back out of the cell. "And get Prieto up here," she called after him.

Joaquim heard the men's footsteps retreat, leaving the prisoners alone with the two women. Piedad eyed him speculatively, as if she wanted to continue the beatings for her own enjoyment. There were people like that, who relished hurting others, some basic thread of humanity in them missing. Piedad might be young, but they'd probably noticed her penchant for violence early on. That made her a tool for the woman named Reyna. With one final—comparatively gentle—slap to Joaquim's cheek, Piedad followed the men.

The other woman came closer and peered into Joaquim's face, then began humming. She'd been beautiful when young, he could tell, and had resorted to cosmetics to maintain the image of youth. Too much rouge, and cherry-stained lips against papery-pale skin. He recognized the faint *call* woven into her tune. Its wispy touch wrapped around him, no more effective than the naval blockade had been. *What is she trying to get me to do?*

He listened closely to the tendrils of magic slipping past him, and felt the urge to lie down and sleep. Joaquim let his body go slack against the ropes that bound him, his aching head falling forward. It made the throbbing of his nose worse, but after a moment of shamming, the woman's hum ceased. Joaquim stayed still.

"Odd that he looks so much like your son, Leandra, yet you deny he's Alejandro's father."

The woman believed him asleep, a small victory.

"He's far too young," Leandra replied. "Perhaps this is one of his brothers."

"And Liliana's father is in Barcelona as well? I assume he was the blond fellow the Mossos beat up. Every time you leave this place you accumulate males willing to suffer for you."

Leandra didn't respond.

"Did you hope they would trade the book for you and your daughter?"

"I know better than to believe you'll let me out of the Morra alive," Leandra finally answered. "I want Liliana out."

That wasn't true, Joaquim realized. If she'd meant for someone to negotiate Liliana's freedom, she would have given the book to Adler and told him the truth. The Americans had enough influence to sway the Spanish government. Instead Leandra had hidden the book and let the Mossos bring her back here. It was an effort to buy time, but for what?

"*We are desperate*," Miss Prieto had said.

"Liliana is our future," Reyna said. "It's one thing to let little Alejandro slip away. He's an *aberración*, not acceptable breeding stock. Liliana, on the other hand, is exactly what we need."

Joaquim felt ill hearing children described as breeding stock.

"That man's right," Leandra responded. "The Americans are going to insist on her, not me. She's one of their citizens. You'd be lucky to get the book in trade at all."

"I will have it," Reyna snapped.

"To force the islands to sell you more of us? Perhaps a few males as well? By now they have to have realized the promised Spanish takeover will never happen."

Reyna laughed. "Minister Raposo is too afraid the book will reveal her willingness to betray her own kind for the mere promise of power. She will negotiate with me, to prevent her own downfall." Joaquim heard her feet move farther away. "If his information turns out to be wrong," she added, "we'll have this conversation again."

Then she retreated as well. After a moment passed in silence, Joaquim opened his eyes and lifted his head. The throbbing in his face ebbed. "Are you hurt?"

It was a foolish question. He had no doubt she was hurt.

"You're awake?" Leandra asked, surprise in her soft voice. "You should sleep for hours."

"My wife's a sereia," Joaquim said.

"Ah, I see. And you've met William Adler? Is he safe?"

"He was stabbed," he admitted. "Whether he lives I have no idea."

"Poor William," she said softly. "You lied about the Americans trading for me, didn't you?"

Could there be someone still listening to us? Joaquim chose his words carefully. "They may have the journal by now. They may not. You were correct, by the way. Alexandre Ferreira fathered me."

Her face lifted, a blur in the dark. "You're the youngest son? The one he could never talk to?"

Other than the dull sensation that he was bleeding all over himself, the pain from his face wasn't too bad. His arm was a different matter. He forced himself to focus on Leandra's words instead. "What do you mean?"

"He told me he had three sons. The eldest was too much like him, the middle too little like him, and the youngest he couldn't acknowledge."

Joaquim chuckled wetly, which set the cuts on his face to burning again. This was the first time he'd ever heard of Alexandre Ferreira admitting his paternity to anyone, and he had to hear it now, in this horrid place. "Yes, I'm that third son," he said. "Joaquim."

"I don't remember much about Ferreira, but for some reason that tidbit about his sons stuck in my memory."

Perhaps it had stuck so that *he* could hear it one day. Joaquim licked his lips, the coppery taste of blood on them. "What happens to us now?"

"They'll take you to the other prison, put you in with Marcos. He's trustworthy. I cannot tell you how sorry I am about this, but we were desperate. We needed you here. I never thought they would treat you this way."

That statement was followed by a fit of coughing that went on longer than Joaquim liked. He could understand her desperate situation better now. When her fit ended, he asked, "How ill are you?"

"I'm dying," she said without inflection.

"Tuberculosis?" He'd seen someone else with it recently. The exhaustion and coughing combined were telling.

"Yes," she said. "Almost three years now."

Most people with tuberculosis of the lungs only lasted a few years once it was diagnosed, enough time to get their affairs in order . . . or plan an escape from prison. Joaquim turned his head toward the cell door. It seemed that the light was increasing, though, as if someone approached with another lamp. Then he heard the jangle of keys. The cell door creaked open again.

Miss Prieto walked into the cell and set her lamp on something behind Joaquim. She carried her bag over to Leandra first and began cutting the ropes that bound Leandra's arms. "What did they do to you?"

"A few cuts," the woman answered wearily. "And Piedad broke two of my fingers. My arms are numb, so I don't know how bad they are. Can you splint them?"

The healer slowly lifted Leandra's left arm and set her hand in her lap. The two outermost fingers were visibly twisted and swollen. "Give it a few minutes and these are going to hurt."

"Check on him first," Leandra said, pointing with her chin. "I think Piedad broke his nose."

Joaquim didn't argue with that assessment.

The healer came to his side and began cutting his bonds, surveying his injuries as she did so. "She used the gauntlet on you, didn't she? She prefers that for men."

Apparently this was a common occurrence in this place. Joaquim's arms fell free and immediately he felt the sting of blood returning to that brand on his arm. "She hits hard enough without it."

The healer shook her head as she looked at Joaquim's nose. "She likes the blood. Yes, this is broken. I'll have to realign it." Her fingers brushed his nose and Joaquim fought the urge to jerk back from her gentle touch. She must be controlling his pain, though, because it didn't hurt nearly as badly as he'd expected. Then her fingers settled on the bridge of his nose, she jerked quickly to one side, and that *did* hurt. Joaquim hissed in an agonized breath, gritting his teeth together until the flare of pain subsided. "Try not to hit your nose for a while," the healer advised.

"I have a feeling your Piedad's going to do it for me," he gasped out.

She turned to the other captive. "Leandra, can you feel your fingers yet?"

"No," the woman said softly.

"Then let's get this done before you do." The healer knelt in front of Leandra, blocking Joaquim's view. He didn't want to see this anyway. He could hear the pop of bone moving against bone at one point, his own fingers curling reflexively into fists. He grimaced, his stomach turning, and that set his cheek to stinging again. Leandra's jaw clenched, but she didn't flinch. *How many times has this happened to her?*

The healer searched her satchel and produced a length of bandage to secure the fingers to the middle finger. "I'll try to ease the swelling," she said as she bound the woman's fingers, "but I can't fix the bones."

From what Joaquim understood of healers, repairing bone was beyond them, so he was stuck with the broken nose as well.

"Prieto." A guard spoke from the cell's doorway behind him. "Is he ready to move?"

Joaquim closed his eyes and pretended to sleep again.

"I'll need to replace the bandage on his arm," the healer protested, "and stitch up that cut on his cheek."

"You can do that at the prison."

Two men hoisted Joaquim to his feet between them and began dragging his limp form from the cell. Apparently it was time to go.

CHAPTER 35

❧

TERRASSA

Marina was still reading when the train pulled into the station at Terrassa. Alejandro looked disappointed when she put the book away, but she needed to prepare her mind for the coming confrontation.

The marquesa had been nothing but unpleasant to Joaquim. Marina didn't have any illusions about the woman helping her. But she knew something about the marquesa that the woman wouldn't want known. The marquesa *had to be* a witch, and the Spanish still imprisoned witches.

Marina didn't think it would come to the point of actually denouncing the woman, but she could make the woman believe she would do it.

Inside the station, one of the clerks provided her with the name and direction of a hotel should they miss the last train back to Barcelona. Once outside the station, she hired a driver to take her and Alejandro to the marquesa's estate. As they rode along in the back of his open carriage, the boy eyed the rows of vines marching up the sides of the hills. "What are those?"

Marina stared at him, startled. That was the first time he'd asked a question. "Grapevines. This part of the country makes wine called *cava*."

"Oh."

That seemed an end to his curiosity. "There are some cork trees farther along," she said. "So I suppose the winery produces its own cork."

Alejandro's dark eyes slid toward her mistrustfully. "Cork *trees?*"

So she found herself explaining how cork was harvested from trees, something she only knew because one of her father's clients grew cork in Southern Portugal. Then she launched into a one-sided discussion on how wine was made. Alejandro seemed to accept everything she said as truth, as if he didn't think she could lie to him.

Marina saw that they were approaching the gate of the estate. Unfortunately, when they reached it, the gate was closed. *Well, we've come this far.* Marina stepped down from the cart, helped Alejandro down, and grabbed her bag from the cart's floor. Once she'd paid the driver and he'd driven away, she turned back to face the locked gate.

Did it mean that the marquesa was out? Or that she was traveling? Marina carried her bag over to the gate and set it down. How humiliating it would be if she wasted an afternoon here when she could be searching out help from someone else.

"Should I climb over?" Alejandro asked.

She shook her head. That wrought-iron fence must be eight feet high, and the spike on the top of each stake looked deadly. "Will she come back?"

He nodded, so she decided they could wait. She surveyed the area around them. To the side of the road she could see a stream, its banks crowded with shrub. She hoped the stream was clean enough that they could drink from it. She didn't have a flask with her, a foolish oversight. She wasn't going to make that mistake again. And when she needed to attend the call of nature—which, given her monthly, wouldn't wait forever—the shrubs would suffice as cover.

So she sat on a green-tiled bench in front of the stone wall where a honeysuckle vine bloomed, spreading its sweet fragrance about them. She tugged out the book, beckoned for Alejandro to sit next to her, and once he was settled, began reading again.

It was some time later when the rattle of a coach coming down the graveled road caught Alejandro's ear. He tugged on Marina's sleeve to alert her, and she spotted the old contraption as it came around the curve into view of the gate. Hoping she still looked presentable after sitting out in the wind, she rose.

The coach was large and grand, with a coat of arms painted on the door. When the coachman set the brake, a stripling in old-fashioned livery clambered down from the back of the coach to unlock the gate. He shot a startled glance at Marina and Alejandro.

"We need to speak to the marquesa," Marina quickly said in Spanish as he passed.

"The lady doesn't have time for beggars," the groom said in a squeaky tenor.

I don't look that bad, do I? "I am not a beggar. My husband and I met with her only a couple of days ago."

The groom averted his face and went to unlock the gates.

The portly driver leaned down from his high perch and barked, "Move on, woman."

Marina's jaw clenched. Furious, she dropped Alejandro's hand, strode over to the coach, and pounded on the door with the side of her fist. "I must speak with you, Marquesa."

The shade was swept aside by a gnarled black-gloved hand. The old woman peered down at Marina, her dark eyes narrowed. "I don't have time to gossip with every beggar who comes to my door," she snapped. "Go to the Church."

"I'm Joaquim's wife," Marina protested. "You met me earlier this week."

The woman squinted at her, waved one hand, and pronounced, "I'll talk to you when I'm ready."

"What?"

"Stand back," the driver called down. He set the horses to motion so quickly that Marina had to snatch her skirts out of the way of the wheels. The carriage rolled through the gate without even waiting for the groom, leaving an irate Marina standing in the dust kicked up by the wheels. The groom closed the gate, his eyes carefully averted.

Marina ran to the gate and grasped the bars. "I have come all the way from Barcelona to speak with her. I *must* speak with her. Please tell her it's about her great-grandson."

Flushing, the groom set the latch on the gate and jogged up the long drive to the house.

"Please!" Marina yelled after him.

He didn't acknowledge that.

Marina pressed her forehead against the bars, trying to decide what to do. Would the groom repeat her pleas to the marquesa? Would the marquesa even listen?

She pushed down the urge to cry. She didn't want to do that in front of Alejandro. And she wasn't going to shake the bars in pointless fury. So after a moment she stepped away from the gate and looked back to where Alejandro stood waiting, his expression unreadable. "She said to wait," Marina said. "We can do that."

Alejandro took off his cap and stuffed it into his jacket pocket. Then he went back to sit on the bench as if nothing had happened at all.

Marina joined him there. "Are you hungry? There's a meat pie left."

His eyes snaked toward the bag on the ground. "Don't you want it?"

Even that brief confrontation with the marquesa had left her stomach in knots. So she dug out the meat pie and handed it over to him. While he ate it, she gazed out at the road in the late-afternoon heat. She hadn't made time to purchase a watch, and now she had no idea how late it was. She glanced at the sun. It was going to set soon. In an hour? Two?

She touched Alejandro's knee. "I'm going to go just off the road over there," she said, pointing to where the stream ran past the road. "Call of nature."

He nodded, so she picked up her bag and headed down to the streamside. She hated leaving him alone, but she couldn't put this off much longer. The little stream was easy to hop over, more a deep ditch than anything else. Fortunately, she found a secluded spot behind some bushes that looked like broom. Once she'd taken care of her needs, she made certain her dress was in order and headed back to the stream to wash her hands.

The water was cool, and after scrubbing her hands in the water, she lifted up a handful to take a cautious sip. It seemed drinkable.

"What do we have here?" a man's voice asked from the side of the road.

Marina spun about, nearly losing her balance and falling into the water in the process. She ended up with one foot in the stream.

A squarely built man stood on the roadside a few feet higher than her, his arms akimbo and his feet wide. His garments looked like a farmer's, a dirt-stained tunic over homespun pants. He had a handsome face, but his hair was unkempt and the look he directed at her could only be called lecherous. "Little lady coming to take a piss in the stream?"

Marina tried hard not to glance at the bag sitting on the ground a few feet from her. It currently held all their money. Every last peseta. Her passport. Her mother's journal with its secrets. "Go away," she said in as calm a voice as she could manage.

He started down the embankment toward her. "What's in that bag, little lady? I bet there's something there I'd like."

She stepped back, putting herself between him and the bag. "There's nothing there for you."

She'd put a touch of a *call* into her words, but it didn't work.

Not when she'd told an outright lie. Her pulse was pounding in her ears now, panic beginning to shorten her breaths. What could she possibly do against a man this size?

He grabbed her arm and yanked her close to him. He wrapped his other hand about her jaw to make her look at him. "Pretty thing, aren't you?"

Marina felt a blaze of fury go through her. She jerked her head out of his grasp and yanked at her arm, but his grip didn't give. "I'm not a thing," she yelled.

His beefy hand connected with her jaw, sending sparks flying through her vision. Then he yowled and released her. Marina stumbled backward, tripping over her bag and landing hard on her rump. Her jaw throbbed, but her vision cleared immediately, showing her that the man now held Alejandro aloft by the back of his jacket. Alejandro clutched a large rock in his hand.

Then the man raised his fist to strike the boy.

Marina hurtled to her feet and threw herself at the man, managing to score his cheek with her nails. "You touch him and I'll scratch your eyes out!"

The man stumbled back, his eyes wide with fear as if he believed that hotheaded claim.

She'd done it without thinking.

She'd used her *call*. She wanted him to fear her, and he *did*.

He scrambled up the embankment on his hands and knees. In her fury, Marina jumped to pursue him, but the heel of her shoe caught in the hem of her skirt. She tumbled forward against the embankment and then fell back on her rump again.

"May lightning strike you!" she screamed at the man's fleeing form.

Her breath was coming in ragged gasps and her teeth were on their sharp edge. She was ready to bite something. Or someone. Only the man was long gone.

She laid her hands over her face, only to discover that her palms were scraped. She pushed up to her knees and sorted out her skirts to rise, but went still when she saw Alejandro's face. He wore a strange frown, his lower lip thrust out. Mud smudged the side of his face.

She wasn't sure what that expression meant. Was he acting now?

She hadn't meant to put him in danger. But if he hadn't come to her defense, she didn't think she would have gotten away from that ruffian. "You were very brave," she said. "Thank you for saving me."

He didn't say anything in return.

So she tugged her handkerchief out of her sleeve and dampened it in the stream. Then she shifted closer to Alejandro. "Here, let me get this dirt off your face."

She moved slowly. Even though the boy flinched away at first, he let her wipe the mud from his cheek, his mouth turned down in that terrible frown the whole while. When she'd finished, she held the handkerchief out toward him. "Do I have any on my face?"

He shook his head. Then his lips twisted abruptly and he choked out a sob.

Marina set her hands on his shoulders, but Alejandro began to cry in earnest, so she wrapped her arms about him and held him close. And then she was crying too.

How could she let him go once they got his mother out of the prison? There would be a hole in her heart when he was taken away.

Marina held him a moment longer, then eased back to wipe his cheeks. He was so guarded and distrustful that she'd almost forgotten he was just a little boy. It was cruel that Alejandro had been raised to be responsible for every ill that befell his mother.

"Don't tell my mother I cried," he whispered.

And there was the little boy peeking out from his hard facade. "I won't if you don't tell my husband I cried."

He nodded. "Or the Vilaró."

"I promise." She brushed hair from his forehead, that thick straight lock just like Joaquim's.

"My mother can't hug me," he said then. "She doesn't want to make me sick. She held my hand but said she shouldn't hug me."

Oh God. How painful that must have been for a boy who just wanted his mother to himself. And how terrible for Leandra, denying a mother's instincts for her son's sake. Marina knew the woman wasn't indifferent to Alejandro, not after all she'd endured to get her children free. She set her hands on the boy's shoulders. "I'm not your mother, but you can hug me in her place . . . whenever you want."

He nodded quickly as if embarrassed, and rubbed his nose on his sleeve.

She didn't even consider correcting him. Not after what he'd just done. Instead she washed her scraped hands in the stream, rinsed out her handkerchief, and collected her bag. "I think you can drink from the stream," she said, and he complied, likely as thirsty as she'd been.

"Did you throw a rock at him?" she asked. "Or did you hit him with it?"

"I hit him," Alejandro said. "On top of his head."

"Well, you saved me," she said. "So I will always be grateful."

He shrugged. "He looked scared of you."

"Anyone who threatens you had better be scared of me."

CHAPTER 36

LLEIDA

The guard hauled Joaquim through the stone hallways of the Morra and up a series of steps. A metal door clanged open after a rattle of keys, and they went up a few more steps into an open building. Joaquim tried to pinpoint any clues that would tell him about the place without opening his eyes, but it smelled of stone as well, although dryer here and swept by wind. Sounds echoed and he smelled a well nearby. Prieto had said they were under the town hall, but he couldn't imagine why there would be a well in it, so they must be in an outer courtyard.

Eventually he heard the noise of traffic, people walking and talking nearby. Still feigning sleep, he didn't bother to cry out for help. For some reason he was needed at the *other* prison. Having seen what Leandra had endured, he wasn't going to fail her.

The guards hoisted him into a coach and dumped him on a seat. He slumped against the wall of the coach and listened as it began to move through the streets, but the guards only discussed an automobile race from Paris to Madrid that would take place next month, as if their captive was of no interest.

On arriving at the prison—easy to discern by its myriad voices and the smell of too many bodies—the guards dragged Joaquim down hallways and up a flight of stairs. One unlocked a door and shoved him inside. His feet weren't under him, so Joaquim fell to the floor, his nose hitting his arm in the process and sending a flare of nauseating discomfort through his intestines. His eyes remained clenched shut as the door lock clicked behind him and he fought the urge to vomit.

"Let me help you," a man said, gently grasping his elbow.

He didn't need to feign sleep any longer. Joaquim wrenched his eyes open and saw he was in a normal room. There were three beds in the room, but it wasn't a jail cell. It wasn't a fine hotel either, not like the Colón, but it wasn't terrible. "Where am I?"

"Lleida Prison," the man said. A handsome man, he was a few years younger than Joaquim himself, with what could only be called soulful eyes. His hair was overlong, pulled back from an angular face, but he showed no sign of facial hair. He helped Joaquim to a chair. "Don't let the appearance fool you. Come on, sit down."

The throbbing in Joaquim's nose was worse now, but his new surroundings were preferable to the Morra. "Who are you?"

"Marcos Davila," the young man said. "Prisoner, like you. Miss Prieto will come around as soon as she can, but until she gets here, it would be best to clean up those wounds." He went to one side of the room and returned with a basin of water and a pair of clean towels. "I see darling Piedad's been after you."

Joaquim choked out a laugh, tasting blood again. "I take it you don't like her."

"She's my cousin, thankfully." The man wet one of the towels and handed it to Joaquim. "Why don't you wipe down your hands, and I'll find you a shirt? Mine should work for you." From a chest at the end of one of the beds, Marcos produced fresh linens and a clean shirt.

Joaquim wiped his right hand, removing the blood from where he'd tried to quench the bleeding of his nose earlier. "Why are you thankful she's your cousin?"

Marcos let out a dry laugh, a desperately sad sound. "They don't expect me to bed her."

Joaquim stopped in the midst of unbuttoning his shirt cuffs.

"I'm the harem," Marcos said. "Currently the only member. They keep me clothed and fed, but if I don't do what they tell me, the woman I love will pay. It's a damnable existence."

If he understood correctly, a sereia-human mating would produce sereia daughters. But if Marcos was Piedad's cousin, he must already have sereia blood. He must be *webless*, like Alejandro, but still a better choice than any of the hundreds of human men in the cells.

Joaquim heard voices from beyond the window, an increase in the sounds. "What's happening out there?"

"One of the wings has been let out to get some fresh air in the courtyard." He cocked his head as if listening to birds singing. "Ah, those are the Catalan nationalists. Their number has been increasing for the last few months. They're the most harmless of the prisoners. Poets, writers, the occasional socialist. That sort," he said dismissively.

Joaquim unbuttoned his shirt and removed it, then carefully peeled his undershirt off over his head, easing the right sleeve over his stained bandage. "Is there any chance of a glass of water?"

Marcos opened an interior door, revealing a toilet stand and a sink with a mirror over it. He pulled a string, and an electric light brightened the tiny space. "My palace," he said bitterly with a dramatic wave of his hand. He poured a glass of water from the tap and brought it over.

Joaquim drank, spotting a hint of red as blood flowed from his mouth back into the glass. "Thank you."

"Truthfully," Marcus said with a sigh, "this is far better than a cell with stone floors, and I have running water and decent food. Most prisoners here would be jealous."

Joaquim didn't doubt that. Once he'd had his fill of water, he went to survey his face in the mirror above the sink. He hardly knew himself. The harsh electric light made the cut running down his cheek look ghoulishly red, with spots clotted dark already. But it wasn't as long as he'd expected, given the amount of blood. A couple of inches at most. His nose seemed swollen to twice its normal size, and the skin under his eyes looked red and angry. He wet the towel and began cleaning, starting first with the blood drying under his nose. He had a day's growth of beard as well, making it harder to scrub his chin. Under the blood he found another cut and gingerly dabbed at it. Everything felt tender.

He cleaned away as much of the dried blood as possible, and once he thought he'd done as well as he could with his face, he washed his hands and wiped down his chest. He still smelled, but he didn't know how much better he could do until he had a chance to bathe properly. He closed the door of the tiny water closet and used the toilet stand, thanking God that he could do so without a guard standing over him. Then he returned to where Marcos waited.

Marcos handed him an undershirt. Although it fit closer than Joaquim liked, it was silk and comfortable. He decided not to put on the offered dress shirt for the moment and instead asked if he could lie down. After being told that the bed under the high window was Marcos', he picked the middle bed and lay down on his back. The throbbing in his nose eased once he was lying flat. He closed one eye and used the other to look at Marcos, who sat on the edge of his bed, his hands dangling between his knees. The young man had near-black hair and dark eyes, a striking combination with his fair skin.

"Leandra said I could trust you," Joaquim said.

"I want to get out of here as much as she does, so yes."

"How long have you been here?"

"Almost three years. They treat me better than men like you, so I've outlasted all the others."

"Men like me?" Joaquim asked.

"Human men." Marcos rolled up the leg of his trousers and displayed a swath of silver skin above his sock.

"You're half sereia," Joaquim observed dully. Now that he was lying down, exhaustion wrapped around him like a smothering blanket.

"Sirena, yes," the young man said, using the Spanish word. "My mother came from this prison."

"And your father?"

"A diplomat, like his father before him, as I'd hoped to be one day. The sirenas here needed someone in my father's sphere of influence, so they sent my mother to seduce him."

"Ah," Joaquim said. "They didn't raise you here?"

"No. I grew up thinking myself a fine Spanish citizen. When my father was assigned as ambassador to the islands, I remained behind in Madrid and went to the university. Three years ago, I was woken in the middle of the night by men who drugged me and brought me here."

"You've been here ever since?"

"Not in this fine room," Marcos said. "At first they put me in a room with another prisoner, a woman named Safira. She wasn't Spanish, I discovered quickly, although she spoke the language well enough when she did speak to me. She'd been beaten, you see, by men on some ship. She was terrified. Can you imagine what that's like? We had no privacy from each other. In time she came to trust me and I, not having any idea what lay ahead, fell in love with her. And that was what my grandmother was waiting for, why we were put together."

"Your grandmother?"

Marcos let off a short bark of laughter. "Don't picture her as a sweet and caring angel, like grandmothers are supposed to be. She runs this place, runs the lives of all of them. She makes the decisions, who's put with whom, who lives, who's no longer useful. Her name is Reyna, but they call her *La* Reyna—the queen. For her everything is about maintaining their place here in Spain, their influence, their power."

"To the point that she would imprison her own grandson?"

316 | J. Kathleen Cheney

"Yes. It's torture. Safira and I have a daughter together, but we're never allowed to see each other."

"And if either of you disobeys, the other is punished."

"Yes, as you've learned already, I see. They use us all against each other. I only see my daughter once a month, but that's enough to make me love her and fear what they might do to her when she is older."

"What is her name?"

"Serafina," Marcos said, "my little angel."

Poor Marcos. Joaquim blinked, his eyes growing heavy. What would he be willing to do to save Marina pain? "Why do they do all this?"

"There are not enough of them," Marcos said. "Not to serve on the ships and to run the prisons. Years and years ago, there was an outbreak of tuberculosis here. When a sirena catches that, she loses her gills. She cannot *call* any longer, and cannot control the prisoners. La Reyna holds back her own people—the sirenas—to influence the right men in government, like my father. But La Reyna wants to convince the humans to let her control all the prisons in Spain, not just this one. She needs more sirenas, and will do anything to them to force them to work for her. Some of the ones brought here, they fight too hard and they die. The ones who give in are sent out with the navy, and many were lost in *El Desastre*," Marcos said, referring to Spain's war with America. "The ones left here are the ones Reyna doesn't trust. She keeps them close so she can force their cooperation. But La Reyna preaches that Spain will soon take over the islands Safira came from, where the Portuguese sirenas are, and then she will have as many as she needs."

"Do you believe that?"

"It may have been true once, but not since 'ninety-eight. Spain has no taste for war now. Yet the old sirenas living in this prison, they tell the same lies to themselves over and over until *they* believe them."

Marcos apparently didn't consider himself a sirena like his mother and grandmother. And Leandra had said he was trustworthy, a relief to Joaquim, since he was having trouble keeping his eyes open now. "What happened to the men before me, the ones who didn't last?"

"They disappear. I've no idea where they end up."

Joaquim knew he should be concerned by that, but at the moment he was just too tired.

CHAPTER 37

TERRASSA

Marina picked the best spot to climb up the embankment back to the road, and waited as Alejandro made his way after her. Once on the roadside again, she first checked her skirt for dust and then Alejandro's trousers, earning an embarrassed scowl from the boy. When she determined they were both presentable, she turned back to the big house. She only hoped her eyes weren't red from crying.

A man stood near the wrought-iron gate. His black cassock proclaimed him a priest, and he watched patiently as they approached. His graying hair indicated age, but Marina wasn't sure how old he was. He had a young face, a pleasant face.

Then she saw that he held their book in his hands.

Alejandro must have dropped the thing when he came to her aid, and Marina wasn't going to let anyone take something Alejandro enjoyed that much. She marched staunchly up to the priest and held out one hand, her palm angry and red. "Please, Father, that's my son's book."

"Of course," the priest said, handing it to her. His dark eyebrows drew together when he saw the condition of her palm. "Are you hurt, madam?"

"A man hit my mother," Alejandro said, managing to sound as

if he were even younger than seven. He stood halfway behind her, hiding behind her skirts. Now that *was* acting.

"I'm fine, Father," she mumbled. "Just a blow to my jaw. I was more startled than hurt. I'm not accustomed to ruffians."

The priest gazed at her sympathetically. "I am sorry you were ill-used, madam. Tell me, why are you here on the road?"

"I must speak with the marquesa," Marina said, hope flaring suddenly. "Alejandro and I have been waiting here all afternoon, but she refused to see me."

The priest set his hands on his hips. "What is this about?"

She was angry enough with the old woman that she relished the idea of provoking this man to share her anger. "A family member of hers," Marina said. "Her great-grandson needs her help, and she would not even hear me out."

"Her great-grandson?" The priest's eyebrows rose. "I didn't know she had grandchildren."

"A schism in the family," Marina said. "Her daughter married without her permission, and she does not forgive. Neither her daughter nor her daughter's descendants."

The priest seemed troubled, as well he might be over such a sign of hardness in a member of his flock. "Perhaps we could go speak to her together, Mrs. . . .?"

"Tavares," Marina said. "My husband's father is Portuguese."

"Ah, I see."

"This is my son, Alejandro."

"So this would be the marquesa's great-great-grandson?" the priest asked.

Do I look old enough to have a child Alejandro's age? She was only twenty-three. With Alejandro being nearly eight, that would have made her a *very* young mother. "He's our foster son," she clarified, setting a hand on Alejandro's shoulder.

"Ah," the priest said. "I am Father Escarrá. Come, let's speak with the marquesa."

Marina was impressed with his surety that the woman would see him on a moment's notice, but a priest often held great influence in the countryside. "Thank you, Father."

When they reached the gate of the house, the priest waited patiently for the old butler to come tottering out again. He very calmly stated that he wished to see the lady, and when the old man mumbled a protest, the priest overrode that by simply striding past. Marina followed, Alejandro jogging along behind her.

The portly butler bade them wait for the lady to join them, asking them to remain in the hallway. He went into the sitting room, giving Marina the barest glimpse inside before he shut the door. He slipped out a moment later and gestured for them to wait for the lady within. The priest let Marina enter first. Not wanting to keep him standing, she sat, bidding Alejandro to sit on the sofa at her side. She set her bag at her feet. "Take off your cap," she whispered to him.

He snatched it off and held it in his lap.

"From where are you visiting?" Father Escarrá asked politely.

"The Golden City," Marina said.

"Ah," he said. "I have visited Lisboa but have never reached Northern Portugal."

"Travel is not always convenient," she said vaguely.

"Yes. I hope you're finding Catalonia to your liking."

To my liking? When Joaquim has been taken prisoner? When I've been struck by a man for no good reason? But it would be impolitic to say that to a man who was helping her. And it was unfair to judge the country or its people by her current circumstances. "It has not turned out exactly as we'd hoped, but it is beautiful here."

"Oh, damnation." The marquesa leaned heavily on her cane, scowling at her visitors. "What sort of trouble has he fallen into? Has he started begging on the street?"

Marina rose, her hands balling into fists. The woman had spoken in Catalan, but Marina caught the gist of her accusations. "Your pardon, Marquesa, but I do not speak Catalan well."

"Learn." The old woman tottered over to her favored chair and sat down, glaring at Marina balefully. "Now, what do you want?"

"I need your help, Marquesa." She could say that much in Catalan, at least. "My husband was . . . taken by the Mossos."

The marquesa groaned. "Just speak Spanish, girl. Better that than listening to your wretched pronunciation. You butcher my language."

Marina felt her cheeks go warm. Most Catalans so far had appreciated it when she'd tried. She supposed it was too much to expect this woman to be tolerant about anything. "Pardon me," she said in Spanish, sitting again. "My husband was taken yesterday morning, to a prison. I believe you can help me get him out."

"Go to your consulate," the old woman snapped, pushing her twisted hands down on her cane to rise again. "Let *them* get him out."

Marina rose with her, but gestured for Alejandro to remain seated. She was not going to let this bitter old woman slip away. "Shall I tell you why he was taken? Or shall we discuss what your servant came in here to do before he let Father Escarrá in?"

The marquesa glared at Marina, but she simply returned the woman's gaze. Marina had glimpsed the servant turning the statue of the Virgin around so that it no longer faced the wall, something she'd seen in her childhood. She'd originally meant to threaten this woman with the knowledge that she had to be a witch, a desperate ploy since it was *possible* the marquesa wasn't even aware of her gift. But what she'd seen the butler do hinted at a far better threat.

The marquesa turned to the priest. "Wait outside in the hall, please, Father," she said, far more politely than she'd spoken to Marina. "This is a family matter."

The priest seemed ready to protest, but nodded once and left the room, drawing the door closed behind him.

The old woman's head snapped toward Marina. "I don't know what you think you're up to, girl, but you have no place disagreeing with me."

"What do I have to lose? My husband is in a prison, not having committed any crime. You are my best hope for getting him out."

The old woman sank down in her chair again. "Why should I do anything to help him? He has no claim on this family."

Marina sat down. "Because the Mossos have every right to take you and put you in that prison as well."

The old woman slammed her cane to the floor. "How dare you threaten me in my own house? You think you're better than us just because your people rule here?"

Marina licked her lips. Joaquim would know just how to turn the woman's words around to get at what he wanted to know. He would know how to make her admit . . . something.

"What does she mean by *your people*?" Alejandro asked in Portuguese, eyes wide.

Marina took his hand in hers. Alejandro's confused look was a fake. At least she *thought* it was. He'd pointed out the marquesa's misstep. If there was anything in this world Alejandro would understand, it would be a threat.

The marquesa hadn't been commenting on the Spanish. *Your people* referred to the Church's power in Spain, the very power represented by Father Escarrá. And that verified what Marina thought she'd seen. The statue of the Virgin *had* been facing the wall.

Marina glanced at Alejandro again. "Some people hide their true faith," she said to him in Portuguese. "Their neighbors might be upset if they learn they're different."

Supposedly that had ended in Spain—and in Portugal—with the end of the Inquisition during the past century. But people were often suspicious of *anything* different. Enough so to make this woman send the priest out into the hallway.

Marina looked up to find the marquesa's hard eyes on her. The woman *knew* she had an advantage. She could threaten to expose the woman's secret to her priest, to her neighbors. They might turn on the old woman, or shun her. It would be just recompense for the woman's unpleasantness not only to Joaquim, but to his mother and grand-mother as well, wouldn't it?

Marina closed her eyes. She'd lived under her aunt's roof for years, hiding her own faith. A Christian on Quitos was as much a rarity as . . .

Would the marquesa be a Jew? Would the Mossos take this fragile old woman and throw her in that prison as well? Merely because she'd turned around the statue of the Virgin?

As unpleasant as the woman was, Marina wouldn't wish that on her. Out of respect for an elder, if nothing else, she wouldn't do that. She *couldn't*.

Jaw clenched, Marina rose from her seat.

"Where do you think you're going?" the old woman snapped.

"I had thought I could threaten you to force you to help my husband," Marina said, her throat tight. "But I can't. I know what it's like to have to hide who I am. I know what it's like to fear expo-sure. I won't do that to someone else, not even to save my husband. He would be so disappointed in me." Her lips began to quiver and she took a shaky breath. "And I won't set that example for my son. We'll find some other way to get my husband free."

I have to get out of here before I break into tears.

Leaving Alejandro to follow, Marina rushed out into the hall-way, covering her mouth with one hand to hold in her sobs. Then she ran to the front door, right past the startled-looking priest. With-out waiting for the butler, Marina threw the door open and stum-bled down the steps.

She stopped on the stone pathway, bent over and clutching at her belly, trying to hold down the anguish that made her want to cast up her meager lunch.

She had ruined her best chance to free Joaquim.

CHAPTER 38

After a moment, the nausea passed, leaving Marina with clammy skin and a pounding in her temples. She drew a few deep breaths, sternly reminding herself she couldn't behave like a child. There was no one here to take care of her, and *she* had to take care of Alejandro.

Calmed by that thought, she turned back and saw he'd followed her. She was glad she didn't have to walk back in there to get him. He clutched her bag in his hands—it must be heavy for him—and regarded her with a worried line between his eyebrows. "Why did you do that?"

Alejandro had grown up with threats. He'd clearly recognized what she'd intended. But she hadn't been able to go through with it. She was weak, just as her aunts had always said.

She wiped her cheeks with her scraped palm, ignoring the sting of the salt tears on her raw skin. "There are some things I can't do, Alejandro." She sniffed. "I just . . . can't. It would be wrong." She took another deep breath. "Why don't you give me that bag? It's a long way back to town."

Alejandro walked along with her, silent as always, his eyes on the rows of vines marching up the hills. When they passed the house's gate, he glanced back. "I thought grandmothers were supposed to be nice."

That made her chuckle. Of course, he'd likely never met a real grandmother, much less his own. "My grandmother is. It was her house you came to out on the islands."

"Oh," Alejandro said, mouth pursing.

"She understands why you stole the book," Marina reminded him. He shrugged, which sent her looking about for another topic.

"Joaquim's mother passed away when he was your age, but his foster mother is very nice. You'll like her." If she could ever get Alejandro to the Golden City, he would adore Lady Ferreira. And she would like him. She liked clever people.

Marina shifted the bag to her other hand. With her aching palms, it was going to get heavy quickly. The sky was already darkening. They definitely weren't going to reach the town before full dark.

Marina paused when Alejandro grabbed her arm. She looked down to see him pointing back toward the house. A one-horse gig headed toward them along the path. As it came closer, she saw the priest was driving. She drew Alejandro to the side of the road, but the priest pulled the horse to a stop next to them, dust settling about the wheels.

"May I give you a ride back to the town?" he asked in a civil voice.

At least she hadn't shamed herself so thoroughly that the priest shunned her. "Yes, Father," she said quickly. "It's later than I thought."

"There's almost no moon, and I wouldn't want you and your son walking into town in the dark," the priest said. "Particularly not after your earlier difficulties."

Marina helped Alejandro onto the gig's bench, put the bag on the floor, and then climbed up herself. She had to pull Alejandro onto her lap, but he didn't seem to mind. "We had thought to stay at the hotel near the train station tonight, Father," Marina said. "Would you be willing to drop us there?"

He flicked the reins and the horse began to trot again, carrying the light gig toward the town far faster than they would have been able to walk. "May I suggest another location?"

"I am not familiar with the town, Father, so I would welcome it."

The priest smiled. "The Sala family takes in visitors," he said. "They have a few smallish guest rooms, serve fine meals, and need the funds more than the hotel does. These last few years have been difficult."

Marina nodded. The Spanish economy had suffered after their wars. "That would be lovely, Father."

"Good, then." The gig rattled past the spot where he'd found them by the stream, and then the road turned so that they could see the edge of the town in the far distance. "The marquesa can be difficult," he said then. "I often help her deal with requests for aid or charity. Can I assume she declined to aid you?"

Marina felt her cheeks flush. "In the end, I didn't ask. I . . ."

The priest regarded her sympathetically.

"I meant to blackmail her into helping me, Father, but . . . I couldn't."

Alejandro glanced up at her face, his elbow digging into her stomach, a rebuke for confessing that, but she was *not* going to lie to a priest.

"Ah," the priest said mildly. "And she, of course, refuses to help because of the schism in the family. The rumor is that her daughter married a Spaniard."

"Yes, that was the case."

Father Escarrá glanced at her again. "I am aware, however, that it was more than dislike of the Spanish. I've always known that the marquesa's ancestors were *conversos*."

Marina stared down at the top of Alejandro's cap ruefully. "I see. I had thought to push her into helping us by threatening to tell you."

"Why did you not go through with your plan?"

Marina sighed. "Because I am not ruthless enough to threaten an old woman, Father."

"You think threatening her would have gotten you what you wanted?"

"I am sorry for using you to get us into her house when I had such intentions, Father."

He shook the reins again to speed the horse. "You had the upper hand, yet you didn't expose her, even when you had so much at stake."

"I have been threatened before, Father. I was the lone Christian among a people who were not. Remembering that made me change my mind."

"That is not weakness, child," he said. "It's compassion. The marquesa is old enough to remember the last time a Jew was tried by the Inquisition, so her fear is reasonable. You could have hurt her terribly, and I'm grateful you did not."

Well, she hadn't made a friend out of Joaquim's great-grandmother, but the priest approved. Not that it would help her situation. "Thank you, Father," she mumbled.

"The lady is," he added, "a good Christian, despite the fact that she honors some of the old ways as well."

That sounded familiar to Marina, much like her own grandmother's adherence to two religions at once. "Where I am from, it is the Christians who hide their religion, rather than the other way around. My parents kept customs of both, so I understand how that can be true."

"Ah. For the marquesa, it is mostly respect for her ancestors, and what they suffered. They were forced to make terrible decisions, whether to abandon their homes, accept a religion that was not theirs, or die. She honors their struggle by honoring some of their customs, and I do not believe it is my place to examine her orthodoxy."

Marina gazed down at her hands, the webbing cut away to protect her *appearance* of humanness. *It's the same, isn't it?* She might have stayed true to her religion on Quitos, but under the ban in the Golden City she'd feared for her life, and had acted by altering who she was. The world was a hard place for anyone who was different.

The priest made a harrumphing sound. "If the Church looks back far enough in anyone's family, they will find *something* to question.

Even mine." After a moment, he added, "So, tell me how your husband came to be taken up."

After all she'd said, she didn't think it would hurt to tell the truth. "The Mossos were trying to catch Alejandro. He escaped, but they took my husband in his place."

Father Escarrá peered at Alejandro speculatively. "And why would they be after a child? Is his mother a Catalan nationalist?"

"No," Marina said. "It's a more . . . complicated political matter."

"How long has she been there?"

"Ten years."

"Ah. That is a long time." He glanced at the top of Alejandro's head but didn't ask further. Her statement made it clear that Alejandro had been born in the prison.

As they were coming into the outskirts of the town, he turned his attention to the road and the other traffic. It was almost dark. He turned south off the main street onto a narrower one crowded with old houses, some in disrepair, as they headed toward the home of the Sala family. "It's not the finest part of town," Father Escarrá said, "but you will be close to the park and the old church of Saint Peter, if you have time to visit there in the morning. And Mr. Sala will be happy to drive you to the train station whenever you need."

Marina nodded as he drew the gig to a halt before a house of two stories with a wrought-iron gate. Flowers bloomed on the balconies above the cobbled street, and lamps lit either side of the doorway. It was cheery and welcoming, and right now that was what she needed.

LLEIDA

Joaquim stumbled back to wakefulness when he felt someone tugging at his aching arm. For a moment he lay there, his head feeling as if it were stuffed with wool that burned. He couldn't breathe properly. And then a sharp stab of pain brought him back to reality.

He opened his eyes. "What?"

"Be still," Miss Prieto said softly. "I have to get this bandage off."

Joaquim blinked, and realized his eyes weren't opening properly because his lids were swollen. He had the taste of stale blood in his mouth. She continued to work on the bandage that the guards had crushed into his arm when they'd tied him to the chair in Leandra's cell. She'd put his arm over a basin of warm water and was soaking it with water. "Would it help if I sat up?" he asked.

"You'd feel better," she said. "It will give your nose a chance to drain."

So she pulled the basin away and waited while Marcos came over and helped Joaquim into a sitting position. The young man placed a pillow behind him and then returned to sit on his own bed, watching with worried eyes. Joaquim thanked him again, and did his best to comply as Miss Prieto repositioned his arm. "This isn't good, is it?"

"No," she said. "I had a poultice on it, but we'll have to see how much damage the ropes did before I can start to cut the dead skin away."

Joaquim didn't bother to complain. Miss Prieto had been branded herself, and Marcos as well. The young man had kept talking, long after Joaquim had drifted too far away to pay attention. He must have mentioned it at some point, though, because Joaquim recalled it was an I, for *inhumano*, rather than a B.

"If you're very lucky, the poultice will have eased off most of the dead skin," Miss Prieto added, actually mustering a gentle smile for him, "and this will just be unpleasant."

The alternative didn't sound good. "Wouldn't it be better to rip it off quickly?"

"Not with a burn. We want to preserve as much skin as possible." Now that the water had soaked into the bandage, she began carefully loosening the bandage with a pair of tweezers. Although the burned area wasn't even two inches wide, it seemed to take forever. When she reached a patch where the rope had driven the gauze into the burned and blistered skin, *that* hurt. Joaquim hissed, but kept his hand still under her ministrations.

Once the last of the gauze was gone, he was confronted with a nasty-looking burn, blackened and blistered skin. It was swollen but roughly outlined the shape of a B—*brujo*. Blood seeped from the spot on the inner edge where the skin had torn, and the remaining poultice was a nasty orangey brown. "What's in your poultice?"

"The primary ingredient is honey," she said. "It protects the surface of the wound and helps debride it as well."

"Debride?" He definitely didn't know that Spanish word.

Her lips twisted as she worked. "All that blackened skin has to go. If the honey hasn't eased it off, I'll have to scrape it off."

Joaquim shuddered. He'd never been particularly strong-stomached when it came to injuries and blood. "Very well."

She patted his knee. "I've seen a lot worse."

I'm sure she has in this place. He focused on the door across from them as she began picking at his wound. "So, why am I here?"

"You're a *finder*, aren't you?" Miss Prieto asked.

"Yes," he admitted, revealing that he'd earned that brand on his arm.

"This prison is full of witches," she said, "or *aberraciónes*, as the sirenas call us—a way to imply that we are inferior. Most of the witches here are harmless, and not a single one of them is a finder like you."

The healer tugged at something that hurt, and Joaquim clenched his jaw, forcing down his reaction. "You need me to find someone," he guessed.

"No, some*thing*. A little over eighty years ago," she said, "a prisoner was deposited in the bottom of the prison, in a cell beneath the courtyard. He was deemed dangerous and secured with magical locks that require a special key. The sirenas, fearing someone would free him, hid the key. Unfortunately, even they have forgotten where it is."

"What did he do?"

"No more than you. He exists, and was careless enough to get caught," she said. "But he's the master of stone. It answers his call."

Joaquim puzzled over what that meant, but logic failed to supply an answer. "And you want to set him free? Is he dangerous?"

"The Vilaró? Not to us. If we free him, he's agreed to free us."

All of them? How? "You're taking his word for that?"

"He's bound by his word," she said. "His kind cannot go back on their promises."

"The key has been lost for eighty years? Are you saying this man, the Vilaró, has been here that long?" He must be very old by now. Strange that the sirenas still feared him so much.

"Yes," Miss Prieto said. "I've been here almost thirty years, and he was here long before me. He's not human, though. I've tried to heal him, but I can't. Unlike a sirena or a selkie, he's simply too inhuman."

"What is he?" Joaquim asked.

"A fairy is what Leandra says," Marcos supplied.

After a dull moment where his brain couldn't seem to work out all she'd said, Joaquim asked, "That's why you call him the Vilaró, isn't it? Because he doesn't tell anyone his real name, because he has fairy blood."

Miss Prieto paused, scissors suspended above Joaquim's arm. "How do you know that?"

"I know someone with enough fairy blood that she doesn't use a name," Joaquim admitted. "We call her the Lady. From what I hear, her husband is the only man alive who knows her name."

"And Leandra is likely the only one who knows the Vilaró's true name," Miss Prieto said.

That implied a relationship between the supposed fairy and Leandra he hadn't suspected before. He contemplated that for a moment, but decided he had bigger concerns. "I don't know if I can find a thing," he admitted. "I find people."

Miss Prieto's lips turned up at one corner, almost a smile. "You *can*. Alejandro says you can."

She cut a last bit of burned skin away. What was left was a blistered mess, blood seeping from the torn spot. "How am I supposed to do that?" Joaquim asked.

She sat back and gave him a strange look. "Did no one teach you?"

"I didn't even know I was a witch until last fall."

Miss Prieto shook her head and reached into her satchel to pull out a tin. "I'm going to put another poultice on this, and bandage it loosely. Try not to be a restless sleeper."

It wasn't likely he was going to roll over onto his swollen face. While she worked on his arm, he pondered finding a *thing*. He'd never tried it, but his ability to find people stemmed from familiarity with them. Still, he'd had no familiarity with Alejandro, yet had tracked the boy by using something he'd touched. "Is there anything the key would have touched?"

She'd begun wrapping his arm with gauze. "The locks, I suppose."

"Is there any way I can touch the lock on his cell?"

"The locks are on him," Miss Prieto said. "In the morning after Mass, I'll come back to check on you again. I'll take you down to see him then."

"Can you just do that?" How much freedom did Miss Prieto have within the prison?

"I hope not to be caught," she said briskly. "God is with us this time."

"Whose plan is this?"

"Mostly the Vilaró's," Miss Prieto admitted. "Leandra and I helped flesh it out, but all the details came from Alejandro. The Vilaró questioned him for months, trying to get Alejandro's gift to give us the steps to follow."

"So Leandra stole the journal . . ."

"Because Alejandro *said* she would."

Seers often struggled with the temptation to act merely because they knew they would act. His cousin Rafael often compared it to passing a house on the street, *knowing* that he would buy it, and therefore doing so . . . without bothering to tour the house first to see if it was sound. It was a dangerous way to approach life, leading to wild and unpredictable decisions. "That's insane."

"It worked, did it not? To get everyone out, we need the Vilaró. To get him free, we needed a finder—you. The possibility of stealing that book only arose a couple of months ago, finally explaining why Leandra and Alejandro would be outside the prison at all. The most difficult part was convincing La Reyna that sending *them* to steal the book was her own idea. Piedad is far easier to manipulate, so we used her to plant the idea."

He suspected that Piedad *was* more predictable. "It's fortunate the Spanish embassy on the islands went along with that plan."

Miss Prieto shot a glance at Marcos.

"The ambassador is my father," the young man reminded him. "He never had any choice."

Joaquim shook his head. *Poor Marcos.* If there was any way to help get these people out of here, he was going to do it. "Aren't you concerned that the sirenas are listening to you?"

"Not at all," Miss Prieto said, tying off his bandage. "They see no need to. It's God's will, after all, that we live out our lives as their servants."

History was filled with those who thought they knew God's will, only to learn they were wrong. Joaquim hoped this was one of those times.

CHAPTER 39

Joaquim had spent most of the early-morning hours unable to sleep. His face actually felt worse than it had the previous day, his arm throbbed, and he was worried about the idiocy of a plan that relied on him to do something he'd never done before. About whether the man in chains could deliver on his promise to free these people. About Marina and Alejandro. They felt *closer* than Barcelona. What were they doing?

To distract himself, he'd talked with Marcos instead. Joaquim couldn't blame the young man for his bitterness. Of a more idealistic bent than Joaquim himself, Marcos had spent his youth among other wealthy boys with few cares to trouble them. Despite being only half human, he'd felt his father's status as a diplomat would protect him from imprisonment. And he was violently in love with this woman, Safira, yet feared that should they both ever be free, she might reject him for what he perceived as his faithlessness, even though he'd only done as ordered to protect *her*.

Considering that he'd spent the better part of three years in this place with nothing to do—there were no books, no paper, not even a deck of playing cards—Joaquim was impressed the young man was still sane.

When the morning's first light crept through his high window, Marcos gestured for Joaquim to come over to look outside. Following the young man's lead, he stepped onto Marcos' bed and stood on his toes to peer out the window, being careful not to touch his swollen nose to the glass. His second-floor window looked out onto a small courtyard surrounded by walls on two sides and fences on the other.

"We're in the back of the prison," Marcos said. "You can see the outer fence from here. This courtyard is only for the ladies and the children. Not prisoners. There's one on the opposite side for them."

Joaquim could see the stone outer fence, which looked twice as tall as any man. Plus, there were guard posts at the corners, although he couldn't see a guard at the moment. "That's not much space."

"No, they don't let the prisoners out often. Once a day. The part we're in is newer, a cross arm like the transept of a church, and the chapel is in the lower floor straight across . . . um, the apse, I suppose. That's where you go to get down to the bottom."

Joaquim peered in the direction he was pointing. "Bottom?"

"Where the Vilaró is. There's some way to get down there from the chapel. I've never been inside the chapel."

"Are you not allowed to go to Mass?"

Marcos laughed bitterly. "No. I refuse to give my word not to attempt escape."

He hadn't been able to tell how far they'd come from the first prison, the Morra, but it couldn't have been far. "Where are we in relation to the town?"

"Near the middle of it, actually. The prison is old and the town grew around it."

Joaquim eyed the fence again. Beyond that the land looked unused, not even for farming. It was an open field, where prisoners fleeing would be easy to see. "I don't see the town."

"We're looking in the one direction in which the town doesn't lie. Believe me, there's a plaza right in front of the prison, and streets on either side."

He supposed that was possible. After all, the prison in the Golden City was in the middle of the city as well, not far from his own flat. "If the Vilaró can break this prison, and you escape, what then?"

Marcos' lips pressed together. "What do you mean?"

"What's to stop the guards from simply catching everyone and bringing them back?"

Marcos frowned. "He has a plan."

Joaquim climbed down off the bed. Either the Vilaró hadn't told them his plan, or no one had told Marcos, for fear he would talk. Or none of them had a plan. "How many are planning to escape?"

"Only a few know," Marcos said. "Most will have to decide when the time comes."

That meant some of the sereia might choose to stay here instead of going home, a strange thought. But people held in captivity for a long time often feared leaving it. After Moses had led them out of Egypt, hadn't many of the Israelites wanted to return to slavery rather than face an unknown wilderness? "And there are children?"

The young man nodded. "That's my job, mine and Miss Prieto's."

"How many?"

"Nine."

An escape with nine children in tow? Joaquim felt his stomach sink.

"Eight," Marcos corrected. "I included Alejandro."

Eight wasn't any better. "And you believe you'll be able to get them all out safely?"

Marcos took a deep breath. "Alejandro said so. I have to believe the Vilaró can create enough chaos to aid us."

Joaquim hoped the young man's faith wasn't misplaced. But so far, Alejandro's insights had been correct, hadn't they? By volunteering to take Alejandro all the way to the islands to steal a book of unknown value, his mother had managed to bring a finder here to the prison. That told Joaquim that Alejandro's gift *had* to be stronger than his own, and likely stronger than Duilio's. He didn't think Duilio could have predicted the turns his path would take to end up here.

They talked on, discussing the numbers of sereia from the islands in the prison. Marcos lumped them in three groups: those who capitulated and served the navy; those who'd resisted and were still in the prison, forced to serve as wardens like Leandra and his Safira; and those who resisted too much and simply disappeared. Far more sereia had been dragged here than Joaquim had realized before.

"What do—"

The ground rumbled and, right before his eyes, the stones tiles of the floor buckled upward, only an inch or so, the movement flowing across the cell like a wave. A second later there was silence.

Joaquim swallowed. *An earthquake?* "What just happened?"

"The Vilaró," Marcos said. "He likes to remind La Reyna that while she controls the guards, it's him in whom the prisoners believe."

"He made the stone floor move?" Joaquim asked, disbelieving.

"Yes. Even in chains in the bottom of the prison, he has that much power. That is why they fear him so. And because the prisoners believe in him, he grows stronger."

"Because of their belief?"

"Yes," Marcos said with a short laugh. "La Reyna cannot kill him. She's tried. Her mother before her tried. Yet every day he grows stronger because the prisoners believe."

"Then why does he need help to escape at all?"

"In time he'll be strong enough to defeat the iron holding him, but that may be a hundred years from now, and Leandra will be dead. That's why he wants to help us escape. She is his favorite, and he wants to save her."

There was no saving her from the sickness that had already taken her gills. Joaquim said as much to Marcos.

"The Vilaró means to take her away to somewhere where she won't be sick any longer. She might live forever there, he says." Marcos crossed himself. "It's wrong to want to escape heaven, but she's a pagan anyway."

TERRASSA

M arina felt far better when she woke. She'd actually gotten a decent night's sleep. The mirror in the bathroom showed her that the blow to her jaw had produced only a yellowish bruising. It wasn't noticeable if one wasn't looking for it. She pinned up her hair and faced her reflection squarely. Even though yesterday had been a failure from one end to the other, she felt hopeful about today.

So I don't have the ruthlessness to be a blackmailer. I don't have the physical strength to fight off attackers without resorting to my call, meager though it is. I don't have the pragmatism to do things I don't agree with.

She pinched her cheeks to get back some of her color.

What I do have is persistence. I will keep asking for help until I have my husband back. As long as it takes.

Today she would send another telegraph and ask for Lady Ferreira's help. Then she would go to the Portuguese consulate in Barcelona and ask for their help. And then she would go to the Americans again. And if she must, she would go to Lleida itself and start over there. She couldn't afford to be arrested—that would leave Alejandro alone—but anything she could do short of that, she would.

Marina headed back down the quiet hall to the room where Alejandro was still sleeping. She lightly touched his shoulder. His eyes opened wide and he tensed.

Will he ever get over that? "It's me," she reminded him.

His shoulders sagged. His straight hair was disordered. "I'm awake."

"I'm going to go down to the church," she said. "I won't be long. Would you prefer to stay here?"

He shoved the blanket away. "No. Don't go without me."

Was that because he had some allegiance to the Church? If she asked him, he would probably say yes, whether or not it was true. Or did he simply not want to be left alone? "Why don't you go down to the water closet and then get dressed? I'll wait for you in the kitchen."

Rubbing at his eyes, Alejandro tumbled out of his bed and headed barefoot down the hall.

In the kitchen Marina found her industrious hostess preparing bread for the day. She asked for instructions on how to get to the church, and Mrs. Sala offered her son as a guide.

When Alejandro appeared a moment later, clothes donned hastily enough that he'd not tucked in the tails of his shirt, Marina took a moment to straighten his hair and then they both followed the tall young man to the church. Along the way he described every building they passed, keeping up a constant stream of good-natured chatter, a stark contrast to Alejandro's guarded silence.

The old church turned out to be three churches built close together, two ancient and plain in golden stone, and the third more modern, but still old. It was to that one that the boy led them. Since early Mass was to begin shortly, Marina quickly made her way over to the stand of votive candles that waited under a statue of the Virgin. She lit a candle and knelt to pray for the Virgin's intercession in securing Joaquim's freedom. She added Alejandro's mother and sister to that prayer, and then rose, surprised to find Alejandro kneeling next to her. He rose with her and followed her silently from the church. The Sala boy ambled ahead of them.

There were others coming to early Mass, down the street while they walked up it, but Marina didn't think they would overhear. "Did your mother take you to Mass at the prison?"

Alejandro shook his head. "The sirenas had Mass, but prisoners don't go."

Marina pursed her lips. It seemed harsh to exclude the prisoners, but it was a prison, after all. "Would she want to go if she could?"

Alejandro's brow rumpled, and Marina wondered if his mother had ever discussed her religious leanings with him. Perhaps not, given how little time they'd spent together. He shrugged then, confirming that.

"What do you think of Mass?" she finally asked, hoping to get some idea of what was going on inside the boy's head.

Instead of answering, Alejandro pointed ahead of them. Father Escarrá strolled in their direction. The priest waved when he saw them and stopped to greet them. "Mrs. Tavares," he said, "I was coming to find you two."

"To find us?" Marina took Alejandro's hand. "Why?"

"The marquesa would like a word with you," he said. "I've brought her to the house, and Mrs. Sala told me you'd gone down to the church."

Marina groaned inwardly. She'd admitted to the priest that she'd been in the wrong. She supposed she could say it to the old lady's face too. "Very well, Father."

Along the way back up to the house, the priest asked whether she'd been satisfied with her accommodations the previous night, and she was happy to tell him of the wonderful meal the Sala family had shared with them. He glanced at Alejandro a few times to see if the boy agreed, but Alejandro kept his opinion to himself.

When they reached the house, they found the marquesa enthroned in the middle of the humble sitting room like a flustered black crow. She clutched an ebony cane in her hands this morning. Her dark eyes looked just as angry as they had yesterday, so Marina suspected this was going to be an unpleasant interview. Mrs. Sala stood to one side, her hands wrapped in her apron and her downturned features strained.

Marina opened her mouth to apologize, but the marquesa spoke before she could get a single word out. She thumped her cane on the wooden floor and snapped, "So, what has the boy done to get himself thrown in a prison?"

At least the woman is speaking Spanish this morning. Marina shot a glance at the priest, who gestured that she should answer. "We came to Catalonia seeking a mother and son who were imprisoned for political reasons. The mother was imprisoned again the day before we arrived, but Alejandro was still free. The Mossos spotted him, and Joaquim tried to prevent them from taking him. They grabbed Joaquim in Alejandro's place."

The woman made a harrumphing sound. "Why would they take my great-grandson in this boy's place?"

"I don't know," Marina confessed.

"And how do you know where they've taken him?"

"We're assuming they took him to the same prison as Alejandro's mother, in Lleida."

The woman mumbled something under her breath. "Lleida, you say? That's the Unnaturals Prison. Why would this woman be there?"

She couldn't see any way to answer that without giving away that Leandra, and thus Alejandro, wasn't entirely human. "Mrs. Sala, is there any way Alejandro could eat breakfast? He's probably starving."

Her hostess looked relieved to have an excuse to escape the marquesa's regard. She quickly swept Alejandro from the sitting room and drew the door closed behind them. Father Escarrá remained, politely waiting.

Marina took a second to gather her wits. This could end up with her being thrown in prison herself. "Joaquim and I came here as a favor to the ambassador of the Portugals to the islands of the sereia."

The woman's white eyebrows rose. "You want me to believe that my great-grandson has friends in high places, do you?"

"He does," Marina said softly. "He regularly visits with Prince

Raimundo of Northern Portugal. They are friends, as strange as that may sound to you. Six months ago the prince's elder brother was assassinated by a representative of the Spanish throne. That woman left a trail implicating the government of the islands of the sereia, but they were able to identify her as a Canary instead, a sirena from the prison in Lleida."

The marquesa glanced at the priest, who nodded slowly. Then she pressed on. "You're saying a fishling killed the Portuguese prince? Wasn't it some botched surgery?"

Marina licked her lips. She wasn't going to argue over the insulting term. "She orchestrated the plot. Her parents were caught up in the first round of executions after the ban in the Golden City, and she wanted revenge." She wasn't going to explain the whole mess to the marquesa, just the political aspect of the conspiracy. "That is what ultimately sent us here. We were to determine who funded her actions."

"But on what grounds did they throw my great-grandson into that prison?" the marquesa asked, thumping her cane for emphasis. "Is he a witch?"

"Of course he is," Marina said, growing exasperated. "He finds things. That's why he was sent to Barcelona in the first place. To find the woman."

"Marquesa," the priest said, setting a gentle hand on the old woman's shoulder, "the less said, the better."

"Haven't you been listening, Father?" The marquesa pointed her finger at Marina. "That one has more to hide than either of us. We can always deny, but that one can't."

Marina noted that the woman said we. The priest had hinted there was something unusual about his family; he must also be a witch like the marquesa, his talent hidden. Given the way the marquesa kept looking to him for verification, Marina wondered if he might be a Truthsayer. "That is true," she said softly. "I am not human."

"And did my great-grandson know that before he married you?"

Marina felt calm settle over her like a blanket. Nothing she said from here out could make this worse. "Of course. Joaquim has known since he met me."

The old woman made a harrumphing sound again.

"He believes in equality," Marina said, "regardless of kind or station or religion. He always treated me as if I were the same as any other woman of his acquaintance, even when it was illegal for me to live in the Golden City."

"Did you bewitch him?"

"No," she said. "He courted me completely of his own choice."

The marquesa's nostrils flared, betraying anger. Or perhaps it was annoyance. Or distaste. She probably didn't approve of Joaquim, an unacknowledged scion of her line, taking a nonhuman for his wife. If the old woman was going to denounce her, she would do it now.

The marquesa pressed down on her cane to rise. She beckoned over the priest with her chin and he offered his arm to steady her. "We'll meet you at ten at the station, girl."

Marina rose quickly. "At the station?"

"If we're going to Lleida, I'm not going to rattle my old bones in a carriage all that way." The marquesa began to stomp and clomp her way out of the sitting room. "Just make sure that boy looks presentable. I don't travel with ragamuffins."

Marina stood unmoving, unsure whether she'd just agreed to something, and if so, what.

CHAPTER 40

✺

ILHAS DAS SEREIAS

The first messenger to arrive that morning bore good news: a written guarantee from the sereia government that the mission was welcome to return to Quitos. After some deliberation, it was decided that Captain Vas Neves and their chief of staff would oversee the move back to the embassy grounds there.

The second messenger arrived a couple of hours later, one of those American embassy guards in his dark jacket and white trousers. He spoke briefly with Captain Vas Neves and left the message in her hands.

"Madam Norton asks that if you decide to take any action," Vas Neves said to Oriana, "she would appreciate being advised. The lieutenant told me they're busy packing up to return to the embassy, or Madam Norton would have come herself."

Oriana opened the sealed envelope, drew out a sheet of paper, and began reading. Duilio watched her, visibly forcing himself to be patient. Oriana read on, a sick feeling growing in her stomach—not morning sickness. When she finished reading, she looked at Duilio. "Joaquim has been taken prisoner, and Madam Norton's nephew was gravely injured in the process."

Duilio's lips pressed into a thin line. "Taken by whom?"

Oriana sighed. "She says they don't have much information at this point. Pigeons, remember?"

One of his eyebrows rose, and he made the sign for frustration. "What about Marina?"

"Marina has the boy," Oriana said, one bit of good news. "She was told to wait at her hotel while the Americans tried to find him."

Oriana didn't know what Marina *could* do in this situation, but her sister had never been one to follow orders.

"We still have almost two weeks left of our retreat, don't we?" Duilio ran fingers through his hair. "I'm going to take Costa and go talk to the captain of the *Tesouro*."

Oriana wasn't sure of the implications of leaving her post, but what was the worst the Foreign Office could do? They didn't have anyone trained to replace her yet, and even if they did, the adoption papers had gone through. They could just return to this house and take up their own lives again.

And she no more wanted to leave Marina on her own than Duilio would wish to abandon his brother. Or brothers. So she nodded, and Duilio walked out of the courtyard to find Costa.

TERRASSA

The train to Lleida was scheduled to leave the station at half past ten. Marina waited patiently, their single bag at her feet. Alejandro stood at her side, wearing his cleanest shirt and trousers. Marina had left double the payment her hostess asked, along with a quick prayer that God would watch over the Sala household.

A few minutes before the train was set to leave, Father Escarrá appeared, accompanying the marquesa along the platform. He carried a bag much larger than Marina's own that must belong to the old woman. The black-clad marquesa plunked her cane on the platform as she walked, swiping at other passengers' feet to get them out of her way. Presently she stood at Marina's side.

"You're a tiny little thing. Did your mother have trouble birthing children?" the marquesa asked, gazing speculatively at Marina's hips.

Marina felt her face flush. "No, Marquesa, not to my knowledge."

"Hmmph."

Perhaps the marquesa hoped she'd die in childbirth, leaving Joaquim free to marry someone more suitable, someone human. The conductors opened the doors to the first-class car then, and after a nod to Marina, Father Escarrá helped the old woman up the steps. Marina handed her bag to a porter and followed with Alejandro.

Soon they were all ensconced in a first-class compartment, Marina and Alejandro sitting facing the back of the train and the priest and the marquesa across from them. Marina was relieved to see that the old woman had brought a pillow to make herself comfortable. The priest draped a large shawl over the marquesa's shoulders once she'd settled, and she seemed, as far as Marina could tell, to drop immediately off to sleep.

Marina managed not to make her sigh of relief audible. She didn't know what to say to the marquesa and frankly she wasn't entirely sure the woman wasn't accompanying her to Lleida to turn her in.

She withdrew Alejandro's book from her bag and opened it up to where they'd left off. Alejandro scooted closer to her and peered at the page when she began reading, so she let her finger trail along the words for him to see. She kept her voice low, not wanting to wake the marquesa.

The train moved out of Terrassa Station and slowly picked up speed as it headed north. Much of the countryside even beyond Terrassa was terraced, vines marching in neat rows up the hillsides. Marina stole an occasional glance at the priest, who looked as though he might be trying to comprehend her Portuguese, but kept reading.

The stop at Manresa would be long enough for them to take on new passengers, so Marina availed herself of a chance to visit the water closet in the station. Father Escarrá had gotten out to walk about on the platform, stretch his legs, and breathe in the fine morning air. When Marina came out, she found him still there, waiting for her. Other passengers stood on the platform, most of the men smoking. From the platform they could see none of the town; they faced a stony ridge covered with trees instead, making it seem as if the station stood in an abandoned spot of countryside.

"It sounds like an interesting tale," Father Escarrá said in Spanish, "although I cannot follow enough to know exactly what's happening."

Ah, the book. "There are also a number of strange words," she added, "words that I'm certain make sense for someone who knows Africa. I'm afraid I do not."

"I see," the priest said. "I should tell you that the marquesa doesn't travel much anymore. That she bestirred herself is an indicator that she thinks this important."

"Did you intercede with her on my behalf?"

The priest smiled. "No, Mrs. Tavares. Your actions alone convinced her. I think if you'd threatened her as you'd planned, you would only have vexed her. When you didn't, she was intrigued."

Apparently her lack of strength had worked in her favor this time. "I am glad to know that."

A gentleman with a cigar walked past them toward the doors of the second car, the scent of smoke drifting along with him and tickling Marina's nose. "Affability is *not* one of the lady's gifts," Father Escarrá said, "but she is unfailingly generous when we need help providing for the poor of the town."

Marina recalled the woman's orders from her coach for Marina to go to the Church for aid. "I was fortunate you came along last night."

"I was coming to join her for dinner," the priest admitted. "I often do."

"Were you raised there?"

"On a farm nearby," he said. "My family's land marches with hers. I often visit to check on my nephew, the son of my older brother."

"Oh. Is your family still here?"

"Only my sister-in-law and my nephew. My brother died a couple of years ago while imprisoned." He crossed himself, and added, "He wrote a poem that was published in *La Veu de Catalunya*. The government took exception to the nationalistic tone of the poem and threw him in prison, which is how I know anything about Lleida at all. I used to visit him there."

"Is that where he died?"

"Yes. There was an outbreak of plague in 1900." He crossed himself again.

There had been one in the Golden City in 1899 as well, shortly before she'd arrived there. "I am so sorry."

The conductors began calling for the passengers to board again, so Marina let the priest help her into the car. She walked down the narrow corridor until she reached their compartment and found the marquesa and Alejandro within, glaring at each other from opposite benches. Alejandro's lower lip was thrust out and his arms were folded over his chest.

"Alejandro, if you stick that lip out any farther," she said in Portuguese, "a bird will come and land on it."

That tore his attention away from his glaring match with the marquesa. His expression hinted that he had no idea whether birds actually did that sort of thing. Marina was glad for once that Oriana had teased her exactly that way when she was a girl.

"So, why are you sulking?" she asked him.

"She called you a *fish girl*."

Well, the priest had said that affability wasn't one of the marquesa's gifts. Marina sat down next to the boy. "Be polite anyway. This falls under the mantle of respecting one's elders."

He settled back against the seat, but the scowl didn't fade.

"That boy needs to learn his manners," the old woman snapped in Spanish.

Marina sighed and put one arm reassuringly around Alejandro's shoulders. "He will, in time, madam. He was raised in difficult circum-stances."

"A child of the prison," the marquesa said knowingly. "I can tell. There are rumors that terrible things happen in that prison in Lleida. That prisoners disappear."

The priest shook his head. "My brother spoke of a place called the Morra, an *underground* prison built centuries ago within the basement of the town hall. The prisoners believed that if you were sent there, you would never return."

The train began to move slowly, jerking out of the station with a loud, screeching whistle. A prison under the town hall? *How very odd.* Marina glanced down at Alejandro. "Is that true? Is there such a place?"

Alejandro nodded slowly, eyes lowered.

Marina crossed herself, praying that Joaquim never found him-self there.

CHAPTER 41

LLEIDA

The morning had crawled by in a haze of annoying aches as Joaquim waited for the promised visit by Miss Prieto. He'd begun to fear she'd been found out, and had only Marcos' dogged belief in the plan to sustain him.

He and Marcos watched the children—only the girls—play in the courtyard below with a few old women in attendance. Joaquim counted five, Liliana being the eldest. "Where are the boys?"

"They do not play. They are used to run errands, scrub floors. Because they are male, they have no value to the sirenas until they are old enough to sire children. Except Alejandro, of course."

Joaquim recalled that Reyna had said Alejandro wasn't acceptable breeding stock. "Why not him?"

"Because he's also a witch. For that reason, he would never have shared my fate."

One of the rare times when being a witch in Spain was a blessing, Joaquim supposed. "The girls look well cared for."

"They are treated like . . . princesses," Marcos said. "They are told all others are inferior to them because God gave them the ability to control men, and one day they may be queen of this damned place. And after a time, they begin to believe it. My poor baby."

Liliana had shown nothing but disdain for her mother—who, with her ruined gills, could not *call*—and Joaquim was certain she'd never been struck before the moment Piedad slapped her.

Later they watched the sirenas file into the chapel for their morning worship, the older girls among them. With the exception of Piedad, most of the sirenas were older women, dressed in matching gray suits, the uniforms of the wardens, Joaquim realized. Marcos confirmed that all the children held in the prison were children of the Portuguese sereia. The daughters of the Canaries—the sirenas— were spread throughout Spain, as wives and mistresses of influential men. The sons apparently thought themselves safe, as Marcos had.

The key rattled in the lock, and Joaquim rose. Miss Prieto slipped inside just as a bugle called outside, summoning prisoners out to lunch in the courtyard. She shut the door behind her and checked Joaquim's injuries. The cut on his cheek—in which she'd put a handful of stitches—seemed less angry. "You do look like you've taken a beating," she said, "but as long as you keep these clean, you'll be fine. I'm sorry that I haven't used my gift to heal these, but I'm saving my strength for afterward."

Joaquim nodded. Fortunately. the swelling in his eyes had gone down and didn't impinge on his vision. "So, what do I do?"

She patted his knee. "I'm going to walk you downstairs and across the courtyard to the chapel. There's a passage that leads off to the cell where the Vilaró is kept. As long as you look like you're supposed to be there, we should do well enough."

"Will the priest be in the chapel?"

"The priest only comes on Sundays," she said. "We had one residing here before, but he's gone, thank God."

It was a strange sentiment, until Joaquim recalled the priest who'd come from this place. "Salazar, you mean."

Miss Prieto's eyes lifted to meet his, her lip curling at one corner. "You know him?"

"No, but I saw him die," Joaquim said. "And Dr. Serpa as well."

Marcos slid closer to the edge of his bed, an eager smile touching his lips. "They're dead?"

It's been over six months, and they don't know?

"Yes. That's what started this quest." Joaquim explained as briefly as he could about the night that Dr. Serpa and Salazar, under Iria Serpa's guidance, had killed the prince of Northern Portugal and tried to start a war between the sereia and the Portuguese. "Someone involved in that plot also murdered my wife's mother to prevent Iria's exposure."

Miss Prieto began repacking her satchel, shaking her head. "Iria had an insatiable desire for vengeance. When their whole plan began to disintegrate, she moved ahead with her part. The others were so intent on pushing Spain to invade that I don't think they even noticed Iria had carried on with her quest until Father Salazar left with her."

"Why was he here to begin with?" Joaquim asked.

"Experiments," Miss Prieto said, "with Dr. Serpa. They tried to combine magic and science, claiming that they were making great advances in medicine. They didn't care how many prisoners died in their quest. After he moved back to Portugal, Serpa returned many times, coming back to further his so-called experiments with Salazar. Salazar used his gift to keep the sirenas alive. He stole strength from other prisoners, killing most in the process. He used that strength to hold the sirenas' illness, the *gill rot*, in check, although he couldn't defeat it." Miss Prieto shook her head. "Now I know why La Reyna was desperate enough to send Leandra to steal that book. She's running out of time. The others were waiting for his return, but she must know the truth—that Salazar won't come back. The sirenas who have tuberculosis will start dying, so Reyna needs that book to force the Portuguese sirenas to send more women here to replace them."

"You can't help them?" Joaquim asked.

Her chin lifted stubbornly. "No. I refuse to do what he did. Killing some so that others might live? It's a corruption of the gift. In a way I'm glad I'm not powerful like he is . . . *was*. I prefer not to be tempted to believe I dispense God's will."

"Why are you here? In prison, I mean?"

"As a young woman I was given the chance to disavow my gift, but God has given me the talent, so I must use it. They brought me here, and I have been trying to serve where I am."

A noble attitude in such a horrible situation. It explained her relative freedom within the prison. "If we are successful, where will you go? Home?"

She shook her head. "It was a long time ago. I have no one left."

"There are healers in the Golden City, powerful ones, but they lack experience." He hesitated to admit that one of those healers was Salazar's natural daughter, who'd not even known she was a witch until her father tried to blackmail her into joining him in his crimes. "Someone of your experience would be helpful in teaching them how to better use their skills."

Miss Prieto gazed at him thoughtfully, then shook her head. "We're running short on time," she said. "We need to go."

Mind whirling, Joaquim pushed off the bed, went to the water closet, and then came back and pulled on his borrowed shirt. It fit passably, although he left the collar unbuttoned. Miss Prieto passed a key to Marcos, picked up her satchel with one hand, and set the other on Joaquim's arm above his elbow. "Pretend I'm escorting you from one place to another."

Joaquim nodded. When Miss Prieto opened the door, he accompanied her docilely along a hallway that looked more as if it were, well, a *prison*. A guard in a plain gray uniform stood at the corner of the hallway where it turned, watching them with unconcerned eyes. When they got closer, Miss Prieto bade Joaquim stay where he was and went to speak to the guard alone. Whatever she said to the man caused a nasty smile to flicker across his face as he eyed Joaquim. She returned to Joaquim's side and took his arm again.

"What did you tell him?" he asked once they were past the guard.

"That I was taking you to the chapel," she said, "to see Piedad."

Joaquim felt his temples throb in time with his footfalls. "Is that what you're doing?"

Miss Prieto didn't pause. "There is always the possibility that she's there. I pray not, but I cannot promise."

"She doesn't strike me as being very Christian," Joaquim observed as they walked down a stairwell at the end of that hall.

Miss Prieto drew him closer and softly said, "Her God is the God of forced conversion. She truly believes that their quest is only to bring Christianity to the Portuguese sirenas by Spanish domination. It is her passion, her reason for drawing each breath. In her eyes, what violence she commits is done for a greater cause."

How many times throughout history had that claim been used to justify evil? "Even striking a child?"

"It got *you* to cooperate," Miss Prieto pointed out.

Well, that was true. They came out of the stairwell and she opened a door that led to an intersection of hallways. As Marcos had said, the building went off in four directions, like a cross. Voices echoed faintly along those halls, and the smell of human filth was stronger than in the wing they'd left. Miss Prieto led him down one hall until he could see the entrance of the chapel. He had a split second of worry that Miss Prieto was indeed taking him to face Piedad again.

Another sirena in gray stood at the doorway, though, apparently on guard. The young woman had auburn hair and shadows under her dark eyes that hinted she'd not slept in days. "Miss Prieto," she said in little more than a whisper. "Is this him?"

"Yes," the healer answered.

How long have they been waiting for a finder to show up?

The young woman crossed herself and then reached out to take Joaquim's hands. "Bless you," she said in Portuguese.

She was a Christian? "You're from Amado?"

A line appeared between her brows. "You know it?"

"My wife was raised on Amado," he said.

The young woman leaned closer. "Does she know . . . ?"

"Safira, we need to go," Miss Prieto insisted. "You can talk later."

The young woman stepped back, nodding briskly, and Miss Prieto pushed open the tall door of a chapel that could hold at most forty worshippers. An altar stood at the front, its altar cloths finely embroidered, but otherwise it was a very plain house of worship, suited to a prison. While the door closed behind them, Joaquim scanned the pews and the aisles, but saw no sign of Piedad, a great relief. "Now what?"

"In the office, there's a stairwell." She led him along the outside aisle to a heavy door and they stepped inside. The office was small and apparently rarely used, but the rug showed a worn path between the door and a closet.

"In there?" Joaquim asked.

Miss Prieto opened the door of the closet with a lopsided smile. "Shall we?"

The inner door opened to reveal a narrow stone stairwell. There were lights in the well, a sloppily strung series of electric bulbs next to old defunct gas fixtures. Miss Prieto lifted the hem of her skirts and started down the spiral, keeping close to the outside. Joaquim followed. The steps were just wide enough for his feet and worn in spots so that they made for treacherous footing. After about two stories, they stepped out into a narrow tunnel, a rough-cut stone passageway that led on for thirty or forty feet. Joaquim followed her down that hallway, glad he didn't have to stoop to do so.

At the end of the tunnel, he expected to find a cell door awaiting them. But there was no door on this cell. To his left the tunnel opened into a wide circular space where the walls, the ceiling, and even the floor were covered in steel, sheets bound together with heavy rivets, reminding Joaquim of a shipbuilder's work. In the middle of that space, lit by the last of the electric lights, stood a man, his arms spread wide, held that way by chains that extended from the ceiling. His ankles were shackled to the steel floor.

This is the man who'd made the floors ripple?

He didn't look powerful. The Vilaró was terribly lean, but not emaciated. His age was difficult to pinpoint, but Joaquim would put him between thirty and forty-five. Joaquim couldn't place his nationality either; European, he would guess. His skin was pale, his dark hair was unkempt but not overlong, yet his nails appeared to have been cut recently. The man wore nothing, but didn't seem concerned by his nudity in Miss Prieto's presence. His eyes were fixed on Joaquim instead, pale eyes that showed cool anger.

"This is the Vilaró," Miss Prieto said.

The Vilaró regarded Joaquim steadily. "So this is our finder?" he said in a deep voice that rumbled. "Let us hope Alejandro was right about him."

"There should be one key to all these locks," Miss Prieto said to Joaquim. "That's the one we'll need to find."

Joaquim turned to the man waiting there. "I've never tried this before."

"Time is of the essence," Miss Prieto reminded him. "We should hurry before anyone shows up in the chapel. We'd be stuck in here then."

And she might be missed, Joaquim realized. So he crossed the metal floor to where the man waited. This close the Vilaró didn't smell, not of anything. Not even of perspiration. The only scent that Joaquim could catch was rusting steel and the musty stone of the hallway they'd just left. The man had no stubble on his jaw, unlike Joaquim's growth of a few days. "I'm going to handle this lock," he warned.

"Fine," the man rumbled.

Joaquim wrapped his hands around the padlock that secured the heavy iron cuff holding the man's right wrist in the air. The Vilaró bared his teeth. Under that cuff his skin was nearly burned away, far worse than the brand on Joaquim's arm. He tried to be gentle as he set his index finger on the lock's keyhole.

He'd found Alejandro with a borrowed item of clothing. Somehow he'd gotten enough of a feel of the boy to track him. He needed to do the same for the key.

"How long have you been here?" he asked the man.

"What year is it?" the Vilaró asked in turn. When Joaquim informed him it was 1903, the man said, "Eighty-one years, then."

Joaquim considered the cuff again. "Have these irons been on you all the time?"

"Yes."

This cell had to have been built for him. These irons had been against his skin, burning his flesh, for more than eight decades. Fairies were supposed to fear iron, weren't they? "Why did they chain you here?"

The Vilaró laughed softly. "To study me."

"He says that Salazar and Serpa are dead," Miss Prieto interjected. "Six months ago."

"Good," the man said, an echo of Miss Prieto's reaction. "Saves me the trouble of hunting them down."

Supposedly, the writer of the book upon which Serpa and Salazar had based their experiments *had* included fairies among those he'd vivisected. The Vilaró didn't show any scars, but given his acid tone, the doctor and healer must have experimented on him in some way. If he'd been here eighty years, he'd been here long before Serpa or Salazar arrived.

"*Are* you a fairy?" Joaquim asked, thinking that might improve his grasp of the builder's logic.

"That is a very broad term," the Vilaró replied. "A human term."

Joaquim decided that was a *yes*, or close enough. He thought about the lock, holding this man for a long time, metal, rusting, but so thick it hadn't worn away. The key that had fit into this lock would have smallish teeth. It would be slender, made of the same metal.

He closed his eyes and concentrated, imagining that key and trying to feel where it was.

He had to do this, because if he didn't, he wasn't sure the chance to escape would come again. He didn't want to contemplate life in this prison, even in Marcos' palace. Marina was coming here, and if he couldn't get out, she and Alejandro were surely walking into danger.

And there it was, burning on the edge of his awareness, a dark light that could only be the iron key he sought. "Miss Prieto, we have to go back up."

CHAPTER 42

Marina set aside the book. Alejandro had fallen asleep, his head slumped against the compartment wall. The marquesa slept as well, snoring slightly. That was the first thing Marina had found endearing about the hard old woman.

The train rattled past more countryside, the view growing more barren as they moved west. It wasn't like the drier areas she'd seen around Madrid, but they were clearly growing closer to that part of the country. She peered at the luggage rack overhead. She would like to use the time to work on deciphering the remaining bits of the code in her mother's journal. She'd figured out about half of the letters, and the remaining ones should fall into place when she studied it further, but Father Escarrá was reading a newspaper and she didn't want to disturb him to get into her bag.

So she glanced down ruefully at Alejandro's book. Perhaps she could start reading this book again from the beginning. She opened the book and thumbed through the first few pages, and then sighed. What she actually wanted was to be done with the thing. She flipped the book to the back instead to see how many pages were left, and paused.

There was writing on those pages.

Neatly inscribed on the blank pages at the back of the book were all the letters with which she'd grown so familiar. Leandra had done the same thing Marina had, only she'd had the journal for several days. She'd had time to decipher the writing while in hiding and aboard ship. And, possibly because she didn't want to misplace it, she'd written it in the other book she'd had with her, the one that Alejandro called his own.

That must be why this book was hidden in the bookstore along with the journal. Even if the Canaries found the *journal*, they wouldn't have known to take this book as well. It was quite clever of her.

Marina read through the deciphered notes Leandra had left.

Her mother hadn't *only* been focused on the woman they knew as Iria Serpa. Instead she'd seen a larger pattern. While inspecting the background of a new applicant to the Ministry of Intelligence—Iria—she'd discovered that a handful of Canaries had slipped onto the islands via the Spanish embassy. Apparently all had found work in the various newspapers of Quitos. Because of the government's tight controls over the press, especially on the main island, they had been easy for her to track once she grasped what she was hunting. She hadn't been able to determine what the Canaries were trying to accomplish, but surmised the Spanish government wanted a foothold on the islands.

Then she'd found more—evidence that this plan had the backing of several prominent members of the ministry. They knew of the Canary spies and were providing them with identity papers and money to establish themselves as sereia citizens. There were even records of a few arrests of those spies, quickly squelched by the then minister of Internal Affairs—the branch responsible for routing out sedition.

Marina rubbed her hands together. They'd started hurting again. That was the branch that accused her father of sedition and had him exiled.

She read on. Her mother had compiled all her evidence and left those papers in a safe-deposit box in the bank at Porto Novo. That information still had to be there, even fourteen years later, because the only people her mother had listed as having permission to open the box were her mate and her daughters.

It was all there, waiting to be discovered.

The cipher recorded in the back of the book ended with her mother's concerns that someone within the ministry itself was moving to block her. She'd made an appointment to see Minister Raposo, but was uncertain whether the minister was involved. So she'd written it all down in her journal, and planned to leave it where her mate would find it should anything happen to her.

She'd known she was at risk, Marina thought.

Would Mother have approached her sisters Valeria and Vitoria about this? She was staying under their roof at the time, yet had chosen to hide the journal from them. Had she suspected them of complicity too? What about her aunt Jovita?

Marina clutched the book close against her chest as the train rattled on. *Thank God I didn't turn this over to that woman in Barcelona.* She'd thought she might find evidence of a single conspirator in their midst. This was far worse.

LLEIDA

Joaquim made his way up the stairs, Miss Prieto close behind him. He came up into the closet within the chapel's office, and stopped to listen at the closet door before he opened it. The office stood empty. He let out a pent breath.

While Miss Prieto closed the closet door behind them, he stood in the office and concentrated. His perception of the key's location held steady. It was *inside* the chapel.

Miss Prieto opened the office door only a crack and peered into the chapel. "We're alone."

He followed her out and pushed the office door closed. "Over by the altar."

They approached the altar, the familiar scent of incense growing stronger and his heart sinking deeper with every step. He could feel it. The key was *inside* the altar.

He peered down at the altar's coverings. One section hung down over the front of the altar, a gold cloth embroidered to depict a young woman with an ax in her right hand—a martyr. "Who is this?" Joaquim asked.

Miss Prieto stood behind the altar where she could watch the door. "Saint Grace of Lleida."

"The town's patron?"

"No, a patron of Spain. She was martyred trying to convert her brother to Christianity."

Joaquim stared at the cloth for a moment, trying to decide what to do. No, he knew what needed to be done. Saying a quick prayer for forgiveness, he carefully lifted the edge of the cloth to reveal a niche in the wood of the altar. Inside that niche was a small casket made of gilded wood.

"What are you doing?" Miss Prieto asked, her voice anxious. "Is it there?"

"There's a reliquary," he said. "I . . ."

How could he explain to her that this went against all his training? Joaquim crossed himself. "It would be desecrating the altar to remove it."

Her eyes met his across the altar. "Let me do it, then."

"Letting you do it is little different from doing it myself." Joaquim licked his lips, wishing that his head didn't hurt. It made him want to ignore his qualms and get this over with. *I'm going to do it*, he thought. *I'm going to desecrate an altar and hope that God will forgive. These people aren't criminals, and I have the ability to help right the wrongs perpetrated against them.*

There *wasn't* another way, not when their entire plan hinged on his doing this. He reached into the niche and removed the gilded box. When he shook it, he heard something inside rattle, too heavy to be a piece of bone. "What is this relic supposed to be?"

"A shard of the ax that killed Saint Grace," Miss Prieto said.

That would sound a great deal like a key. He looked at the box, trying to find hinges or a latch, but there was no way to open it. *I've gone this far.* He set the box on the floor in front of the altar and stomped on it. It broke apart with a dry crunch, the wood under the gilding fragile and powdery. Joaquim knelt down and dug through the ruins of the casket. He pulled away a sheet of gold and splintered wood to reveal the relic hidden inside. No saint's finger bone or splinter of a cross. Joaquim lifted it and showed it to Miss Prieto.

She let out a quiet laugh. "Thank God."

It was a slender key, old and made of iron just like the locks that bound the Vilaró.

"I'll go back to Marcos," she said. "I need to help him with the children. Give us a few minutes to get ready before you release the Vilaró."

"How will you know when I've set him free?"

"*Everyone* will know," she said, laying one hand on his unin-jured arm. "Be cautious. If all goes as planned, we should meet again outside."

Without waiting for an answer, she turned and walked swiftly out of the chapel. Joaquim stared down at the key, amazed that so much seemed to hinge on such a small thing. He stuck it in his pocket and headed toward the door of the office.

Joaquim had almost reached it when the chapel door opened again.

Piedad stood at the threshold of the chapel, one hand still on the door. "What are you doing here?"

Joaquim's heart beat hard against the walls of his chest. He could surely incapacitate Piedad if he had to, but he would prefer it not come to that.

But it will come to that, won't it? Piedad could *call* every guard in the prison to this chapel. Every prisoner within these walls would throw themselves at the bars of their cells trying to reach her, to *protect* her. The moment she became suspicious, he was going to have to fight her.

And there was no good answer he could give her. "I came to see the chapel."

Piedad came toward him, a sly smile on her pretty face. A smile that didn't show her pointed teeth, Joaquim noted. "The queen says that I get to keep you for now," she said. "But if you disobey, do you understand what will happen?"

"You'll hurt that little girl again."

She'd reached him by then, and laid one hand on his chest. He saw for the first time that her fingers were scarred from the surgery to remove the webbing, but so slightly that it was barely visible. It must have been done when she was young. "Yes, you understand very well." Her head tilted. "How did you get out of your cell?"

"I made the healer let me out," he said.

"And you came *here*? Why?"

He could feel it then, like a wisp of cigarette smoke drifting about his head. She was trying to use her *call* on him. Not like the sereia who'd *called* him from the naval boat, who'd tugged at him from a distance. This was more like Marina's *call*—subtle and powerful up close. And yet like smoke, it drifted away, ineffectual. "I wanted to pray."

Her eyes narrowed, as if she'd not expected that answer. No, she'd expected the full truth out of him.

He knew that women could be just as dangerous as any man, but he still didn't like the idea of hitting a woman. Even one like Piedad, so clearly a woman of violence. Then he thought of Captain Vas Neves and her soldiers, and the sereia naval officer on the boat that had intercepted them.

His mother and Lady Ferreira had raised him to respect women. Not to treat them like inferiors. And here he was, holding off on hitting an enemy merely because she was a woman.

Joaquim moved half a step back and punched her, his fist con-necting with her jaw.

Piedad didn't collapse. She swayed with the punch, pointed teeth bared.

Joaquim didn't wait for her to get in a swing. With one foot, he swiped her legs out from under her—a trick learned from Alessio. She hit the wall next to the office door floor face-first. Joaquim grabbed the back of her neck and slammed her forehead onto the wall again. She dropped like a rag doll then, still hissing in fury. For a second she huddled on the floor, clutching her forehead.

Damn. I didn't hit her hard enough.

Joaquim took a step toward her. Now he was going to have to hit an opponent who was already on the floor.

That was when she lunged toward his leg. Her fine, pointed teeth caught the back of his ankle and she bit down. That *hurt.*

Joaquim planted his weight on that foot and kicked her head with his other heel. It loosened her hold, but he felt something tear in his ankle. That made him kick her again, harder. If that didn't break her nose, he didn't know what would.

Her teeth loosened enough that he managed to yank his ankle free. Still lying on the floor, she clutched at her face.

I know exactly how that feels. Joaquim didn't wait to find out whether she could *call* in this state. He stumbled back into the office and slammed the door. He dragged the chair against the handle to block the door, opened the closet, and began hurrying down the stairwell. His ankle burned and about halfway down the blood in his shoe made him slip. He slid down the last steps and landed on his rump on the tunnel floor, hitting hard enough that he could feel it in his nose.

For a second he sat there, waiting for the wave of pain to subside. Then he felt that *call* again, the tendrils of Piedad's influence trying to pull him back, slipping away because his heart already had Marina's seal on it. He laughed dryly and pushed himself off the floor.

His ankle was *bad.* He could tell that now, but he would deal with it later.

He made his way down the tunnel to where the Vilaró waited. The man's pale eyes fixed on him as he approached. Joaquim gazed at him in return. "If I let you go, are you going to help these people escape?"

"Yes," the Vilaró answered in his deep voice.

Joaquim drew the key from his pocket and tried the key in the lock that held the man's right hand. The tumblers grated as he turned it. "How?"

The Vilaró chuckled. "You sound like Leandra, who gave me conditions, and names of those who must not be hurt."

"I want assurance that you'll not simply kill everyone here. I've already done things this morning I would never have contemplated before. Don't make me regret freeing you."

With a crunch, the last tumbler in the lock turned and the hasp sprang free. Joaquim opened the lock, pulled it through the holes on the cuff, and dropped it on the floor. Then he opened the cuff and let it fall. The chain dangled from the ceiling.

"Give me the key," the Vilaró said, holding out his hand.

The man's wrist showed livid burns, and in one spot Joaquim thought he saw bone. "Can you touch it?"

"Give it to me," the Vilaró insisted.

Joaquim laid the key in the man's hand, only to hear flesh sizzle. But the Vilaró's hand clenched around the key. He shoved it into the keyhole of the lock binding the cuff on the far side, turning it far easier than the first lock. He freed that wrist, then squatted down to unshackle his ankles. Joaquim smelled burning flesh. He could see the man's hand blackening, and fought down a surge of nausea.

A moment later, the Vilaró stepped free from his chains. He walked across the steel floor and out into the stone hallway. He placed his tortured hands against the stone wall, and as Joaquim watched, he was *transformed*.

Light flowed about the Vilaró, coalescing into garb that mimicked what Joaquim himself wore. The man's gaunt frame filled out, almost like air filling a bladder, and his blackened hands became whole again. He turned his face back toward Joaquim. "My bargain was with Leandra, not you. Because you brought me that key, I'll kill as few as possible."

And then he stepped right into the stone wall, as if it were a sheet of water instead.

Joaquim stood in the cell, his breath coming hard. His ankle had begun to stiffen, so he shifted his weight to the other leg. He could still feel the tendrils of Piedad's *call* tugging at him, unable to find purchase, but otherwise it was silent in the abandoned cell.

And then a boom shook the earth. Dust from the ceiling settled in the tunnel. The lights flickered and went out. Left in utter blackness, Joaquim limped toward the tunnel, hands outstretched in search of the wall.

He needed to get out of here before the ceiling caved in on him. He hit the edge of the cell with his wounded arm, and hissed in another pained breath. But at least he knew where he was now.

The wispy grasp of Piedad's *call* abruptly stopped. Joaquim paused for a second, feeling liberated by its absence. Then cool hands settled on his shoulders.

Before he could cry out, he was jerked away from the world.

CHAPTER 43

※

ILHAS DAS SEREIAS

When word had reached them via the Americans that Joaquim had been taken prisoner, there hadn't been any question in Duilio's mind. He was needed in Barcelona.

His gift told him he wouldn't arrive in time to rescue his brother. But he had to *try.*

So now Duilio stood on the docks of Porto Novo in trousers, shirt, and jacket. Shoes, even. He rather enjoyed that, although he suspected the nostalgic feel of Portuguese garb would wear off quickly and he'd then be chafing at the restriction of waistcoats and neckties again.

Oriana dressed the part of a Portuguese gentlewoman, wearing a lovely teal suit that his mother had ordered made for her the year before, although she'd had to have the waist let out. As she'd worn human clothing for two years in the Golden City, she bore it without too much discomfort. Inês, on the other hand, looked uncomfortable in the simple white shirtwaist and black skirt she'd worn at the Spanish embassy. Her expression betrayed her suffering, although every time Costa glanced her way, she managed a halfhearted smile. Duilio felt sorry for the young woman. The prospect of going to Portugal to beg the permission of her mate's family must be daunting.

The fifth member of their party stood to one side, watching silently. Oriana's aunt had sent Lorena Evangelista, her investigator, to join them. Fortunately, Inês confirmed for them that the woman was indeed the same one who'd contacted her months before. Evangelista was to collect any evidence she could, and take Leandra's statement whenever they located her. The minister hoped Leandra's story would help convict those who had sold her to the Spanish, even if Leandra chose never to return to the islands.

"We're almost ready to cast off," the first mate of the *Tesouro* said. "Is your luggage aboard?"

"Yes," Duilio said, "but please let the captain know we're waiting for one more traveler."

The first mate made his way back up the gangplank to the ship.

"Are you sure she's coming?" Oriana asked, leaning close.

"Yes." Duilio turned to watch the traffic on the main street, and as he did, a carriage pulled to a stop and a woman in a white outfit stepped down.

After some wrangling with luggage, Madam Norton strode down the pier to the ship with one portmanteau in her hand. One of her aides followed, a young woman in plainer attire, clutching two portmanteaus and a briefcase. The two women in blue uniforms of the Signal Corps came last, carrying a large trunk between them. That had to be their mechanical arm. Good news, since that meant they could contact Barcelona and let them know the *Tesouro* was on its way.

Madam Norton walked directly up to Duilio and Oriana, clutching her straw hat to her head with one daintily gloved hand. "Madam Paredes, Mr. Ferreira, I'm grateful for your inviting me along. I hope there's better news about my nephew when we arrive." She turned to Duilio, one eyebrow lifted speculatively. "You say that I'll be needed there. Could you tell me why?"

Duilio wasn't going to admit his gift had told him that. He'd rather have some secret in reserve for future interactions with the clever ambassador. "You have your ways, we have ours."

LLEIDA

The train finally drew up to the platform at Lleida as the sun crept toward the mountains in the west. The station at Lleida was another simple one, a small building with a metal canopy like Manresa's. A river flowed toward the town, along the road from the station. To the east, an ancient cathedral rose on a hill. It looked more like a fortress than a church to Marina's eyes. The whole town had that brownness she was beginning to associate with central Spain. She felt a sudden surge of homesickness for the often-foggy streets of the Golden City.

Father Escarrá immediately went to find a cab to carry them to the town hall. He returned a moment later with a large coach and, after a short discourse with the marquesa, helped her and Marina into it. Alejandro obediently climbed up and sat by her, keeping his knees well away from the old woman's. Once they were all settled, the driver headed down the road that followed the bank of the river. It wasn't like the Douro, deep and dark and powerful. Instead it seemed a lazy river, tamed, and more suited to this city with its bright sunshine and sandstone walls.

"What do we do once we get to the town hall?" Marina asked.

"I will speak with the . . ." The marquesa rattled off a phrase that meant nothing to Marina.

"That's their title for the mayor here," Father Escarrá said after seeing Marina's baffled expression. "*Paer en cap.*"

The marquesa tapped her cane against the floor of the coach. "Who's the bishop now?"

"Meseguer," the priest supplied.

"He's a good man. If the *paer en cap* won't produce my great-grandson, the bishop will."

Marina wished she felt as sanguine about the marquesa's chances. Nobility wasn't as much a guarantee of cooperation as it must have been in the old days. "What do you need *me* to do?"

The marquesa's eyes narrowed. "Keep yourself and that boy out of the way. I'm not prepared to fight two wars at once."

Alejandro's face remained expressionless. He was probably accustomed to hearing himself spoken of in that way. Marina wasn't. She looked away at the river they were passing along, but then the coach turned from the wide main avenue onto a narrower street.

The street was lined with older buildings, the same beige stone predominating on either side of the street. Like in the Golden City, the buildings had small balconies that overlooked the traffic, wrought-iron rails guarding them. The coach finally pulled to a stop in a wider area in front of a stern building with tapestries hanging beneath trios of narrow arched windows.

"The town hall," Father Escarrá said to Marina as he helped her down.

It didn't seem a very grand building, but that was often the case in older parts of cities where one would find a church or museum crammed in between houses or shops.

Marina waited while Alejandro jumped down from the coach, landing on the paving stones in his worn shoes. His eyes shifted around the square—it was more a wide area in the street rather than a true square—and he stepped behind her. He was coming back to his prison. He couldn't like being here. She took his hand. "We'll be fine."

His expression was doubtful. His jaw clenched and he looked away.

The marquesa stomped toward the hall, passing under the

archway on Father Escarrá's arm. Marina followed with a reluctant Alejandro hanging on to her hand. The inside of the building was stately, the stone cast into a golden glow by the rings of lights hanging from the high ceiling and sconces on the walls. An arcade of arches surrounded the room, one covering a stairwell that led upward into what must be the areas of the building where the business of the city took place. The impressive main room in which they stood was nearly empty save for a few pieces of dark furniture under the arches and, incongruously enough, what looked like a well to one side.

The marquesa surveyed the room with a jaded eye and began banging her cane against the stone floor. A guard in ceremonial livery with a gold and red patch on his cap hurried over, his eyes wide with alarm. "My lady, how can I help you?"

The old woman peered up at the tall young man. "Get me a chair, you fool. And bring the *paer en cap* here. I want to speak with him now."

"There are chairs in the waiting chamber upstairs."

She snapped her cane against the young man's shins, causing him to flinch. "I am not climbing those stairs, boy. I am the marquesa of Terrassa-Montcada. I am a grandee, and your mayor will come to me."

Marina pursed her lips. *Grandee?* Surely Joaquim would know exactly what that meant. Whatever it was, it had the desired effect. The young man hurried off and returned carrying a heavy wooden chair. He set it on the floor and the marquesa settled into it with a satisfied huff. "Now, where is your mayor?"

"I've sent for him, lady," the young guard said.

"Adequate." The marquesa settled both of her gnarled hands atop her cane.

Marina glanced down at Alejandro, who rolled his eyes. She clamped her lips together to keep from laughing. It was the first time she'd seen him show such exasperation. He must share Joaquim's egalitarian sentiments. She laid one hand on his shoulder instead. *How long will we have to wait?*

Joaquim took a great gasp of air. It seemed as if he'd been imprisoned in rock, stone filling his lungs. He blinked, dazzled by the light about him. *How did I get here?*

He was in a courtyard, he realized, the reflection of the one that Marcos had shown him this morning—the prisoners' courtyard—but there was *no* wall. Where the wall should have been, rubble sprayed away from the yard. In the distance Joaquim saw men running toward the town, the streets he'd not been able to see from the other side of the prison. A handful of men in worn clothes huddled in the court despite the missing walls, gazing past Joaquim with frightened eyes.

"Where is she?" the Vilaró demanded.

Joaquim turned as much as his aching ankle would allow. The Vilaró stood to his left, open hands held wide at his side. "What did you do?"

"Where is Leandra?" the Vilaró asked again.

Joaquim swallowed, tasting dust. "How did I get here?"

"I moved you through the stone," the Vilaró said. "Now find Leandra for me, witch."

Moved him *through* the stone? What exactly did that mean? "Why?"

"Because if she's still in the Morra," the Vilaró added, "we need to get her out of there."

Ah, he hadn't thought of that. Joaquim closed his eyes and recalled Leandra's face the last time he saw her, bloodied like his own and exhausted. She was far enough away that she wasn't in *this* prison. "She's still there."

The Vilaró moved so quickly that Joaquim didn't have a chance to jerk away. He set his hand on Joaquim's shoulder, and the world went dark again.

Then they were standing in a dim room of all stone, blocks roughly hewn. The smell was mustier, as if it was wetter here, but still carried the undeniable scent of human filth. This was the Morra. He recognized it by the smell, even if he hadn't seen it before.

Joaquim coughed, trying to get the taste of dust out of his mouth. "What did you just do?"

"I moved you through the stone," the Vilaró said again.

This place was lit by lanterns rather than electricity. They were on a lower level, in a central atrium that had stairwells leading up on either side. As the Vilaró hauled him toward the wall beside one of the stairwells, Joaquim closed his eyes and caught his sense of Leandra.

She's in the same cell as before.

"If I get you a set of keys and a gun," the Vilaró asked, "can you get her out of here?"

Joaquim gazed at the man, his stomach cramping now. The Vilaró's hand, the one that had seemed burned to the bone, now looked whole. "What happened to your burns?"

"Why do you keep asking questions?" the Vilaró snapped. "I can feel the guard's feet on the steps. I'll retrieve his keys and gun, but you need to help Leandra out of this place."

Joaquim heard the footsteps of the guard above them now, clomping in heavy boots down the stone stair. A brawny man with curling hair came off the last step and turned to survey the atrium where Joaquim and the Vilaró stood. He turned his head one way, as if trying to spot something out of the corner of his eye, and Joaquim realized the guard couldn't see him.

The Vilaró was hiding them, making them invisible even though they stood in plain sight only a few feet away. Back in the Golden City, the Lady could do the same, as could Prince Raimundo. That told Joaquim they all had common blood.

But the guard clearly recognized there was danger. He drew a dagger, then advanced. The man had a pistol in his sash but hadn't chosen it, wise in this stone-walled space where any missed shot would ricochet. He paused again, expression puzzled, only a few feet away from where Joaquim stood.

Joaquim felt the Vilaró's hand on his shirt slacken, and when he glanced back, the Vilaró was gone.

And in that same instant, the guard saw *him*. "Who are you?"

Trapped against the wall, Joaquim made his choice. He lowered his shoulder and rammed forward into the man's stomach. The guard went down, Joaquim atop him, and let out a groan when his head hit the hard floor. As Joaquim grabbed at the dagger, the man's head lifted, his teeth bared. He huffed cigarette-smoke-laden breath in Joaquim's face as they wrestled for the blade. It hit the floor with a clatter. Joaquim reached for it, only to gasp in pain when the guard's hand closed around his burned arm. The guard pushed, throwing off Joaquim's weight. Joaquim's back hit the floor, his head striking the stone floor hard enough to send stars flaring through his vision.

By the time he got his eyes to focus, the guard had rolled to his feet and now loomed overhead, pistol in hand. At this distance, he couldn't miss. He took a step toward Joaquim, but then abruptly jerked away with a loud cry. Joaquim rolled onto his side and used his elbow to lift himself. The Vilaró held the guard against the wall.

The guard's eyes were wide with terror. "No," he pleaded with his captor. "No, Vilaró, don't hurt me. I swear I will let you out of here."

Joaquim couldn't see the Vilaró's face from this angle, but he heard a low laugh. Then the guard faded back into the wall, as if falling through it. The Vilaró continued to push him until all that was left were the guard's splayed hands, and then those were gone too. The Vilaró's arms emerged from the stone wall as if they were coming out of water.

Joaquim swallowed, tasting blood from a bitten tongue. *What did I just see?*

His breath short, Joaquim pushed himself into a sitting position against the hallway wall and regarded his savior with trepidation. In a low tone that he hoped wouldn't carry, he asked, "What happened to him?"

The Vilaró merely said, "I wouldn't think about it too hard."

Joaquim glanced downward. His sleeve was bloody now where the guard had grabbed his arm, the brand bleeding again. It burned anew.

"There's your gun," the Vilaró said, pointing.

The guard's pistol lay on the floor. He must have dropped it when the Vilaró grabbed him.

The Vilaró pushed his hands back into the stone, looking as if he was feeling about in the dark. When he withdrew his hands from the stone, one of them gingerly clutched a ring of large old keys. That hand was sheathed in stone. The Vilaró dropped the keys and the stone about his fingers dissolved into a cloud of dust that drifted to the floor.

Joaquim's eyes slid toward where the guard had disappeared. "He's dead, isn't he? The guard?"

The Vilaró smiled benignly. "Very much so. I could have left him half in, half out. I was merciful, to spare your sensibilities, not because he deserved that mercy."

Joaquim regarded the Vilaró, a prickle of fear running down his spine. He hated to imagine what this man thought *just* punishment looked like. "What did that guard do to you?"

"Nothing," the Vilaró said. "But I tell you this, the sirenas of the prison are off-limits to the men. If a guard attacks one of them, he will die slowly. That same protection was never given to any of the human women here. Ask Miss Prieto when you see her next. Don't bother praying for that man's soul."

Joaquim didn't intend to ask. He had a very good idea what could happen to a woman in a prison.

"Now, I promised Leandra I would help the others escape, so I must go back. You help *her* escape," the Vilaró ordered.

Then he walked away through the wall.

Joaquim was alone. The Vilaró was gone, distant, he could tell. Probably back at the prison. But Leandra was upstairs in one of the cells, and he had to get her out. So he picked up the pistol and the keys and headed up the stone steps.

CHAPTER 44

The walls of the underground prison were cool and faintly damp, smelling of moldering stone. The cell was the only one on this level, with an iron-barred door like that of the cell Joaquim had woken in. Inside the darkness of the cell, Joaquim could see a still form lying on a bare bunk. Trying to be as quiet as possible, he tried several keys until he located the correct one. He pushed the door inward.

Leandra lay on her side, her unbound hair straggling off the edge of the narrow bed. Her swollen hand was swathed in bandages. Joaquim shook her shoulder gently.

Her eyes opened. "What are you doing here?"

"The Vilaró brought me to get you out."

She started coughing. Joaquim helped her sit up and waited until the coughing fit passed. "They weren't supposed to worry about me," she said.

"Apparently, the Vilaró doesn't see it that way," Joaquim said.

She laughed diffidently and pushed herself off the bench. "If I asked you to leave me here, would you?"

Joaquim didn't bother to answer. "Do you have any idea how many guards there are?"

"Two or three. No need to have more. I'm the only prisoner here right now."

Make that one or two, Joaquim thought, thinking of the one the Vilaró had dispatched. "Where would they be?"

Leandra walked like one half-dead. Joaquim suspected if he offered to carry her, she would only insist on walking on her own. "At the door," she said.

"The door?"

She stopped at the edge of the cell and peered out into the dimly lit hallway. "Out the hall, to the left, and up one flight of stairs. Door to the ground level."

The same path along which they dragged me out of here. "Do you have a plan for this?"

"No," she admitted. "I expected to be left behind." The hallways were preternaturally quiet. As they left the cell, Leandra stumbled and set one hand against the wall to balance herself.

Joaquim wrapped one arm around her waist. "Why did the Vilaró not just take you out of here, the way he brought me? Through the stone?"

"Because he keeps his word," Leandra said with a dry chuckle. "He promised me he would make certain the others were free first before he came after me. Since he brought you here to get me out, that still conforms to the exact terms of our deal."

They headed for the stair that would lead up to the surface. There would be a landing, he recalled, then an iron door, a few more stairs, and a gate. Then they would be in the echoing area with the well. He was glad he'd been paying attention when the guards dragged him out.

Once at the stairwell, Joaquim helped Leandra up the first couple of steps, stopping when he thought they might become visible to the guards on the landing. He let Leandra go so she could lean against the wall.

Crouching down, he climbed as close as he dared and peered over the edge of the landing. Only one guard waited there, seated at a desk near the large iron door. To one side Joaquim saw a sereia, her gray dress giving away her identity as one of the wardens. Was she with them, or was she Spanish?

Joaquim felt for the gun he'd shoved into his belt. How close could he get before he had to strike? The guard would be impeded by the desk, so the sereia would have to be the first target.

Then she looked at him, taking away any option. She opened her mouth and began to *call*.

It was a low tune, the words unintelligible. It carried her yearning, her exhaustion, endless weariness bearing down on Joaquim's bones, but her magic slipped past him. The guard's head lowered to the desk's surface instead.

Joaquim trained his gun on her. He hated shooting people.

The sereia stepped closer to the sleeping guard and reached down to take the man's gun, still watching Joaquim's face. The words of her *call* continued to flow past him, some taking shape now. *Sleep*, she sang, just as Reyna had sung in the cell, but . . .

Portuguese. She was singing to him in Portuguese. This was one of the women from the islands. Her *call* had stopped, he realized then, but the guard slept on. In her hand she now held the guard's gun, but pointed it past Joaquim—at Leandra.

Leandra had reached the top step by herself and stood leaning against the wall. "Aline, let him go."

"What's happening here?" the sereia asked.

"The Vilaró is loose. He's helping us escape."

The sereia's chin lifted. "And once you're gone, what becomes of us?"

"I would suggest abandoning the prisons altogether," Leandra said wearily. "You'll never be safe from the Vilaró here. Even if he doesn't kill you, he won't forget what was done to him, and he'll live a very long time."

"And if I let you out?" the sereia asked. "Would you take me back to the islands?"

"I'm willing to try," Joaquim offered.

"Make up your mind, Aline," Leandra said. "Which side are you on?"

The sereia gazed at Leandra, tears glistening in her eyes. "I want to go home."

Leandra nodded once, and Joaquim followed her lead. She knew this woman; he didn't. But somehow the woman's statement rang false in his ears. Not that he had a Truthsayer's talent; he'd simply had too many people lie to him in his work for the police. He'd seen faked tears before.

"He has the keys," she said to Joaquim, motioning toward the guard slumped over the desk, now snoring lightly. Slipping his gun back into his waistband, Joaquim went around the desk and tugged a ring of keys loose from the guard's belt. But when he rose, he saw that Aline now held Leandra's arm twisted behind her, her gun held to Leandra's side. He considered the tableau, weighing the odds.

Leandra wasn't afraid of death; he had no doubt of that. Her eyes were flatly unconcerned.

Would the other woman actually shoot Leandra? He felt sure that Aline didn't want to. But if he went for his gun, she could easily kill Leandra before he got off a shot. Instead he threw the keys directly at Aline's face.

She flinched, dropping her grip on Leandra at the same time. Leandra didn't hesitate. She elbowed the woman in the side of the neck, directly on her gill slits. The woman fell to her knees and clutched at her neck. Then Leandra brought her knee up, catching the other in the face.

It wasn't pretty, but it *was* effective. The woman on the floor began to moan, a *call* woven into it, sending spasms of familiar discomfort flickering down Joaquim's spine. That was pain, and he'd heard a sereia *calling* in pain before. Even the protection Marina had given him didn't block that completely.

"Give me the keys," Joaquim managed through gritted teeth.

Leandra leaned over, having to rest against the wall to do so, but fished the keys out from under the other woman's skirts. She kicked Aline's gun away, and it slid under the desk. She handed the ring to Joaquim as he came to help her to the door.

"Will there be a guard on the other side of that door?"

"I don't know," Leandra admitted.

Joaquim glanced at the iron door's lock and selected one of the five keys. He tried the first key, his fingers fumbling as Aline's keening grew louder. It didn't work. How soon before the guard woke and came to Aline's rescue?

Joaquim stuck the second key in the lock.

A flurry of activity alerted Marina to the approach of the mayor as he bustled down the stairwell to greet the marquesa. It appeared that in addition to a pair of guards, he'd brought along a couple of assistants. When the man saw the marquesa enthroned in the middle of the hall, he rushed over toward her, trailing attendants.

The *paer en cap* was an older man with slicked-back hair and spectacles, the sort one would expect to be an accountant, with a too-tight collar. He looked distressed before he reached the fuming marquesa's side. Marina had met enough of this sort of person while working for her father, a man trying hard to do the right thing while caught between too many expectations. The mayor bowed to the marquesa and launched into a formal introduction of his two assistants.

The marquesa waved that away with one hand. "There is a prison below this hall," she snapped. "My great-grandson is being held in it. I want him brought up to me immediately."

The man blinked a couple of times, as if no one had ever mentioned a prison to him before. "But the Morra was closed up, Marquesa," he said firmly. "Ages ago. No one goes in or out."

The marquesa's jaw hardened. She glanced over at Father Escarrá, who nodded, and turned back to the mayor. "Even in Terrassa we've heard rumors that the Morra is in use, that prisoners are brought here from the prison, never to return. I assure you, my great-grandson is down there. As I have heard no charges against him, I want him released now."

Marina held her breath. The marquesa was the source of

Joaquim's gift of finding, so she must know where he was. Perhaps she had a sense of him below. Marina barely restrained herself from looking down at the floor.

"Do you pretend you don't know?" the marquesa went on. "Or is it more convenient to let those fish girls run your prison for you and close one eye to their other actions?"

The mayor blinked rapidly. "I have not been told of this."

Father Escarrá nodded when the marquesa glanced his way.

"I have sent a message to the king with my protest," she announced. "You would do well to satisfy my demands before I speak to my cousin in person."

"The king?" the man asked, paling.

"I sent him a telegram myself. This place may have suited the world of the nineteenth century, but this is a new century." She turned to the priest, who stood at her side. "Father Escarrá, go fetch Bishop Meseguer for me. He'll want to know what's been going on under his nose."

The *paer en cap* whispered something to one of his adjuncts, who dashed back up the stairs. "There's no need, Marquesa," he said. "We'll get to the truth of this immediately. I've sent for the keeper of the keys. If the underground is being used, we'll find out now."

Marina glanced down at Alejandro, whose lips were pursed. Getting them out didn't guarantee they would *stay* free.

A man in a different uniform, a plain gray one, came jogging into the hall, breathing hard as if he'd run a long way. He began speaking to the mayor in urgent, low tones.

"He says the wall about the main prison has fallen down," Father Escarrá whispered to Marina. "Like the walls of Jericho, it simply fell. The prisoners who were in the courtyard fled in all directions, and the guards cannot chase them all down." He paused, listening. "He says the bad prisoners—he means the violent ones, I think—the hall they're in is intact, but the nationalists are escaping."

The man continued to talk to the mayor, and the priest's head cocked as he listened. Then he whispered to Marina again, "The mayor asked why the sirenas who run the prison haven't *called* the escaping men back, and the guard said they're busy with something else."

The adjunct who'd gone upstairs returned with a barrel-chested man in the fancy livery of the city guard. The mayor, still talking with the guard from the prison, waved for him to go on. The large man paraded past them toward a walnut railing under one of the arcades. He opened out an iron gate and then disappeared down a flight of steps.

His nerves rattled, Joaquim tried the next key. Aline pushed herself back up to her knees, only one hand to her throat now. Her pained *call* had shifted to the *call* he'd heard before: *come, come.* It was yearning, pure and simple, trying to drag him away from the door.

The guard who'd been asleep at the desk shook his head blearily. He gaped at the *calling* sereia, only a few feet from him, then rose and helped her to her feet, gazing at her worshipfully.

Leandra tugged the key ring out of Joaquim's hands, freeing him to draw his gun again, and pushed the next key into the hole. This one turned in the lock, clicking as it went around. Joaquim kept his gun trained on Aline and the guard.

The sereia woman saw the gun under the desk then and bade the guard to retrieve it. He dove under the desk.

"I've got it!" Leandra tried to shove the door open, and Joaquim reached past her, pushing the iron door ponderously outward.

Aline grabbed the gun away from the guard and shot wildly, but the bullet found its mark, searing its way into Joaquim's calf. He cried out, his right knee buckling. He hurtled forward and landed atop Leandra. They both fell onto another stone landing.

A muscular man in a different uniform—not the prison guard's gray—stood a few feet away on the landing above them, his mouth gaping. Joaquim rolled away from Leandra, lifting his borrowed pistol. He turned it on the sereia. Aline was already coming after them. She lifted her pistol again, her second bullet firing wide. It hit the low wall near the unknown guard's feet. He cursed vehemently.

Joaquim trained his gun on the woman. "I'm a much better shot than you are, Aline. You'd better drop that gun."

Marina heard the guard's startled exclamation. "Stay right here," she told Alejandro.

She dashed across the hall to the walnut railing and peeked over it. At the bottom of the stairwell, the large guard stood frozen in indecision. A few feet away, Joaquim sprawled half across a woman who must be Leandra Rocha, pinning her to the floor with his weight. Joaquim had a gun trained on someone beyond Marina's field of vision.

She grabbed up her skirts and ran down the stairs, halting next to the guard. On the other side of the iron door, a woman in gray walked up the steps, a gun in her hands. Her eyes were fixed on Joaquim.

"I don't want to shoot you," Joaquim was saying.

"Do you think I can let you get away now?" She raised her gun. "If I fail Reyna . . ."

Marina didn't wait to hear what the woman had to say. She laid her hand on the town hall guard's arm and worked a *call* into her whispered voice. "Shoot her."

The guard drew his gun and fired.

The woman tumbled back onto a stone landing on the other side of the heavy door. Marina darted past the befuddled guard to kneel at Joaquim's side.

He regarded her as if unsure she was real. "Marina?"

Marina saw blood staining his trouser legs. "Are you injured? Can you move?"

Before he could answer, she spotted movement farther down the stair, beyond the door. A gray-garbed guard like the one who'd come from the prison had been helping the unknown woman, but he glanced up, his eyes meeting Marina's. He started toward the steps, patting his holster . . . only to find it empty.

Marina didn't wait for him to locate his missing gun. She jumped up and pushed the iron door, groaning when she realized how heavy it was.

But the town hall guard stepped over Joaquim, caught the edge of the door, and shoved it closed with one hand. Then he locked it, an effective means to cut off the combatants and prevent any more shooting. He glared down at Joaquim and grabbed up the pistol and keys that lay on the steps near him. "What's going on here?" he barked.

Joaquim held out one hand to Marina and she did her best to help him up. He hissed when he put his weight on his right leg, though, and ended up stretching one arm over Marina's shoulders. Once Joaquim's weight was off her, Leandra rose slowly. She ignored the guard's hand when he moved to aid her. She'd been beaten, one eye swollen almost all the way closed. One of her hands was heavily bandaged and she moved as if exhausted. Even so, she looked very formidable.

This is Alejandro's mother, Marina thought, feeling a sudden pang of loss.

Her jaw clenching tightly, Marina turned away. She drew Joaquim up the steps to the ground floor of the hall. She wanted to find a place where she could inspect his injured leg or, better yet, get him to a hospital, but she didn't know whether they were safe or not.

"What are you doing here?" Joaquim asked.

Marina touched his swollen cheek. "I'm here to rescue you."

CHAPTER 45

Joaquim surveyed the hall as Marina helped him up the stairs. It was an impressive place of arches and arcades like the construction below, but made of far finer stone than the prison beneath. Seated on the far side in a large wooden chair was his great-grandmother. A bespectacled man argued with a handful of attendants nearby, and a priest waited at her side. Alejandro stood with the priest, his expression unreadable as he looked toward Leandra.

The man in civic livery had followed them up the stairs, his gun in his hand. He gestured forcefully for Joaquim and Leandra to stay where they were and went to report to the gentleman in spectacles, adding to the confusion.

"What is happening here?" Joaquim asked.

"They say the prison's walls fell down," Marina whispered as she drew his left arm over her shoulders to help carry his weight. "Like the walls of Jericho, they just fell down."

"I saw it," he admitted. Sounds drifted in from the entryway of the hall, growing louder by the moment. A ruckus was building outside, and Joaquim spotted the shadows of people running past the arcade beyond the outer door. If they knew the prison walls had fallen, the citizens had good reason to flee. The commotion outside built, a low voice now leading the flood.

Ignoring the guard's order to remain where they were, Leandra walked toward that doorway, stumbling against one of the hall's arches and pausing to catch her breath before continuing on. Since the guard didn't seem to have noticed, Joaquim steered Marina toward the doorway as well. She held out her free hand toward Alejandro, who jogged to join them and took Marina's hand as if she were his mother instead of Leandra.

They emerged from the hall into the sunlight of a small square, with more arcades of arches lining the street. People crowded under those arcades, watching as if they feared attack. Joaquim stopped when they drew abreast of where Leandra stood, heavily leaning against one of the arches.

"Oh gods, they don't have her," Leandra whispered.

In the center of the square stood a clump of people, mostly women dressed in the gray of the prison and young children. Joaquim was relieved to see Marcos among them, but didn't see Alejandro's sister there, or Miss Prieto.

Standing squarely before the group was the Vilaró, his hand wrapped around the back of Piedad's neck, his fingers digging into the edges of her gills. From what Joaquim knew of sereia, that would be terribly painful. Piedad remained very still, her angry eyes wide. Her face, already bruising, looked nearly as bad as his must. Joaquim wasn't sure whether he felt guilty about that or gratified by the symmetry.

They were waiting, Joaquim realized, to make their case to *someone*. They had walked from the broken prison to the town hall, so the distance must not be great. But surely this was the only place they could beg for mercy. To whom could they turn other than the town's authorities?

"We will speak before the city's ruler," the Vilaró said, as if he'd repeated that request before.

The officious-looking man from inside the building came out into the square, his guards and two of his attendants in tow. He gestured for them to remain under the arcade and then placed himself in front of the Vilaró, his jaw working. "Sir," he said. "I am the *paer en cap*. I must insist that you release that woman."

"He's the mayor," Marina whispered to Joaquim.

The Vilaró turned toward the mayor. "Do you control the prison?"

The mayor raised his chin. "I do not. The wardens of the prison work for the Spanish government."

Joaquim felt sorry for the mayor. The poor man was an elected official, faced now with a creature he had no hope to control, escaped prisoners, and a mutiny in a prison he didn't run.

The mayor waved one hand toward the gray-suited women grouped protectively around the children. "Are these not the wardens of the prison themselves?"

"I am not Spanish," one of the women cried aloud. "I am *not* one of them. I have been held hostage in that prison for four years, forced to serve them like a slave for fear they would hurt my daughter."

Others in that group raised their voices, shouting similar charges. Joaquim saw that Marcos looked pale. Among all of them, he *was* Spanish.

Farther down the street, onlookers moved back under the arcades to clear the way for a contingent of prison guards hurrying toward them.

"Guards coming this way," Joaquim said aloud, hoping the Vilaró would hear him.

The Vilaró waved his free hand, and at the edge of the square, the paving stones peeled off the ground like the skin of an orange, sending the nearby onlookers running in all directions. Screams filled the street as that layer of stone rose until it reached twice the height of a man, completely blocking off the square.

Joaquim held his breath for a second until it was clear that the stones were not going to fall. Dust flew in the breeze, a choking cloud of unsettled dirt and ground-down mule dung and bits of refuse. The Vilaró blew softly into that wind, and the dust instantly dropped to the ground.

The remaining onlookers—the ones who hadn't fled in terror—fell silent at that demonstration of power. Even the mayor looked cowed. Had he known what was hidden in his town all these de-cades?

Leandra looked over at Alejandro. "Stay with them," she said, ges-turing toward Marina. Then she walked slowly to the Vilaró's side.

"Why have you come here?" the mayor asked in a breathy voice. "What is it you want?"

"The queen of your prison is holding one more child hostage," the Vilaró said. "I want that child in exchange for this woman I hold, and then these people will leave this place."

"I must insist that you return my streets to order," the mayor said.

The Vilaró shook his head. "When I have what I want, I will do so."

The marquesa had finally reached Joaquim's side. She stood next to him, leaning heavily on her cane. "Who are all these people?" she demanded in a cross tone, as if everything had been done to incon-venience her. "Why is the street broken?"

"I came to Barcelona to find this woman," Joaquim told his great-grandmother, pointing with his chin toward Leandra. "But she's not the only one of my wife's people who was held captive here. All of these others are captives, just as she was, just as Alejan-dro was."

Marina clutched the boy to her side.

The marquesa slammed the tip of her cane on the stone of the square. "Children being held captive? In a prison? I will not put up with such an offense." She turned to the mayor. "Have your guards fetch this other girl immediately, man."

Leandra looked at the marquesa for the first time, as if baffled by the woman's intervention. The mayor seemed taken aback as well, but after a second of indecision, he sent his guards out the back of the arcade with orders to find the warden and the missing girl.

And for a moment, silence reigned in the square.

"When they bring the child," the marquesa said loudly, "these people will need to be transported to the train station. We will need six cabs, I think. And I want the first-class carriage cleared for us. Send one of your men to do that as well," she added, clearly speaking to the mayor now. "I won't sit in second class with a horde of smelly children."

Joaquim did his best not to look surprised at her presumption. But the mayor dispatched his remaining aides to fulfill the marquesa's demand.

Then Joaquim heard the sound of a child screeching somewhere beyond the walled-off square, sooner than he'd expected. Reyna must have come in pursuit of the Vilaró herself. She could not have gotten here so quickly otherwise.

The Vilaró waved one hand, and a part of the new stone wall about the square opened like a door. Reyna entered the walled-off square, her regal bearing leaving no doubt that she thought her name apt. Next to her, Miss Prieto dragged a clearly uncooperative Liliana by one arm. A livid bruise on one side of her jaw marred the girl's pretty face—Piedad's work.

"No! You can't make me go with her!" Liliana screeched.

The queen glowered down at the girl. "We're keeping our part of the bargain."

It was a mark of Reyna's fear of the Vilaró, that she'd given in so completely.

"No!" Liliana screamed, the sound sending gooseflesh along Joaquim's arm.

"You have to stay with your mother," Miss Prieto said quietly, "or the Vilaró will kill them all."

"That's not fair," the girl shouted. "It's not my fault."

Joaquim glanced down at Alejandro, and saw him eye the girl with distaste. Joaquim couldn't blame the boy. After all Leandra had done to get the girl free of the prison, Liliana should be grateful. But he suspected that gratefulness wasn't something the sirenas had instilled in her. He doubted Liliana had any idea she should be grateful.

Miss Prieto drew the girl toward Leandra, who stepped forward.

The girl turned her face away, but then confronted her mother. "You let Piedad hit me," she said bitterly. "Look at my face."

"Piedad hit you," Leandra said. "Not me."

"And Piedad enjoyed it too, I'm sure," the Vilaró said, glaring down at Liliana. "You're an obnoxious child."

"Vilaró, don't bait her," Leandra said, no real anger in her voice.

"You agreed to free Piedad," Reyna insisted.

"I agreed not to kill her," the Vilaró replied. "I can bury her ten feet under the ground, still alive, and leave her there. So tell the man in charge what I want. I'm sure Miss Prieto made my demands clear."

Bristling, Reyna turned to the officious-looking man. "These people," she said, pointing at the group of women and children, "are not to be returned to the prison."

The Vilaró shoved Piedad away from him. She stumbled a few steps before she turned on him, teeth bared, but stone lifted from its bed and crumbled to wrap around her feet, trapping her there. She hissed in fury as she struggled to wrench her feet loose.

Dust swirled around her, rising from the ground and pulling off the old walls of the building. A slender column coalesced within the dust, rising like a cobra poised before Piedad's face. "Cross me," the Vilaró said, "and the dust will seek out your lungs. It will grind your teeth away, scratch your eyes to blindness, fill your gills until you cannot breathe and your organs until you are stone itself."

Joaquim swallowed. He'd set the Vilaró free. He was responsible for what this creature did now. "Vilaró, your promise!"

The Vilaró's pale eyes flicked toward him, but then he turned to Leandra. "My bargain was that all of you would be freed in return for Piedad's life. If they try to take any of you back, *all* their lives will be forfeit."

Leandra nodded her understanding.

Piedad struggled, but the stone encasing her lower legs didn't give. At least she didn't dare open her mouth again.

"My grandson will stay," Reyna said, turning calmly to the mayor.

Joaquim heard the hint of a *call* in her words. "They are trying to take away my own flesh and blood. My grandson and great-granddaughter are Spanish citizens."

Marcos looked horrified, mouth agape.

"No!" one of the women cried out. Joaquim recognized the young woman who'd stood guard outside the chapel. She clutched a black-haired imp in her arms that must be Marcos' daughter. "You *threw* him away. He belongs to me now."

"My deal," the Vilaró rumbled, "was for *all* of them. Including Marcos and Miss Prieto."

Joaquim saw relief on Marcos' face. Even if Reyna didn't respect any claim Safira had on Marcos, the Vilaró's threat should make her relent.

The mayor, caught between the warden and a creature with far more power, stepped closer to the Vilaró's side, as if that would protect him from the warden's *call*. "You will have what you asked for," he assured the Vilaró. "I've sent for cabs, but they won't be able to enter here until you return my streets to normal, sir."

"We will *all* walk out of here," the Vilaró said to Reyna. "These people will board a train and travel to Barcelona. If they do not leave here safely, I will destroy the prison and take each one of your sire-nas down with it. If there's any attempt to take them into custody before they escape Spain, there will be repercussions. They are un-der *my* protection now, and a town like this, made of dust and stone, is mine to destroy. Your prison can become your tomb. Do you un-derstand that, Reyna?"

She stared at him and nodded once, regally.

The Vilaró waved one hand and the broad cobbles sank back to the ground like dough being rolled out. When the dust settled, Joa-quim was relieved to see that the Vilaró had managed not to hurt anyone. Most of the prison guards had scattered, but a few remained in the center of the street. The shaken *paer en cap* raised his arms to warn them back.

The stones at the center of the square abruptly heaved, pitching Piedad to land at the queen's feet. Piedad scrambled to her feet and lunged toward the Vilaró, but Reyna slapped her across the back of her head. Not hard, but enough to startle Piedad into stopping. The queen said something softly to her, only a couple of words. With one last disdainful look, Piedad turned and walked away. She gestured as she walked past, and the prison guards followed her.

"You've won for today," Reyna said to the Vilaró, "but God will destroy you."

The Vilaró regarded her disdainfully. "In one day's time, I will return here. If there are any guards or sirenas left in the Morra below, I will feed them to the stone. I will restore the walls of your prison once these people are safely beyond the shores of Spain."

"And our lives?" Reyna asked.

"And your lives, such as they are, will be spared," the Vilaró answered.

The queen nodded her agreement, clearly grasping that she had no choice at all.

CHAPTER 46

Once they were off the platform and safely ensconced on the train, the *paer en cap* appeared satisfied that *his* part of the bargain had been upheld and his town was now safe. The Vilaró stayed on the platform as well. He would remain in Lleida to ensure that the conditions of the deal were kept. Given that the train was mostly iron, Joaquim suspected that the creature would find the trip uncomfortable anyway. He had no doubt that the Vilaró had some other way of getting to Barcelona.

The marquesa marched down the narrow corridor of the first-class car, assigning each compartment as she desired. Leandra, Miss Prieto, and the sullen Liliana were in the first, leaving the second for the marquesa and the priest. Joaquim, his leg temporarily bandaged by Miss Prieto, was put in there as well. After she'd introduced Joaquim to the priest, Alejandro came and joined them, apparently preferring *their* company to his sister's.

Marina sat back against the squabs and watched as Joaquim and Alejandro consumed between them half a dozen meat pies from the full tray the mayor had procured while they waited for the train to arrive. Joaquim looked terrible. In addition to his bandaged leg and arm, his face was bruised, and he had a few days' growth of beard. He smelled too, although she wasn't going to complain about that. It was a relief to have him back.

"Did you actually send a telegram to the king?" Marina asked once the marquesa settled in her seat, apparently having reorganized the escaping group how she wanted them.

The marquesa barked out a laugh. "My husband might have been a grandee, but that doesn't mean what it did when I married him. The young man on the throne would have no interest in an old lady's complaints. The bishop *might* have come when I asked, only because he's a good man. Once you're my age, you can say whatever you want, and no one dares to contradict you."

It had all been bluster, Marina realized, but very convincing bluster.

Joaquim shifted, trying to get comfortable. "I am grateful you came, Marquesa. We weren't managing our escape well."

The old woman gripped the silver head of her cane. "No, you weren't. A good thing you have such a persistent wife. You should call me Grandmother."

Joaquim nodded slowly, grasping Marina's hand in his own. "Thank you, Grandmother."

The marquesa harrumphed and plumped her pillow preparatory to feigning sleep. Evidently that was the only concession Joaquim was going to get today.

Once the train started into motion, Marina saw Joaquim's shoulders relax. She couldn't blame him.

"How did you convince her to come here?" he whispered, pointing toward his great-grandmother with his chin.

She launched into the story of her visit to the marquesa's home with Alejandro, and then their next morning's conversation in Terrassa, all in whispers. A knock on their compartment door came just as she'd finished. The Spanish nurse had come to check on Joaquim's injuries again.

The woman smiled and ruffled Alejandro's hair first. "I'm glad you're safe, Jandro."

He nodded but didn't say anything, looking a bit sulky.

"Your mother wants to see you," the nurse added, "but Liliana's being difficult, so it may have to wait until we get to Barcelona." Marina put her arm around Alejandro's shoulders and hugged him closer. She had no doubt that—what was the word the Vilaró had used?—*obnoxious* girl was going to be a problem. She was embarrassingly relieved that Liliana wasn't in this compartment with them. Marina gazed down at the top of Alejandro's head. If she understood what he'd told her so far, he'd had very little to do with Liliana, and what few encounters he'd had with his elder sister hadn't been pleasant.

Father Escarrá went to stand in the corridor so the nurse could sit across from Joaquim. She gently surveyed bandages on his arm. "This has ripped open. You're going to have an ugly scar after all. The leg will need attention, but I think it bled out most of the contaminants left by the bullet. The ankle wound is another story. That's going to need a thorough cleaning when we get somewhere safe. I've stopped the bleeding, and I can block the pain if you want, so you can get some sleep, but you'll have to be careful not to aggravate either injury further."

Joaquim glanced over at Marina and she nodded. He looked as though he desperately needed the sleep. So the healer placed her hand at the outside of Joaquim's elbow and appeared to concentrate for a moment. Then she laid her other hand on the back of his knee. He sagged visibly, as if he'd been holding himself stiff to stifle the pain.

"It will wear off in a few hours," the healer said to Marina. "With a bite we have to worry about infection."

Marina agreed, noting that Joaquim seemed ready to nod off already. Had the healer made him more sleepy? Or was it just a cessation of pain combined with a full stomach? "Thank you," she said to the healer. "We're very grateful for your help. Is anyone else hurt?"

"They're mostly frightened," Miss Prieto said. "Getting out of the prison is not the same as escaping Spain."

Marina knew that all too well. "We'll manage somehow."

The healer smiled at her, patted Alejandro's head again, and left them.

"I wish my mother didn't go back for Liliana," Alejandro said in little more than a whisper.

Marina leaned closer to him. "It doesn't mean she loves you less. It's just that Liliana needs her more right now."

"That's what she said," he returned.

"Would she lie to you?"

Alejandro shook his head, which was better than a shrug, Marina supposed. She glanced over and saw that Joaquim had indeed fallen asleep, his head against the wall of the compartment and his wounded leg stretched out.

She wished she could have some time alone with him. Now that they were getting away from that town, she wanted to put her arms around her husband to assure herself she had him back. Alejandro wanted much the same from his mother, she suspected. She hugged the boy again and drew out the book. They would finish it before they reached Barcelona, but she hoped that at some point his mother would come back and see him. He needed that.

By the time they reached Barcelona, hours later, Joaquim was fevered. When Marina shook him awake, he responded, but looked so disoriented that she wasn't sure he understood what she said.

It was dark already, and the group gathered on the train platform, some arguing that they should immediately go to the harbor to find a ship heading away from Spain. Others were quicker to realize the extent of their problem: they had no funds to book passage anywhere, a large hole in their plan.

"It is late," the marquesa snapped. "And my grandson needs to rest. We will go to a hotel and they will serve us dinner. In the morning we will sort this out."

"We were at the Hotel Colón," Marina said quietly. "They're holding our room."

The marquesa banged her cane on the platform, catching the attention of the arguing sereia. "It's decided, then. We will all go to this hotel. *Now*. Everyone off the platform."

Father Escarrá picked up the marquesa's bag and then Marina's. "She's a bully at times," he whispered, "but that *can* be helpful."

Marcos helped get Joaquim to his feet and down the corridor to where a porter waited to help him out to a horse-drawn omnibus. The children had never seen a city before, save from behind the walls of the prison. The older ones were fascinated by the lights . . . and the horses . . . and the omnibus as well. As some of them climbed to the top level, Miss Prieto counted, making certain they had everyone. Marina was thankful someone had the skills to organize this retreat—she had no idea what half of them were named, even, or to whom they belonged. The porter helped Joaquim into a seat on the lower level and Marina sat next to him. Alejandro settled on the nearest bench.

The hotel was close to the train station, and a few moments later, they straggled into the lobby, hoping to book enough rooms and beds that they could all sleep—those who weren't too afraid of being taken back to the prison, that was. Marina left Joaquim sitting in an upholstered chair in the foyer and went to the front desk in the marquesa's wake.

The clerk at the desk looked appalled at the state of his unexpected guests, but quickly regained his professional aplomb when faced with the marquesa's sharp glare. When she demanded that he clear rooms next to the one Joaquim and Marina had, he stammered, "But . . . but . . . that hall has been booked, ma'am. We can provide other rooms, but those rooms are *already* being held for Mr. Tavares." He waved at Marina as he said that last part.

"We didn't have the entire hall," Marina protested.

The clerk turned to her. "Not before, Mrs. Tavares, but Lady

Ferreira's agent sent another telegram yesterday morning, and she arrived just this evening."

"Lady Ferreira is here?" Marina asked, suddenly feeling limp with relief. But she couldn't stop now, not while decisions needed to be made.

The clerk turned and checked the keys on the wall. "Yes, Mrs. Tavares."

"Then may we have the keys?"

Marcos and Father Escarrá helped Joaquim up the stairs to the second floor, and the commotion of herding several exhausted and overstimulated children up the curved stairs was enough to alert Joaquim's foster mother that they'd arrived. Lady Ferreira emerged from one of the rooms on the hallway, a picture of elegance in her fine brown suit and ivory lace. She ran down the hall to join them, brown eyes wide.

Joaquim blinked at her blearily, as if he feared he was hallucinating.

Lady Ferreira stroked the side of his face. "Filho," she said, "what have you done to yourself?"

Then she smiled down at the boy silently clinging to Marina's hand. "And you must be Alejandro. I am pleased to meet you." She turned back to Marina. "Dear, why don't you get Joaquim settled in his bed, and we'll sort out your entourage? We have twelve rooms on this floor. . . ."

Drained, Marina was more than happy to leave everyone in the capable hands of Lady Ferreira, even the cranky marquesa. While the chatter continued in the hallway, Marina opened the door to their suite of rooms and let the men carry Joaquim inside.

The healer followed immediately, instructing the men where to lay him and what to fetch. When they'd brought her everything she needed, she shooed them off and turned her attention to Joaquim's ankle, where one of the sirenas had bitten him. It had scabbed over, but even Marina could see that the tears in his skin were ragged. "Will it heal?"

The healer set a basin under his foot and proceeded to sponge it with warm water. "Bites are always nasty. Now, Mrs. Tavares, why don't you leave me to this? I've handled plenty of injuries like this before. And I suspect that Alejandro is hungry. . . ."

Marina only then realized that Alejandro had followed them into the bedroom. He sat in a chair to one side, eyes worried. "Alejandro, why don't we go see if we can find some food?"

He rose at her suggestion and followed her out, casting one glance back at Joaquim. "I'm sorry he's hurt," he whispered.

Marina stopped and touched the boy's cheek with one hand. "Don't worry," she said as firmly as she could manage. "He understands why he had to go there. He'll be fine."

She was relieved her voice wasn't shaking. Joaquim had better not disappoint her.

The hallway was empty for the moment, so Marina cocked her head to listen and decided that the refugees were gathered in a room farther down the hall. She led Alejandro that way, only to pause again when she saw a woman coming up the steps—the woman her aunt Jovita had sent to follow them. She had to have been watching the hotel. Marina grasped Alejandro's hand in her own.

The woman stopped on the landing and inclined her head politely. "Your aunt will be most pleased to see that you've returned safely. And you've brought the boy back with you. Were you successful in finding his mother?"

"Yes," Marina said, "although she's very ill."

"I see. How unfortunate."

Marina kept her eyes on the woman's face. The woman might not know Leandra Rocha, but she should at least put a *little* sympathy into her voice in front of Leandra's son. "Yes, it is."

From a room a few feet farther down the hallway, the marquesa emerged, clutching her cane in one hand and leaning on Father Escarrá's arm. They came toward the stairwell.

"Since you've located the boy's mother, I'll need you to turn the journal over to me. For safekeeping," the woman added, ignoring the marquesa's approach. "Subminister Paredes wouldn't want anything to happen to it, and I can get it back to the islands safely."

Marina wasn't certain whether or not to trust her aunt's emissary. She'd left the journal in her handbag, though, back in the bedroom. She turned in that direction, but a glance at Father Escarrá's expression stopped her. Still a few feet from the woman, he mouthed something at Marina, the word *mentirosa*—liar.

She turned back to the woman. "I don't think so. We've secured it in the hotel safe," she claimed, "and it will remain there until we book passage out of here."

The woman's head tilted, as if that confused her. "Your aunt asked me to bring it back to the islands as soon as possible."

"It can wait," Marina said firmly.

The woman leapt forward and shoved Marina toward the stairs. With a cry, Marina fell. She managed to grab the railing with one hand and fetched to a stop against it. When she got back to her feet, she was three steps down.

But at the head of the stairwell, the woman held Alejandro to her side, a small gun in her free hand. "Let's try again. You'll go down to the safe and get that book for me. I'll trade it for the boy. Simple enough."

Marina gazed at the woman, her heart pounding in her chest. She couldn't give up the journal. Her mother had died for it. But she wasn't going to let this woman hurt Alejandro. She swallowed, and everyone seemed to stand still as if the world waited on what she would do.

Alejandro's eyes were wide, his lips turned down. He was going to do *something*, just as he'd done with the man at the stream. Behind him, the marquesa's expression was one of annoyance, her lips twisted in disdain. Father Escarrá watched the gun in the woman's hand. Even farther down the hall, Lady Ferreira had emerged from her room and stood still, knuckles white on her handbag.

Marina's eyes slid back to the woman's. The journal wasn't in the safe anyway. She would have to return to the bedroom to retrieve it. "I have to go back to my room to get my key," she said in a calming tone, "to prove to the desk clerk who I am. Don't hurt him."

The woman's head inclined, and she took a couple of steps back from the stairwell, dragging Alejandro with her. Marina walked back up the steps to the landing and paused, facing her adversary. "If you hurt my boy," she whispered, "I will claw your eyes out."

The woman made a scoffing sound. "Get me the book, and I'll give you the webless brat."

Marina made as if to turn toward her bedroom, then fell on the woman's right arm, letting her weight push the gun away. "Jandro! Run!"

The woman grimaced, shaking her arm as if to get rid of Marina's weight. Alejandro took advantage of her distraction to jump onto her instep with both feet. Marina clung to the woman's arm, but the woman swung her other arm at the boy, knocking him back against the wall. He hissed and looked ready to fling himself at her again when a heavy *thwack* sounded and the women's eyes rolled up into the back of her head. She crumpled forward, bearing Marina to the landing with her.

Marina struggled to get out from under her, pushing the dropped gun to one side with her foot as she did so. She let loose a sigh of relief when she saw that Father Escarrá had Alejandro safe in his grasp. The woman remained slumped on the floor, the frail marquesa standing over her, gripping her ebony cane in both hands like a club.

"Thank you, Marquesa," Marina said breathlessly.

"Stupid woman," the marquesa grumbled. "Turning her back on me because I'm old. It's my legs that are weak, not my arms."

Marina reminded herself never to underestimate that woman.

Lady Ferreira approached and, without a word, picked up the

gun that lay on the carpet. "I take it that I should shoot her if she moves?"

"She's not going to move for a good long while," the marquesa muttered.

Lady Ferreira shrugged, checked to be sure that the safety on the gun was off, and tucked it into her cummerbund. "Well, then, I will just keep an eye on her until the guards arrive."

Marina stared down at her crumpled adversary. She would have clawed the woman's eyes out if she'd hurt Alejandro. She'd meant those words. But she was glad she didn't have to take on her enemies alone.

"Guards?" she asked Lady Ferreira, wondering if she'd heard that correctly.

"Yes, dear. From the Portuguese consulate. They should be here shortly. Before I left the Golden City, I informed the prince that Joaquim was in trouble. He didn't ask for details, just sent word to the consulate here that they were to provide whatever we needed. I had a porter place a call directly after you arrived."

Marina closed her eyes and said a quick prayer of thanks. It was a wonderful thing to have friends.

CHAPTER 47

Since Joaquim was still sleeping under Miss Prieto's watchful eye, Marina carried a lunch tray down to the last bedroom on the hotel's hallway. The Portuguese consulate guard standing at the end of the hall nodded smartly to her and, after knocking, opened the door for her.

She'd been putting this off, this difficult talk. But she needed to make her position clear. With the children gone to a park under the watchful eyes of Marcos and a handful of guards, and the women about to leave on an excursion to a shop, they would have some time uninterrupted.

So Marina gathered her nerve and carried the tray inside the room where Leandra Rocha lay still abed, her face bruised but composed. The woman had bathed, and her dark hair was braided neatly. Her splinted hand lay atop the covers. She pushed herself into a sitting position when Marina entered, moving slowly, as if in a fog.

"Can I help you?" Marina asked, setting the tray on the table next to the bed.

"No, please. I'd rather you keep your distance," the woman said in her soft voice as she finally sat with her back against the wooden headboard. "How is your husband faring?"

"His fever has broken," Marina said, "although the healer wants to keep him asleep for now in hopes that his ankle will heal faster if she can keep him off it."

"I never meant for that to happen to him," Leandra said. "I am sorry. We never thought he would be treated that way. We assumed he would be taken to the main prison like any other prisoner."

Shaking her head, Marina lifted the tray again and set it across the woman's lap. "You cannot plan for everything, even with a seer aiding you. Now, you need to eat, to get your strength back."

"Do not worry about me," Leandra said. "I'll be gone soon."

Marina felt her stomach go hollow at that pronouncement. "You shouldn't say that. We know healers in Portugal, terribly strong ones. One of them healed her husband's tuberculosis. Surely she can help you."

They *would* reach Portugal before Leandra became too ill. They'd had word from the Americans that a Portuguese ship would arrive tonight from the islands to take the former prisoners to the Golden City and from there to the islands if they wished. Consequently this would be a day of rest for them all, something they sorely needed, although the sooner they got away from the shores of Spain, the happier these women would be.

Leandra shook her head. "The more quickly this is done, the better. I don't want my children to watch me linger on for months. Once I've made out my will and we've gotten them safely out of Spain, the Vilaró will take me elsewhere."

Marina sat in the chair near the bed. "To die?"

Leandra gazed down at the food on the tray and began awkwardly cutting her sausage.

"Let me do that," Marina said, gently pushing away the woman's bandaged hand. She took the plate with the sausage, set it on the table, and began cutting the sausage into manageable pieces to put in her soup. "You would be far more comfortable at the . . . at *our* house in the Golden City. There's no need for you to be alone."

"No," Leandra said. "I won't stay in the same house as my children. I won't risk infecting them, or everything we've worked for will be for naught."

Marina passed the plate back to her and Leandra slid the sausage into her soup. "Then where will you go?"

A hint of a smile touched Leandra's lips. "He says he will take me to a place where I won't be sick any longer. I would never be able to return, but he claims I will be able to watch my children grow from a distance."

Something about her expression struck Marina. "Do you love him?"

"The Vilaró? Yes, rather foolishly," Leandra said, "as I don't think it's possible for him to love me. He doesn't seem to possess that manner of sentiment. But he is very fond of me, and enjoys being adored. It makes him stronger."

That sounded like a strange relationship, but she wasn't going to criticize this woman's choices, not after all Leandra had been through.

"What about William Adler?" Marina asked. Mr. Pinter had brought the news that Adler was still recuperating in the hospital, but was now expected to make a full recovery.

"William is, I'm afraid, the same young man he was when I met him a decade ago, whereas I am . . . a thousand years older. That is why I'll be leaving Liliana in his aunt's care rather than his, if she'll accept. She would be a far better guardian for a capricious child such as Liliana."

Given that the girl was also a sereia and coming into her powers, Marina had to agree that Ambassador Norton would be a better choice. Adler would be defenseless against his daughter's *call*.

But the part of this conversation she'd most feared lay before her now. She dreaded asking the question. "So she'll take Alejandro back to the islands as well?"

Leandra suddenly began coughing. She covered her mouth with

a handkerchief while Marina pulled the tray away from her. The fit passed after a moment, and Marina returned the tray so Leandra could resume eating.

"I was hoping," Leandra said wearily, "that Alejandro would live with his family in Portugal. I didn't know his father was dead."

"You don't want them raised together?" Marina asked, trying to keep the delighted note out of her voice.

Leandra shook her head. "They barely know each other as it is. And I want him to have the advantages that human males have, even if he's half sereia."

"We would willingly raise him," Marina said before Leandra went any further.

"I saw you with him," Leandra said. "You're good with him, and that's what he needs. He needs someone who will love him, and not care that he's only half human."

"Joaquim and I both want him to stay with us. We plan to—"

"Madam," came a velvety voice in the hallway, "I do wonder why you think those *fish girls*, as you persist in calling them, would want you along on this excursion."

Marina hid a smile. Lady Ferreira and the marquesa were bickering again, the lady in a soft tone, and the marquesa in her usual raspy growl. Despite the fireworks, they seemed to like each other, and Lady Ferreira had already invited the marquesa to visit with them at the Ferreira house so that she could meet Joaquim's brother, Cristiano. Father Escarrá had returned to Terrassa that morning to have the marquesa's maid pack for her. "They're taking the women to a shop to purchase new clothing," Marina whispered to Leandra, "so they won't have to wear the uniforms from the prison."

"They *are* fish girls," the marquesa insisted from the hallway.

"As your great-grandson is married to a *sereia*," Lady Ferreira returned, "perhaps you should learn the proper term. Also, the proper name for a seal girl is a selkie, if you were contemplating bandying that one about."

Leandra actually smiled.

"When did seal girls enter this conversation, you foolish woman?" the marquesa snapped.

"You are speaking to one," Lady Ferreira said regally.

The marquesa grumbled something unintelligible in answer, and then said, "Come over here, young man, and help me down those stairs. . . ."

The voices moved off down the hallway, leaving Marina and Leandra in silence again. Leandra sipped a spoonful of soup and then said, "I will list you as Alejandro's guardian, then."

Marina sat back, feeling as if she could breathe freely for the first time since she'd seen the woman on the steps of the town hall in Lleida. "Then will you tell me everything? I need to know what family you have back on the islands, about your execution, how you escaped the first time, what you remember of Alejandro's father, what the prison was like. I need to know *everything* so that I can tell Alejandro when he's older."

"Will he want to know, do you think?" Leandra asked wearily.

"Yes," Marina said. "I will make certain he never forgets you and all you sacrificed for your children."

EPILOG

In the front sitting room of the Ferreira home on the Street of Flowers, Oriana sat with Duilio, making their farewells. Fortunately, the Ministry of Foreign Affairs had given Oriana permission to stay in Portugal a few days longer than originally planned so that they could attend Saturday's festivities: Rafael's wedding to Miss Jardim and the small private ceremony that followed in which Duilio's mother married Joaquim's father. But with those ceremonies behind them, it was time for Oriana and Duilio to resume their duties on Quitos. Costa and Inês Guerra, recently married in Lisboa under his grandmother's auspices, would return with them.

Madam Norton, with a still-sulking Liliana in tow, had departed earlier on an American vessel bound for the islands. For her part, Liliana had actually seemed happier once under her great-aunt's firm control, perhaps recognizing that she couldn't wrap the woman around her finger. Oriana suspected that the girl would soon learn to see her great-aunt as an ally rather than adversary.

The Spanish healer had ordered Joaquim to stay off his feet, so he and Marina wouldn't accompany them to the quay to see the *Tesouro* off for its return voyage to the islands. While Joaquim had made it through Saturday's festivities, leaning heavily on the silver-headed ebony cane his great-grandmother had left for him when she'd returned to Spain on Wednesday, Oriana suspected he needed the rest.

Duilio scanned the headlines of the newspaper Joaquim had handed him before passing the paper to her. Oriana glanced at the headline. "It just sank?"

Joaquim nodded, leaning back in his ivory brocaded chair. "The harbormaster said the sand crept out to the ship and devoured it. That was the word—*devoured*."

A steam corvette at dock in Ferrol had sunk overnight. The suddenness of the sinking had caused enough sensation to make the newspapers in Portugal. Oriana had no doubt what ship that was— one that usually flew dark sails, had a mermaid figurehead, and a recently replaced bowsprit—the ship that had carried Leandra to slavery in Spain. Oriana wasn't surprised. Over the last week, word had been filtering back of women across Spain being exposed as sire-nas. The Spanish government was taking careful steps to figure out which government officials had been compromised, and there was already talk of forcibly repatriating the sirenas. For her part, Oriana doubted they would like being returned to the Canary Islands. "I suspect your Vilaró was making a point."

"He's not *my* Vilaró," Joaquim said. "He has refrained from kill-ing anyone, but he's done his part to make the Canaries' lives mis-erable."

Duilio just shrugged, likely finding it more amusing than Joa-quim did. Joaquim felt responsible for the man's—or fairy's—actions since he'd *chosen* to release the Vilaró.

"The conspirators over on the islands are going to have it far worse, I suspect," Oriana said.

"I thought things had settled down," Marina said, a line of worry appearing between her delicate brows. "Is it safe for you to go back?"

"There will be trials. There's ample evidence now to convict those involved. Aunt Jovita guaranteed our safety there."

Not only would Jovita have the message from their mother's journal, but most of the sereia from the prison were returning on the *Tesouro* and planned to testify in the trials. They'd received promises of amnesty from the government and there was even talk of reparations, both for them and their children, but also for the families of those sereia who'd died in the prison or aboard Spanish ships. Jovita Paredes was holding true to her word; the newspapers on Quitos had already printed parts of the story, sparking outrage among a populace that placed the importance of bloodlines above politics. In time the anger would die down, but it would likely be years before a Spanish mission was allowed back on sereia soil, a boon for Portuguese traders daring enough to sail there.

Marina had given her statement to Evangelista as well, and handed over a *copy* of the information in their mother's journal. She'd decided to keep the original—along with the book that held Leandra's notes—in Portugal, and Oriana didn't argue that decision. Marina had fought to keep the journal out of the hands of an agent of the ministry, a woman who'd claimed she was working for their aunt Jovita, but actually worked for the previous minister of Intelligence, Raposo. Either way, Oriana now had the information about a safe-deposit box in Porto Novo that she hadn't known existed before, and that would likely prove to be the journal's true treasure.

That was one reason Oriana wanted to return to Amado. She wanted to see all the information their mother had collected, and make sure that Jovita got what she needed to prosecute whoever had killed their mother, every person involved with the selling of sereia women to the Canaries, and anyone who'd helped the Canary spies on the islands.

She would miss the Golden City, and this house. She'd come here almost eight months before, alone and afraid. The Ferreiras had taken her in, kept her safe, and when she had nearly died, Duilio and

Joaquim had come after her to save her. She hoped that she and Duilio would be able to visit here often in the future. She wanted her children to know this side of her family, to play in these halls with their cousins.

A high-pitched voice in the hallway warned them a second before the sitting room was invaded by two-year-old Serafina, her dark curling hair wild and her webbed hands smudged with chocolate. Giggling, she ran to Joaquim and wrapped her stubby arms around one of his legs—fortunately the uninjured left one.

Joaquim sighed and set one hand atop the girl's head. Duilio suppressed a laugh at his brother's long-suffering expression, since he was likely to be in a similar position in a couple of years and life had a way of repaying misbehavior. The child belonged to Safira Palmeira and Marcos Davila, the only two prisoners who'd decided to remain in Portugal. They were currently moving their meager belongings into Joaquim's old apartment, too small for a family with a boy Alejandro's size, but adequate for *their* needs while they decided whether to move to Amado to live with Inês' family on the beach or stay in Portugal. While Duilio easily kept up the pretense of subservience, and Costa apparently didn't mind letting Inês take the lead, apparently the prospect of living among the sereia daunted the young Spaniard, Marcos. Oriana couldn't blame him.

Predictably, Alejandro peered around the doorframe a second later, unable to see the girl from his location. "Is she in here?"

The boy still carried around a hint of melancholy, provoked when his mother disappeared in the company of the Vilaró only a day after arriving in Portugal. It had been hard on Alejandro, but he was a resilient child, and had a family who would take care of him now. Oriana just hoped that the woman who'd suffered so much for her children was happy *somewhere*.

"Yes," Duilio said to the boy. "She's clamped on to your brother's leg like an octopus."

Alejandro rolled his eyes dramatically. "She's a pest."

But he came into the sitting room anyway and began detaching the girl from Joaquim's leg. The girl relinquished her hold on Joaquim only to wrap her arms around Alejandro instead, earning another aggrieved look. Marina laughed, picked up the girl, and sat on the beige sofa again. She patted the seat between herself and Oriana, and Alejandro joined them.

"We were helping Mrs. Cardoza stir," the boy explained, grabbing one of the toddler's chocolate-smeared hands, "and she ran off."

Marina tugged a handkerchief out of her sleeve, and the boy used that to scrub the little girl's hands. In addition to football, Duilio's new brother was fascinated by every aspect of life in an active household, including the cook's work. Joaquim also said Alejandro showed great aptitude for reading. He'd been teaching the boy since he was currently held captive in the house by his injured limbs. Joaquim was confident that Alejandro could attend a school later that year, once he'd caught up to other boys his age.

Alejandro tried to catch Serafina's other hand before she wiped chocolate onto Marina's white shirtwaist.

The butler rapped gently on the doorframe. "Mr. Duilio, the driver's waiting out front."

So Oriana and Duilio rose, waiting as Joaquim pushed himself to his feet with his borrowed cane. While Marina extricated herself from the children, Oriana went and embraced Joaquim and then leaned down to kiss Alejandro's cheeks.

Duilio hugged his brother, sharing a wish that they would be able to visit again soon. Then he turned to the boy. "You will make sure Joaquim doesn't reinjure himself, won't you?"

"He won't," Alejandro promised blithely.

Duilio's own gift had told him that, although it would be a long road for Joaquim with an injured tendon. He'd told Oriana that Joaquim might be left with a limp. Fortunately. Gustavo Mendes, who'd taken over Joaquim's job in the meantime, was more than willing to bring files to the house to discuss with him while it healed.

Duilio turned back to Joaquim, who was straightening an object on the side table with his free hand, a silver frame that contained a single worn playing card that looked as though it had come from Miss Felis' old deck. "You'll write," Duilio said, "to let me know how you're all doing?"

"I will," Joaquim promised, glancing up at him. His eyes slid to Marina as he said that, and she smiled back at him. "But there's no need to worry," he added. "We're going to be fine."

Duilio smiled, and signed to Oriana that his gift told him that was true.

ABOUT THE AUTHOR

J. Kathleen Cheney is a former mathematics teacher who has taught classes ranging from seventh grade to calculus, with a brief stint as a gifted and talented specialist. Her short fiction has been published in such venues as *Fantasy Magazine* and *Beneath Ceaseless Skies*, and her novella, *Iron Shoes*, was a Nebula Finalist in 2010.